LOVE LETTERS HOME

LOVE IN A TIME OF WAR

1942-1945

CHAPMAN DEERING

REDZEPHYR

Redzephyr
45 School Street, Suite 170
Barnstable, MA 02635

Printed in the United States of America

First Printing, 2018

Deering, Chapman, author
Love Letters Home / Chapman Deering

Library of Congress Control Number: 2018940573
ISBN-13: 978-1-7322115-0-6
ISBN-10: 1-7322115-0-7

1. Historical Romance 2. World War, 1942-1945 3. Army Air Force—N. Africa, Sicily

Cover Illustration / Book Design by Adira Burchard

For MJV & JM

TABLE OF CONTENTS

Acknowledgements vii

Introduction ix

Chapter 1 • Boston • Fort Devens 3

Chapter 2 • Mississippi • Keesler Field 13

Chapter 3 • Missouri Aviation Institute • Kansas City 33

Chapter 4 • Missouri • Air Corps Training Detachment • Kansas City .67

Chapter 5 • Missouri • Jefferson Barracks 95

Chapter 6 • New Jersey • Fort Dix. 109

Chapter 7 • Boston. 139

Chapter 8 • England. 149

Chapter 9 • North Africa 157

Chapter 10 • North Africa 177

Chapter 11 • Boston. 213

Chapter 12 • Sicily 241

Chapter 13 • Italy 257

Chapter 14 • Eastern Europe 277

Chapter 15 • Boston. 341

Chapter 16 • Naples 375

Chapter 17 • Boston. 421

Epilogue. 427

Time Line of World War II. 429

ACKNOWLEDGEMENTS

I want to thank all those who assisted me in the process of writing *Love Letters Home*. It's been a seven year journey from first discovery of the letters, through selection and transcription from the originals, followed by all the writing, editing and reviewing that goes into making such a volume come to life.

Friends and beta-readers from all across the country including the states of California, Colorado, Florida, Illinois, Maine, Massachusetts, North Carolina, and Virginia gave valuable feedback and insights.

I am especially grateful to my fellow "BarFlies" from the Cape Cod Writers Center: Marianne Shafer, Gail Nickerson and Ann Specht. Your encouragement and wisdom helped make this volume a reality.

INTRODUCTION

It was at least fifteen years ago when she found a cache of letters hidden in the attic of her family home. Her mother had died and her father was moving into assisted living. Everything in the house had to go and the box of old envelopes was just one more thing to toss into the rubbish. Just more paper for the recycle bin, she thought. But then, just by chance, one of the letters escaped the box, slipped from its envelope and landed on the old wood floor in front of her.

Her father's handwriting was still clear. The letters were private but she couldn't help herself as she started to read. She had stumbled upon a real treasure trove: love letters from a soldier sent home to the woman he had left behind. She couldn't just toss them out. They were worth preserving.

It took her nearly three years to read and transcribe the more than 400 pieces of correspondence: Airmail letters, VMail, telegrams, yellowing lined pages—each in its original envelope and neatly organized according to the date received. The box contained one side of a nearly four year correspondence. All the letters she found were written by her father to her mother, during World War II—the war years of 1942 - 1945. Unfortunately, due to constant reassignments, and limited space, her father had not saved any of the letters her mother sent to him. They had been discarded before he returned home at the end of the war.

. . . She had to imagine her mother's side of the conversation.

- Chapman Deering

1942

CHAPTER 1

BOSTON

FORT DEVENS

The streetcar was late again. It was always late on Tuesdays. Who knew why? Who knew anything any more? The whole world was going crazy. The air was cold and the sky still dark when Ruth stepped onto the crumbling station platform at Neponset. The thin fabric of her worn overcoat did little to keep out the harsh morning air as she buried her hands deep in the pockets and pulled the front of her coat ever tighter against her body.

"I should have worn a hat," she berated herself, as she stamped her feet on the hard stone surface, trying to stay warm. She waited.

As she slowly paced back and forth on the nearly deserted platform, a young newsboy stepped out from the alley behind the station house, two heavy bundles of the *Boston Daily Globe's* first edition weighing him down.

"Morning, Miss," he called out, and grabbing the first clean copy from the top of one bundle, he headed straight for her. "Paper, Miss?"

Ruth handed him three pennies and added another penny for his trouble.

"Thanks, Miss. Thanks a lot." He grinned and backed off down the platform.

She looked down at the headlines. The news wasn't pretty. "New York and Detroit Can Be Attacked, Roosevelt Warns." "Tension Grows in Sweden." "Japan Pincer Pushes Southeast." She could only read the large print in the dim light. The rest would have to wait until she got on the trolley where she could devour all the details. World politics had never interested her before, but now that her Jim had joined up, every news item was important.

She folded the newspaper and put it into her satchel, glancing at the outside pocket where she had carefully placed the latest letter from Jim. Ruth had already read it five times, but she had brought it to read again on the way to work. The ride to downtown Boston took about a half hour. Plenty of time for both the newspaper and Jim's letter, provided no one bothered her.

Why, she wondered, had he volunteered? Ruth was still angry. Her sister's boyfriends were still around. They were talking about enlisting but she knew they were stalling. If they waited any longer it was likely they would be drafted. And that would be a mistake.

What Jim didn't understand when he walked into the enlistment office was that as soon as he signed his name to the papers and solemnly swore to defend the USA, he was no longer his own man. In the front door and out the back. He was measured for a uniform, given his kit, lined up and marched to a waiting bus. No going back.

Jim's first letter, written from Fort Devens, arrived the day after he had been inducted. Ruth still carried it in her satchel, but she found it difficult to read.

He left without saying goodbye.

His family had called her to say he had left and that was that. He was off on the great adventure of his life and she could not help but feel abandoned.

Monday, February 9, 1942

Dear Ruth,

Please excuse this ruled paper. It is all I could get (borrow) in the barracks. We have been ordered not to leave the building.

I passed the exam. The last man to examine me was a French doctor. He was swell. He told me I was a good specimen. I was surprised myself.

We were shipped to Devens at 12:30 and arrived here in the pouring rain. I had on an old pair of shoes. We had to walk to the barracks from the station where the trucks unload and did I get wet!

As I am an enlisted man, we were pushed through ahead of the

4

draftees. Eight of the original eighteen sent with me from Boston are still with me in the barracks. All except one are out for the Air Corps. The 8th is going to be a parachutist.

I'm sorry I had to leave without saying goodbye. But I couldn't stay very long on the phone and so I killed three birds by calling my home. They phoned the office to tell them I was joining up, and I told my mother to phone you.

The barrack that I'm in is for enlisted men only. The selectees are in different barracks. There are showers and dressing facilities—a mirror and washbowl.

I may be here 8 days, but I really can't say how long. Eventually we will be shipped to training stations and assigned to a regular company.

Ruth, thank you very much for the wonderful picture and frame. I'm crazy about it, and about you too as a matter of fact. I can't take that picture along however. I treasure it. Thank you darling. I shall let you know when I am to be shipped out.

Please excuse my writing. I'm using the top of my toilet set as a desk, sitting on top of my bunk. The Sergeant took one look at my toilet set and asked me how long I expected to keep it in this _____ hole. They issue a kit anyway.

Well dear, there's the bugle for late mess. I've got to sign off. I'll write again soon. Please write me.

With love, Jim.

The only connection now with Jim would be his letters. This morning, waiting in the cold for the next trolley to Boston, Ruth felt more isolated than ever.

Her work as a commercial artist kept her busy enough during the week but evenings and weekends were quiet. She wasn't exactly engaged to Jim, but Ruth knew he was the one guy for her, and she had decided to stop dating anyone else seriously. She would wait for Jim to come home from the Army, even if it took a whole year! Besides there was always the crowd of friends to go dancing if she wanted to go out. But she didn't want to.

All she could think about was Jim and how far away he was from her right now.

It had only been a few weeks since he enlisted, but already several letters had arrived.

Wednesday, February 11, 1942 - Heading South

Dear Ruth, Well, we're leaving here today.

I have not received any mail from anyone. If you haven't written yet, why not hold off until you hear from me further. I don't know where I'm going. There are all sorts of rumors but no one really knows.

I've been through what the boys call "The Mill"—that is, outfitted, examined, and interviewed along with an IQ test.

I was given three shots this morning so I feel a bit off "high gear." My right arm is a bit sore but that will go away soon.

I'm feeling fine. We have reveille at 4:30 am, ½ hour to dress and make bunks. I learned to make my bed, and are they fussy! We then stand out in the Company Street for roll call. Mess is at 5:30 and details are at 6:30.

I was assigned to a detail at the Quartermasters Supply Store. My job was to measure the men's feet as they stood back against a pole. There was an army regulation chart right on the floor. I merely put their heels well back against the block and shouted out their size to a sergeant. They were then issued socks. As I was going along and getting weary, somewhere around the thousandth man, one guy yells down, "Hello Jim!" It was Harry Black, a draftee. Was I surprised! I haven't seen him since, as the draftees got pushed right through.

Please write me now, when you get my new address. I mailed my letter to you last Saturday night. I've gone to confession so I'm ready for what comes.

Give my regards to the folks at home. I miss you terribly. This is 100% different from civilian life. I get pretty tired at night from a full day's work so I retire at 9pm - lights out.

Keep writing and send me your picture. I'll write again soon.

Bye Darling.

With love, Jim.

Until now the war had not been real for her. The battlefront was always happening someplace else—in a world on the other side of the globe, far away. Now that Jim had enlisted, the war was very real, and the realization that he might be killed or injured fighting this thing put fear in Ruth's heart.

By the time the 7:35 streetcar finally arrived, the platform was filled with commuters heading into town. She headed for the last car, which she knew was usually less crowded and found a seat next to an older gentleman in a rumpled coat who looked half asleep. Ruth opened her newspaper and settled in for the ride.

She had only begun to read when she felt a hand on her arm. The man leaned over and whispered, "Don't read it." His breath was heavy with the smell of whiskey. "Don't read the news. It's all bad. All bad. Damn war will be the end of us."

Ruth looked at the man's hand on her sleeve. Scar tissue ran like rivers across the pale surface. He looked older than his years. And very sad.

"I don't read the papers anymore," he continued. "Not since Pearl Harbor." He looked at her. "You shouldn't read 'em either. Pretty girl like you. You shouldn't be filling your head with all this world war nonsense. Read the fashions. Read the comics."

"My boyfriend is over there. At least he will be. He just joined up and I need to know what's going on," Ruth answered.

The man turned away. "Stupid, stupid, stupid."

"I don't think he's stupid," Ruth countered. "I think my Jim is brave to join up."

"Brave?" The man twisted in his seat and glared at her directly. "You don't know what you're talking about. I was there. I know. I was there."

"Where?"

"There. I was right there in the thick of it. 1918. France."

Ruth wasn't sure what to say.

"You got any idea what your boyfriend is in for? Huh? You got any idea? He's not brave. It's the stupidest thing he could have done. Joining up. He's going to get himself killed. That's what he's going to do. It's the smart ones who are staying out of the war."

"But we've been attacked. Thousands of people are dying. Somebody's got to stop Germany and Japan from taking over the world," Ruth argued. "War is awful. I'm sure it must be. But someone's got to stop Hitler. And I think it's brave for someone like my Jim to step up and do his part."

The man shook his head and turned away. "Rubbish," he mumbled. "All rubbish. That's what's happening. Rubbish."

Ruth did not respond. Clearly, the man was convinced the world was going to hell in a hand basket, and her Jim along with it.

She put the paper down and shut her eyes. She tried to picture Jim and the last time they had been together.

He had taken her to dinner in town at a small pub they liked, just down from her Milk Street office. The place wasn't fancy but it served good food that didn't cost much. Being together was more important than the surroundings. Ruth would have sat on a park bench eating sandwiches in the cold if that's what it took to be with Jim.

They talked about the war. Jim couldn't get enough of it. He was thinking of joining up. "The guys in the crowd are all talking about going down to the recruitment office, Ruth. Even my friend Jerry's thinking of going in, but I think he's going to wait awhile. If he holds off until he graduates in June, he can start right off in officer's training school."

"I know it's important, Jim, but do you have to be the one to go? Maybe it'll all be over before you know it and if you only wait a little while longer, you won't have to join up at all."

Jim poked at the meatloaf he had ordered. "This war's not going to go away. Haven't you read the papers? Hitler is only getting stronger and we've stayed out of this mess for too long. It's time the country took a stand and I mean to be a part of it."

"When will you go?"

"I don't know. I was thinking of joining up right after the Japs went after us in December, but wanted to get through the holidays before I did. One guy in the office enlisted a couple of days ago. He came in to show off his uniform. You should see it. Guy looked real smart. But he was Navy. I'm thinking of going for the Army where the real action is. None of this floating around at sea for me. I hear they've got a whole new division they call the Army Air Force and they're looking for engineers. They say if you enlist instead of waiting to get drafted, you can choose what you want to do. So that's what I'm thinking." Jim looked at Ruth. "I know this is hard for you to understand. But I've just got to go."

Ruth reached out and touched his sleeve. She could see the worn edge of his shirt cuff and a loose thread barely holding the button in place. She wanted to grab Jim right then and keep him from going to war and leaving her behind. He was not a rich man, but Jim was smart. If he wanted to enlist and become an engineer, he would join up no matter how she felt.

Ruth studied his face. "I have faith in you, Jim. And I know you'll do the right thing. But..." she hesitated... "but please, don't go without telling me. Make sure you let me know when you're going to join up."

"Don't worry," Jim sipped his coffee. "I'll be sure to give you plenty of warning. Besides, I'm not even sure when it'll happen. Got to do some asking around first."

That was a month ago. He had gone down to the recruiting station to ask a few questions, like he said he would. But once they got a hold of a willing subject, they were not going to let him go. Jim was signed up, sworn in and shipped out within an hour of walking in the front door. Now, riding on a cold trolley to Boston, remembering their last meal together, Ruth could only sit back in her seat and sigh.

Half an hour later she walked up Milk Street and entered the Sunley Building where she rented a small office space on the fifth floor. Actually, it was more of an office corner. Her desk, with its tilted workspace, was pushed up against a back wall facing out. Surrounded by shelves full of inks, pens and paper, she could work on her designs and still see everyone coming and going in the office. It was noisy, but she liked that. Ruth had tried the quiet, isolated office they had first given her in the back of the building, but it almost drove her crazy to be so alone. She liked the hustle and bustle of people around her. Working for herself as a solo commercial artist was difficult enough. No sense working in isolation.

That's how she had met Jim. He worked upstairs as a clerk for one of the accounting firms. She ran into him on the stairs one day and he seemed like a nice guy. From her desk she could make out the landing of the fifth floor's staircase and once in a while he would stick his head in to "just say hi," on his way up or down stairs.

Shy at first, it took some persuading and a little bit of her feminine guile to get Jim to ask her for a date. He eventually did and since that first time more than five months ago, they had gone out at least once every week to a show or, more often, a dance hall.

Their favorite place had been Norumbega Park's Totem Pole Ballroom in Newton. Almost every Saturday they would take the trolley that ran between Boston and Auburndale and spend the day walking around the amusement park, stopping to eat a picnic lunch Ruth had packed, or if Jim had just received his paycheck, they would eat at the park's Pavilion Restaurant, then rent one of the canoes and take a paddle down the Charles River. Norumbega was always crowded with young people and by evening they would arrange to meet friends at the ballroom and dance the night away.

All that was before the war.

Once at her desk, Ruth took out her pens and focused on putting the finishing touches on a box design for the Polar Ice Pack Company. Big blue letters stretched across an art deco style image of a polar bear sitting on an iceberg. She was almost done when she heard a knock at the open door. David Doherty, Jim's older brother leaned against the door frame.

"Hey, Ruth. Thought I might find you here this morning. We got a letter from Jim and there was another letter addressed to you stuck inside the envelope. I knew you'd want to open it right away." David grinned. "Don't know why Jim put the letter in with the one to Hazel, but..." he shrugged. "Anyway, here's the letter. Unopened. Safe and sound." He held out the envelope.

She could see her name neatly scrawled across the front. Jim's handwriting was small and precise and she recognized it immediately. No postage mark. Perhaps he had simply tried to save Uncle Sam a few pennies and put two letters into one? It didn't matter.

She wanted to open the letter, but not in front of David. Jim's letters were personal and she always tried to savor each and every word in private.

She held the envelope gently. "Thanks, David. I appreciate you bringing the letter." She paused and then, when he didn't move, "Well, I have to get back to work. I'm almost finished with this special job and it's due by five tonight." David still didn't move. "Maybe we can meet for lunch another time?"

Suddenly, as if a light bulb went off in his brain, David finally got the hint. "Oh sure, Ruth. No problem. It's time I return to the station." He turned to go, "Hey, you want to come over to dinner this Saturday? Hazel invited Eddy's new girlfriend to come. I think you should come too. We'll have a lot of fun."

Ruth hesitated. Eddy was Hazel's son and Jim's step-brother. They didn't get along. But if Jim's family were inviting her over, it would be smart to say yes. If her future was to be Jim's wife, and she strongly suspected that would be the case, offending his step-mother Hazel was the last thing she wanted to do.

"I think I could make it Saturday."

"Sounds good. I'll tell Hazel to expect you. I'll pick you up at your place. How about five o'clock?"

She nodded and he was gone.

CHAPTER 2

MISSISSIPPI

KEESLER FIELD

R uth looked down at the envelope. Should she open it now or wait? Sometimes waiting made the reading all the sweeter. It had been almost two weeks since Jim's last letter and she was eager to know where he was and what was happening to him. Using her pen knife, she sliced across the top of the sealed opening and carefully unfolded three sheets of paper.

Saturday, February, 14, 1942 - Valentine's Day—
Air Corps Technical School, Keesler Field, Mississippi

To My Valentine:

She looked again at the date. He had written the letter over a month ago! Why had it taken so long to get to her?

Ruth darling, I'm many miles from you now. We shipped Thursday and arrived here 2 hours ago. I'm still dirty (but fed) from the trip. What an airfield. You could put East Boston Airport in the corner and lose it. The weather here is about like Boston in June. And the fellows say that today is cold! (It's about 50.) By the way, I don't think I'm going to like the southerners.

Seriously, they actually gritted their teeth and gave us some pretty dirty remarks at chow. We are the first group of any size to arrive here from the North. *They booed and cat called us from their barracks when we marched in from the station about 1 1/2 miles. But I'm going to make them like me. I felt funny marching along carrying my heavy overcoat and traveling pack and then looking at the peculiar and sometimes unpleasant expressions on their damn rebel faces.*

That drawl of theirs can be dirty. I'll be all right tomorrow after a night's rest. We're right down on the delta, you couldn't get much farther south, except maybe Florida.

I get feeling a little alone now and then but all I have to do is think of you. If I could only get a letter from you soon telling me about those little things that only lovers understand. I guess I got it bad.

Since I just arrived Ruth, I can't tell you much about the place, but we did get our general orders from the commanding officer and it looks as though the picnic is over. We're really going to buckle down now. I'm glad I enlisted while the opportunity was there.

New Orleans is quite near, but we were warned that venereal disease is prevalent there. Not that I would partake of any illicit relations (I love you too much for that) but there's always the chance of being touched or touching things or people.

There are theaters and ball fields on the post. I'm told we will be kept quite busy studying. Reveille is 5:00 am. Must be in by 9:00 pm. Lights out at 10:00 pm. No leaves will be granted for 15 months.

We might as well both understand now that we will be away from each other for a long time, unless I'm fortunate enough to be transferred north again. Maybe Mitchell Field or Boston?

I don't have much time to write letters (other than yours). Will you send me your picture and tell me about your family and of course about you? You know how I look forward to knowing everything you are doing. I'll write again. I think you're the sweetest person alive.

With love,
Jim

Ruth put the letter down as she felt tears begin to well up. He loved her. And he missed her terribly.

She closed her eyes and tried to picture Jim in a barracks, hunched over, writing his letter on the back of his shaving case, dozens of soldiers in the background. She could only imagine what it was like for him to be so far away.

Their lives were going in very different directions.

Saturday morning dawned—the day of the Doherty family get together. All week she had debated whether she would go or not. She knew she should; it was Jim's family after all. He had never said outright what his childhood with Hazel as stepmother had been like, but he had hinted enough around the edges of the story for Ruth to get an accurate picture.

Jim's mother had died when he was only eleven years old. His father, John, saddled with four teen-aged children didn't waste any time finding a new wife. Hazel's husband had died suddenly, and according to the neighborhood rumor mill, she was determined to find a new one as fast as she could.

John always stopped into Tuckerman's Pub for a few pints on his way home from his job at the Ironworks and it was there that Hazel and he met. Whatever magic spell Hazel wove, Jim never knew, but within a week of their first encounter, John was bringing Hazel home to meet Jim, his sister Brigid and brothers David and George. A month later, John and Hazel were married and she moved into John's Jamaica Plain flat, bringing her eleven-year old son, Eddy, along with her. Jim was relegated to the attic and Eddy got Jim's bedroom for his own.

"We have to be nice to Eddy," John ordered his son. "He's family now. And he's new here. He needs your room. You," and he pointed to the ceiling, "you set yourself up above. And don't be complaining."

It didn't take long before all three of Jim's siblings moved out. George and David rented a small room in Davis Square and Brigid decided to visit a cousin in New Hampshire for the summer. Eleven-year-old Jim was left behind to fend for himself.

Things did not go well. Eddy and Jim were constantly fighting about one thing or another. If they had been blood brothers they might have patched things up, but instead they became fierce rivals, and neither would give an inch on anything. Hazel was constantly breaking up one confrontation or another, and more than once, John took the strap to Jim to keep him in line. As the years went on, the divide between the boys grew even deeper. Once Jim reached the age of seventeen he was out of the house for good.

He tried living with his brothers, George and David, but there was very little room in their small apartment and he only lasted two weeks before they kicked him out. His sister Brigid and her new husband, Herb, had set up housekeeping in Arlington, north of the city. Jim asked if he could stay with her for a while. Reluctantly, the new bride agreed. "But you'll have to sleep on the couch, Jim. We only have the one bed."

That arrangement didn't last a month.

Finally, Jim moved into the YMCA and there he stayed, calling his tiny room "home" for the next year and a half until he graduated from English High, got a job and could finally afford his own place. Once he was out on his own Jim's relationship with his father and stepmother improved a bit, but things were never quite smooth.

By five o'clock Ruth was dressed in her best dress, the one with the small daisies at the collar that Jim liked. She stood at the bay window, winter coat over her arm, looking up Bromfield Street, waiting for the first sign of David's '32 Ford Sedan turning the corner. He was nowhere to be seen.

She put on her coat, stepped out onto the wide veranda and pulled the collar up against the cold.

It was half past five and Ruth was getting nervous when she finally caught sight of David's car as it turned into the far end of the street. He pulled the Ford to the curb, and rolled down the car window. "Sorry," he said. "Got a flat!" He pointed to the left front tire."

Ruth studied the tire. It seemed all right, but there was some odd kind of patch on it.

"I fixed it temporarily. Should get us to Jamaica Plain, I think." He paused and looked at Ruth. "You ready to go?" She nodded. "Well, then, get in. We're off to another family drama!"

David drove up Bergin Parkway and headed north into town. They were already a half hour late. He stepped on the gas and the old Ford cut out into traffic. "What time is it?" David asked.

"Almost 5:45. How long will it take us to drive there?"

"Don't worry. We'll be ok. Hazel may be stern, but she's not totally unreasonable. Besides, my Dad will act as a buffer zone. By this time they'll both have had a drink or two so things will be fine."

It took the better part of an hour to drive the rest of the way to Jamaica Plain. David made a wrong turn somewhere near Huntington Avenue and they ended up circling through the Arborway in the wrong direction. By the time they reached Marker Street, both David and Ruth were a little nervous. One thing they both knew for certain, you didn't keep Hazel waiting.

As Ruth got out of the car, she looked up at the top floor of the three-decker. In the dim light from the street lamp near by she could just make out John Doherty leaning over the wooden porch railing, a tall glass of beer in one hand. He had on his old fedora hat but no coat.

"Hello, you two!" John shouted down at them. "You're late!"

"Sorry, Dad." David called up. "Got a flat."

"You shoulda taken the bus." John lifted the glass to his lips. "No matter. Hazel's got everything ready. We've been waiting on you. Come on in."

David and Ruth hustled up the front stoop and entered the front door. There was no need to knock or ring. The door was always left unlocked so the other tenants could come and go. As she hurried up the two flights of stairs, Ruth caught a whiff of corned beef and cabbage boiling on a stove. It would be traditional Irish fare.

"Hello, hello," Hazel cried out as they entered the apartment. She held open her arms towards Ruth. "Sure and it's good to see you, darlin'." Ruth was swallowed in one strong embrace as Hazel wrapped her arms around her and pressed Ruth to her ample bosom. "'Tis good at last," she repeated. "And about time too." She stepped back and studied the two of them.

"And what took you so long, David, I'm asking?" Hazel's thick brogue was hard for Ruth to understand, but there was no mistaking her intent as she slapped David's shoulder. "You know my dinner is nearly ruined, thanks to the likes of you."

"Sorry, Hazel. The Ford got a puncture. Took a while to fix it."

John came in from the porch. "Oh leave the boy alone," he said. "A flat could happen to anyone." With that, he put an arm around Ruth's shoulder. "And how are you doing, miss pretty? Still doing that art thing of yours?"

"Oh yes, still doing that art thing."

"Don't understand how you can make a living drawing such doodads," John drawled, "but I guess somebody must need what you do."

David took her coat and with his own, hung them both in the tiny hall closet. "So, what's for dinner?" he asked Hazel.

"Now, don't rush me, young man. Plenty of time for that." She smoothed the flower print on her apron. "Why don't we sit a bit in the parlor, first."

She led the way into the front room and pointed to an oversized stuffed chair near the door. "Put yourself down there, Ruth, and we can chat a while. Have you heard anything from Jim?"

Ruth glanced over at David as he settled onto the couch. He was busy fussing with the pleats in his trousers and did not look up. Ruth was hoping for a signal from him. Should she tell Hazel that Jim had already written to her several times? She knew instinctively that it would make Hazel jealous to think her step-son was not putting his family first on his correspondence list.

"Yes, he sounds well and very busy. I don't think he gets much time for letter writing."

"Hmph. You'd t'ink he'd have a little more time for his own family." Hazel responded.

Ruth fell silent. She didn't know where to go next with this conversation. Luckily she didn't have to, as at that moment Eddy, the infamous favorite son, came bounding up the stairs, his girlfriend in tow.

"Sorry, we're late, Mum." Eddy crossed the room in two steps and planted a big kiss on his mother's forehead. "How you doing?" He turned to John, ignoring David and Ruth.

"Fine. Fine. David here got a flat in that old rattletrap of his." John gave a laugh. "Shoulda taken the bus, I say."

Eddy turned to his girlfriend. "You remember Laurel don't you, Mum?"

"Certain I do." Hazel smiled warmly and held out her arms. Laurel was given a proper bear hug.

Eddy looked around, finally noticing David and Ruth. "Oh, hello you two. Looking fine there, Davey boy." He turned and took Laurel's hand. "You remember my girl, Laurel?" David and Laurel exchanged nods of acknowledgment. "And this here," Eddy gestured towards Ruth, "this is my brother Jim's sweetheart, Ruth. She's an artist."

"Really?" Laurel exclaimed. "A real artist? Like with paints and things?" She was clearly impressed.

"I'm a commercial artist," Ruth replied. "I do a lot of work in advertising for companies and the stores in Boston."

"Oh," said Laurel, her voice dropping a notch, clearly disappointed. "So you're not a real artist."

"She's a real artist, all right," David interrupted, "and she's talented, too." He encouraged Ruth, "Tell 'em some of your clients, Ruth—who you work for."

"Well, I don't think..." Ruth's answer was suddenly interrupted. John had entered the room, holding several bottles of beer in his fists.

"Come on, everyone. Have a beer. Enough of this 'getting to know you, stuff.' Here Laurel, have a Pabst!" He handed a tall neck bottle to Laurel and steered her towards an empty chair. Eddy grabbed another and plunked himself down on the nearby ottoman.

"David, you'll have a beer?" He handed a third bottle to David and then turned to Ruth. "And what'll you be wanting, pretty lady? How about a beer? Or would you want something else? We have whiskey, a'course."

Ruth hesitated. She didn't like the taste of beer, but it was a better alternative to the whiskey he offered. "I'll have a Pabst, thank you." She hesitated as John handed over a bottle. "Could I have it in a glass, please?"

"O'course." He looked around, puzzled. He had already downed a few bottles of his own before his guests had arrived, and now he appeared to not know where a glass could be found.

"Now, let's not get fancy, here." Hazel crossed the room to the corner hutch. "Here's a glass for ye." She handed it to Ruth. "One thing we have in this house, is lots of glasses," she chuckled. "Wouldn't you say that, Eddy?"

"Yeah, Mum. Lots of glasses for every drink you can name." He raised his beer bottle high. "Hey, let's have a toast!" He looked around the room, eager to have everyone join in.

"And what shall we toast, Eddy boy?" asked John.

"I say we toast to ourselves, and all good things to come."

"And to Jim, too. Let's toast to Jim." Ruth chimed in.

"Hear, hear. Sláinte!"

"And to all the boys who are going off to war," added Eddy.

"Let's toast to a quick end to this war," said David.

"That's for sure. Here, here." They all added as they raised their bottles high and clinked and clanked bottles against bottles and glass.

Finally, the room was quiet.

"So," John spoke up, "what's the news from the front?" He turned to Ruth. "We got a couple notes from Jim after he left Boston. Do you know where he is now?"

"I'm not exactly sure, I did just receive a letter, but it was dated some time ago. He was down south—Mississippi, I think. He's not overseas yet. That's certain."

"Maybe he'll be lucky and this whole damn thing will be over before he has to go," Eddy said.

"I don't know about that." David remarked. "It's sounding as if things are going to get a lot worse before they get better. I was reading in the paper that Germany is sending more troops into Poland. The Russians are determined to knock 'em back.

Laurel turned to David. "Are you planning on joining up?"

John and Hazel exchanged glances, embarrassed for David. But he answered her directly. He was getting used to the question. "No. I tried to join a few weeks after Jim did. But they won't have me."

"Why ever not?" Laurel asked.

"I have a medical condition," David replied. Laurel suddenly looked sorry she had asked. "Don't worry, it's not life threatening, Laurel. I have flat feet."

"That's all?" she asked, incredulous. "That doesn't seem like a good enough reason."

"It is when you consider how many miles you have to walk as a foot soldier." David took another sip of his beer. "I didn't think it was a big deal, either, but they explained that a guy with flat feet can't keep up with the unit. He becomes a burden to the other guys. So that's that. If you've got flat feet they don't want you."

"Oh." Laurel sat back in her chair, thinking. She turned towards Eddy. "And do you have flat feet too?"

Eddy's face flushed beet red. "Laurel, I told you why I'm not going in."

"You mean, that secret thing you told me about?"

Eddy didn't know where to look. "Laurel, just drop it, ok. You know why I'm not joining up."

"No, I don't Eddy." Laurel prodded. "At least I didn't think you meant it. What you told me."

The rest of the room was now listening intently.

"What's this all about, Eddy?" John asked. "I thought you were planning on going down to the recruiting station last week. I don't want to see you off to the war, but it's your duty, and you've got to at least let them know you're willin'."

Eddy held the beer bottle close to his lips as he answered. "I didn't go down to the recruiting station. I know, I should, but I didn't. Some of the guys at the shop were talking about waiting a bit more to see what's going to happen."

"But if you don't sign up, they're sure to draft you." John warned.

"We'll see. I may not have to go in any case."

"What are ye talkin about?" Hazel asked.

"It's nothing, Mum." He looked at the worried look on his mother's face. "I wasn't feeling so well the other day and checked in with the shop doctor.

Seems I've got some kind of problem with my breathing. They think I've got some form of asthma."

"You think that might have something to do with the fact you smoke?" John spoke sharply. "I've told you to quit dozens of times. It's a nasty habit."

"If smoking keeps me from breathing right and keeps me out of this rotten war, then I'll keep smoking," Eddy shot back.

Laurel reached out and touched his arm. "Don't talk to your father like that."

Eddy pulled his arm away. "He's not my father." He turned on John. "You have no right to set after me. If I want to smoke, I'll smoke."

"Now stop all this, you two," Hazel cut in. "I won't have you ruining a perfectly good family meal, talking about this sort of thing. Eddy, show Laurel where the loo is and wash your hands. I'm laying the table." She turned on John. "And you leave him be. He's my son and I'll not have him under your thumb. Now go wash up."

Hazel headed towards the kitchen, John to the back porch and David and Ruth sat quietly waiting for dinner to be served. One thing Ruth remembered from all that Jim had shared with her, family dinners at Hazel's were always guaranteed to be full of some sort of drama. This evening was not an exception.

Jim's next letter arrived a few days later. Ruth took it to work so she could read it again during her morning break.

Saturday, February 21, 1942 - Air Corps Technical School, Keesler Field, Mississippi - 5:45 pm

Dearest Ruth:

Things haven't been too well down here the past couple of days. We got a double dose of typhoid toxin and oh boy what an after effect. Six fellows in our barracks alone were taken away in ambulances. The shot in the arm kicks up about 5 hours after injection. It runs a fever and there is quite a pain in the arm. What a night I spent.

I couldn't get comfortable because of the pain and my fever was growing until about 3 in the morning. I thought I had caught something or other. And the sight of those stretcher bearers lugging out the fellows didn't help any. I pitched and tossed all night. I was in a sort of semi conscious state. I remember trying to get to sleep by thinking of holding you in my arms. It usually works every time. But the pain kept me awake.

In the morning there were 3 more fellows who were unable to get up. Well, we fell out in the Squadron area at 5:30 for setting up exercises and sure enough another fellow flops over.

It's cold and damp around here in the early morning and the fellows began to complain, but the sergeant just told us that we were supposed to be soldiers, not boy scouts.

Some fellows believe we are jinxed because we shipped down here. Friday the 13th on a 13 car train and we're housed in Block 13. But I'm not suspicious.

I got a letter from my friend Steve today. He just got a shot for yellow fever. He should be in these parts and get a double dose of typhoid along with 2 shots of tetanus, 1 shot for diphtheria, 1 shot for yellow fever, 1 shot for scarlet and a blood test along with a test for venereal diseases fever (to protect us from that O'Hara gal.)

So help me, I feel like a guinea pig. And I understand there is a peach of an injection waiting for the fellows that go further south - that one is a special injection for malaria. You hit the floor when that old needle stabs.

Ruth couldn't imagine what it was like to get so many different needles all at the same time. No wonder soldiers were dropping like flies.

I heard from home today. They mentioned having called you up. Well dear, you know I'm writing you the most and I send them a letter every four or five days. Should I write them more? I suppose it would be asking you too much to call them occasionally and let them know the latest, or would that make them feel sort of left out of things? What do you think, honey?

My brother David wants to keep your picture. What's the penalty for murdering a brother? Now, don't get ideas! I'm not going to tell you any more about him.

I miss you dear, but there will come a time when I can see you again. Just write me whenever you can. Give my regards to your folks.

Jim

Ruth carefully folded the letter, put it back in its envelope and placed it in the front pocket of her satchel. This was the fifth time she had read it over, savoring each and every word. She missed Jim more than she thought she could ever miss anyone. His being so far away and out of reach felt like some heavy burden sitting on her chest, not painful really, just an ache that wouldn't go away.

Now, sitting in front of her work easel, with piles of paper and bottles of inks scattered about in front of her, she began to organize her desk. It was always easier for her to think while she distracted herself with tidying up.

David had promised to take her dancing at Norumbega Park later in the month. She wondered if she should mention that to Jim. Would he be jealous? Maybe he was kidding around, but Ruth could read hints of unease between the lines of Jim's letter. He did want her to have fun while he was away. She knew that. Just not too much fun.

She would have worked right through the lunch hour if Helen from the office one flight up, had not stuck her head in the door. "Going to lunch?" she asked. "Girl's gotta eat sometime."

Helen was one of Ruth's closest friends and the best fashion critic she knew. Tall and stylish, Helen could always be counted on for honest advice, whether about the latest trends in women's wear or how to handle the opposite sex.

Ruth looked down at the half finished ad layout. It was due the next morning. She'd have enough time if she wasn't gone too long.

"Where were you thinking of going? I only want a sandwich. Nothing big. And I can only take a few minutes. Got to finish this ad before the end of the day."

Helen came closer and glanced over the drafting board at Ruth's drawing. "Who's it for this time?"

"Jordan's. They've got a big sale on handbags for spring coming out next week. This is just one of a dozen ads we're running." She turned the sheet so Helen could see it more easily.

"Nice look. Not leather though. I hear they're beginning to ration that."

"I think they call it some sort of faux leather. It's made of crocodile or alligator or something. It's supposed to be very durable which is smart. Since this war began we have to make everything last a lot longer. There's also a whole collection of canvas bags that are coming out too."

"Hope they've got one that'll go with my old best dress," Helen wondered. "I don't think there's going to be a new Easter outfit in my future this year. But at least I can buy a new bag." She paused, "So, are you coming to lunch, or not?"

"Let me get my coat," Ruth answered. "Let's try that new deli on the corner of Devonshire and Franklin. I hear they give free pickles with every sandwich."

"Now, that sounds like a plan." Helen agreed, and the two friends headed down the stairs and out to Milk Street.

Three days later, Jim's next letter arrived. Ruth saved it to read on the trolley ride into town.

Saturday, February 21, 1942 - Air Corps Technical School, Keesler Field, Mississippi - 7:10 pm

Dearest Ruth,

The reason I can write this now is that we were forced to quit drill because of a terrific downpour and it will last several hours. This is the rainy season down here now, and it pours three or four days each week. The cotton is all planted and this rain will get it growing. They have terrific lighting storms. The other night I saw a bolt of lightning strike the top of the huge water tower. There was a big flash and a noise like the cracking of a whip. "Crack - Boom" and I said "whew" pretty close.

I'm sorry if I said the southerners were hostile. That was my first impression. But now, I understand that they usually give rookies the razz anyway. But they keep much to themselves. Outside of an occasional wise crack, everything is peaceful.

24

Ruth had to smile, imagining Jim struggling with the weather, the accents, and southerners in general. He had never traveled much and she knew what a homebody he was, always more comfortable with the known than the unknown. She looked out the window as the trolley rattled past row after row of three-deckers lining the tracks. She tried to picture Jim so many miles away.

We march in review tomorrow in full ceremony. They are dedicating Keesler Field and graduating the first class to go through the school. I wish you could see the field and hangars. They have 6 hangars and a great big runway in several directions. They also have a building they call the test block. They set the engines in this building and test them. What a roar! You'd get a kick out of seeing the P40s and 41s flying up and down. Any day I expect to see them smack into the ground the way they bank after taking off. A lieutenant was killed here 2 months ago.

Say a little prayer that I'll get into technical school. I'm still in basic training here and after 4 weeks will either go to school or ship out. A crowd of fellows (2,700) shipped out at 3 am today. They were fully equipped for a trip south—mosquito netting and sun hats - khaki etc. They think they are going to Trinidad, but then again, who knows?

Don't worry darling, I'll tell you in plenty of time what's going on. You don't mind me getting into aviation mechanics do you? I have already been classified as office clerk but am trying to see if I can't pick up a trade and see if I can succeed. I'm fighting for you honey, all the way. You understand that once in the Air Corps you cannot transfer to any other branch since the Air Corps is considered Highest Rank. I'd like to work on those big bombers and "keep 'em flying."

We got our third shot of typhoid today. It is not as tough as the second, but my arm is a bit sore. My cold is much better thanks, it's just in my head a little now. I didn't have any medicine, just plenty of water and tried to get as much rest as possible. You see, sick calls go on your service record and I'm trying to keep that as clean as possible.

Besides, unless you're pretty sick the usual remedy for colds, stomach

aches, headaches, backaches, and general fatigue is a good dose of
GI pills. (Castor Oil.) Boy, what results!

We are all set for three years on typhoid shots but will get tetanus
every 21 days. I guess by now you think that all we do is eat, sleep,
and take the needle, but this stuff is just what the recruit must go
through at the start.

Ruth carefully folded the letter, slipped it back into its envelope and placed it in the inside pocket of her satchel where it would be safe. She sat back and rested her head against the hard metal edge of the trolley seat. The weather had turned and through the foggy window she could just make out Boston Harbor in the distance. The rain was steady now; a cold, hard, early spring rain, the kind that seemed to pierce the toughest weather gear. Ruth had nothing more than her thin winter coat.

She couldn't help thinking of Jim, somewhere in Mississippi, watching his own rain fall, warm, hot and humid. They were separated not just by time and distance but by the weather. How different their worlds were becoming. She, in Boston, working on ads to sell handbags to women who already had too many handbags, and Jim learning how to repair plane engines so that bombers could keep on flying and drop bombs on foreign cities.

"This war is going to change everything," she thought.

By the time the 7:35 reached South Station the rain had turned into a downpour. Passengers disembarked from the car and ran for cover, scattering like beads on glass, running into the shelter of the cavernous central station or into the doorways that lined Atlantic Avenue. Ruth grabbed the newspaper from her satchel and holding it flat above her head as her only protection, joined the crowd surging towards the first available entrance into the station's rotunda. By the time she got inside, the newspaper was a mass of wet pulp and her coat was soaked. The dampness seeped through the coat's thin woolen layer. It would take hours for her clothes to dry out.

"What I wouldn't give for a cup of real coffee, right now," she mused. Coffee was becoming harder to find as it was one of the first foodstuffs to have been rationed. The lunchroom in South Station was now selling a coffee substitute called Postum, made from wheat bran and molasses. She didn't like it.

Ruth looked across at the marble mosaic in the center of the rotunda. Tiny puddles trailed after an old woman heading across to the ticket counter, her umbrella dripping as she padded along. Gathered near the newsstand on the far side were dozens of men in uniform heading out for who knows where, their canvas duffel bags stuffed with army regulation gear. They all appeared so eager and full of excitement for the adventure ahead. She silently wished them well and god speed. One of them, a boy who looked no more than eighteen, approached her.

"Got a light, ma'am?" he asked. He held a cigarette between the fingers of his right hand and gestured with it. "Got a light for a future hero?" he grinned down at her. He was tall and lanky and too thin for the uniform he had been issued. She instantly felt a wave of compassion for him. This kid had no idea what he was in for. His life was going to be altered in ways he could never imagine. What would he see? What would he be forced to do? Would he even survive? She shook her head. She couldn't think about all that. Not with Jim soon going into the thick of it.

"Sorry, I don't smoke. But you should be able to find a book of matches at the Tobacconists." She pointed to the small shop at the far end of the station.

"Thanks, ma'am." The boy started to walk away.

"Wait." Ruth stopped him. "Where are you boys headed? You just join up?"

"Heading south, ma'am. Biloxi, Mississippi they tell me. Supposed to be hot there. I can't wait to get out of this rotten New England weather."

"Well, good luck." Ruth answered. "I hear from my boyfriend, Jim, that Mississippi is ok. People are nice and friendly." She decided not to tell him of Jim's first impressions. What was the point? All soldiers, both north and south were the same. They're all in this together.

She glanced up at the large arched windows that faced towards Summer Street. Enormous blackout curtains had been drawn back for the day and she could see that the rain was still coming down. She decided to order a cup of tea at one of the counters. This rain can't last that much longer, she thought.

She took one of the empty stools that were up against the far counter in the lunch room, and settled in to wait out the rainstorm. She took out the letter from Jim and continued to read.

He had written this portion of the letter a couple of days after the first.

Good news tonight honey. I passed the entrance examination for Aviation Technician and will begin school soon after my basic training period. I hope I'm doing the right thing.

As you know, I was classified as clerk and could probably earn a rating with more pay in the finance dept. But I feel I'd like to branch out into a trade to see what it's like. They don't advance you as fast in the early stages of the game simply because it takes quite a while to become expert with airplane engines. If I were a clerk with my education and experience I could knock off a corporal rating inside 3 months. Then to a sergeant and possibly staff sergeant but not likely much higher.

Against this though, I have the possibility of being proficient as technician and a first class mechanic gets the same pay as First Sergeant although he has no stripes. A first sergeant makes $84 per month. I doubt if I'd make this in the finance dept. I understand there is politics there and the fellows who have a little cash on the outside seem to get the breaks. Perhaps I shouldn't say this because I have no proof, but it's the general opinion of the non-coms, some of whom have been in the army quite awhile.

But darling, it's not the idea of being a big shot in the Army that counts. It's my idea to see if I am adapted to that type of work, and as I say, if I can become expert at it, I could probably use my training quite advantageously in the outside after this damm mess is over.

A first class mechanic is not a grease-monkey. He is the man responsible for the performance of the engines on ships to which he is assigned. A ship cannot leave the ground until he approves the action of the engines, because it's his neck if they conk out "up there."

He directs a crew of men in the breaking down and overhauling and servicing of the engines. They have what they call flying mechanics also. They travel on large bombers, the engines of which can be repaired while in flight. It all sounds interesting and sort of appeals to me, so I hope I'm doing the right thing in choosing the trade instead of finance.

He had decided to become a mechanic and go back to school? It seemed a bit of a waste not to use all the education and experience he already had in accounting—but if learning a new trade fixing airplane engines kept Jim in school stateside, then Ruth thought it was a great idea.

I'm enclosing the insignia of the Air Corps at this field. Keep it, won't you? Darling, I miss you so much it hurts. If I go to school here (5 ½ months) at least you'll know where I am for a while. Your letter gave me a lump in my throat where you say your eyes are blurry. I wish I could have been there to see them. I would have kissed the blur right out of them. I'll write again very soon dear.

Good night my love. Jim.

Ruth couldn't help feeling pride at Jim's success in getting into the aviation class. She could tell he was feeling pleased with himself. His family couldn't afford to send him off to college, and she knew he had barely kept himself clothed and fed with his small salary as a clerk. But Jim was smart and now that he had found a subject he really seemed to love, she knew he would succeed. Not only that, but she realized he was already making plans to advance up the military ladder as far as he could go. As she fingered the small blue cloth insignia he had enclosed in the letter, she had to smile. She was proud of his ambition. Her Jim was going to be okay.

"And so am I," she thought. The rain was starting to ease up and the sky beginning to brighten. She glanced at the great clock above the concourse. She would have to hustle. Her best client was expecting her with new design sketches within the hour.

A long letter from Jim arrived by post the next day.

Sunday, March 1, 1942 - Air Corps Technical School, Keesler Field, Mississippi

Ruth my love:

I just have time for one letter tonight and although I should write my folks, I feel as though Sunday should be given over to thoughts and remembrances of you. I have to shampoo my hair and wash some clothes. It's raining pretty hard out so I will dry them over my bunk. Nothing can be left hanging in barracks after 7 am. They are pretty strict here as to the making of bunks, hanging up outside clothing, having shoes placed just right and floor spotless. We have foot-lockers in which we keep various clothing and equipment. Everything in the locker must be just right.

Of course there is nothing difficult about this; if you follow instructions and obey orders.

We were issued a large amount of summer clothing and a flight jacket and summer flight cap. I got a pretty good fit in everything except a pair of off duty trousers and shoes.

Our meals are wonderful. We can have as much as we want. Steak, chops, everything is there for us.

Biloxi is a little Boomtown due to the location of this field. I saw quite a few southern gals here Friday. It was visitors' day and they were the first girls I have been near since I joined the Army. It gave me a funny feeling to see the southern fellows taking their girls arm in arm and showing them around.

I wanted so much to have you down here then, so I could walk you around. I'd show some of these Rebels what a real girl looks like.

Ruth reread this last paragraph and shook her head. Her Jim was becoming a true romantic. She had never expected it from him as his outward demeanor was often a bit rigid. In fact, her sister Justine had long questioned what Ruth saw in him.

"He's so... so... , I don't know—stiff, Ruth. He stands like an undertaker at a funeral parlor! Have you ever seen Jim relax?"

"He's perfectly relaxed when he's with me. You just need to spend time with him and get to know him a little better."

"And he's so religious! All that church stuff he's always talking about. Is he serious? Does he really go to church every morning?"

"Jim grew up in a very Irish Catholic family. His mother was a real churchgoer. I think he takes after her just to keep her memory alive."

"Well, as long as you don't turn into one of those church widows with their husbands always hanging about with the priests or passing the baskets at every service on every weekend all year 'round. Remember what happened to Mrs. Flaherty down the block. Her husband might as well have joined the monastery for all she ever saw of him."

Ruth laughed. "No chance of that with my Jim. He likes his church all right, but he has more important things on his mind." She remembered her last conversation with him before he joined up. He was focused on only one thing that night and it had nothing to do with church! In fact, it was the type of conversation you didn't mention in church unless it was in the confessional. She had to suppress a laugh as she continued to read.

Ruth, will you please send me one of your handkerchiefs. I'd like to have something like that of yours, as a lucky piece. You might also put the imprint of your lips in one corner. I'm blushing, while I write this, but it's what I want. I hope you don't think I'm silly. I got it bad I guess.

The other day the fellow that bunks next to me showed me something quite confidential. It was a combination of clock mirror and picture. On the back of the picture of his girl he had the impression of her lips and a lock of her hair. I thought that would be just what I would like from you. Dear, I'm way down here and I've got to have something of yours to cherish and sort of look at once in a while.

Ruth paused. What could she send him? A lock of hair seemed a little too dramatic to her, but if that was what he wanted, then she could easily send him a bit in her next letter. Perhaps she could buy a small wallet to keep it safe. She wondered if the army would approve. She guessed Jim would be happy for any small token from her and made a mental note to check in Jordan's next time she was downtown.

I have finished my basic training here today. I was notified today that I would be shipped out tomorrow. I am going to a private school many miles from here. They want to train us as quickly as possible and the school here is filled already. Why we particular men were selected I do not know. I will be able to tell you more of course when I get there.

The boys are planning a little blow up tonight in the squad room.

We can buy canned beer at the canteen. You know, a sort of farewell to the fellows left behind.

I've met a few nice fellows. But I doubt if we will become real chummy until we are stationed at our permanent bases.

We think we are going to get different uniforms since the Air Corps is a separate unit. Rumors are it will be similar to the R.A.F. Marine blue or something, with Gold Braid. Sam Brown belts and everything, I betcha.

I met a fellow last week that knew my friend Eddie Barry. This morning I saw him marching as a prisoner under guard. He had told me he was going over the hill and he did but got caught.

Don't work too hard dear. I think you're quite wonderful. I better cut out thinking thoughts of you so much or I'll be driven to "go over the hill."

But seriously, I'm glad I have a girl like you at home. I know I will stay on the straight and narrow.

Good-bye for now my lovely one. My next letter will be from ?

Jim.

Ruth stared at the question mark in the letter's last line. Jim was being moved. But to where? Would it be to a base near enough to Boston to visit him? Unlikely. The only Army base near by was Fort Devens and there was no school located there as far as she knew. It was an embarkation center where the men who were drafted were trained before being sent overseas. At least three of the old crowd had been sent to Devens when they got the call. Charlie Bates, Mike Provo, and Louis Bridge had been shipped out from there.

Charlie's girlfriend, Midge, had been very upset that she never had a chance to say goodbye. The Army was moving the men through training so fast, there had been no time for the usual farewells.

CHAPTER 3

MISSOURI

MISSOURI AVIATION INSTITUTE • KANSAS CITY

our months had passed since war had been declared and the one thing Jim still had going for him, Ruth realized, was that he was still in the country.

"Tuesday, March 3, 1942 12 noon – Air Corps Training Detachment, Missouri Aviation Institute, Kansas City, Missouri."

Ruth, my darling—I dreamt about you last night. It was just a "short feature." You were sitting on a sofa, and I was on the arm and I was teasing you about something or other. You bit on my fingers and I woke up. I'll get you for that, you wait and see if I don't.

Ruth wondered what he had been drinking the night before. Jim liked his beer well enough, but he must have had a toot too much! She shook her head and kept on reading.

The class in structures finished last night and today we begin the study of hydraulics. I understand if you can draw well you will get a good mark. There are something like 63 drawings of parts to be made.

You people are having quite a few blackouts aren't you? I don't imagine Kansas City will ever have one. They don't even have a Civilian Defense Committee here. They really don't know a war is on. And if I stay here long enough I won't either. Everything is so peaceful like. Not many soldiers. No army trucks banging through the streets. Absolutely no sailors. Very few bar rooms. This is quite the city. Their city hall is a bigger building than your Boston court house.

I would sure like to see you Easter morn. I bet you will look real beautiful. I hope the day is sunny. I'll be thinking of you all the day.

Goodbye now dear, and have a nice Easter.

Jim.

Ruth put the letter down and looked out her bedroom window at her neighbor, Mrs. Wilson, working in her garden across the street. The cold rains of early spring were finally over and the last few days of sunshine had had the effect of drawing everyone out of hibernation for the first time since the last hard frost.

The next day she stopped by the accessories counter in Jordan's and purchased a small, inexpensive wallet. That evening when the house was finally quiet, she snipped a short lock of her hair, tied it with a thin gold ribbon and carefully placed it inside the wallet and wrote Jim a short note.

My darling, Jim

Here is a lock of my hair for you to hold as a keepsake. I send it with all my love and wishes for you to return safely to my arms. Stay happy and healthy until we meet again.

Yours, Ruth

She did not know how long it would take for her little gift to be delivered to Jim, but determined that it be delivered before the holiday, she mailed it first class.

✳

"I'm going to walk up to the corner store, Mother," Ruth stuck her head into the kitchen where Mrs. LeBlanc was mixing something in a large bowl. "You need me to pick up anything for supper?"

"I could use some sugar if they have any," Mrs. LeBlanc answered. "I think you'll find at least a few ration coupons in that drawer." She pointed a large mixing spoon in the direction of the kitchen cabinet.

"What are you making?" Ruth asked, poking her head around her mother's shoulder to view a doughy brown lump in the bottom of the bowl.

"A surprise," her mother answered. "I've never made this before. Found the recipe in the morning paper. It's supposed to be a substitute for angel food cake, but without the sugar, I'm not sure how it will taste. Ask Mr. Mazzioli if he can manage a small bag of sugar for us just in case."

"Ok," Ruth answered. She found the ration book and removed a few stamps. "I'll see if these will work. I'm still not sure how many we need."

"It changes all the time. But Mr. Mazzioli will know. Ask him."

It took only a minute or two to walk to Mazzioli's. The small grocery had been at the corner of Bromfield and Wollaston for decades. Everyone in the neighborhood stopped in for the essentials of life: newspaper, bread, milk, and of course, the latest gossip.

"Hey Missy LeBlanc!" Mr. Mazzioli called out as she pushed open the old glass door. The small bell above the transom signaled her entrance to the one or two patrons standing at the counter. She recognized one of them as Mrs. Evans, the widow from across the nearby playground. Her son Charlie had gone off just before Jim had signed up and Ruth knew he had already shipped out to the South Pacific.

"Morning. Mr. Mazzioli. Mrs. Evans." She nodded to them both.

"What can I do for you this beautiful day?" Mr. Mazzioli was eager to please.

"Any chance you have any sugar? My mother's making a new recipe and it calls for sugar or something we can use as a substitute."

"We don't have any sugar in stock. Getting harder and harder to come by." Mr. Mazzioli shook his head. "But some cooks are using corn syrup instead. We have lots of corn syrup!"

"But you have to be sure to use enough syrup," Mrs. Evans interrupted. "You need at least two cups for a recipe that calls for a cup of sugar. And be careful not to use too much. The syrup gets too gooey. The last time I baked was for little Jessie's birthday. No matter how I tried, the cake was all runny and wouldn't settle. Try maple syrup instead."

Now Ruth was confused. Corn syrup, maple syrup? Which was better? She turned to the grocer. "Which is better for baking a cake?" She looked again at Mrs. Evans. "I guess I'll try the maple syrup." Mrs. Evans nodded her agreement.

"Any word from Charlie, Mrs. Evans? Any news?"

"We got a letter a bit ago. He's off to fight the Japanese somewhere in the Pacific. But no details. They're being very strict about details." Mrs. Evans continued. "But he sounded fine and I think he's with a good group of men. Most of them are from New England. They all signed up together, and that's a good thing, don't you think?" Mrs. Evans grasped her shopping bag a little more tightly and Ruth could see she was uncomfortable talking about her son and his being so far away. "How's your young man? Jim, isn't it?"

"He's fine, thanks. He sends letters all the time. He signed up for the Army Air Force and is in training somewhere in the Midwest."

"That sounds important." Mrs. Evans responded. "Is he a pilot?"

"No, he'll be working on the engines and keeping the planes flying."

"So he won't be going overseas?"

"I think once he finishes his training they will send him wherever they need him. Here or over there. No word yet."

"Well, let's hope it all ends soon and he won't have to go at all." Mrs. Evans paused and Ruth could tell she was on the verge of tears. "I want all them boys to come back home. Now. You'd think they could settle these things without them killing each other. Makes no sense to me."

"Now, Mrs. Evans," Mr. Mazzioli spoke up. "We got to fight to stop Hitler and those people who bombed us back in December. We have to fight back. Look at the headlines." He pointed to the stack of newspapers on the counter top.

"Brits Bombed Again" "Navy Convoy Losses Mount" The extra bold type filled the entire top of the page. Just under the headline was a large photo of a bombed out street and people running for their lives. Ruth's stomach gave a lurch. This was the world her Jim was about to face.

"You're right, Mr. Mazzioli. And I realize we have to go over there and stop it. I wish there was another way."

"No other way, Missy LeBlanc. Too late for that now. If we don't stop Hitler..."

"And that Mussolini character from your Italy," Mrs. Evans interrupted.

"He is not from my Italy!" Mr. Mazzioli countered. "Mussolini—he is a fascist! A traitor to my family and all of Italy." His voice was getting louder. "Do not tell me about this Mussolini. Don't talk about him."

Mrs. Evans was too stunned to continue. "I'm sorry, Mr. Mazzioli. I only just heard on the radio..."

"The radio lies. It tells nothing but bad things about my country. I don't listen no more." He paused, realizing his voice had betrayed his anger. "I'm sorry to be so mad, Mrs. Evans. Not your fault." He began to stack her few parcels on the counter to ring them up. "Is this everything? You need anything else?"

"No, nothing else, Mr. Mazzioli." Mrs. Evans handed the storekeeper a canvas sack and together they bagged her groceries.

Ruth turned away and walked down the center aisle of the small store in search of a jar of maple syrup. The shelves were still full of products but there were a few spots where the tins were beginning to thin out. Ruth had heard rumors that prepared foods were becoming scarce and she guessed from the look of these shelves that the rumor was true. No sugar, no tins of coffee, and in the spot where there were usually racks of candy bars and sweets, bags of pretzels were spread out to give the appearance of a fully packed shelf.

She found the maple syrup on the top shelf at the end of the aisle and was heading back to the counter when she remembered why she had headed to Mazzioli's market in the first place. She needed nylons. A one stop shop, Mazzioli's wasn't the biggest market, but it was one of those places that always carried at least a few of everything you might need in a pinch. And Ruth needed nylons. Her last pair had a ladder just above the knee that she knew was going to show beneath her skirt's hemline in no time.

Mazzioli kept the personal care items like nylons, and hair brushes on a rack near the pay phone at the front of the store. Maple syrup in hand, Ruth headed back towards the front counter. The rack where nylons were usually displayed was totally empty.

"Mr. Mazzioli, where are all the nylons? You usually have a whole variety."

"Gone, Missy LeBlanc. "All gone. Two days ago the salesman came in and told me that was it. No more nylons for ladies. Everything is going to parachutes for the war."

"What?" Ruth was incredulous. "You've got to be kidding."

"That's what the salesman said. No nylons. And I don't know when more come in. But we got socks. Lots of socks. Bottom shelf on the right." He pointed in the direction of the bottom shelf, but Ruth was not interested in socks and shook her head no.

All the way home Ruth turned this latest piece of information over and over in her mind. This war was getting serious. No nylons. All materials going to parachutes? What was she going to do?

Justine was equally incredulous. "No nylons? What are they thinking? What are we supposed to do without nylons? Go bare legged? I can't do that."

"Well, we've done it before. When we were kids, we always went bare legged."

"Right. But we were wearing ankle socks and Mary Janes, Ruth. I can't wear heels without nylons. What do they think we're going to do?"

"We'll just have to make do with what we've got I guess." Ruth thought about her one last pair of nylons that she was saving for special occasions. They were in her second drawer carefully wrapped in white tissue paper. She decided they would stay there.

"I've got a ladder starting on the pair I've got on now, Justine. Do you have any nail polish or a bit of glue I can use to stop it?"

Justine sighed. "This is the way it's going to be from now on, isn't it? Patching this, taping that, no nylons, no sugar, no new leather belts. My friend Judy was telling me her dad's car ran out of gas on the way home yesterday, and they won't have new gas ration stamps until next month. He's really upset."

"I guess he'll have to take the bus like the rest of us."

"He's putting in for an exemption. He's in sales, after all, and he's got to keep driving or there won't be any sales. No sales, no money. No money, they'll all be out on the street."

"Now you're exaggerating, Justine." Ruth was losing patience with her sister. Justine had developed a very narrow view of the world that only revolved around her little group of friends and their best buddies. She was still too young to know anyone who was off to war, though a few of her high school friends were very likely to be drafted once they graduated in the spring. That would change Justine's view for sure, Ruth thought.

That evening the family gathered for supper and Mrs. LeBlanc's angel food cake a la maple syrup was a great hit. Though the cake was gooey and a little hard to cut, the maple syrup supplied just the right amount of sweetness. They all agreed that one good thing that might come out of the war would be alternative recipes for old favorites.

✿

During the next two weeks Ruth waited anxiously for Jim to write. She checked the small table by the front door each time she went in or out of the house, but no letters arrived. Worried he might have already been shipped overseas, she began to scan the newspapers for news of troop deployments. So much information was kept secret from the public. It was the not knowing that was driving her crazy.

Finally, on Saturday, when the morning mail arrived, there were two letters from Jim, both of them postmarked from Kansas City. He was still in the states! At least he was when he posted the letters.

Anxious to savor Jim's words in private, Ruth pressed the precious envelopes to her heart and hurried up the stairs to the quiet comfort of her bedroom. Grabbing Aunt Cora's quilt for warmth, she fell into the overstuffed armchair by the window, and settled in for a long read.

Wednesday, March 4, 1942 11:50 pm -
Air Corps Training Detachment,

Missouri Aviation Institute, Kansas City, Missouri

Hiya Honey:

You won't get this until Monday so allow me to say I hope you spent a pleasant Sunday.

My buddy, Ray, is playing the mouth organ so instead of just lying in bed waiting for him to shut up, I thought I'd utilize the time and drop you a word or two. Today we started our new class in "Hydraulics." We had to make 6 drawings of various parts.

The only thing that bothered me today was the standing in one spot all the time. The subject itself I don't think will be too difficult. It's lots cleaner work than engines. This morning, not having too much work to do, I went downtown and viewed a Messerschmidt 109. It was quite a sight. It is a very fast plane.

I don't think the construction on German planes will equal our ships however. It is of a very simple design and they didn't take great pains in putting the fuselage together. It didn't have half the rivets that are in our ships.

An Irish lad shot this one down over London. The German pilot was an Ace. He had five veterans marked on his vertical fin.

Every night, I drop off to sleep thinking of you. It works every time. It's because I can become fully relaxed when I dwell on pleasant thoughts. What could be more pleasant.

Love, Jim

Ruth folded the letter back into its envelope. She tried to imagine Jim sleeping in his bunk, the sound of a far-away harmonica softly wooing him to sleep. If only she could cross over time and space and be with him in that bunk. How warm and tender that moment would be. She sighed and opened the second envelope. Jim had written it the following day.

Thursday, March 5, 1942 - Air Corps Training Detachment, Missouri Aviation Institute, Kansas City, Missouri

Dearest Ruth,

I tried to start this letter while waiting for chow but I just got the date down and had to run for it. You have to fall out when that call sounds or you don't eat.

When we came back to the barracks after mess we were called out again for special detail. "K.P." I washed pots and pans for 6 hours, served the stuff at the evening meal, and went back to pots and pans until 9:15 pm.

Tuesday we spent the whole day in rough country. Early in the morning the drill instructors called for 12 volunteers to train in skirmish fighting so that they in turn could train a squad of fellows. This was necessary because there is a shortage of drill instructors at this camp. I volunteered and he gave us full instructions as squad leaders. Then, I was given charge of 11 men and told to take them anywhere in the area and run through skirmishes.

I got my marks from that test. I was second highest in our barrack. Imagine me getting such a mark in a mechanical test, after studying accounting! There were 20 questions in math and as many as you could answer in 40 minutes in the subject of machinery and gears. I guess I have what they call "mechanical aptitude" or sheer luck - maybe.

Thank you darling for the picture. It was exactly what I wanted and fits my wallet perfectly. I glance at it many times during the day. I feel excited every time I look at it. How I long to run my fingers through those lovely blond tresses, and hold my face close to yours. I'm in love with you darling, and it's the grandest feeling I have ever yet experienced. I miss you very much, my sweet, but I keep telling myself, "I'll go to her soon."

Have you got the family buggy all fixed? I was sort of planning to have some fun with you this summer. We could go on some picnics, and moonlight sails, and kind of spoon under the warm summer moon. If you ever find yourself spooning with someone else darling, please don't mention it. I don't know what I'd do but the thought of it depresses me.

Love is certainly a funny thing. It can be just as painful as it can be pleasant. I never want to be jealous; I'd rather have any sickness you can name than be sick at heart from jealousy.

Be watchful of men in uniform. Especially if they have been confined for a length of time in camp. That song of "From Taps to Reveille" fits me fine. Pleasant dreams,

Good night my love, Jim

Ruth reread the letter. Did she detect hints of jealousy between the lines? If anyone had encouraged her to get out and have a good time while he was away, it was Jim. She liked his brother David all right and was happy to join the crowd each weekend at one of the local dance halls where she and Jim used to go, but there was no one she was interested in more than Jim. Still, she was secretly pleased Jim at least considered the possibility he could lose her.

Ruth's hope for an early end to the war was crushed the next Sunday morning when she picked up the newspaper from the front porch. "Hitler's Forces and Hirohito's Battalions Hope to Join Hands in India," screamed across the page. There were pictures and first person accounts. The paper was full of it. This war was not going to stop any time soon.

"Did you hear the news, Mother?" Ruth asked as she tossed the paper onto the kitchen table. "The Germans are joining up with the Japanese."

"What are you talking about?"

"Look. Just look at the headlines this morning. It's awful. This war is just getting worse and worse. At this rate, Jim will never come home."

Mrs. Leblanc stopped beating up scrambled eggs and wiped her hands on her apron. "Let me see." She reached for the paper and read the large print. "Oh dear," she muttered. "It's horrible what's happening. You must be worried, but you said Jim is still in that school? Maybe they'll keep him there? School can take a long time, you know."

"Jim's a very smart man. He'll learn everything they have to teach in no time and be on the first ship out." She pulled one of his last letters out of her dress pocket. "He's learning all about planes and engines and how to fix them. They wouldn't be spending so much time and money on him if they weren't going to ship him out."

"You may be right, dear, but no sense worrying about it today. Jim's safe at the moment, and that's something.

Fr. O'Brien's sermon that Sunday was all duty and patriotism and doing God's will—an about face for Fr. O'Brien. Up until the bombing of Pearl Harbor the priest had been dead set against the country going to war. His solution was to pray for those who were fighting, but otherwise stay out of it! He wasn't alone. There had been a lot of talk about remaining neutral and just not getting involved. Politicians and priests together had warned about the dire consequences of committing the country to the battle. But with the Japanese attack on U.S. ships in Hawaii, all opposition disappeared. Now both politicians and the church were calling for a full frontal effort. Justice demanded action. Ruth felt that Fr. O'Brien's changed attitude was one of the reasons Jim had responded so quickly to the call to arms.

After Mass, Ruth headed down Hancock Street towards home. It was unusually warm for an early spring day and she felt like taking the long way home. The sky was a deep blue with just a few wispy clouds, and the early afternoon sun made everything seem fresh and new. Spring crocuses were just beginning to appear along the Wilson's foot path, and the bright yellow forsythia in the Babcock's front yard was just coming into full flower. If the warm weather kept up everything would be in full bloom by mid-April.

Rather than take her usual route down Mason, Ruth continued down Beach Street towards the sea wall and Wollaston Beach. So much had happened in the last four months. She needed time and a long walk to just sort it out.

Top of the list: she had definitely fallen in love—and with the most unlikely guy—Jim, the accountant from the sixth floor office. For the better part of the fall, Jim had been part of the Saturday night "crowd"—dining and dancing every week at one night spot or another. But then, just before Thanksgiving, they had begun dating seriously, just the two of them; meeting for lunch downtown, visiting each other's homes and meeting each other's families. When Pearl Harbor happened, Jim was one of the first in his crowd to answer his country's call for men to fight back.

Now that he was gone off to war, Ruth realized how much she loved him. She missed his laugh, and his smile and the funny way he had of standing so still, you'd think he was a mannequin. One day while Jim was waiting for her to finish Christmas shopping in Filene's, Ruth saw a woman shopper actually feel the lapel of his jacket thinking he was a store model. Jim moved, the woman screamed and quickly ran off down the aisle. They had laughed about that for days.

As Ruth reached the end of Beach Street, she crossed over the wide boulevard and headed for the bench near the sea wall. Families on the sand below, sauntered by in small groups, the children running and circling the adults, the sound of their laughter carried to her on the soft on-shore breeze. Ruth sat down and lifted her face to the warm spring sun. "Where is Jim today?" she thought. "What is he doing?" "Does he miss me?"

She knew the answer to that last question. Jim's last letters were full of his longing to be with her again. She hadn't realized what a sentimental man he was. The words had not been easy for him to say when they had been together, but his true feelings flowed in rivers of emotion in his letters.

Monday, March 2, 1942 - Air Corps Technical School, Keesler Field, Mississippi

Dearest Ruth,

I haven't written anyone yet about my leaving. I have my duffel bags packed and they are plenty heavy. We had to lug them quite a ways to the shipping station. I hear all kinds of rumors about the place we are going

A bit of sad news, don't spread this around. We lost four men (all northerners) from sickness - colds - nervous breakdowns. Now I haven't seen anything official on this, but news like that is bound to get around the Squadron. It's very damp here. You see this place is built on the site of a swamp. The continual rainy season, the inoculations combined with fatigue due to drilling and detail, have just about floored a couple dozen fellows who came here with us. Of these, 4 have died. But you take the number of men here and that would be a small average.

One guy from another squadron jumped in front of a big truck and was killed. I don't think they told his family it was suicide but the fellows say he deliberately ran out and fell in front of it. That could happen anywhere. You meet all kinds of people in an Army camp.

There are many times when I don't like it, but to grin and bear it will see me through much better than just crabbing.

Kansas City is really wonderful. Very modern. Their City Hall, Court House, Police Dept are 3 skyscrapers. The girls? Much better than those Southern ladies. I was getting just a little fed up on that Southern drawl. These girls up here are city girls (from the country) and they look more like you girls up North.

I reside in a second class hotel, have 2 meals in the dining room here and one meal at the Airport. My school hours are from 2 pm to 11 pm. Bed check at 12:30 pm. But, I don't have to get up until 8:15 am. Working nights (I'm glad) I will be sure of behaving. Girls are all over the place here (in the lobby, on the piazzas) and I understand they are there to keep us entertained. Their movements are sponsored by some society who are supposed to be taking care of the soldiers.

Actually, we are treated very well. You know we are rated as second in importance in the Air Corps. As I said before, we are going to come out of here as technicians or you might call us troubleshooters. Do I sound as though I'm bragging? We all are so darn relieved to

*get away from that Mississippi weather that some of us think we are
in a dream. No kidding, it's from the extreme to the sublime.*

It won't be a picnic. We got a talking today on just what we are in for.

*It's so pleasant writing to you and so much more pleasant getting
letters from you. I guess it will be a few days before I get another
one. So long for now, Ruth dear, and please take care of yourself*

*I really love you- with all my heart. Please call my home. I will write
them tomorrow.*

Lovingly yours, Jim.

Ruth closed the letter and slipped it back into her purse. Thank goodness he was still safe and in school. Kansas City, Missouri of all places. She
imagined her city boy standing in the cornfields of Missouri with all those
pretty mid-west girls around to entertain him!

Jim was only teasing her by mentioning the girls from what she imagined was the USO. She knew there wouldn't be any funny business with
Jim. He was just too "Catholic" to take a chance on ruining his immortal
soul.

Ruth turned her coat collar up a little higher as a cloud crossed the sun
and she felt a momentary chill off the ocean.

"Mind if I sit down?" a familiar voice asked. Ruth turned to look. It was
Jim's brother, David.

"Good morning, or should I say good afternoon?" she responded.

"Afternoon," David looked at his watch. "Just after 1 o'clock."

"Really?" Ruth stood up. "I didn't realize. I've just been sitting here gazing off into space. I've got to go. Mother's got dinner on the table by now."

"Oh." David hesitated. "Well, if I can't sit down, can I walk with you?"

"Of course. In fact, why don't you join us for dinner? I'm sure they'll be
enough. Mother always goes overboard on a Sunday."

"Even with rationing?" David seemed uncertain. "We always seem to be
a little short at the end of the week at our house." Ruth took his arm and
together they crossed the boulevard and headed back towards Bromfield
Street. "Hazel does well, but somehow we run out of one thing or another."

"I'm sure she's doing her best but it isn't easy keeping everything straight.
There are always changes and new regulations. Mother just has a knack for
managing things and making substitutions. If she doesn't have one ingre-

45

dient she'll use another. Somehow it all works out."

They walked another block in silence. "How is your business doing these days?" Ruth asked. "With so few cars on the roads, I hope your garage can still survive."

"We do okay." David assured her. "Thankfully, between Quincy and Boston, we have enough doctors, police and politicians to keep us busy. The important people can have all the gas they want. The rest of us don't do too badly right now, but the OPA, the Office of Price Administration, is going to get stricter. The big deal right now is tires. Since they put in the rule that you're only allowed four tires plus a spare for every car, we've been real busy fixing flats. No new tires available unless you're one of the top dogs in city hall. And even they have to ask for special treatment. It's getting crazy, and this war has only just begun."

Ruth patted her purse. "Jim wrote me. He's just been shipped to a new technical school in the middle of Missouri. They're teaching him how to fix airplane engines. He says it's pretty important stuff."

"I'd say it is." David turned and together they continued to walk. "We don't hear much from Jim these days. I guess you're the one he writes to mostly."

"Almost a letter every week. Sometimes two or three." Ruth paused. She realized this was not what David needed to hear. "But he always tells me to pass on the information to you all. I'm sorry, I guess I haven't been too good at that."

"No problem. Just as long as Jim's okay. But I think Hazel would like a more frequent update if you can manage it." He paused and then continued. "Hazel and Jim are not the closest. What with her coming in and taking things over so soon after our mother died. Jim was only eleven and I don't think he ever really got over losing Mom."

"I know the story, David. It was a real tragedy for you all. But thank goodness for Hazel. She wasn't your Mother, but she did help make it a home for you."

"I guess you could say that." David stopped talking and it was clear he had nothing more to say on the subject.

By now they had reached the front of number 180 Bromfield. "Please, David, come in for dinner. Everyone will be pleased to see you."

"Can't say 'no' to delicious home cooking."

Sunday dinner was always a big affair. Mrs. LeBlanc had spent a lot of time preparing a wide variety of dishes. "I'm doing some testing on a few new ingredients and recipes," she declared, scooping large servings of root vegetables smothered in some sort of cream sauce onto their plates. "I want you to try a little of each and tell me what you think."

David looked down at what he suspected was a mash of turnips, parsnips and potatoes. "Looks delicious, Mrs. LeBlanc," he declared, but he did not pick up his fork. Ruth caught his eye and smiled.

"Looks almost good enough to eat, Mother."

"What's that supposed to mean?" Mrs. LeBlanc questioned. "I'm experimenting with mixing things up a bit. Just try it. If you don't like it, we can always give it to the neighbor's dog."

"No way is the dog getting any of this," Mr. LeBlanc declared, entering the dining room. "Food is too precious to hand it off to an animal." He settled his large frame into the chair at the head of the table and let his gaze fall across the fancy serving platters steaming in the center of the spread. "Looks fine, Bertha. Everything looks delicious." He tucked a large white dinner napkin into the collar of his shirt and reached for the nearest dish.

"I see we have Spam as our main attraction today." He turned to Justine, sitting next to him on his right. "Please hand me the mustard, will you? Mustard's the only thing that makes this stuff edible."

Justine passed the small jar to her father and then leaned towards David. "How's the garage going these days, David? My friend Mark, over in Quincy, just picked up a nail in one of his wheels last Saturday and he can't buy a new tire anywhere. I told him about your garage, but I'm not sure if he made it that far. How much does a new tire cost anyway,?" Justine didn't wait for an answer. "I guess things are just going to get tighter and tighter for all of us if this war keeps going the way it's going."

David opened his mouth to answer Justine's question, but she just kept on talking, unaware that no one was really listening.

"I think it's just awful the way they have us rationed for just about everything, don't you think so, David?" At that moment she paused long enough to swallow a spoonful of vegetables and almost gagged. "Mom, what is this stuff? What did you put on it?" she asked, holding the spoon filled with the vegetable mash up so her mother could see.

"They are perfectly good vegetables. I just combined them and added a little honey and Karo Syrup to add some sweetness."

"Why didn't you use sugar?" Justine complained. "They taste awful."

Mrs. Leblanc glared at her daughter. "Because sugar is too precious to use on vegetables. I save the little sugar we have for special occasions. Just eat and be glad you have something to eat. Lots of people don't have as good, and remember our soldiers." She glanced at her oldest daughter.

"Remember Ruth's Jim. He's in the Army now and who knows what he has to eat."

"Actually, Mother," Ruth interrupted, "Jim is doing just fine. I got a letter from him yesterday. He's eating better than we are."

David chuckled and shook his head. "Leave it to Jim to manage the best for himself." He looked over at Ruth and gave her a wink. But she didn't seem to notice.

"What do you think about starting a Victory Garden in the backyard this spring?" Mrs. LeBlanc asked. "I've been doing a lot of reading and I think it's the patriotic thing to do. Mrs. Carlton from next door and I were talking and I think we can buy all we need from the hardware store." She looked around the table at her husband and daughters. "Don't you think that's a good idea?"

David spoke up, "Sounds like a fine idea. Some of our customers at the garage are talking about setting up something in the empty lot over by O'Neil Field. They're asking all the neighbors to chip in. Going to make it some sort of a cooperative. Anyone who helps plant and weed gets a share of the harvest at the end of the season."

"That sounds like a fine idea, but we don't need to go all the way to O'Neil's." Mr. LeBlanc interrupted. "We've got a lot of room in our own backyard. We can start our own Victory Garden right here."

"And you'll help with it, Frederick?" Mrs. LeBlanc asked eagerly.

"I'll dig the patch and get you started, but as far as planting and weeding, that's women's work. You girls can do all that."

"Sure. We do all the hard work and come harvest time, you'll eat all the profits, I'm sure," Justine teased.

"Well, isn't that the way it should be? We men do the heavy labor, and you ladies take care of the details." He chuckled and flashed a wide toothy grin at everyone at the table.

By the time dinner was finished everyone had had quite enough of Mrs. LeBlanc's experimental dishes. They declared the chicken with honey was a hit, but the vegetable mash was a bit of a disaster. And the boiled Spam? They all agreed she should try frying it up next time. As the women began to clear the table, David and Mr. LeBlanc moved into the front parlor.

"So, tell me David," Mr. LeBlanc slowly walked to the large bay window that looked out over the front yard, "you hear all the local gossip from those damn politicians who stop in at your garage. What's really happening with this war and these rules and regulations they keep tossing at us? First it's gas, then car tires, next it'll be my car! How am I supposed to live without a car to get around?"

David didn't have an answer. Instead, he just shrugged his shoulders, dug a pack of Lucky Strikes from his breast pocket, and pulled a cigarette out from under the foil. He lit the cigarette and took a long, slow drag, filling his lungs with the heavy, white smoke.

Mr. LeBlanc studied David before continuing, unsure how to ask him what was on his mind. "You must be sorry to be missing all the action. Your brother Jim is off making a mark on the world and doing his part for the war effort and here you are stuck fixing flats and pumping gas."

David gave him a hard stare. "I'm not sorry. Not one whit. There's plenty to do here on the home front to keep life and limb together." He took another drag off his butt. "The way I've got it figured, we're all soldiers one way or the other. Besides, I've just volunteered as an airplane spotter."

"Really?" Mr. LeBlanc was surprised. He didn't know David very well, but from what he had observed, the man was a bit of a lazy lout.

"Joe Meany set me up with the GOC just last week. That's Ground Observer Corps run by the Army Air Force. Same crowd as has Jim working on engines. We've got a few weeks of training to get us up to speed, but then it's all ahead full."

"Well, I must say, David, I'm impressed. Glad you're doing your part."

"It's a lot to learn, Mr. LeBlanc, and it's important. I might not be able to fight on the front lines, but with us living right along the ocean, making sure we don't have enemy planes coming at us, well—it's what I can do." He took one last drag on his cigarette and looked around for an ashtray.

Mr. LeBlanc handed him one of Bertha's candy dishes. "Here, use this. The missus will kill me if you get those hot ashes on her carpet."

"Thanks." David crushed the cigarette against the bottom of the dish. "Listen, you don't think Ruth would be interested in this plane spotter thing, do you? All kinds of people are volunteering now. Women especially. I guess they figure it's one way they can help out even if they're not on the front lines. The Captain asked us to spread the word. Connecticut got the jump on us here in Boston and there are spotters now, up and down Long Island Sound. With all the coastline we've got here, we need more volunteers and I thought Ruth might be just the one."

Mr. LeBlanc rubbed his chin, thoughtfully. "I don't know why one of my girls can't help you out. I think I heard Justine mention something about joining some group going out to Quincy Point or maybe it was Nantasket? Can't remember." He scratched his head slowly. "Why don't you just ask 'em. I'm sure they'd be interested."

"Interested in what? What plot are you two cooking up?" Ruth asked as she entered the parlor.

"Plane spotting." David answered. "I was just telling your Dad, we're looking for more volunteers."

"Really? You joined the Corps."

"Just did, actually. And I think it's something you'd be splendid at. You've got such a fine eye for details and all that."

"Thanks for the compliment, David, but I don't really know anything about planes or spotting or anything like that. What is it you have to do?"

"It's really quite simple. Every few days we go out and watch the skies for a couple of hours. Any plane that comes over, we look at these spotting cards they give us, match the silhouette and then if it's not one of ours, we call it in to headquarters and they send out the gunners."

"You're kidding." Ruth looked shocked. "They bomb the plane?"

"Well, no, not exactly." David looked a bit sheepish. "I'm exaggerating. But it's roughly the same thing. All I know is we call it in and they—the Army Air Force, takes care of the rest."

"I see," Ruth replied. "Well, it sounds exciting, I guess. But I still don't know a thing about planes."

"Oh, the GOC will teach us all that. It takes a couple of weeks to learn the ropes but then we're ready to go. They'll assign us a spot right here along the coast. I'm thinking, if you're willing, we could do this together." He turned to Mr. LeBlanc, "I'd make sure nothing happened to Ruth, especially if we were sent out on a night patrol."

Mr. LeBlanc nodded his approval. "That's the only way I'd let one of my daughters go out searching the skies for the enemy. Doesn't sound too dangerous, but these days, you have to be careful."

"When do the classes begin?" Ruth asked.

"Next Thursday. If you're really willing to do it, I could pick you up after work and we could go to the class together. They're being held at the Quincy Armory."

"Let me think about it, David. I do want to do my part, but I'm awfully busy at work. I'm not sure I could spare the time."

David looked at her with a steady gaze. "Jim couldn't spare the time, either. But he's given the country the next who knows how many months or years fighting for us. I think two or three hours a week looking out to protect our skies is not too much to ask."

Ruth was surprised at how firm David was, but she knew he was right. Volunteering a couple hours of her time every other week was a small sacrifice she could easily afford. And with David at her side, what could go wrong?

"Ok, David, I'll do it. I think Jim would approve. I'll write him about it tonight."

❊

Ruth sat at her office desk, sipping tea, re-reading the latest letter from Jim. It was full of details she didn't need to know, but his fascination with the aircraft made her realize how much he loved his new job.

Sunday,

April 12, 1942 - Air Corps Training Detachment, Missouri Aviation Institute, Kansas City, Missouri

Dearest Ruth,

Please say a little silent prayer that I'll pass the exams with high marks.

We had the thrill of a lifetime yesterday. One of the P-38's came in while we were out in the field for "break."

He circled the field three times going somewhere around 300 mph. Boy, what a streak. Banks way over on his left wing and zooms it down for a pretty little landing.

It has a landing speed of about 100 mph. When he goes over your head you don't hear a thing. After he is past, you can hear the "whoosh" just coming to your ears. It sounds more like a whistle than a "whoosh."

One of the instructors flew an A-17 the other day. We thought sure he'd hit the hangars at the end of the field. He flew about 10 feet from the ground the entire runway and then just cleared the tops of the hanger. He shot straight up then banked it left—a "chandelle" maneuver. A pretty good sight for us because that is one of the aircraft in the school.

We heard some sad news as well. One of the army transport planes - a Stratosphere Liner that was parked on our field for a week, took off last Friday. We saw it go. They found it later in a heap in the mountains. There were 5 soldiers in it but you won't read about it in the papers. Those planes are the big babies, bigger than your B-24 or B-17.

I have just come back from something quite terrible. I had to stop writing. I was called out for guard duty. A B-25 came down just outside our field. As the story goes, it was being tested. The right engine failed only 200 feet off the ground and however it happened, the pilot couldn't keep it up long enough to clear a railroad track which is built up at one side of the field. He came down in a heap, and I mean heap. All five boys were burned beyond recognition. When we got there, there wasn't much left that would tell you it was a plane. The engines were scattered all over the place. If he could only have cleared those tracks. It has sort of taken the sunshine away for the rest of the day.

Ruth folded the letter and carefully placed it back in its envelope. Sitting at her desk and re-reading it for the fourth time, she couldn't shake a deep sense of foreboding. The image of all those men going down in a fiery crash had burned into her mind and she couldn't dismiss it. It was little comfort that Jim seemed almost casual about the tragedy as if these things happened every day. Well, maybe they did, but she hadn't heard of such things. And if what Jim wrote was true, this kind of news never got out to the public. What else was going on they never heard about?

She glanced at the front page of the morning's *Boston Post* that was still open on a nearby shelf. Every article had something to do with the latest Japanese attacks on remote islands in the Pacific. American troops were under fire, but no one seemed to know what was going on. In any case it did not sound good.

"Hey Doll face! Got time for lunch?"

Ruth looked up to see David standing in the doorway. "David! You startled me," Ruth exclaimed. "What are you doing here?"

David leaned his tall lanky body against the door frame. "I'm here to take my brother's girlfriend to lunch, if you can spare the time." His smile was disarming. "Actually, I was delivering a car to one of the top brass in the bank next door, and thought I'd take a chance you might be hungry right about now. It is nearly lunchtime."

Ruth had to laugh. Since she and David had been taking plane spotter lessons together, he had become a lot more friendly, and had started stopping by unexpectedly to invite her to one adventure or another. Last week it was a ride on the swan boats in the Public Garden, and now, lunch. With all this extra attention she was beginning to wonder if he was more interested in her than the plane spotting. Not that it really concerned her. They got along well, and he had a quirky sense of humor that Jim lacked. She liked being with David, but as far as she was concerned, her relationship with Jim was not in any danger. And right now she was hungry. If David wanted to take her to lunch, that was fine with her.

"Give me just a second to finish this." She looked down at the design she had been working on. "I've only got one more bit to do."

"What is it?" David moved closer to see what was on the piece of vellum.

"Another ad for Jordan's. I'm just finishing the logo." She quickly made a couple of strokes with her pen, adding the final swish to the last letter. "I've drawn this so many times I could do it in my sleep."

"You make it look easy, but I guess that's because you're so good at your job," David said, admiration in his voice.

"True. I am good at what I do. That's why they pay me the big bucks!" She laughed. They both knew she was kidding. There were no big bucks for the work she did so well. There was a war on and everyone was pinching pennies.

"Well, I think you deserve the big bucks, even if the boys down at Jordan's don't think so." David grabbed her coat off the coatrack.

It was a short walk to the Devonshire Deli. The place was crowded but they were able to find a table near the wall at the back. Once seated, Ruth pulled out Jim's latest letter.

"I just got another letter from Jim. He's doing fine, and really enjoys learning all about planes and engines."

"Jim's a natural engineer. I think he's finally found his gift. No way should he be an accountant or pencil pusher. Give him a machine to fix and he's in his glory."

"I guess so, and he does sound like he's doing well. It just sounds so dangerous. They just had a couple of planes crash right there at the base. Ten soldiers died." She handed David the letter and pointed to the passage she had read earlier.

David read the section. "Sounds horrible." He looked up at Ruth. "But that's what happens in war. Things go wrong and people die."

"But if this is what can happen here at home, what's happening overseas? What's happening on those islands in the Pacific I read about in the paper this morning? I'm scared, David. I'm scared for Jim. I'm scared for all the men that join up or get drafted into this mess."

David reached out and touched the top of Ruth's hand. She didn't pull away. "I know it's hard. It's hard on all of us. But Jim is just doing his bit, and I think you should be proud of him."

"Oh, I'm proud all right." Ruth raised her eyes to David. "I really am glad he's doing what he can do to make this war end quickly. But I can't help but worry."

"Well, don't worry too soon. Remember, Jim is still stateside. The time to worry is when he gets shipped out. Does he say anything about that in his letter?"

"They keep a pretty tight lid on all that information. He's in Missouri for at least a few more weeks. There's a chance they'll give him leave before he goes overseas, but everything is very uncertain."

David gripped her hand more firmly now. "Don't worry, Ruth. We'll get through this one way or the other."

She didn't have a chance to respond before the waitress came to take their order and she pulled her hand away. David looked over at the chalkboard menu that hung on the far wall. "We'll both have the same thing. Pastrami on rye with hot mustard. And a side of fries I think and two cokes." He turned to Ruth. "That okay?" he asked.

"Sounds fine," Ruth answered. The waitress left.

"So, what's happening at your garage? You said you just fixed the bank president's car?"

"Not the president, but someone high up. I think it was the manager. Doesn't matter. Those guys get to keep their cars running, while the rest of us walk and take streetcars."

"I don't mind taking the trolley." Ruth countered. "It's a lot cheaper than paying for a car's upkeep."

"If you had your own car, Ruth, I'd keep it humming away, top notch. No charge."

"David, stop it. You don't have to promise me anything. Besides, you know very well I don't have a car and most likely never will."

"Maybe. Once this war is over, things are going to start changing. I'll bet every adult male or female in these United States will own a car one day, and it won't take forever to see it happen."

"You are a dreamer, David. But that's what I like about you. Always looking out for the next great thing coming down the road."

The waitress arrived with their sandwiches and for the next few minutes, food became their focus.

"Are you going to Norumbega, this weekend? Rumor has it they've got a new band. Supposed to be quite the thing." David used his finger to wipe a bit of mustard from the corner of his mouth.

"Sal Marcusio called and told me." Ruth took a sip of soda before she continued. "I think our crowd is going to meet up at the train in Wollaston and head over together. Why? Are you interested?"

Ruth was a little puzzled. Norumbega was the site of the Totem Pole Ballroom, the biggest dance hall in the area, and a place she and Jim had often gone for a night out. David had never shown much interest in dancing before. In fact, the one or two times Jim had asked if he wanted to tag along, he always had had an excuse.

"Sounds like fun. But there's no need to take the train. I can pick you up and we can drive to the park together."

"But what about Sal and the others?" Ruth asked.

"We can bring them along too." David took a sip of coke. "How many are there in your crowd?"

"Too many to fit in one car."

"Well, we can take as many as six, including you and me. Three in the front, three in the back. Just let me know who, what, when and where, and I'll be there."

Ruth tentatively agreed. She knew the others would be thrilled to have a car and driver take them to the dance, but it all depended on who was planning on going. She didn't want to leave anybody out.

"Let me talk to Sal and get details."

"No problem. Just as long as I can take you, I'm a happy man." David gave her a playful wink. At least it looked playful. Ruth could not be sure.

※

By the time Saturday night arrived, Ruth had sorted out all the transportation. Sal and three of the girls would meet them at the station and David would drive them all to Newton.

Ruth picked out her favorite spring dress to wear—the light cream one with the puff sleeves and rose pattern.

"You're looking mighty smart, there, Ruth. Pretty dress." David grinned broadly when he came to pick her up Saturday night.

"Why, thank you Mr. Doherty. Your compliments are most welcome." Ruth tossed her hair back as she got into the front seat of David's Ford sedan. "I've been looking forward to this all week! I told Sal we'd meet him and the others at the station."

They picked up Sal, his girlfriend Louise and her cousins Bettie and Rita in Wollaston and headed for Newton. They arrived at the park just as the band returned from their first intermission. No sooner did they settle their coats, grab a table and order refreshments, than the band started playing one of their favorites. Quickly the dance floor filled with eager couples.

"Come on, Ruth," David reached for her hand. "Dance with me. This is one of the best." The music was "String of Pearls" which was easy to dance to. David took her in his arms and the two of them moved easily into the crowd. As they danced, Ruth suddenly felt an unexpected wave of sadness come over her. She couldn't help but think of Jim. Here she was dancing with his brother David, enjoying herself, while Jim was off somewhere getting ready for war. She pulled back a little and David felt her hesitation.

As if he could read her mind, David leaned in close to her ear and whispered, "I know you're worried about him but there's no reason. Jim's fine. Nothing you can do about it tonight anyway. Just relax and enjoy yourself. I'll take care of you."

Ruth gave a little nod.

"Just look around. We're here, dancing. We've got a great band playing, you're out with friends. Everything's going to be fine. Jim would want you to have a great time. And I intend to give it to you."

Ruth had to smile. David was right. She was out with friends at one of the best dance halls in the area. She resolved to stop worrying.

At that moment, Sal tapped David on the shoulder. "Cutting in buddy!" Sal slipped his arm around Ruth's shoulder and before she knew it, they were dancing to "Chattanooga Choo Choo," a dance with a lot of swing. She decided to just go with it and didn't resist when Sal dipped her at the end!

The night turned out to be glorious. They all danced 'till just before midnight. Rather than get into an overcrowded car, Louise and Sal decided to go back by train. David offered to drive the others, but before leaving the park, Rita ran into a friend who said she could take two of them back to Wollaston. That left David and Ruth to find their way to Bromfield Street alone.

David hummed softly as he drove south. There were so few cars on the road at that hour that they made it back home in no time.

Next day, Ruth stood in the front hallway, her coat and hat still on, sorting through the unopened mail. A letter had arrived that morning after she had left for work.

Wednesday,

April 15, 1942 - Air Corps Training Detachment, Missouri Aviation Institute, Kansas City, Missouri

Dearest Ruth,

I received a very nice letter from you today so I thought I'd best say hello before retiring. I am a bit groggy from school and I still have a slight chest cold. But no matter what I go through, I just think of you, and of the nice things we have seen and done together, and I snap right out of the blues. You are my sunshine darling and there is nothing I like better than basking in the rays of such a sun light.

I got a letter from my friend Hank. He has heard again from his draft board and is afraid he is done for. He says that he is going to find out where he stands and then enlist if it looks dangerous.

Ruth scanned her memory. Jim must be referring to Henry Carter. He had been trying to dodge the draft for the last two months. Henry was a nice enough guy, but a little too eager to avoid work. His mother had been supporting him while he focused more on his tennis game than looking for a job. Maybe the Army would straighten him out.

I must write my friend Jerry Brennan. He doesn't know about me moving here. He has a surprise coming I guess. You know the night we left, over 3,000 fellows left Kessler bound for New Orleans with full pack. They were sailing to Trinidad to go from there to build Air Bases. They were the poor chaps who didn't succeed in getting into school. Everyone can't be lucky. But don't worry, darling, the war isn't in Kansas City. They won't waste much time shipping us to Airfields when our training is up. That's why I hope they will give us a furlough after graduation.

I'm glad to hear your work is progressing so favorably. How is the family? Are there many fellows still around? Hank wrote to say he went to the dance Saturday night and saw plenty of eligibles in civvies. Ruth darling, please write again soon, and in the meantime, take care of yourself.

I love you very much. Bye for now, Jim

Plane spotting sessions were held after work at the armory in Quincy. It was just getting dark when she walked in the large front doors and checked in with the reception desk.

"Good evening, Miss," the civilian officer greeted her. "Class is being held in the downstairs reception hall this evening." He handed her a schedule and a new deck of spotter cards. "You'll need these for the class."

The downstairs hall was nearly filled as Ruth entered and took a seat near the far wall. She looked around for David, but he was nowhere to be found. Class was well under way when he finally made his appearance. She tried to catch his eye, but he was too busy trying to sneak his way around the back of the hall. She watched as he took a seat three rows back, directly behind her.

Classwork was intense. The instructors took the volunteers step by step through a series of games using the spotter cards. Silhouettes of all the major war planes were printed on the 52 cards in each deck. Set up like regular playing cards with thirteen cards in four suits,—each suit focused on one country's war planes. American aircraft were pictured on the suit of spades, British planes were on the cards marked with hearts, the Germans were on the diamond suit, and the Japanese war birds were pictured on the clubs. The idea was that plane spotter volunteers could learn to recognize the different planes while playing card games.

Ruth was partnered for the class with three women she recognized from her neighborhood. Each was trying to impress the others with her knowledge of civil defense procedures.

One woman dominated the conversation. "My cousin Charles is in the Coast Guard in Hull and he showed me how they do things down at the Pemberton Point station, just off the coast. They are constantly practicing and training for sea rescues and such. Very impressive. And they're always watching out for those U-boats the Germans are sending over."

Ginger, a petite woman who was intently taking notes and chewing the end of her pencil, looked up, shocked. "There are U-boats here? In Boston Harbor?"

"That's what my cousin tells me. I don't think they want the general public to know about it. They think people will panic. But he told me because I'm in this class. We're supposed to keep an eye out."

"But I thought we were only looking up at the sky. Are we supposed to keep an eye on the oceans, too?" asked Ginger.

Ruth chimed in. "I think it depends on your spotter location. I'm assigned to be a plane spotter on that hill in Hull that overlooks Boston Light. It's a perfect spot to check out both the sky and the ocean, so I'm guessing I'll be doing both."

The fourth woman looked through her paperwork. "They've assigned me to a spot in Waltham, far away from the ocean. I guess I'll be focused on planes most of the time."

"There's always the Charles River you can watch," Ruth kidded. "Maybe a U-boat could get in that way!"

"It'd have to be a pretty small U-boat to make its way up the Charles as far as Waltham," the red-head remarked.

They all laughed at the thought of tiny U Boats sneaking up the Charles River.

"We should practice memorizing these cards," Ginger suggested. "I think they're going to give us a test at some point." She turned to Ruth. "Who are you spotting with, Ruth? Did they give you a partner?"

"I think I'm with David Doherty. He's the fellow who convinced me to volunteer. We joined up together."

"He's a good looking guy. Won't your fella be jealous?"

Ruth laughed. "David is Jim's brother."

"Whatever you say." Ginger looked over at the other women in the group and gave an exaggerated wink as they all exchanged knowing smiles.

"Don't you think it's time we got down to business?" Ruth cut off any further discussion.

At this, the women began studying each of the cards in the decks. It wasn't easy. Each card had both a silhouette of the warplane pictured from below and one from the front. Ruth reasoned that was so they could recognize the planes as they flew directly overhead or if they were flying in from a distance.

The pilot would have to be aiming right at me to see a plane at this angle, Ruth thought to herself.

She sifted through her deck until she came to the B-25 silhouette. "Jim's working on this plane right now," she thought. "This is the bomber that he's learning to repair." Ruth stared at the silhouette pictured on the 7 of spades. "Seven. That's a lucky number." She stroked the card gently and said a silent prayer as she shuffled the card back into the deck.

The instructor gave the students another series of quick drills to identify the images, and encouraged each of them to memorize the information and test each other by flipping the cards one by one, asking for proper IDs. It was a lot to memorize. By the time the class was done, Ruth was tired but had a good grasp on the American set of images. The others in the deck would have to wait.

She grabbed her coat and looked around for David. The last time she had seen him, he had been sitting in a small group in the far corner near the door. She scanned the crowd moving into the hallway, but he must have slipped out early.

Oh, well, I'm sure I'll see him before next week, she thought and headed for the exit. She had half hoped David would offer to drive her home, but it seemed he had taken off. Ruth headed for the door and the train station. If she could catch the 9 o'clock, she'd be home in a half hour.

No sooner had she reached the street corner then she heard a familiar voice call her name.

"Hey Ruth, and where do you think you're going?" It was David. He was in his car, driving slowly along the curbside, following her. "Hop in. I'll give you a ride home."

"I thought you had taken off."

"And leave you stranded to ride the rails? No way." David reached over to open the passenger door. "Come on, I'll make sure you get home safe and sound."

Ruth didn't hesitate. "You are most kind and very gallant."

"We aim to please."

Ruth settled into the front seat as David reached across her to close the door and lock it.

"I can do that." Ruth protested.

"No bother. Just want to be sure you're safe. This lock has been acting up and sometimes it just doesn't click into place."

"You should find an auto mechanic to fix it," Ruth teased. "I know a good one if you're looking."

David laughed. "So do I. But he's been very busy lately learning air spotting and just doesn't seem to have the time."

"Well, he should make the time if he wants me to ride in his car without taking a chance I'll fall out onto the street."

David chuckled, put the car in gear and slowly pulled away from the curb. There wasn't much traffic at this hour but with all the drivers using blinders on their headlights to comply with the blackout rules, he had to be extra careful. He turned the car onto the beach boulevard and five minutes more, he had Ruth delivered home.

※

"There's another letter from your boyfriend," Justine greeted her when Ruth walked in the door. "He sends you a letter almost every day!"

"That's because he loves me madly," Ruth countered, smiling. She hung her coat on the rack and reached for the letter her sister held in her hand. Justine pulled it back, teasing.

"You two could support the United States Postal Service all by yourselves with the letters you send back and forth," she laughed.

"Give it over, Justine." Ruth playfully made another grab for the letter. "You're just jealous."

"Not jealous, just impressed. This guy Jim must be something. A regular Shakespeare with all the writing he does."

"He is. He really is." With that, Justine relinquished her prize and Ruth headed upstairs to her room and a chance to read Jim's latest letter in private.

Monday, April 13, 1942 - 10:02 am - Air Corps Training Detachment, Missouri Aviation Institute, Kansas City, Missouri

My Darling Ruth:

I have just come back to my room from chow and when I opened the door the first thing my eyes laid upon was your letter. A very pleasant feeling crept through me. A very confident one at that. I just said to myself "What a girl, still writing." I'll make it up to you someday, love, I promise I will.

Today we began the study of propellers and you'd be surprised how much there is to know about them.

You know, dear, I became awful lonesome Sunday morning. A couple of fellows were down in the street blowing a horn in a big Chrysler. They were out all night with two pretty gals and I could see them clinching down there, having plenty of fun. Do I miss a pair of arms. Boy oh boy.

These two boys in particular are regular woman chasers. They have several women calling the hotel for one or the other many times. I answered the phone one Sunday morn, and it was a girl calling for Mac. She said she missed him awfully bad, and just had to call to see how he was. She had a sweet voice and I mentioned that to Mac. But he replied "Oh her, I'm not seeing her anymore, I saw her twice already." What a guy.

He's one of these Southern Gentlemen and sure has a line. I know, I watched him work it at the U.S.O. He was making $75. a week before joining up and has shown me several pictures of his home, family and prospective wife. I didn't ask him what he was doing gallivanting around with such a nice girl waiting for him back home. It's better not to ask.

Boy, they do plenty of "grassin" out here.

I thought they were bad in Central Park but they pitch plenty of woo in K.C.

I love you Ruth, with all my heart.

Yours, Jim.

It was nearing midnight and Ruth still could not sleep. She kept re-reading Jim's last letter in her mind. He seemed so alone. At one thirty she looked at the clock, tossed the blankets aside and got up.

She crossed the room to her desk, flicked on the small lamp and sat down. Writing to Jim might calm her mind.

Dearest Jim,

Just received your latest letter. You sound very busy and happy with the work you are doing. I am so very proud of you. And proud of all you boys who are training to help save our country. Please know that.

For my part, I've joined the local Civil Defense Group and am training to be a plane spotter. David is also in the group. We met this evening for our class at the Quincy Amory. A great crowd of people. So many want to help with the war effort. It was encouraging to see them all.

David and I have been assigned to the same spotter's location in Hull. Once a week, our job is to watch the skies and call in any suspicious aircraft that flies over. We have two more weeks of lessons and then we start. We will be looking out over the harbor and Boston Light, so even if there is no activity in the skies, it's a beautiful spot to have a picnic.

Remember the time you and I had lunch there? I have a very clear picture of a handsome young man who joined me on a blanket for an afternoon nap. Just thinking of that day makes me realize how much I miss you.

Ruth paused and re-read the last few lines she had written. A flood of memories washed over her. She could picture Jim smiling at her in the autumn sunshine, his lanky body stretched out across their blanket. It had been a warm day and his shirt was open. She remembered his pale skin and how much she had wanted to caress it, to run her hand across his chest. She wanted to touch him and feel his strength and power beneath her. She knew for certain, without any words being said, that he wanted her in a way she had never been wanted before. And she had been willing. If it had not been for the dog that came bounding across the grass at just the wrong moment, things might have gone further. But they didn't. The tension was broken as the dog's owner invaded their privacy.

"Apologies. Sorry. Looking for my dog."

Jim pointed away and down the hill. "Thanks so much. Sorry to disturb you two love birds." He gave Jim a wink and turned away.

Now, writing the letter so many months later, the memories were still fresh and warm and Ruth remembered the deep longing she had for Jim. It was a physical yearning deep inside that she couldn't explain.

Much relieved, Ruth turned out the light and returned to her bed. She would finish the letter later.

❧

She slept soundly till the alarm clock woke her and the smell of morning coffee reached her bedroom.

Coffee might be on the ration list but everyone in the family agreed it was one luxury they could not do without in the morning. For the rest of the day, they settled for Postum, Ovaltine or tea, but first thing in the morning, it had to be coffee.

Mr. LeBlanc did not cook, but he always insisted on making the coffee each morning. "You always heat the water too hot," he told his wife. "You don't want the water to boil. It does something to the molecules. For tea, you boil. For coffee, you don't."

Mrs. LeBlanc didn't agree with his theories, but it was easier to just give in to his compulsions than argue. "You want to make the coffee? You make the coffee. I don't care. Boil the water, or don't boil the water. It's not important to me. You do what you want. Otherwise, stay out of my kitchen!"

The two of them were in the middle of their usual morning back and forth by the time Ruth poked her head in at the kitchen door, already in her hat and coat. "I'm off to the office early. Got a lot to catch up on. "

"What? No coffee?" her father asked. "I just made a fresh pot. Just for you. Here, take a cup for the train. I can put it in a thermos. This stuff is precious. You don't want to waste a drop."

"No, Dad. I'm fine. I'll pick something up downtown."

"That's nonsense. Why spend good money on a cup of coffee if you can even find it, when you can get it here for free?" He paused and reached for the thermos he kept behind the bread box. "Here, takes just a second." He began to pour the rich dark liquid into the container. "You take milk? I can never remember."

"Yes, Dad. I take milk, but just a little."

"You've got to start saving every penny, you know," her mother chimed in. Mrs. LeBlanc stood with her arms across her ample breast, her kitchen apron tied on over her brightly flowered housecoat. She was dressed for a day of baking. "Every little bit helps. Even the dimes and pennies." She paused, gathering her thoughts. "During the last war, we had to scrape and save. I can remember when..."

Ruth knew this speech and she had no time for it. "Mother, I know. Life was tough for everyone back then." She reached for the thermos, and leaned over to give her father a quick kiss. "Thanks for the coffee, Dad. I've gotta run or I'll miss my trolley. See you both tonight."

She felt a little guilty leaving them in such a hurry. But right now what she needed was to be alone with her thoughts. The new feelings she had uncovered writing Jim the night before filled her with a strange and wonderful sense of certainty and hope, and she wanted to savor the moment alone.

She loved Jim. And she wanted to marry him if he asked. Any doubts she had had were now gone, and she felt somehow very certain in a way she had not felt before.

Sitting on the streetcar, holding the thermos on her lap, Ruth could feel the warmth of the coffee through the metal of the canister. It was a very old thermos and was not going to keep the coffee hot for long. "I should probably drink it," she thought. But by now the trolley was crowded. The rocking motion of the car as it clacked along the old tracks would make it impossible for her to drink without spilling the hot liquid all down the front of her coat.

It would have been easier to buy a cup of coffee at the deli on the corner, she thought. But Mother is right. I have to save every dime I can. If she and Jim were going to be married some day, she would have to start saving money now.

In one of his last letters to her Jim had suggested she might come and visit him in Kansas City. She had already investigated travel options to Missouri. She could go by bus, but that would take two days and the cost of plane fare was out of the question. They would have to wait till Jim was stationed a little closer to Boston. There was a very slim chance that once he finished training he would be assigned to one of the army bases state-side, but Ruth knew how unlikely that was. As she rode into work that morning one thing became certain. She would go to Jim before he shipped out, no matter what. But there was no sense making plans until she knew more.

CHAPTER 4

MISSOURI

AIR CORPS TRAINING DETACHMENT • KANSAS CITY

Jim continued sending Ruth letters, at least two each week. They were filled with local news about his life in Kansas City, his classes and stories about the other fellows in the platoon.

Jim's friend Roy surprised everyone by proposing to a girl he had only just met. They married within a week. Jim didn't go into details, but Ruth could read between the lines. These men of the Air Corps were facing war and a very uncertain future. Some were desperate to live their lives as fully as possible. And if falling madly in love and running off to get married made Roy feel right about himself, well, Jim was not going to find fault with it.

She wondered when Jim would pop his own question to her.

Tuesday, May 19, 1942 - Air Corps Training Detachment, Missouri Aviation Institute, Kansas City, Missouri

Hello Hon:

We are wearing our summer dress now, and it wrinkles very quickly. If you lounge around at all it gets terribly sloppy looking, but its light and comfortable.

We are having our final exam tonight on engine repair. The way I feel about this phase, I don't care what I get as a mark. I didn't like the instructor. He was about 4'5" short and had an inferiority complex which he took out on 6 footers like me. A big fellow in the last class picked him up like a child and put him on a table. He has been mad ever since.

He didn't teach us anything really. And of course I didn't know enough about the damn engine to ask him. His assistant, an old army mechanic was very nice, and I learned a lot from him.

How is every one at home anyway? Your sister Justine seems to be a busy little creature with all her dates. Why don't you double date with her dear? I'd rather have you do that than stay home alone. If you love me like I love you, I need have no fear of anyone stealing you.

I meet lots of girls at the USO dances and they have boyfriends who have gone away. They are trying hard to entertain other girls' lonesome boys. If it weren't for these dances many fellows would get in with the wrong people. So I want you to help the boys stay happy just the way these girls are trying out here.

Some of them of course are really headhunting. There is something like 3 or 4 marriages in the outfit every month. Some of these are to girls back home, but most are to girls the soldiers have met out here.

The local girls on average are healthier than eastern girls. They are corn fed and a great majority sprung from the rugged early pioneer breed. Irish blood is somewhere in most, since the Irish settled here in the Middle West. Even the Protestants have real Irish names.

I think you're the sweetest and loveliest girl on the whole East coast and I love you very much.

Yours, Jim.

Ruth sat on her bed and read the letter again, especially the part about all the boys marrying up. Jim's attitude seemed very passive. It was clear he loved her, and she trusted that. But would he ask her to marry him?

Maybe he was just taking their arrangement for granted. He wanted her to date other guys and help out at the local USO, entertaining the soldiers. He had mentioned it several times in his letters. But how seriously should she take his suggestion?

It was one thing to go out with the crowd and dance up a storm for an evening. But was Jim really encouraging her to start seeing other men?

When her friend Irene called her two days later and told her about the big dance on Saturday night at the USO in town, she decided to test Jim's sincerity. She told Irene she'd be happy to join her.

"I think the USO might be a lot of fun. Jim's told me about the great times they're having at the dances in Kansas City. Why shouldn't we help out the boys here in Boston?"

Irene convinced her Father to lend her the family car. He was reluctant at first. "Gas costs a lot of ration points, Irene, so don't you go driving off in any direction. You pick up Ruth, you go and come directly."

"Don't worry, Papa, we promise to behave ourselves." Irene gave her mother a wink, grabbed the car keys off the front hall table and was out the door before her father could change his mind.

The drive into town only took a half hour and the two friends easily found a parking spot not far from the entrance to the dance hall. Dozens of sailors in their bright white uniforms crowded around the doorway, checking out the local women as they approached the building. Ruth heard a couple of high pitched whistles.

"This is going to be interesting." Ruth pulled her sweater a little more closely against the cool night air.

Irene looked at Ruth's worried face and linked their arms. "Don't worry. These guys are all just making noise. I've done this a dozen times. We smile, we dance, we say goodnight. It's a chance to give these fellows a good time before they ship out. Nothing more. Come on, this is going to be fun."

Once they got by the sailors and entered the lobby, Ruth began to relax. The dance hall was filled with young women, soldiers and sailors, all talking and milling about. On one side of the hall a tall woman was standing behind a long table, serving cold drinks and donuts. On stage a small band was beginning to tune up and a man in a tuxedo was setting up a microphone and sound system.

"Listen Ruth, I think we should split up. These guys always seem a little intimidated if the girls cling to each other. Besides I see somebody I know." Irene let go of Ruth's arm. "You go, and have a good time and we'll meet back here at the drinks table, say around 9ish. Ok?"

Irene didn't wait for an answer. Ruth watched as her friend headed across the hall towards a group of soldiers and tapped the best looking one on the shoulder. She couldn't hear what "Mr. Handsome" said over the sound of the crowd, but it was clear he knew Irene and was glad to see her again.

"Hey doll! Where you been all my life?"

Ruth turned quickly and found herself facing a sailor wearing the broadest grin she had ever seen.

"That's a crazy pickup line," she laughed. "You use that one often?"

"Yup. That's because it works." He paused just as the band began to play. "My name is Arno. Wanna dance?"

Ruth shrugged. "Sure. That's why I'm here."

Arno slipped his arm under Ruth's and guided her to the center of the floor. Other couples quickly joined them and within moments everyone was out on the dance floor swinging to the "Jersey Bounce!" It was a fine tune to start the evening. It had a strong swing beat, but not so fast as to exhaust the dancers before they even had a chance to introduce themselves.

"Where are you from, Arno?" Ruth asked.

"Wisconsin. Just south of Red Wing." He looked down at her and grinned. "Ever been to Wisconsin?"

Ruth shook her head. "You're the first person I ever met from Wisconsin."

"It's a wonderful place. You should visit sometime. Lots of farmland, beautiful rolling hills. And of course, the Mississippi River. We live just up the road from the river. We're farmers."

Farming was far from her personal experience but Ruth tried to seem interested. "What kind of crops do you grow?"

"Not that kind of farm, missy. Cows. Holsteins, mainly." Arno spun her around, grabbing her hand and pulling her a little closer. "You ready to dip?"

There was no time to answer. Arno pressed his hips tight against her, and with one smooth move, arched her back, tilting her head dangerously close to the floor.

"Yeehaw!" He shouted, and pulled her back up, now holding her closer than ever.

Ruth's head was spinning. "Don't do that!" She grabbed her forehead as if she were going to faint. Arno just grinned at her.

"At least give me some warning." She felt dizzy and exhilarated at the same time.

"You don't like to dip?" Arno asked. "Why, dipping is my very favorite part of dancin'." And with that, he spun her around and dipped her again.

"Woowee. You sure are a pretty little thing when you're dizzy!"

Ruth tried to smile. "I think, maybe we should skip the dipping for a bit. I'm not feeling very stable."

"Whatever you say, doll." He grinned again. "We won't dip, at least for a while."

Fortunately for her, the "Jersey Bounce" ended, and the band started in on one of Ruth's favorites, "Moonglow." Arno easily transitioned from his aggressive dipper style to the smooth foxtrot rhythm of the music, and led Ruth around the crowded dance floor.

"You're a very good dancer for a farmer from Wisconsin."

Arno laughed. "Thanks. My ma taught me. She used to be one of those fancy dancers when she lived in New York. We'd dance up a storm almost every night. She told me it was the best way to meet girls." He smiled down at her. "And I guess she was right."

Arno was quite a character. He was tall and not bad looking, with a thick neck and broad shoulders that Ruth suspected could only come from years of lifting heavy bales of hay on his daddy's farm. His blonde hair was buzz cut to meet the military requirements. If nothing else, Arno was confident. He might seem like a simple farm boy from Wisconsin, but she suspected he was quite the smooth talking rascal beneath the surface. Her suspicions were confirmed when ten minutes later he asked her to take a walk outside.

"Just for a little bit. It's getting hot and stuffy in here."

"I think we girls are supposed to keep circulating. Not spend too much time with just one guy."

He leaned in very close, his lips just brushing her hair as he whispered into her ear. "But I really need some fresh air. Wouldn't you like to get some fresh air with me?"

Ruth shook her head. "Arno, I think you can walk outside on your own. Go to the door and take a deep breath. You don't need me for that."

"But I do. I need you to hold my hand while I take that deep breath." It was clear he was looking for more attention than Ruth was willing to give, and the darkness outside the hall would be just the spot for the "breathing exercises" he might desire.

Ruth looked around the dance floor. Where was Irene? she wondered. "Listen, Arno, I'm sure you're a nice guy, and I wish you all the luck in the world. But I'm not interested in anything more than a dance or two with you. I already have a beau. He's in the Army Air Force."

"But I'm here right now, and heading overseas in just a day or so. It's wartime. Your guy is far away. I'm sure you're missing him, but hey, spend a little extra time with me. He'll never find out. Besides, you don't even know what he's up to. I bet he's getting a little something from the girls wherever he is." He was beginning to plead. "I need a little attention here, before I shove off—maybe for the last time."

Arno was right. She didn't know what Jim was up to, so far away. He wrote about all the beautiful girls he had met at the local dances. His friends were falling in love every day. Even his best buddy Roy had gone and got married. All she had to go on were Jim's letters. He said he loved her, but was it really true or just the passionate words of a man facing war? He could be away for years. He might be shot or even killed, and then she would be alone. Who knew what might happen.

Maybe giving Arno a little extra attention might be the kind thing to do? Ruth hadn't seriously dated anyone in months and though she never spoke of it, realized how much she missed that attention. She needed a little affection as well.

The temptation to give this man what he wanted was strong. But not convincing. She looked at the lonely sailor and shook her head. "Arno, I'm sure you do need the attention. But you'll have to find it someplace else. You're not going to get it from me." And with that, she turned and walked away.

Helping out at the USO wasn't all it was cracked up to be. It wasn't easy being a one-time dance partner. These boys were shipping out. Who knew how many would ever get home again and some of them, like Arno, were desperate for one last fling. The USO could be a dangerous place if you weren't sure of yourself.

She decided to tell Jim about it the next time she wrote. Little did she realize what a hornet's nest that would raise.

Friday, May 29, 1942- Air Corps Training Detachment, Missouri Aviation Institute, Kansas City, Missouri

Darling Ruth:

I got your letter this morning dear, and it has made me both sad and glad. Gosh darn it; I'm sort of peeved, here.

Darling, I miss you and want you so much. I suppose I shouldn't go off the handle like this but after reading your last letter about that guy at the USO dance, I had to leave and go-downstairs for a Coke to cool off.

I'll pray for you dear if it makes things much easier for you. I'm afraid you'll need my prayers if you intend to continue going out with the type of character who casts up to you the fact that you don't know what I'm doing. "The rat."

I'm burning up again. All right you don't know what I'm doing. "So what!" If you really love me you won't have any doubts in your mind as to my faithfulness.

I always said and I'll say again, I'll have nothing to do with any girl who can't keep her skirts clean. That's probably big talk but the girl I love and the girl I marry is going to be the mother of my children. I want someday to say to my sons and daughters that their mother came to me a virgin and that I expect them to do the same. I better stop writing for a few minutes and cool off again.

Really dear, I get upset to think that some foul minded so and so is trying to break down your resistance. I want you to go out and enjoy yourself, go dancing if you like, but if they invariably lead up to parking, remember that Jim who is in Kansas City loves you the way you are now but will not love you the way you'll be if you don't follow the straight and narrow. I'm putting it right up to you, Ruth. Either you do or you don't.

Ruth felt her temperature rising. Who does he think I am? A pushover for the first handsome sailor who comes along? Ruth fumed.

I know that you have desires the same as I but that should strengthen us, not cause us to fall to pieces.

I'm not beating around the bush; I'm talking straight from the shoulder. This separation of time and distance is going to prove something and is the best that could happen to us providing it is not too long.

You have got the right idea darling when you say you have too much at stake and will not toss it over your shoulder for a little cheap pleasure. Pleasure? I doubt it. The real pleasure that is derived from those relations is much more than actual physical contact.

There is an extreme pleasure mentally when the two people really love each other. Then and then only does it become a union where both become one. You cannot have this feeling when the relations with each other are cloaked in sin. Then it becomes seconds of pleasure but in lawful wedlock it is minutes and hours of the highest form of love. It's worth waiting for. I think so anyway.

You are a good girl and have principles and more than that—a conscience. Just think dear what it will cost you and you will realize the price is too high.

Maybe I should have been a priest? Huh?

Thanks darling for writing me but please, please, stay away from such characters. They'll break you down if you let them, because they're after one thing and it's not your heart. I love you Ruth so just hold out, please.

Yours, Jim

Ruth re-read the letter for the third time, using every bit of will power she had to not rip it into shreds.

Who did Jim think he was, railing on about virginity, faithfulness and motherhood. Was he a virgin? He seemed to imply it. But how could she be certain? And who cared anyway. She certainly didn't. In fact, she hoped he had had a little experience in that department.

His letter sent her into a tailspin. She had written Jim about her encounter with Arno and the USO dance, asking for his advice, never expecting the kind of response she got back. Perhaps she had explained herself and her feelings in too much detail. Jim had taken it all too seriously and brought the situation to a level she had never intended.

"Maybe he should have been a priest!" That line really caught her attention. What was he thinking? She knew he was religious, but his ideas seemed old-fashioned and out of step with reality.

She shook her head in wonder. Who was this man? And what right did he have to challenge her this way? He should know her well enough by now to realize she had no intention of giving herself away to the first sailor to ask. Did Jim think she was "easy pickings"—like those girls he had seen in Kansas City, hanging around the dance halls hoping to hook a soldier boy for a husband?

The more Ruth thought about his letter, the angrier she got. There was no way she could let Jim think he could dictate to her how she should live her life. She had to nip this in the bud before it had a chance to grow. Who did he think he was, challenging her morality this way?

It took several tries and at least ten sheets of false starts, but Ruth finally got her thoughts down on paper and sent off a short, direct letter to Jim.

June 1, 1942

Dear Jim,

I don't exactly know how to respond to your last letter. Your attitude and the questions you raise about my integrity, morality and how and when I meet other people has left me angry and hurt.

I thought we had an understanding between us. In fact, you are the one who encouraged me to go out and meet other people. I thought you would be pleased with my helping out at the USO. I would never do anything to hurt you or our relationship and I would hope that you could trust me in this.

I don't know where we go after this. If you persist in this attitude, then I think our relationship is at an end. This war has made it very hard on both of us. Ruth

She made a conscious choice not to sign off with anything but her signature. She hoped that would get Jim's attention.

It did.

Within two weeks of sending off her response to Jim's tirade, Ruth received a letter that could only be described as Jim "eating his words."

Thursday June 11, 1942- Air Corps Training Detachment,

Missouri Aviation Institute, Kansas City, Missouri

Dearest Ruth:

The past few days have been days of suspense. After I mailed the last letter and began mulling over its contents in my mind, I realized that what was in that letter had been on my mind just a few moments before. Speaking one's mind has its faults, but writing one's thoughts on paper has definitely proven to me now that a person should never write with a troubled mind.

I'm wrong, I'll admit that first thing, but regardless you still have exactly my thoughts at the time I composed the letter. I can't explain myself out of the situation because there is no reasonable alibi aside from the fact that I was perturbed by your letter. If my words contained such composition as to form an ultimatum it was absolutely unintended. I believe I once told you that I had no right to tell you what to do, or to condone your actions or even suggest certain steps to be taken to alter a situation.

Allow me again, please, to clarify myself: Although I am interested in your life to the extent it will affect our future I have no authority whatsoever to attempt to guide its conduct with the purpose in mind of subjecting it to my mode of living. That will have to be a mutual understanding between us at all times.

But, I have every right to say what I want to say, that is, saying what will remain within the category of language used by a gentleman.

You understand me now, don't you that I am not backtracking on the ideals I set forth. I am merely attempting to show you where I was wrong in twisting my words into what you understand to be an ultimatum.

In other words I was not trying to provoke ill feeling but on the contrary was trying to give you a lift by showing you how serious I was in keeping our lives above those of the dubious class.

However, I seemed to have failed miserably and in addition caused you to write a letter the like of which I hope never to receive from you again.

Allow me to say here I am terribly sorry and want to apologize to you. Please accept my apology. It is now a closed chapter.

Understand dear, that I don't want to get into any more deep discussions with you unless I am holding you in my arms or at least very close to you.

Then and then only, can we both understand each other. I'm trying to study here and get the best out of it. I do not want to be troubled with affairs of the heart. There is no reason why our letters cannot give each of us a lift to keep us going.

So, beautiful, I shall leave you now with one thought in mind. I love you and I hope I can keep you.

With all my love, Jim

Clearly, Jim regretted the letter he had written. But did he really understand how much he had stepped over the line? Or why she was so hurt by his lack of trust? She doubted it.

What was going on in this man's mind? Where did all this righteous attitude about what was right and wrong come from?

Several days later, a small package from Jim and another letter arrived in the same delivery. The package contained a gold bracelet with one charm in the shape of a small plane. There was no note in the box, but Ruth knew what it was—a peace offering.

Friday June 12, 1942- Air Corps Training Detachment, Missouri Aviation Institute, Kansas City, Missouri

Darling Ruth:

Your picture is before me and I am admiring your features. How I long to once again put my face close to yours and look into those soft brown eyes. I'd like to whisper into your ear all that is in my mind. My longing for you, sweet Ruth, is everyday becoming a dull pain. I never wanted anything so badly as I crave to hold you once again in my arms. Wouldn't it be nice to just sit in the dark and hold hands? Just to know that you're near would give me that sense of possessiveness that every fellow likes to have. Oh for the day when I can take your hand in mine and I say to myself, "She's mine."

Dearest, that would be the climax of my life. From then on you could make or break me.

We don't know what is in store for us. Who knows what will happen. Life has been so good to me thus far. I have come through childhood without any mental or physical mishaps. The death of my mother did not affect my life psychologically speaking the way it did my brothers and sisters because I was too young. But, it did affect my life, socially speaking.

If my mother had lived she would have gotten me through "Tech" by hook or by crook. She was like that, Ruth. I never did talk about her to you, did I?

Well, my mother was born in Ireland of English Irish parentage. Her name was Elizabeth Dever. Everyone called her Liz. Her father was quite a horseman and the skill of riding seems to have passed down through two generations for I am never more at home than when in the saddle. She was the second oldest of 13 children. The oldest child is my Aunt Dorothy now residing at 71st St. New York.

Thirteen children! Ruth wondered at how any woman could manage such a family. Jim's mother came from strong Irish stock, for sure.

Liz had the most education of the brood and was quite the businesswoman. She had her own establishment in Ireland merchandising cosmetics or something similar—I forget now what it was. But as fate would have it; someone started the rumor that gold was to be found in the States so off went ambitious Liz. And do you know with every cent she earned here, she used it to bring over her mother and 7 of her brothers and sisters.

Her father was a Protestant but her mother was a devout Catholic and she brought all the children up in the faith. My mother was a very pious woman, always reading the scriptures.

Liz was real clever and could have married well, as I understand from my cousins. But love has its ways and she married a common ironworker who turned out to be true blue to her until she passed away. My father, John, traveled from Chicago to New York once a month to court her. That was quite a trip in those days so I guess he was sincere in his wooing.

My father was born on Prince Edward Island and his early life was one of extreme hardship. He had no education, leaving home at a very early age and striking out on his own to make his fortune. Of course, having had no schooling whatsoever, he was practically illiterate. He learned to read and write from an old missionary who was living among the Indians on the island. He has cut lumber, worked as a fisherman, cabby, chauffeur (all horses of course). He drove a double hitch coach for Mr. Chase of Chase & Sanborn, and told me of the many cold nights he sat atop his hitch waiting for the Old Arlington St. opera house to empty. He is rather quiet about his early life however, and I never attempt to egg him on.

He got into the building business eventually and soon found himself. He was a steel worker, which required a lot of heavy lifting and climbing. He is pretty much busted up now like an old bronc rider. He has two bad legs and has the use of only 4 fingers, two on each hand. He has fallen from buildings, was hit by a train and had the flu and double pneumonia. He finished off Boston's Custom House tower in Boston and had my mother up there the day it was dedicated. That shall remain for me a monument to both of them.

I started out telling you how good life has been to me. It sure has. Fate has brought me to your doorstep Ruth, and I beg to come into your heart and sit before its fire of love and warm myself.

Boy, that was five dollar stuff. No kidding though Ruth, I'm sold on you and think you're the tops. I'm sending you a small token of my affection: a bracelet with a charm. I hope you like it and wear it to remember your Jim.

I hope we are not separated too long dear, but in the meantime live your normal life and do not hide away. That won't prove anything. If you live normally Ruth, your heart will give you the answer as to how long to wait. I love you Ruth darling but find myself restricted at present in saying more.

Give my regards to the folks. I'll write again soon, beautiful.

Yours, Jim

For all its intimate family details, the letter was surprisingly matter of fact, and Ruth realized that as far as Jim was concerned all was back to normal between them. She searched for any reference to the infamous Arno, requirements of moral behavior, or Jim's attitudes about faithfulness. Nothing. It was as if he had gotten all that out of his system. And now it was over and done.

Jim had never talked much about his childhood. She knew he had lost his mother at an early age and suspected her death had had a major impact on him. The fact that he claimed in this letter that—what had he written?—*"The death of my mother did not affect my life psychologically speaking the way it did my brothers and sisters because I was too young. But, it did affect my life socially speaking..."*—that his mother's death had had no real affect upon him? Ruth realized this was not true. No one could lose a parent that young and not have it leave a lasting imprint on his life.

The Jim she knew was a fine man, fun and outgoing on the surface, always ready to go out dancing and join in the crowd. He was eager to please and sometimes generous to a fault with his time and his money. People loved him. She loved him. But there was something hidden—a deep sadness behind his smile. She was certain it was somehow connected to his mother and her religious devotion.

His clear ultimatum to her about "staying pure" had rattled her to the core. He had apologized but the mistrust and questions still lingered. And the bracelet? She knew it was his way of trying to say he was sorry.

In her next letter to Jim, she would try to keep things light and newsy. The last thing she wanted was to stir up anything that would cause Jim to lose focus on the one thing he needed to do: stay safe and come home in one piece.

Tuesday June 16, 1942– Air Corps Training Detachment, Missouri Aviation Institute, Kansas City, Missouri

My dearest Ruth:

Darling we are back in the game again aren't we? Your letter received this morning has made my heart beat much faster. Ruth, I love you so much it hurts. The more I love you, the more I miss you and it's getting just like a dull ache somewhere in me. I can't seem to put my finger on it, but the way I feel is just this. I'd like to sit in the dark with you tight in my arms and then I would sort of relax knowing that you're with me. I shall never fully relax until that happens.

We have #1 engine on the test block. It is a radial engine from a pursuit ship. My knowledge of magnetic timing worked out well. The other fellows openly admit they could never get that darn thing wired in such short order. I know I'm bragging darling, but I feel so good this morning. Hard study is now proving worthwhile. That engine had not been started running in any other class before three days at least.

We worked Saturday putting it all together up onto the block and I supervised the whole thing.

This test stand is the thing that fascinates me. Putting these engines through their paces. The boys stand outside the building while the instructors gum up the works then we come in and "trouble shoot." Great fun. Sometimes it takes two minutes or two days.

Good for you, Jim. About time you got some credit for all the work you're putting in. I'll have to tell Jim's family.

Really darling, you have made me feel so good this morning with what you said in your letter. Do you remember what you said? I bet you don't.

Well, you said you wished you could have been in my arms to say "Thank You" for the gold bracelet. That is a real nice thought. That would be worth giving you a thousand bracelets. I hope you like it dear; it is a real nice one. I want you to be happy sweetheart. I wish I could give you more and someday I will.

I meant the bracelet for more than a peace offering. I want you to have things about you that will keep you in mind of me. Even when you're dancing, I shall be represented if you wear the bracelet.

I guess I better sign off now sweet. Take care of yourself and keep writing please. I'm dreaming about the time when I can hold you close to me again.

With all my love. Yours.

Jim

Ruth touched the small airplane charm that hung from the gold bracelet on her wrist. It wasn't a very expensive piece of jewelry, but as it probably cost him at least a month's army wages, Ruth appreciated it all the more.

During these last confusing weeks, she had been undecided whether or not she should visit Jim before he went overseas. Now that things seemed to have settled down between them, she determined to make plans to go to him, wherever he would be stationed. She hoped it wouldn't mean traveling all the way to Kansas City, but if it did, so be it. Ruth would travel anywhere to give Jim a proper send-off.

Next morning, she picked up the local paper to check on schedules and the cost of a round-trip ticket on a Greyhound bus. She could afford the fare if she put aside a little bit each week for the next month or so. Not knowing when he would be shipping out, she determined to start saving immediately.

"Kansas City is a long way to travel," Helen remarked when Ruth shared her plans. "You'll need at least two days on a bus to get there. I sure hope this guy is worth it."

"Oh, I think so. Not that I haven't had my doubts. Jim does have some very strong religious convictions, but that isn't necessarily a bad thing. I'd rather have a beau who had a moral backbone than a guy who was wishy washy about things that matter."

"I guess." Helen paused, wondering if she should ask the question both of them were avoiding. "If you do go to visit Jim, will you stay with him?"

Ruth tried to look shocked. "What do you mean?"

"You know exactly what I mean. If you go all that way to see your fella, he's going to expect a little extra on your part, don't you think? Especially if he's heading overseas."

"Jim's not like that. Besides, I don't think they let soldiers have their girlfriends stay on base."

"So you'll get a hotel? Jim can stay with you." Helen was matter of fact about it all.

Ruth didn't want to give Helen the wrong impression. She had, in fact asked herself the same question. If she traveled all the way to Kansas City to say goodbye to Jim, wasn't that a sign that they were serious? Wasn't that as good as saying they were engaged? And if they were engaged? Well, things could move pretty quickly in the love making department. But Jim had made his feelings pretty clear about what he wanted in a wife. She wondered if it mattered to him when she actually lost her virginity, as long as it was with him.

"I'm not sure what arrangements Jim will make. But I'm sure it'll all work itself out. Lots of girls are visiting soldiers. The Army must have some arrangement."

"I guess you'll have to wait and see. But I expect you to tell me every-thing as soon as you find out." She gave her friend a knowing wink. "I better get back to work. Mr. Gibson will be wanting his monthly balance sheet delivered by the end of the day." With that, the two friends parted, Helen to her adding machine and Ruth to work on another fashion ad.

Two hours later Ruth finished the advertisement and went in search of Helen. "I have to deliver this ad to Jordan's marketing department over on Willard Street. Want to go for a walk? It's a beautiful day out there. I have enough lunch for two and we can go down to the Public Garden to eat and watch the ducks."

Helen leaned back in her chair and looked out the tall oversized window. From the sixth floor she couldn't see the street below without stretching, but it was clearly a beautiful warm day outside. The stuffy office suddenly seemed oppressive. "You're on. Gibson'll get his numbers on time. But I need a break. Let me go and freshen up and I'll be ready in a jif."

Within fifteen minutes they had delivered the ad to Willard Street and headed back down Washington, crossing over to Boylston towards the Public Gardens. The sidewalks bustled with shoppers and workers happy to be out for a quick lunchtime stroll in the warm fresh air. It wasn't until the two friends settled on a wooden bench near the duck pond that Ruth continued the conversation they had started at the beginning of the day.

"Helen, before you were married, did you and Gary ever... I mean, did you... before you were married?" She let the question hang there, hoping she didn't have to explain what she meant.

Helen bit into her half of the tuna fish sandwich Ruth had shared. "You mean did we have sex before the wedding day?"

"You know what I mean," Ruth prodded. "You two had been together for ages. I was wondering."

"Of course we did. Everybody does. They just don't go around broadcasting it." She looked at the confused look on Ruth's face. "Don't worry about it. If it's supposed to happen between you and Jim, it'll happen. It's not something you really plan. It just sort of happens."

"Jim is a planner, I'm afraid. And he has some strong convictions about such things."

"You mean, he wants to? Or he doesn't want to?"

"I'm not sure. He's hard to read sometimes. He certainly doesn't want me to do anything with anybody else." Ruth decided to tell her friend about the latest confusion. "Jim asked me to go to the USO dances to help make the boys going overseas a little happier before they ship out. My friend Irene and I went to the Quincy USO dance a couple of weeks ago. I met this sailor from Wisconsin." Ruth went on to describe the evening, how she had written to Jim asking for his advice. "Jim was really upset. I know he sent the letter on the spur of the moment and didn't mean half of what he wrote, but he was really angry, thinking I might have 'slipped' as he put it." She paused, "He said he would never marry a girl who wasn't a virgin."

Helen sat bolt upright.

"He didn't actually accuse me of anything. I mean, I didn't do anything wrong. But his attitude was very clear and very self righteous."

"And now he wants you to go all the way to Kansas City to visit him?" Helen asked. "What does he think is going to happen if you two are together for a weekend?"

"That's why I'm confused. I can't read the man."

"Hmmm." Helen took a moment before answering. "Go visit him, and let him take the lead. See what happens. You do love the guy, so whatever happens, it'll all be fine."

"I guess you're right. And like you said, it's not something you can plan."

As it turned out, the Kansas City trip was canceled before it began.

Saturday morning, Ruth returned from the corner store to find a stack of mail on the front hall side table. Immediately she began going through the pile of cards and bills. Jim's letter was the last one, tucked in at the bottom of the stack.

She checked the postal mark. He had mailed it on the 16th. It usually took only a couple of days for his letters to get to her, but for some reason this one had taken a full week to arrive. She knew Jim would be panicked at not hearing back. He must be thinking all sorts of possible scenarios by this time. Well, he can wait a bit more. I need a cup of tea.

She went into the kitchen to put the kettle on and found a note from her mother on the counter. "We're at the Victory Garden on Willet Street. Back by noon."

Good. I can read my letter in peace without everyone hanging over my shoulder asking questions.

She settled into a kitchen chair and using her fingernail, sliced through the sealed edge of the envelope. Jim's usual scrawl filled three pages of lined paper. I have to buy this man some proper stationery, she thought. He's using sheets from his school notebook!

Friday June 19, 1942- Air Corps Training Detachment, Missouri Aviation Institute, Kansas City, Missouri

Ruth dearest:

Time is flying along now. Engine testing, although hard on the ears and nerve system, is pretty interesting. It took us 3 hours to locate 4 troubles that the instructor put in our engine yesterday, but we got them. As crew chief I do all the report writing and logging of the test. A fellow in engine change class got hit with a prop kicking back on him. Luckily it hit his arm and not his head. He was sent to Leavenworth for repairs.

Squads 15 & 17 are now in Canada. They were shipped first to Michigan and outfitted with big fur jackets, packs and helmets— in fact all equipment necessary for a combat command. Being in Canada would indicate they were going to Northern ports—either Alaska or Ireland.

That's the way it is in the Army dear, one class goes to Miami to continue training, and another class goes on combat duty as soon as they leave here. You can't figure it out, but that's the way the Army works.

I'm sorry dear, if I did not tell you before, when I am leaving here. Please understand that I do want to see you and hold you in my arms oh, so very much. You have been very sweet to me thus far, with your writing me such nice letters and remembering me all the while. After all, we love each other. It takes a little time for two people to really understand each other. And that is where the trouble usually sets in. People are sometimes too self-centered to really want to understand their mate.

I don't ever expect to have an ideal marriage state. It probably would lead to boredom, but I do not ever want to feel I made a mistake and that, dear, is why I want to understand the person I take for a wife.

Life is just getting interesting. It's sort of a challenge to me to take on a big job like building a family. Oh, I know millions of people are doing it every day but it sure makes me begin to think.

So, my dearest, you just pray when you have a spare moment and I will too, and we both shall request that I come out of this mess unscathed and with the idea of settling down to the real business of life,—building a home—our home.

It only took the time for the kettle to boil for Ruth to reach the last paragraph of the letter. Just as the pot's whistle began to screech, she read:

Well, I've said it dear. I want to marry you someday. And I can hardly wait for that day to come. I was sort of planning on asking you when you came here but...

She read the paragraph again.

I want to marry you someday. And I can hardly wait for that day to come. I was sort of planning on asking you when you came here but seeing as how you are unable to make it before I leave, I'm doing my best on paper. Not the most romantic method, but Ruth, it's genuine. I love you darling and want to be with you always. Please say you will dear. I want you because I need you and love you.

Hoping to be really yours, Jim

It took a minute for Ruth to fully comprehend what Jim had written. The piercing sound of the kettle's whistle finally broke through, just as Justine ran into the kitchen, holding her hands to her ears.

"Turn off the kettle!" she shouted at her sister.

"Huh?" Ruth looked up, still unclear at what was happening.

Justine "I said, turn off the kettle!" Ruth didn't budge.

"Oh, leave it to me!" Justine reached the stove and flipped off the burner switch, quickly moving the kettle to the hot pad on the counter. She turned, hands on her hips and stared at Ruth. She saw Jim's letter in her sister's hand.

"What, don't tell me? Lover boy sent you another letter?"

Ruth stared at the sheets of lined paper, and finally looked up at Justine. "Jim's asked me to marry him."

"You're kidding." Justine was stunned. "He asked you to marry him in a letter?"

Ruth nodded and as the reality of Jim's question started to sink in, she began to smile.

"I can't believe it." Justine shook her head. "Leave it to Jim to do it in a letter. Do you know what you're going to answer?"

"Justine, I only just read the letter. I need a little time to figure this out." She looked at her sister more closely. "Besides, I thought you were going to the beach this morning. What are you doing home?"

"Forgot my book." She held up a thin paperback, the cover pictured a couple of lovers in a heated embrace standing in front of some bombed out building.

"Another steamy romance?" Ruth asked.

"It takes my mind off things" Justine countered. "At least for a while." She paused, waiting. "So what's it going to be? Do I hear wedding bells in your future?"

Ruth didn't say anything to Justine, but she already knew what her answer to Jim would be.

※

Ruth sent a letter to Jim in the next mail pickup. His return letter took a few anxious days to arrive.

Friday, July 3, 1942- Air Corps Training Detachment, Missouri

Aviation Institute, Kansas City, Missouri

My dearest darling:

Ruth dear, your originality overwhelms me. What a surprise it was to receive that little red heart with the message that I had so anxiously waited for. Oh sweetheart, I'll really try to make you happy. All I ask is that you have confidence in me and stay just as kind as you have been. More than anything else, money or fame, I want to have your love and in turn, give you mine.

Jim was so easy to please. Her answer to his marriage proposal was set inside a small red heart she drew on a piece of card. She had added a bit of extra filigree to the edging to make it a little fancy, and though it had only taken her a few minutes to create, Jim seemed genuinely impressed.

Things may be all mixed up around us honey and they may keep us apart, but you and I now have our own little world where we can plan for our future. I have wanted you for so long Ruth and I strove to win you over. I'm justly proud now that I have gotten myself the loveliest girl ever. You can't realize how it gives me a lift when you say you are rooting for me. Your devotion is what I long for. I'm so happy darling, I don't care what comes along now, I know your heart is with me.

It's funny, but I feel different already. I'm going to watch my health pretty closely now, and my pocketbook too. Before this, I didn't much care what I did with either but now my aim is to have myself in tip-top condition so I can love you like a man should love. It's really something to strive for, and that's what I needed, a goal. What a goal I picked out for myself! I'm the luckiest guy in the states.

We will be happy won't we? We have plenty of opportunity to talk things over by mail, so let me have all your ideas. We are going to put forth all our opinions on home making so we can iron out the differences. It's a 50-50 proposition first of all, isn't it?

Jim was so earnest. He wanted to charge full steam ahead into their marriage! Let's solve all our problems ahead of time! How did he put it? "...

so we can iron out the differences." He was being a bit unrealistic, but she couldn't help smiling at his enthusiasm.

> *I'm so happy Ruth, I'd give anything to be able to hold you in my arms and look into your big brown eyes and whisper sweet nothings in your ear. Especially would I like to bury my face in that crown of gold you wear. What a beautiful head of hair you have. I remember it so well, shining in the sun on a warm summer day. And then, New Year's Eve, across the table. I'll never forget how lovely you were that night, and how I made up my mind to have you.*

> *Tomorrow is the Fourth of July. This is sure going to be a glorious Fourth for me, and I hope I have made you happy.*

> *Above all dear, I don't want you to deprive yourself of any fun. Go out as often as you wish. I trust you implicitly. Furthermore, it will assure you of your love for me, because I want our marriage to be a life contract.*

She couldn't help but recall the USO dance, her encounter with Arno and Jim's negative attitude. If she ever did decide to go out for a bit of fun, she certainly wasn't going to broadcast it to Jim.

> *I hope I'm not sticking my neck out, but if someone does take you away from me it will at least make you happier than if you considered staying with me and loving another.*

> *So dear, lets both be broad minded and live normal lives. If you really love me and I really love you, we will get together eventually. If not, we'll charge it up to fate or just life.*

> *I guess the feeling I possess now comes but once in a lifetime. When a young man asks for the hand of the one he loves, and she accepts. It's a very tender feeling and a shame you can't be with me to see just how I react.*

> *I hate to leave you sweet, but duty calls, so I'll say so long for a while. Give my regards to all the family.*

> *With all my love, Jim*

Now that their engagement was official, Ruth was eager to tell Helen as soon as she got to the office the following Monday.

"Well, it's done. Jim has asked me to marry him, and I've said yes!"

Helen clapped her hands together. "Oh Ruth, that's wonderful news." She gave her friend a big smile, and pulled her close into a warm embrace. "I'm so happy for you. In fact, I'm delighted."

"Thanks. I wanted you to be the first to know."

Helen shook her head and pushed back a little from Ruth so she could see her friend's face. "You've told your family, right?"

"Not yet. Justine knows he asked me, but she doesn't know my answer. She's going to give me a hard time. She always does."

"She's just jealous," Helen countered. "But you've got to tell your mother and dad."

"I know, I just want a little time to think it through."

"Why? Is there a problem? They like Jim, don't they?"

"Oh, sure. They love him. He's Irish and poor, but they love him." She hesitated. "It's just that my mother had always hoped I would marry someone rich and elegant. She'll be happy for me, but I think she might be a little disappointed that I chose Jim."

"Who else is there? I thought Jim was the only one." Helen questioned. "He's the only one you've been talking about for the last six months, except for David and he doesn't count."

"There is no one else but Jim. At least not anymore."

"Why, Ruth LeBlanc. You've been holding out on me." Helen's voice was full of mocking scorn. "Who else did you have in mind?"

"It was a couple of years ago." Ruth wondered if she should go into any detail. "And it's long over." She paused, calculating how much she should tell. "His name is Sal. I never mentioned him, because it never amounted to much. We only went out a few times. "

"And what made this Sal so special?" Helen probed.

"He comes from a very wealthy family. His father started a business right after the stock market crash of '29 and made a fortune picking up the pieces other businesses left behind. A very smart man." She sighed. "Anyway, the plan is for Sal to take over when his father retires. Marrying someone like Sal would make my mother very happy."

90

"Did he ever ask you?" Helen pointed out.

"We never got that far. He's a wonderful guy. We still see each other once in a while when the old gang gets together. It might have gone somewhere, but then I met Jim." Ruth answered. She looked at her friend. "Jim is the right guy for me."

"Well, if you're happy, that's all that counts." Helen hugged her friend again. "But now that you've told me the news, you really have to tell your family."

"You're right." She looked at all the paperwork on her desk. "But not right now. I've got three ads to create today. And if I don't finish by the end of the day, Jordan's will be on my back for sure."

Helen laughed. "Then you better get started."

※

Ruth waited till after dinner that evening to tell her parents the news.

"Well, I think that's great, Ruth," her Dad declared. "I've always liked Jim. He's a good man."

"He's Irish and poor," her mother chimed in. "He doesn't have much to offer. Are you sure you really love him?"

Justine was still putting away the last of the dishes. "Oh, she loves him all right, mama. The two of them have been writing love letters back and forth like there's no tomorrow."

Mrs. LeBlanc looked at her daughter. "Ruth, is this true?"

"I do love him," Ruth answered. "I really do. Jim doesn't have a lot of money right now. But that will change."

"Not like that friend of yours, Sal you were dating a while back," Justine interrupted. "His family's loaded."

"But Jim's an honest man, Justine. Someone who will work hard and do his best to take care of me and our children."

"Children?" her father interrupted. "You two haven't... " he let the question hang.

"Dad, don't even think it. It's not even possible. Jim's been away for six months."

Her father looked rather sheepish. "Sorry, just being sure."

"Besides," Ruth continued, "Jim is very religious. Almost too religious. Nothing's happened, and nothing will until we are married."

"You never know," Justine mumbled. Ruth stared at her.

"Look, mother, I know Jim is not quite what you hoped for me, but he's a good man, and I love him, and that's what really counts." She paused, "Can you be happy for me?"

"Of course, we are happy for you." Mr. LeBlanc answered. He looked at his wife. "We're happy, right?"

Mrs. LeBlanc placed the last of the dinner plates in the cabinet, and turned to her daughter.

"Jim is a good man. If you love him and he loves you, then that's all there is to it. You may never be wealthy and have the finer things in life that I wished for you, but if you're happy with Jim, then, there's nothing more to be said." She looked at her husband and daughter. "We will be happy for you."

"Thanks, mother. I needed to hear you say that."

"So have you thought about when this wedding will happen?" Justine asked.

"I don't know. Jim is still in school and who knows when or where he will be sent once he graduates. He could be assigned to someplace stateside, and if that happens, well, I'd like to get married sooner rather than later."

"Is there a chance Jim could stay in the states?" her father asked.

"He's doing really well. They've made him a crew chief, which I think means he's in charge of a lot of the men. So maybe they'll make him an instructor? If that happens, he might get to stay home. I don't know." She looked at her mother. "This war has made everything so hard. You can't count on anything anymore."

"If he's that good," her father remarked, "they'll need him overseas right away. I read in the papers this morning, things are not going so good for our fly boys. I hate to say it, Ruth, but it's more likely than not Jim will be needed overseas."

"You're probably right." Ruth agreed. "I just wish this war was over."

"We all wish that," her father responded. He looked at his watch, tucked his newspaper under his arm and headed for the front parlor. "Bertha, bring the tea into the front parlor. I don't want to miss the news." He glanced at his daughter. "You should listen too."

"I'll be there in a minute, Dad."

Once her parents were out of earshot, Ruth turned to her sister. "Justine, I'm going to need your help. I don't want Mother and Dad to worry, but I want to go and visit Jim, and I need you to support me."

Justine couldn't help smiling. "I had a feeling you'd want to take a special trip to the man of your dreams."

"Don't make fun, Justine."

"Not making fun. I'm actually happy for you. Jealous too, of course." She gently touched her sister's arm. "If you think he's the best man for you, then I'm all for it."

"Oh, Justine," Ruth hugged her sister. "I needed to hear you say that."

"So now what?" Justine asked.

"I'm waiting to hear from Jim. His squadron is bound to be leaving soon. Once I know where and when, I can begin to make plans."

Ruth expected a letter with some hint of Jim's next posting. But the letter he sent made clear to her how foolish it was to make any plans at all.

Thursday, July 9, 1942- Air Corps Training Detachment, Missouri Aviation Institute, Kansas City, Missouri

Ruth my darling:

I don't know what's in store for me and I don't want to influence your life if anything does happen, so I plan to leave you unattached in the eyes of the public until this war is over.

That way if anything did happen you would not be embarrassed by changing your plans because of some defect I might have. That's pretty strong talk darling and I don't like to mention it but its' the sanest way to look at it.

Did this mean he wanted to keep their engagement secret? She had already told her family and Helen of course. All her friends would know by now.

The movies play up this hero returns home stuff but you wouldn't want to marry a cripple and I wouldn't marry you if I were. We have not only our own lives to think about but the lives of the children we might bring to the world.

So you have every reason in the world if you really love me to want me to return home safe and sound.

And I don't care what the wise guys say about getting a little practice before you marry—that's the bunk. I want my marriage spotless and I'll blast all their theories about practice before marriage to bits.

At last I have the chance to get what I wanted most. A lovely girl that I can honestly be proud of and put on a pedestal.

A pedestal? she wondered. I was afraid he would try something like this. I'm not perfect and I don't want to be put on any pedestal. Jim has such high expectations. I'm sure to disappoint him.

Oh how I wish we could be together again if only for a few hours. The time draws near when I leave old Kansas City behind and all its good times and new friends made here. But wherever I go I'll never leave you behind. You're with me in spirit, I know. I never knew I could feel this way about anyone but it's got me I guess.

Goodnight for now, darling.

With all my love, Jim.

Over the next month Jim continued to send letters filled with plans for their life together. His ideas ranged from very practical strategies for saving money to how they might handle disagreements, questions about sleeping in twin beds, how many children they should have and the church's teaching on birth control. She added each letter to the growing stack she kept in the bottom drawer of her dresser.

CHAPTER 5

MISSOURI

JEFFERSON BARRACKS

Towards the end of July Jim graduated from the Aeronautics Institute and the squadron was sent to combat training.

Monday, July 20, 1942- In Transit

Dearest Ruth:

Please excuse the handwriting as I am writing on the train. I'm sorry. I didn't write sooner but I was real busy finishing up school and trying to find time to say goodbye to the many good friends I have met here.

This darn train. The boys are raising Cain. About half are drunk and the rebels are ribbing the Yankees as usual. A few minutes ago a rebel, the funniest of them all (Italian, too) yells out, "Hey boys, look thar's some good Yankees." It was a cemetery.

I guess you're interested in where I am going. Everyone is excited about our destination because it may be overseas. Roy feels pretty low because of leaving his new wife, but he'll get over that. We were the first class to be shipped from the school under sealed orders.

We're heading for some special combat training. We were given some pretty gruesome tales of what happened to the ground crews in Batan and the Philippines at the hands of the Japs. The ground crew there had no chance for survival because they had no training in defense.

They were good mechanics but not soldiers. It is our purpose here to learn by that sad experience. Darling, I'll have to tell you now or later, so I'll tell you now. I am going overseas following this training.

So it was done. The Army was really sending him to war. Any hope she'd had for a state-side posting evaporated.

I've been assigned to the "Fighting 27th" Squadron as the officer told us yesterday. We are going to receive commando training under special instructors so that we can give a good account of ourselves if our air field is attacked by parachutists. We are all given "Tommy Guns." The only group in the U.S. Army to receive them will be the ground forces of the Air Corps in foreign duty. We were given a lecture on what is ahead of us under the special training. It goes like this:

Pistol practice with the 45 caliber automatic; training and sentry duty with Springfield Rifle; bayonet practice and learning "the Spirit of the Bayonet;" gas chamber drills; obstacle course, practice with the "Tommy Gun," a weapon every man will be equipped with and finally training with the 30 caliber MM Heavy air cooled machine gun.

We will be trained to take cover and camouflage ourselves and to run uphill wearing gas masks. We carry gas masks and canteens on cartridge belts with our raincoats slung in back all the time. It sure is hot down here and we have to carry salt to ward off heat prostration.

The plan is for the Squadron to take three hikes: 10 miles, 15 miles and on the last few days we go 20 miles and bivouac out under the stars. We were told we would become real tough if we applied ourselves conscientiously. I certainly hope so, because I'm not a fighter by nature.

How can a fellow fight with love in his heart? Perhaps I could if I thought that you or my family were endangered.

We've been issued new equipment: a gas mask, first aid pouch and kit, a canvas field bag, a helmet, a pair of heavy duty leather gloves, a fur lined hat with big ear flaps and of course, gun belts and a few small things I need not mention.

The fellows are more sober now about the whole thing. We are now joined in with many other fellows. You should see the 27th darling.

Row after row of tents—all Air Corps men. I'd say we will be here about 30 days roughly speaking, but we were told that we are subject to a 24 hr. shipping notice. Remember dear, your lover is a member of the "Fighting 27th." I am proud to be here because that outfit gets plenty of respect from the rest of the camp. They know we are training in earnest while they are rookies the same as we were down at Keesler. We are called the "Soldiers of the Post."

I have so much to be thankful for. I have had the exquisite delight of holding you tightly in my arms and caressing those soft lips with mine. What more could a fellow want for memories? I used to look at you and just try to imagine how it would be to make love to you.

Dearest, please write me. I'll need your encouragement now more than ever before. Call my home and tell them where I am and that everything is O.K.

Please say you're with me darling. I love you as much as I can possibly love anyone.

Jim

A package arrived at the same time as the letter. In it were all the letters Ruth had sent to Jim since he left for war. He had carefully wrapped them in brown paper and tied the package with string, It made Ruth cry to touch them now. Jim had clearly treasured them. Written in the bottom left corner of each envelope in his small, tight script, Jim had marked the date each had arrived. It was his way of keeping things organized. Such a small gesture, but it showed great care.

Jim had packed a copy of the Kansas City newspaper from the day of his graduation and included a large picture of the Squadron, dozens of young men all standing smartly at attention. He had added a line and circle around the head of a small figure in the back row. It was impossible to tell, but Jim claimed it was himself. Ruth was proud of all he had accomplished. But now she was also beginning to worry.

His description of their new training brought the reality of war into stark focus. This was no longer just an exercise in education. Jim was learning how to handle a gun, wear a gas mask and fight with bayonets. The thought of him fighting his way through some tropical jungle on an island in the Pacific terrified her.

She began to scour the daily newspapers searching for the latest news on troop assignments. It was unlikely a Boston paper would mention the Fighting 27th out of Kansas City, but you never knew. Some of Boston's finest men were in that squadron, Ruth thought. They deserved some attention from the local press if she had anything to say about it.

By the end of July there was no doubt, Jim's troop would be heading overseas. But to exactly where, was still unknown. The letters he sent were filled with details of their training for war.

Monday, July 27, 1942- Air Corps Technical School, Jefferson Barracks, Missouri

Hello Ruth darling:

I am going to write to you every chance I have. You can't realize how I look forward to mail from you. I even rented a post box so I could get your mail without waiting for it to go through the flight headquarters. So far though I haven't rec'd any mail in it and I've made 3 trips a day to it. It's a half-mile walk from my tent.

Monday morning we hiked 3 miles with normal pack to a place far in the woods for a gas drill, and there I found a new love, my gas mask. We drilled for two hours just putting them on, then adjusting and testing for gas on the ground. We were told to relax and then suddenly the cry "Gas!" would sound and immediately every man holds his breath, tucks his hat under his mask pack, rips out his mask and puts it on, testing for fitness, etc. Then he takes a breath. It's all done in just a few seconds. After this drill we were double timed in single file to the gas chamber to give our masks the acid test.

The chamber is made of 4 tents tightly laced together in such a manner to be gas tight. After a certain number of men entered, the flaps were closed and it became quite close in that small space with over 50 men. There were three burners in the center of the floor which emitted the gas. I began feeling a burning sensation against my throat and hand and even my ankles, but inside my mask everything was o.k. except it was quite warm. What an eerie sight it was with everyone silently standing around, masks on, appearing like monsters from Mars.

We were asked if we thought there was any gas in the tent but no one doubted it. We remained there about 5 minutes until everyone was sure their mask didn't leak and now comes the fun. Just to make the men appreciate the mask we were given an object lesson. We had to remove the masks 10 men at a time in the tent and walk out. Boy, oh boy, I was number 20. Did you ever have someone throw pepper in your eyes? Better yet, the best description would be like holding your eyes very close to an open bottle of ammonia. I couldn't see worth a darn and tears were streaming down my face. I got out of that place o.k. but it took me 10 minutes before I could open my eyes. Right then and there I caressed my mask and baptized it "Ruth."

Quite an experience, but it's nice to know my mask is gas proof. Of course there are gases that no mask can protect you from but I'd rather think of something more cheerful.

Ruth, I'll write more later dear, I have some washing to do before lights out. So I'll say goodnight darling. I hope I dream of you.

With love from your Jim.

A day later another letter arrived. Knowing he was definitely heading overseas, Jim had begun making plans "just in case," and he wanted Ruth to know all the details. Things were beginning to move more quickly and the troop's combat training was becoming more intense.

Wednesday, July 30, 1942- Air Corps Technical School, Jefferson Barracks, Missouri

Good morning darling

I have but a few moments to write you because chow call will sound very soon. I have just come back from 6:30 Mass. The little chapel is only about a ¼ mile away and I hurried with my tent duties and dashed down. I received communion with several boys, all members of the 27th. I feel swell darling because my mind is at ease about everything. I have no regrets, instead I hold the sweetest memories ever.

We had bayonet drill all day today under that hot Missouri sun. Honest hon, I think this is the hottest state in the union. Boy, I was sweating gallons and on top of that, the drill isn't a pleasant thing to go through. They don't want us to just stop the enemy, they want us to act like berserk butchers and massacre the poor sappy Japs.

I will not attempt to describe this in detail as I did the gas drill because it isn't pleasant. But boy, it was hot. Two fellows had to be taken away in ambulances. There was a large sprinkling truck going over the drill field to keep the dust down and as it came by a few of us ran right under the spray. Gosh that felt good. We are told to limit ourselves to 2 canteens full of water per day in order to get us used to little water. But it's terribly hard to have to carry that water and not drink it.

"Do you think they're afraid?" Ruth asked her father that evening.

"Of course, they're afraid, Ruthie. What do you expect? But they're being well trained. We have the best army in the world. Those boys will learn how to take care of themselves."

"I'm not sure, Dad. Jim wrote to say some of the men are getting desperate. Listen to this." Ruth read from Jim's latest letter.

One entire tent in our squadron have deserted and gone home. Funny, both men were known as "the tough guys in the unit." The officers went wild when they had roll call the next morning and the tent remained dark and its two occupants were not standing at attention outside. They will show up in a few days no doubt, but I am afraid for them. The command promised us they intend to make an example of these chaps.

But they were no different than the rest of us. We are all getting fed up on the steady diet of army life and gosh, it really has not started yet. Those boys had wives and children home and were likely to ship out any day. So they resolved to see home once more. It's hard to condemn them for their act but the officers painted them as traitors and deserters. They will no doubt become prisoners and be confined to the guardhouse. I hate to leave them behind because we had many good times together in K.C. All this was a complete surprise to me.

"Cowards!" grunted Mr. LeBlanc when Ruth finished reading the passage.

"Sounds like they just wanted to go home to say goodbye to their families," Ruth countered.

"Sounds more like they were trying to escape doing their duty." He shook his head. "This is a rotten business, no doubt about it. But we all have to do our part." He looked at Ruth. "You should be proud of Jim. He's a very brave man."

"I am. But I'm also afraid for him. In the beginning I think he thought of going off to war as some great romantic adventure. He's beginning to realize this is real. And he's certain to get shipped out." She waited a moment before continuing. "Father, if Jim asks me to visit him, to say goodbye, I'm going to go to him. No matter where, and no matter what it costs."

Mr. LeBlanc looked at his daughter. "I see." He scratched his chin thoughtfully. "Well, you're a grown woman, Ruth. You'll do the right thing by Jim. But don't get caught up in it, without thinking things through. Men going off to war can do some foolish things and I wouldn't want to see you get hurt."

"Jim would never do anything to hurt me, father," Ruth answered.

"I'm sure you're right."

"I hope that the Army Air Force takes good care of him," Ruth continued. "They're doing a lot of testing with new types of airplanes. He sent along a photo of one of the experimental planes he's been working on. Read what it says on the reverse."

Ruth handed her father the photo and pointed to the short message Jim had scrawled across the back. *This little plane is a Y.P. 29 A -an experimental ship. Only three of them made and this one nearly killed 2 pilots. It has a tendency for nosing over. I was crew chief on this crate and put it together and made it run.*

Mr. LeBlanc read the message, shook his head and handed the photo back. "I sure hope those boys know what they're doing."

Ruth could only hope it was true. "Jim has to learn everything about dozens of these planes. I'm glad he stays on the ground most of the time and doesn't try to fly them."

Ruth wondered how she could keep Jim's spirits high. Now that the time for shipping out was getting closer, her concern was on how to keep Jim's attitude positive. In her next letter she made sure to share all sorts of neighborhood news and included photos of herself and the family.

But when his return letter arrived, she couldn't help but worry. Living in such close quarters with so many men was turning into a pressure cooker atmosphere for Jim. The smallest things were becoming major issues.

Sunday, August 2, 1942- Air Corps Technical School, Jefferson Barracks, Missouri

My darling:

Gosh dear I am tired and a little bit disgusted. Don't be alarmed. I am not ill but feel terribly disgruntled about something that happened today. I got stuck with latrine detail and what a mess.

Ruth, the way I feel now, I wish you were here so I could get off in a quiet little corner with you and just lay my head in your lap and just look up at you. I need some loving, darling. (Honey, I miss you dreadfully.)

What I wouldn't give to just put my face close to yours and look into those big brown eyes. Boy, I better stop thinking such things or I'll be going A.W.O.L. By the way those fellows are not back yet.

Well, my lovely one, there is the call for lights out. I'm going to dream about the day you come and we are together.

Yours, Jim

Ruth read the last line again. Any doubt she may have had about visiting Jim vanished. They needed to spend time together before his squadron shipped out. There were so many things she wanted to say, things she couldn't put in a letter. And questions, too, and a few inner doubts. If she did go to Jim, what would happen? She wanted to be with him as much as he wanted her. Nothing was clear or certain. She needed to talk to Helen.

Next morning, a stack of freshly delivered art supplies greeted Ruth when she got to her desk. After sorting through the boxes and double checking order slips, she finally had a chance to take a break. She walked up one flight to Helen's office.

"Got time to talk?" Ruth asked her friend. "The deli on the corner had a sign in the window. They've got coffee today and I'm buying."

Helen stopped working her adding machine long enough to answer. "Sure. I can't get these fool numbers to add up correctly, anyway. Maybe a cup of joe will clear my head."

The two friends headed to the local coffee shop on the corner of Milk and Federal Streets. It was crowded with workers and shoppers taking time off from the bustle of the city.

"I'll get the coffees," Ruth told her friend. "You go find us a table."

Five minutes later they were settled in a corner booth with cups of steaming black coffee.

"Hope you take your coffee plain. They're out of sugar," Ruth explained.

"Everyone's out of sugar, these days," Helen mumbled, and took a long sip. "Okay, so what's on your mind?"

"It's a little embarrassing, Helen, but I have to talk to someone, and what with you being a married woman—you have experience, and I can't talk to my mother about these things." Ruth was talking faster than usual.

"Is this about sex again?" Helen smiled. "I wondered when you were going to ask."

Ruth struggled to find the right words. "Jim's writing to me constantly. His squadron is going to be shipped out any day now and, some of the men are getting furloughs to go home and say goodbye to their families. If Jim gets a furlough or even some time off at the base, I want to go and be with him." She looked at her friend, pleading for understanding.

"You want to know if you should sleep with him before he ships out?"

"We're engaged, Helen. It just seems like the next step. But I'm not sure what Jim wants. In one letter he tells me he loves me madly and wants me right this minute and then in the next he writes that he wants his wife to come to him a virgin, set up high on a pedestal. I can't be both."

"Sounds like the man is confused." Helen took another sip of the dark steaming liquid. "Are you sure this is coffee? Tastes like it's half Postum."

"They might be mixing the two to make it stretch." Ruth wondered. "Coffee is getting more and more scarce."

She toyed with her cup a moment, then continued. "I think if there was half a chance, he'd want to get married now, before he leaves." She paused, took a sip of coffee and continued. "But I'm not sure I'm ready to get married."

"He's a man, Ruth. And he's heading to war. And he wants you however it happens. He's thinking about everything that will happen after the war, when you're married and the two of you are together. He's probably focused on that just to avoid thinking about the actual war and what's waiting for him."

Ruth sat thinking about what Helen said. "You're probably right."

"So what are you going to do?"

"I'm not sure. I love him. But get married now, before he ships out? I'm not sure."

"But you're going to go see him if you can?"

"Yes. Wherever he is. I think I need to do that."

"Okay. As long as you're sure." She sipped the last of her coffee and gave her friend a long look. "This could get interesting," she said, smiling.

Thursday, August 6, 1942- Air Corps Technical School, Jefferson Barracks (TENTS) - Don't you believe it!, Missouri

Ruth dearest:

If this letter appears stained, it's because I can't find a spot in this d—tent that's dry. It's pouring buckets and I mean pouring. The wind is trying to carry the tent away but the way the water is coming in I don't think it will make a great deal of difference. This rain will probably hold us here for a while so I am taking advantage of it and writing the girl of my dreams.

I can hear rapid firing coming from the rifle range. Those chaps that went out early are firing in the rain. We carry our raincoats all the time and the storms around here come up awfully quick and are over the same way.

You will send me an occasional snapshot or two won't you dear? I am crazy to see you honey. It will be 6 months tonight since I held you in my arms. You said three little words that night darling that I can still hear as plain as day. In fact you said them twice, so you must love me double.

It looks like Uncle Sam is going to keep me busy but when my work is finished and he says, Soldier, you can go home now, I won't waste much time before tying the knot, that is if you will still have me.

We've been given the word that we are shipping out in a day or two to Fort Dix in New Jersey. I guess our embarkation date will be soon. My next letter will probably be from there. Please don't forget to send me a couple of snaps of you.

All my love, Your Jim

Ruth carefully folded this latest letter, placed it in the envelope and added it to the growing stack of mail. I should let his family know that Jim's being moved again, she thought. I could call them but I'll tell his brother at our next plane spotter's meeting.

A couple of days later, Ruth shared Jim's news with his brother David.

"Thanks for telling me. If it wasn't for you keeping us up to date, we'd never find out where Jim is stationed. As long as he lets one of us know, that's fine, and you're practically family, now, with you and Jim being so tight. That hasn't changed has it?"

Ruth hadn't told anyone except Helen and her immediate family that she and Jim were engaged. Now might be the time. "We're still tight. Jim asked me to marry him about a month ago."

"Really?" David let the question hang.

"And I said, 'yes.'"

David crossed his arms. "So that's that." He rubbed his chin, pondering the news. "Well, I can't say I'm surprised. Congrats to you."

"Thanks, David. I'm glad we have your blessing."

"Blessing?" David asked. "You've got my blessing, I guess. Jim's a lucky sod, that's all I can say." He waited and then continued. "Can I tell the family? Or do you want to? If we wait for Jim to write and tell us the news, we'll be waiting till the end of the war!"

"I haven't told anyone yet, except my best friend Helen and of course my mother and father."

"Why don't you come to dinner next weekend and we can tell the Doherty clan your good news."

"That might be a good idea." Ruth hesitated. "You'll be there, right?"

"Wouldn't miss it."

Ruth wasn't sure if Jim was prepared to tell his family about their engagement, but now that she had told David the news, she knew she had to let Jim know the word was out.

Another letter from Jim arrived the next day. Ruth had scheduled a dental appointment that morning and had stayed home from work. She was still in Wollaston when the mailman arrived and handed a stack of bills and letters to her mother.

Rather than leave the letters in their usual place on the front table, Mrs. LeBlanc walked directly to the kitchen where she knew Ruth was still eating her breakfast.

"There's a letter for you from Jim. Looks important." She handed the envelope to her daughter.

Monday, August 10, 1942 - Air Corps Technical School, Jefferson, Missouri

Dearest Ruth,

I only just wrote you and would have included this information if I had known it ahead of time. The squadron is on the move again and it looks like we're getting ready to ship out. It'll happen soon enough but the brass isn't telling us when or to where. The best I know is that we're going to be at Fort Dix in New Jersey for a couple of weeks while the rest of the boys arrive and everything is prepared.

We've been given the word that if we want anyone to come visit we should let them know right away. I could ask the family to come, but there is only one person I really want to see. Can you guess who?

Is there any way you can come to see me off? That would be the greatest gift a man could wish for. I think there are buses that come down from Boston. I know it might be a lot of money, but I'm hoping you can make it. I've been able to save some money and will pay you back for the cost of the trip. Don't argue. I want to do it. You are worth every penny.

We should be at Fort Dix in a day or so. If you call the Fort and ask for information for visitors they should be able to tell you details for travel and entry into the Fort. Leave your name and travel arrangements and I will check with them once we arrive. Please say you will come. I love you more now than ever and can't wait to see the sweetest girl ever.

With all my love,

Jim

"Jim's at Fort Dix in New Jersey," she said with surprise. "He's being shipped out and he wants me to go see him off." Ruth looked at her mother. "I'm going to go, Mother. I'm going to Fort Dix."

"Now Ruth, is that wise? It costs a lot of money to travel that far."

"We're engaged Mother. I'm going to be Jim's wife. If he wants me to go to Fort Dix, I'm going."

"Hmmph." Mrs. LeBlanc made a disapproving sound. "Does Jim's family know about all this?"

"David knows. I told him last week when we met for plane spotting. He's invited me to visit their family this weekend. Of course, I'll have to cancel that if I'm going to Fort Dix."

"Who else have you told about your engagement?" Mrs. LeBlanc questioned.

"The only person I've told besides David is Helen at work." She stood up, placing the letter in her skirt pocket. "I'm sorry if you don't approve."

Mrs. LeBlanc shook her head and moved to give her daughter a hug. "Of course, I'm happy for you. It's been hard for you, what with Jim being gone. You need to go to him, I realize that." She sighed. "Who knows what will happen once he's overseas."

The two women embraced. "Oh, Mother," Ruth said quietly, "who knows what the future will bring for any of us?"

"What's all this?" Mr. LeBlanc appeared in the kitchen doorway, morning newspaper under his arm, an empty coffee mug in hand.

"Ruth just told me..." Mrs. LeBlanc looked at her daughter. "You tell him. You should be the one to tell your father that you're traveling all the way to Fort Dix."

"What? What did you say?" He looked from wife to daughter, puzzled.

Ruth continued, "I got a letter this morning from Jim. They've moved him to Fort Dix in New Jersey and I'm going to go visit him before he ships out."

"Fort Dix? New Jersey? That's a long way to go." He thought about his car and the price of gas. "You're not thinking of taking the car, are you?"

"No Dad. Not the car. Jim said there's a bus from Boston that goes that way." She looked at her parents. "I need to call the bus terminal and make arrangements. I need to pack. I need to leave word for Jim. I need to call Helen." She paused, trying to think through all the things she would need to do.

"Don't forget to call your clients." Mr. LeBlanc declared. "You've got to tell them you'll be away."

Ruth was already heading for the door. "Yes, Dad. Thanks for the reminder. There's so much I need to do." And she was gone.

CHAPTER 6

NEW JERSEY

FORT DIX

By eight o'clock the next morning, Ruth was seated on a Greyhound bus out of South Station heading towards Fort Dix, New Jersey. The 300-mile journey would take the better part of the day, but she should be at Fort Dix well before nightfall. The woman at the visitor call center had recommended a small hotel not far from the base.

"You can't stay on base, I'm afraid, Miss LeBlanc. I can recommend a number of pleasant hotels in town. There's a bus line in town you can take to Fort Dix most anytime you want to visit. It goes right down Main Street."

"May I leave a message for my fiancé? His name is James Doherty. He's with the 27th Squadron out of Kansas City. They should have just arrived. I want to tell him I am on my way and I'll contact him when I get to town." The woman promised to pass the message on.

Ruth called and reserved a room at the Barlow Hotel in Jobstown, about five miles from the base. The clerk at the front desk promised it was a perfect location for a single woman visiting the area; safe, comfortable, and not too expensive.

Traveling by bus had always been something of an adventure for Ruth. She didn't mind the long distances as long as she had a good book or the chance to grab a bit of sleep. But this time there was no chance for either. The bus was jammed with passengers: men in uniform and women either alone or with children filled every seat. It seemed everyone was headed to an army base in New York or New Jersey. Soldiers were either returning to duty or hoping to spend one more day with their family before heading overseas to war. The mood was a mix of excitement and somber reality.

"My guy is at Fort Drum near Watertown, NY," the woman seated next to Ruth declared. "It's a long way, but he's worth it."

"You must really love this soldier." She paused, then asked, "Did he tell you when he'll be shipping out?"

"No. Nobody's talking. But it won't be long now. I figured I should take the chance to visit him when I can. What about you?"

"Same story I guess. I'm heading to Fort Dix in New Jersey. Hoping for a day or two with my fiancé."

"That's nice. New Jersey is nice. Paul was living in Philadelphia before the war and they sent him to Fort Dix after he enlisted. He was only on base for a few weeks, but I had to see him."

"Can you tell me about the place?"

"The only thing I remember is that Fort Dix is big—like a city inside a city, but kind of ugly. Lots of buildings that all look the same. I was only there one night and we didn't spend a lot of time on the base, if you catch my meaning."

Ruth knew exactly what the woman meant.

After a few more minutes of small talk the two women settled into a comfortable silence and Ruth turned to read the latest edition of LIFE magazine she had purchased in the terminal for a dime.

The cover photo was a close-up of General MacArthur's four-year-old son, Arthur, in a French beret. It was a beautiful picture, but Ruth had no interest in reading about the boy. Instead she flipped through the pages to the entertainment section featuring the latest photos and gossip from the world of Hollywood. "I need a break from the war," she thought and settled in to read. Within a few minutes she had dozed off.

When she woke several hours later, her seat companion was gone and a soldier in a rumpled corporal's uniform was sitting in the seat beside her.

"Where are we?" she asked.

"We're almost to Philadelphia," the soldier replied. "You've been asleep for a while. Sure hope you weren't planning on getting off in New York City."

Ruth shook her head, still a little drowsy. "No, no, I'm on my way to Fort Dix."

"Fantastic. That's where I'm heading. We can go together." With that, he grinned, snapped a large piece of gum he had been chewing and stuck out his hand. "Name's Charlie. From Brooklyn New York. Don't you worry, I'll make sure you make it to Fort Dix, safe and sound."

Charlie was as good as his word. It took a couple of hours and a local bus ride, but by three in the afternoon Ruth found herself at the Fort Dix Visitor Center talking to the sergeant at the front counter.

"I'm here to visit Private James Doherty. He's with the 27th Squadron that arrived from Kansas City. They should have arrived a day or so ago."

The sergeant nodded crisply and began to search through some papers on his desk. "That name sounds familiar. I think I have a message for you, the soldier dropped it off a little while ago." He continued talking while he searched, "His unit arrived Tuesday evening if I'm not mistaken. We've had so many troops come in over the last few days. Almost impossible to keep track." He looked up at Ruth and gave her a thin, tight smile.

Ruth watched as the soldier continued looking through a stack of yellow paper. Finally, "Here it is. From Private James Doherty, 27th Squadron to Miss...." He looked at Ruth who finished the sentence. "Miss Ruth LeBlanc. I've come in from Boston, Massachusetts."

"Do you have any identification?"

Ruth was surprised the soldier asked, but realized at once, that they had to be certain she was who she said she was. "Of course." She fumbled in her purse, found her wallet and pulled out her driver's license. "Will this do?"

The sergeant took the card, looked at the signature and asked Ruth to sign the visitor's log.

"Will I be able to see Jim today?"

"I can't say, miss." He handed the license back with Jim's note. "Perhaps his message will give you the information you are looking for."

"Yes, of course." Ruth replaced the license into her wallet and stepped back from the counter to read Jim's note. He had folded it three times to keep the contents from the prying eyes of the sergeant, but it was unlikely it had stayed private. There was little she could do about it now.

"Hi Dearest.

If you're reading this, you must have arrived. I did my best to wait for you at the visitor's center but after pacing back and forth for a couple of hours I have to go back inside. This note will have to do to welcome the most beautiful girl in the world to ever step foot onto Fort Dix. Am I blushing? You betcha.

I have to be on guard duty until chow at six o'clock, but will come *right to the front gate when I get off. I won't even go to the mess. I couldn't eat anything anyway knowing you were nearby. Please wait for me at the front gate. There's a little park with a bench that seems to be very pleasant for such things.*

I have so much to tell you and cannot wait till you are in my arms, sweet.

Jim

She folded the note again and walked back to the counter. The sergeant was waiting. "The little park is just across the way to the right." He pointed towards the entrance.

Ruth looked at the clock on the wall. Four o'clock. "I'm going to be staying at the Barlow Hotel nearby and would like to settle in before I meet my fiancé." The sergeant gave her a blank look, but Ruth continued. "Can you tell me, Sergeant, how to get to the Barlow from here?"

"Fastest way is a taxi. The hotel is on the bus line, about four miles down the road. A lot of our lady visitors stay there." He gave Ruth a bus schedule. "You can pick up the bus right at the gate. Or you can call a taxi. You can use the visitor phone in the waiting room if you wish."

"Thank you, I think the bus will be fine."

It took all of two hours for Ruth to wait for the bus, travel to the Barlow, check into her room, unpack the few things she had brought, freshen up and finally return to Fort Dix. By six thirty Ruth was walking towards the small green patch of grass Jim had called a park.

A soldier was standing near the bench, his back towards her, his hands deep in his pockets as she approached. He was tall and slim, his khaki uniform smartly pressed, fitting snugly across the muscles of his broad back. Jim had never been one to exercise—in fact Ruth always thought of him as a little too skinny. This soldier was the right height to be Jim, but was strong and very fit. She hesitated before calling out.

"Jim?"

The soldier turned around. It was Jim. He didn't say a word but the look of joy on his face told her everything. He quickly crossed the dirt path, threw his arms around her and pulled her close, his lips seeking hers in a frantic embrace.

"My darling." His words muffled against her cheek.

She returned his kiss with equal passion. It had been far too long.

"I've missed you so much." Jim held her tightly to his chest. "You have no idea."

Ruth chuckled softly. "I think I do." She looked up at him, closed her eyes, and sought his lips once more. "I've missed you so much."

They stood together, arms entwined, holding tight to the moment, oblivious to everything else.

Suddenly a jeep filled with enlisted men drove through the nearby gate. The driver gave a long honk on the horn. "Hey soldier, leave some of that for the rest of us."

Jim looked up and shook his head at the driver. "No way, buddy." He called out. "This girl is all mine."

He gave Ruth a quick kiss on her cheek before setting her free. "Don't worry about those guys. No way is anyone going to take you from me now."

"You look wonderful, Jim." She pulled back a little to get a better look at him. His uniform fit him well, and the peaked cap he wore gave him an almost jaunty air. "You've gained some weight. You look so strong. I wasn't even sure it was you."

"They keep us busy exercising. If nothing else, this army has taught me how to take care of myself." He paused. "I don't want to talk about all that. You look so pretty." Jim looked at Ruth closely. She had gone to a great deal of trouble and expense to look her best for him. "You wearing a new dress? For me?"

Ruth smoothed one hand along her waistband, making certain the belt was centered. "Bought it at Jordan's last week. It's a new style, made of rayon, which is all the rage. You like it?"

"Sweet, I love you." He leaned close again and pressed his lips to hers. "I like everything you wear." He kissed her forehead. "I have missed you so much."

He touched a golden curl that had escaped one of Ruth's hairpins. "What have you done to your hair? It looks lighter." He paused, wondering, "You're not coloring it, are you?"

"Heavens no. This is all natural." She shook her head, the hair softly covering her shoulders. "Number one, I can't afford color, and number two, even if I could, I don't have the time. If my hair appears lighter, well, the sun must be doing it."

"Well, whatever you're doing, keep it up. It looks great. And so do you." And with that, Jim lifted her chin and planted one more kiss on her up-turned lips.

Ruth took Jim's arm, pressing her body close to his side. "So, here I am at Fort Dix. Where are you going to take me first?" Ruth was eager to explore the base and learn everything she could about Jim's troop, his friends and his work. "I want to see everything."

"I'm afraid there isn't much to see." Jim said. "Just a lot of guys march-ing around, practicing drill formations. In fact, I have guard duty later tonight, so I'm afraid there won't be much time for any sightseeing today."

Ruth looked crestfallen. "Guard duty? Tonight? What time? Can't you get out of it?"

Jim looked down at this woman he loved. "One thing you learn in the Army, sweetheart, is there is no getting out of anything." He pulled her a little closer. "Don't worry, I don't have to be back until eleven tonight. And we've got the rest of the weekend to be together. I thought I might spend the next few hours walking you back to your hotel. We need some time alone."

Ruth blushed. Did Jim want to take her to bed the first night she was in town?

"When I knew you were staying at the Barlow I called their front desk. They have a nice little restaurant, right in the hotel lobby. We could have dinner and catch up. I want to hear about everything that's been happen-ing in your life since I've been gone."

Ruth was a little embarrassed that the first thing she thought of was a tryst in her hotel room, and was going to say something to poke a little fun at Jim. But when she saw the innocent look he gave her, she thought better of it.

"There isn't a lot to tell," she said. "I've told you all the latest news in my letters."

"Hearing the words rather than reading them makes a difference," he countered. He put his arm around her shoulder and gave her a gentle hug. "Come on. Let me take you to dinner. It's a beautiful night and the hotel isn't far."

"It's four miles away!" Ruth protested.

"That's nothing for me. We take ten mile hikes everyday." He looked at Ruth. "Too far for you? You must be tired after all that traveling."

She nodded.

"Okay, tonight we'll take the bus. My treat." He took Ruth's hand and the two headed for the main street and the bus that would take them to the center of town.

Dinner was simple but filling. Jim ordered the homemade chicken pot pie for both of them. It came with a side of vegetables and a large basket of dinner rolls. "Would you like some wine with your dinner? We could order a small bottle if you want."

"No, I'm fine. I'll have water. And maybe a cup of tea later." She straightened her napkin. "Do you like wine? If you want a glass of wine, please go ahead."

Jim shook his head. "Actually, I prefer beer. That's what all the boys drink whenever we have a chance to go to a local bar. I've gotten used to it." He saw Ruth's lips tighten ever so slightly. "Don't worry. I never have more than one or two. Not like some of these jokers. I don't like the way it makes me feel when I have more than that." He paused, wondering if he should continue. "I guess I learned that lesson from my dad."

"About beer?"

"About drinking too much." He decided he might as well just plunge right into the truth. "I don't know if I told you, my dad had—has a bit of a drinking problem. Sometimes he has a little too much."

Ruth recalled the last time she was at the Doherty's home, soon after Jim had left for the army. John ended that evening asleep in one of the overstuffed living room chairs. She had dismissed it, thinking the man was overtired. But now that she thought about it, he had never been without a full glass of beer in his hand, and the party had gone on till nearly midnight.

"He used to call it his 'medicine.' And when I was a kid I believed him." He nervously shifted the position of his glass. "He's retired now, but when he was back working for the ironworks in Boston, he'd finish his shift, head straight for Tuckerman's Pub and spend most of his paycheck on whiskey and beer. I remember my mother would go down and haul him home so he wouldn't spend it all." He paused, embarrassed. "He wasn't the only one. Most of the men in our neighborhood were the same. And all the wives would go down with their brooms and sweep out the pubs and order their husbands home. It was a regular Friday ritual." He gave a soft chuckle under his breath, remembering.

"I've told you about my mother. I mean my real mom, Liz?"

"Yes, you wrote to me a while ago about how she had come here from Ireland, looking to make her fortune selling cosmetics or beauty products. But things never worked out for her."

"She met my dad when she was summering on Cape Cod as housemaid to some wealthy New York family. He was working as a mechanic for the hotel where they stayed. I guess it must have been love at first sight, because they were married before the summer was over."

"And they moved to Boston after that?"

"They were actually married in Brooklyn where my grandmother and aunts were living. When Liz came over from Ireland she sent money back to bring over the rest of the family. She had twelve brothers and sisters and most of them came to America thanks to her."

"Where are they all now?"

"Not sure. Most of them went south to Georgia to work as farmhands and maids for wealthy landowners. This was back in the late 1890's, but when my mother died we lost all touch with her side of the family."

"That's a shame. Just think, you probably have family all over the south by now."

"Maybe so." Jim thought a moment . "I still don't like those southern boys making fun of us Yanks. And believe me, they do. They can be mighty mean when they want to be."

"You should do some investigating and find out where your long lost cousins are. That would be something."

Jim reached out and gently stroked Ruth's hand, tracing the edge of one finger as it lay on the white linen tablecloth. "I have better things to do with my free time than search for long lost cousins."

Ruth felt a slight tingle run through her. She was about to say something, when their waiter appeared with their dinner. For the next half hour both Ruth and Jim were focused on enjoying their meal. The waiter could see that the young couple were clearly in love and although there were several couples waiting for a table, he let Jim and Ruth sit undisturbed for most of the evening, checking only once or twice to ask if there was anything more he could do for them.

At close to nine o'clock he approached the table. "I'm sorry, but it is almost nine o'clock and we will be closing shortly. Can I bring either of you a night cap, or tea?"

Ruth had already had two cups of tea with lemon and Jim still had guard duty to look forward to.

"Thank you, but no thanks. I think we're both good," Jim answered. He turned to Ruth, "I'd better be going back to base. I'm on duty in a little over an hour and I have to walk back."

"Why don't you catch a bus?" Ruth asked.

"I think I need to walk off some of this energy I'm feeling. Just knowing you're here with me has got me pretty excited."

He took her hand as they walked to the hotel front door. "Get a good night's sleep tonight and sleep in late tomorrow if you can. I want my girl to be well rested."

"Don't worry, Jim. The trip has pretty much left me beat. I'll be fine by morning."

He caressed her hair and moved closer for a good night kiss. "I'll call you tomorrow and we can make plans to meet. Okay?"

"Okay." Ruth gently nodded as she kissed him back. "I'll be waiting for your call. Be careful tonight."

"Don't worry. Guard duty stateside is easy enough." Jim waved as he walked down the path and headed north into the dark towards the army base. "Love you."

Ruth slept much later than she had intended. Thankfully, she had hung the outfit she had chosen to wear for the day on the wardrobe so that it didn't require any ironing. The bright electric blue cotton dress would be perfect for a summer stroll on the fort's parade grounds, she thought. By the time she finally came downstairs to the hotel lobby the clock above the reception desk read 9:15 a.m.

"Is it too late for breakfast?" she asked the woman behind the reception desk.

The clerk looked up from a stack of index cards she was sorting. "Good morning. miss. I hope you had a good night's sleep," the woman inquired.

"Yes, thank you. Perfectly fine. I was really tired." Ruth answered. "Can you tell me if the hotel restaurant is still serving breakfast?"

The woman glanced across the lobby at the restaurant's entrance. "I believe so. They usually stop serving about ten o'clock, so you should be fine."

"Thank you." Ruth started to walk away, then asked, "Do you have a copy of the morning news?"

"There should be a few copies on the counter in the restaurant. We leave them out for our guests to read each morning."

"Thank you. That's very kind." Ruth crossed to the restaurant and looked in. Most of the tables were occupied but one by the window was free. She walked by the side counter and picked up the only copy left of the *Times of Trenton*.

The waiter from the night before was just coming out of the swinging doors that led to the kitchen. "Good morning. I'll be with you in a moment."

Ruth settled into a chair at the window table and began to scan the headlines. There was news from Europe as well as the Pacific. She was about to turn to the local pages when a woman's voice interrupted. "Do you mind if I join you?"

Ruth looked up at the source of the voice, and for a moment couldn't think of a thing to say. The woman was very tall and was dressed in a white and blue suit, that didn't quite fit her shape. The vertical stripes of the jacket only made her seem even taller. But that was not the worst of it. The woman had the most shocking red hair Ruth had ever seen. It was almost purple it was so red. She has to color it, Ruth thought.

She folded the newspaper and placed it next to her place setting. "Uh, no, not at all. Please, join me." She gestured to the opposite seat.

"Thanks. I just arrived in town. Hope I'm not too late for breakfast. I'm absolutely famished." The woman spoke very fast, in quick clipped sentences. She stuck out her hand towards Ruth. "I'm Alice. Alice Peppertin from Long Island, New York. Just got off the bus."

Ruth shook the woman's hand. "I'm Ruth LeBlanc."

"Glad to meetcha." Ruth noticed that she seemed to bounce up and down a little when she spoke. "You been here long?"

"I arrived yesterday afternoon," Ruth answered.

The woman looked around. "This is a nice place. I'm surprised. My boyfriend told me about it. But he has horrible taste. He could live in a barn." She chuckled. "In fact, I think that's where he lives when he's not in the Army." She reached for a breakfast roll. "Did I mention he's in the Army. My boyfriend, Tony. He's the best guy in the world."

"I'm here to visit my boy friend as well. He's at Fort Dix."

Alice paused and swallowed. "Oh, that's where Tony is. Fort Dix. I'm a little mixed up being here at The Barlow for the first time, I usually stay in a place a little closer, but Tony told me the base is right down the road."

"I plan on visiting the base later today. I'm waiting for Jim to give me a call." Ruth explained.

"Oh, is Jim your beau?"

"He's my fiancé!"

"That's really swell." Alice remarked. "I've been on Tony's back to ask me to marry him, but he's said, what with the war and all, we should wait. But I don't want to. I don't see the point, you know? I mean, if he's going to get shot and die, it'd be a shame if we didn't get a chance to tie the knot ahead of time. I mean, what would happen to me if he should get shot and die? I'll never find another guy like Tony to marry me."

"I'm sure that's not true," Ruth began.

"Well, I don't know what to think." Alice took another bite. "I want to get married. And I want to get married now. I mean this weekend, you know. I don't want to have to haul my tail down here again before they ship out."

"Do you know when they're leaving? Did your boyfriend tell you?" Ruth ask.

Alice shook her head. "Only rumors. Tony pretends he knows something, but I think he's just showing off." She grabbed a small menu from the table stand. "Say, have you ordered yet? I'm really hungry."

Ruth reached for a menu. "No, actually I haven't had a chance to look."

"I think I'm going to have the Patriot Special. I'm hungry and I haven't had waffles in a month of Sundays." She paused, turned the menu over one more time, and then called out to the waiter who was crossing to their table.

"I'm ready to order."

The waiter nodded at Alice but turned to Ruth first. "Have you made a selection?"

Ruth looked up. "I think I'll have tea and an order of wheat toast with some Oleo and jam if you have it. You don't have any fresh fruit do you?"

The man scribbled her order into a small black notebook. "I'm afraid not, Miss. Not today. Perhaps tomorrow." He turned to Alice. "And you, Miss, what would you like?"

"I'm going to go all out. I'll have the biggest breakfast you've got. Give me the Patriot Special."

The waiter left to put in their order.

"So where'd you say you were from, Ruthie? I can call you Ruthie, can't I?" She didn't wait for an answer. "I figure you're from Connecticut or somewhere near there. Or Boston! That's it. I can tell from the way you speak. All those broad A's." She mimicked Ruth. "Pahk the car in Hahvad

Yahd." Am I right? I bet I'm right. You're from Boston."

Ruth answered, smiling. "I'm from a small town south of Boston but I work in the city. I'm a commercial artist."

"Oh." Alice tilted her head slightly. "I'm not sure what that is, but it sounds interesting. I'm in sales."

Alice continued rattling on about her work at Macy's glove department but Ruth heard none of it. Instead she was thinking of Jim and wondering when he would call and where they might spend the day. She only came back to Alice and the conversation when two waiters returned with their orders.

"Any bacon?" Alice asked. "The menu said there might be bacon."

"I'm afraid we are all out of bacon, miss. Bacon and sausages have become very dear," the waiter apologized.

Alice looked at Ruth. "I guess you can't expect everything."

"Can I bring you anything else?" the waiter asked.

"Thank you," Ruth answered. "I think we're all set." She suddenly remembered, "Could you give a message to the front desk? I want them to know I'm here in the restaurant just in case a phone call comes in for me. Ruth LeBlanc is the name."

The waiter gave her a quick nod. "Certainly," and went off in the direction of the lobby.

"You expecting your boyfriend to call?" Alice asked, as she began pouring what looked like honey onto her pancakes.

Ruth didn't bother to answer as Alice just kept right on talking. It was amazing how she could keep a constant monologue going while she ate. But she did.

"I really have to go," Ruth finally interrupted. "Thank you for the lovely breakfast but I really must go. I'm certain my fiancé has called by now. Jim was going to call with directions and a time and place we'd meet."

"Don't count on that happening," Alice said. "The Army always thinks up something to keep the boys busy, especially when there are girlfriends around."

"What do you mean?" Ruth asked, walking towards the lobby. Alice followed, sticking to Ruth like glue.

"The last time I came down to visit Tony, he was supposed to be off all three days. That didn't happen. Guard duty, rifle range, running in the woods, there's always something they've got to do. Training, training, training. All the time. You'll be lucky if you manage to have one night with your man."

Ruth didn't want to believe her. Jim would make sure they had time together. He had promised.

She checked at the hotel's front desk. No message from Jim had arrived. But there had been a phone call for Alice.

"Came in about an hour ago, from a Corporal Antonio Marini." The clerk handed Alice a small card.

As she read the note, Alice's smiled widened. "Leave it to Tony! He's worked it so he's got the whole day off. He wants me to meet him at Hostess House. There's a big USO dance there tonight." She looked at Ruth who couldn't conceal her disappointment. "You should have that boyfriend of yours take you to the dance, too. We can go together!"

Ruth shook her head. "I don't want to make any promises. It all depends on what Jim has planned."

"Now don't you worry." Alice tried to sound encouraging. "Your Jim is going to get the day off. I'm sure of it. Let's plan on getting together at the dance tonight."

With no word from Jim, Ruth spent the next hour exploring the town and nearby shops, checking back with the hotel's concierge. Jim finally called at eleven and left a message. He could not be free until late afternoon, but would meet her at the hotel at six o'clock.

By noon the August heat was taking its toll. Ruth was hot, tired and hungry. Not far from the hotel she discovered a small deli. The booths were filled with families and soldiers. She took a seat at the lunch counter.

"I'll have a grilled cheese sandwich please, and a tall glass of iced tea if you have it." The woman behind the counter nodded. "No trouble. You want it with lemon or sugar?"

"Lemon will be fine."

The woman scrawled her order on a small sales slip. "Good. 'Cause we ain't got no sugar." She clipped Ruth's sandwich order to a hook above the grill. "One grilled cheese sandwich!" She demanded.

An old man at the far end of the counter stood up and straightened the front of his dirty white apron. "One grilled cheese, coming up!"

Ruth looked at the cook. He was at least in his sixties, his white hair disheveled under a small white cap. His chin was covered with a scruffy beard and dark circles under his eyes told a story of long sleepless nights.

What time did he wake up this morning? Ruth wondered.

"You want a pickle and chips with your sandwich? That'll be extra," the woman behind the counter asked.

Ruth did some fast arithmetic. 20¢ for the sandwich. 10¢ for the iced tea. "How much for the pickle and chips?"

"10¢."

"I'll skip the pickle and chips." Ruth figured the savings would pay for the bus ride back to the base the next morning.

"You here visiting a soldier?" the woman asked, pouring a tall glass of iced tea from a large pitcher. A slice of bright yellow lemon plopped in with several ice cubes. She handed the glass to Ruth. "Them boys keep coming and coming. Buses full. How many you figure they have at that base by now? Must be hundreds."

"I'm sure there must be at least a few thousand."

The woman wiped her hands on a hand towel. "So where's your soldier today? What's so important he's let you sit at a lunch counter all by yourself?"

"My fiancé only just arrived." Ruth answered, a hint of defensiveness in her voice. "He's on duty right now, otherwise he'd be here."

"Shame they wouldn't give him the time off. What with you being here to visit and all."

"The army has its own rules, I guess. I'm here for a couple more days. We still have time to be together."

The cook handed the sandwich plate to the woman who placed it on the counter in front of Ruth. "Well, I sure hope it all works out for you." She paused. "You want ketchup or anything?"

"No thanks. I'm fine. Tell me, is there a library or movie theatre within walking distance?"

"Looking for something to do, are ya?"

"Well, I do have a few free hours this afternoon."

The woman pointed towards the street. "If you go out the door, head north, that's left out of here, and take the third street on your right, that'll be Wickham. There's a movie theatre on the corner of Wickham and Pleasant. I don't know what's playing, but they always have a double feature on Friday afternoons. And the movie theater's air conditioned. You can escape this heat for a while."

Ruth looked at the clock. It was nearly one thirty. "I've probably missed the first show by now, but thanks for the tip." The woman smiled and moved away down the counter, wiping the surface as she walked.

Ruth ate her lunch quickly and left a 5¢ tip for the woman. It was a big tip for Ruth to leave, but the woman had been very helpful.

The Wickham Playhouse was exactly where the woman had said it would be. A sandwich board just in front declared the feature for the afternoon: *Mrs. Miniver* with Greer Garson and Walter Pidgeon.

She was in luck. *Mrs. Miniver* was one movie she wanted to see. Ruth paid the 27¢ price of admission, entered the theatre and found a seat on the right aisle near the back.

It took a few minutes for her eyes to become accustomed to the dark, but the light from the large movie screen revealed she wasn't the only one that had sought out the cool of the movie house that afternoon. The theatre was half full. "It must be a good movie, after all," she thought.

She loved the movie. *Mrs. Miniver* was almost two and a half hours long, and a real tear-jerker. She could hear quite a few people sniffling around her when the young bride, her body riddled with bullets from enemy fire, died in Greer Garson's arms. As she watched, Ruth felt grief for everyone in the family, but especially for the young British pilot when he discovered his new wife had been killed. The movie would have ended on a tragic note if not for the final scene, when the whole town gathered in the bombed out church and sang "Onward Christian Soldiers." Ruth couldn't help but join in as everyone in the theatre stood and sang along. It was inspiring.

As she began to walk the short distance to her hotel, she was filled with a new sense of conviction and pride. Yes, her country was at war with an enemy that was cruel and inhuman, but those with faith and courage would overcome all adversity, and they would prevail. She suddenly felt confident that somehow America would win this war and that her Jim would come home safe and sound. The thought lifted her spirits.

It was nearly four thirty when she finally reached her hotel room. If she was going to freshen up and meet Jim at six, she had to hurry. The movie theatre was just a few blocks from the hotel, but the short walk in the heat left Ruth feeling light-headed. Maybe a short nap would be good, she thought. She kicked off her shoes and lay down. It was the sound of a nearby church bell tolling six o'clock that finally woke her.

She looked at her watch. Oh my gosh. I'm late!

Ruth quickly changed clothes. She had chosen a bright pink flowered dress with square shoulders and a sash at the waist. It was brand new, and she knew the style flattered her. She had splurged on the pink canvas shoes. They matched the dress perfectly.

Now, I just have to put on my face and I'm done, she thought.

She quickly applied lipstick, brushed her hair, added a silver hair pin, grabbed her purse, and headed down to the lobby.

Jim was standing near the reception desk, anxiously watching the staircase.

"Hey, good looking," he grinned as she approached. "Ready for some grub? I thought we could eat here at the hotel before we head out. I'm famished."

"That'll be fine," Ruth answered. She took Jim's arm and the two of them walked to the door of the restaurant. Ruth's favorite waiter approached.

"Good evening. Table for two?"

"The one by the window, if available," Ruth answered.

Ruth noticed a few heads turned as she passed by and couldn't help but feel self-confident. She was a good-looking woman, on the arm of the man she loved and most everything in her life was going well. She had to smile.

"What's so funny?" Jim asked, once they were seated.

"Oh nothing," Ruth answered. "I was just thinking about the movie I saw earlier, *Mrs. Miniver.* Greer Garson was so glamorous, and I just loved her hats."

"Is that the English movie that takes place just as the war is breaking out? Before we got into it? They showed it at the movie house on base a few nights ago. Things look pretty bleak, but this family manages to survive, except for this young girl who gets herself killed. She was a rich kid who married a young pilot, right?"

"Yes, that's right." Ruth sipped her water. "It was all very sad."

"There was one scene towards the end, the one where the plane crashes just in front of the car they're driving. I'm not sure how realistic that was. Seemed a little contrived to me." He shrugged. "What do I know about movies?"

"The main point of the movie is that this family survives, and that things are going to be all right after all. I thought it was very inspirational."

Jim reached out and took Ruth's hand. "I thought so too. If it gives you hope that everything is going to work out, well, then, that's good enough for me." He paused, then continued, "I was thinking, there's a USO dance tonight at Holiday House back at the base. I thought we might go. Would that be alright with you?"

"Sounds like fun."

He looked at his watch. "Almost 6:15. We should probably order now if we want to get a good table at the dance."

Dinner went rather quickly. Fish & Chips for Jim, but Ruth preferred the Haddock and they had to wait a little longer as it was cooked to order. By seven-thirty, Jim was beginning to feel anxious. "The dance hall opens at eight. I think we should leave soon."

Ruth stood up. "I need to go back to my room for a minute. I'm just going to check with the front desk for any messages, first."

"Are you expecting any?" Jim questioned.

"No. I'm sure everything's fine at home. I'd just feel better if I made sure."

"Ok. I'll grab us a couple of sodas. It's going to be a warm bus ride back to the base." Jim headed for the small concession stand on the other side of the lobby. He returned with two cold bottles of pop.

Ruth was busy writing. "I'm leaving a note for Alice. She's the woman I met this morning at breakfast. I thought she and her boyfriend Tony might want to sit with us at the dance." Jim's face revealed disappointment.

"Do you need them for the company?"

Ruth shook her head. "What are you talking about? You think I'm not happy being with you? Just the two of us?"

Jim shrugged his shoulders.

"Jim Doherty, you are more than enough for me. I came all this way to be with you, and you alone." She held the note in her hand. "I just thought it would be a good idea, if she was at the dance we might sit with her and her boyfriend, Tony. If you don't want me to leave the note, I won't."

"No, of course leave the note. That's a good idea." Jim shook his head. "I'm just being foolish. It's been so long since we've had time alone..." he let his voice drift off, his face filled with a longing he didn't know how to put into words.

Ruth caught his meaning. "Come with me, soldier," she said smartly. She took Jim by the arm and led the way to the staircase. "I hope you're up for a little hike. My room's on the third floor."

Jim laughed softly, and leaned in against Ruth's arm. "No problem. I'm up for a little hike and a lot more."

Ruth gave him a sly smile and quickly began to climb the stairs, taking two at a time. Jim was right beside her. When they reached the third floor, both were laughing and out of breath.

"Which room is yours?"

Ruth jingled her room key in his face, tempting him to grab it. "The one at the far end. Number 314."

"I'll race you."

"No you won't." Ruth turned and walked as quickly as she could down the hallway, Jim tight on her heels, both laughing all the way.

She reached the door first and Jim slumped against the wall, waiting. He opened his bottle of Coke and took a long drag, offering the second bottle to Ruth.

"Later," she answered. "Let me get the door open first."

At first the key wouldn't fit the lock. "Don't tell me it doesn't work!" Jim said, frustration creeping into his voice.

"Hang on, it's just a little tricky. It's an old door. I had to fuss with it earlier." The lock suddenly clicked. "Got it!" Ruth exclaimed.

"Thank god."

Ruth pushed the door open and Jim followed.

The room was simple enough. A large double bed took up most of the space. The only other pieces of furniture were a small desk and chair and a tall dresser pushed up against the far wall. Light still streamed through the linen curtained windows, throwing dark shadows across the bedspread.

Jim, both hands still holding their cold drinks, closed the door behind them both with his foot.

"Here, let me have those." Ruth took the two bottles and placed them on the top of the dresser.

Jim stood quietly, still catching his breath, watching Ruth. Her hair caught the golden light of the setting sun. The features of her face were cast in shadow but he knew she was looking at him, expectantly.

"I have waited so long for this moment," Jim declared, "if that lock didn't work, I swear I would've kicked the door in."

"And I would have had to pay for it." Ruth said wryly.

"Maybe, but I doubt it." He took her in his arms and held her close. "From now on, I'm paying for everything, Ruth. Especially if I break it," he laughed softly.

"Whatever you say, darling."

He began to stroke her hair, and gently followed the curve of her cheek with his fingers. Everywhere he touched, Ruth felt a surge of heat run through her, a deep well of longing that demanded to be satisfied.

"I love you so much, Ruth. I've loved you for so long. I want to show you how much. Will you let me?"

"I know, Jim. I know." She pulled him closer, her lips grazing his ear as she whispered, "I want you to show me."

He took her hand and led her towards the bed. "I'm not sure we're going to make it to the dance tonight, after all."

"Why, what do you have in mind?" Ruth answered. Her quiet laugh was all the encouragement Jim needed.

※

The next morning Ruth bumped into Alice at breakfast.

"Hello, hello. Sit down." Alice declared, waving at the empty chair, opposite. "And where were you last night? I got your note. Tony and I saved seats for you at our table, but you never showed up." She took a sip of her Postum, rested her elbows on the table and demanded, "So tell me, what happened? Where were you two?"

Ruth wasn't sure she wanted to answer. After all, what happened between her and Jim was private. But she knew Alice wasn't going to stop asking until she got a satisfactory answer.

"Jim and I had every intention of going to the dance," she hesitated. "We had dinner first and then I went up to my room just to fix my hair and, well, things just went from one thing to another, and we decided to just skip the dance."

"Oooooh!" Alice let out a little shriek. "That sounds delicious! Tell me everything."

Ruth felt her face flush red. "Alice," she said firmly. "I'm not going into details. Just let's say, we got to know each other a little better."

"Sounds just fine to me," Alice declared. "Good for you!" She took a large bite of toast. "So, tell me, how was it? On a scale of 1 to 10 with 10 being out of this world, how was it? Tony and I always rate our experiences."

"You've got to be kidding," Ruth answered, stunned.

"We do. It gives us motivation for the next time."

Alice took another bite. "Rating the experience is a perfectly reasonable thing to do. I've done it with all the fellas I've been with. Puts everything into perspective. And I have to tell you, of all the men I've rated, Tony is tops. That's why I'm going to marry him." She gave Ruth a mouthy grin.

Ruth was grateful when the waiter came over to take her order. The whole time Alice kept right on talking about Tony and performance levels and who knows what. Thankfully, the subject had shifted focus from her night with Jim and onto Alice and Tony and the conversation stayed there for most of the meal.

"So where is your guy, now?" Alice asked. "Is he sleeping it off?"

Ruth looked at Alice. She suddenly realized how little she wanted to continue this conversation. Alice was loud and rude and, well, obnoxious in so many ways.

"Jim had guard duty again last night, so I'm assuming he's on the base right now. As for sleeping it off, I couldn't say." Ruth stood up. "Alice you've been very kind. But I have to go. I hope you and Tony will be very happy."

Alice ignored the obvious brush off. "Are you going to the base this morning? I'll go with you."

Ruth paused before answering. "I'm not sure what I'm doing. I think I may stay here for a little while."

"Oh, well, I see." Alice was a little confused. "Tony and I are getting together later. One of his friends loaned him a car for the afternoon. Tony's coming by around noon. If you want a ride back to the base, I'm sure we can drive you," Alice said encouragingly.

"That's very kind. But I'm really not sure what time I'll be going back. It all depends on Jim."

"Okay, just give me a wave. I'll be in the lobby at noon."

Ruth didn't think twice about her next decision. She was going for a long walk. She needed to take some time alone just to think and shake off a little of Alice's frenetic energy.

Last night had been wonderful. She had never felt so close to anyone as she did lying next to Jim. He had wanted to go "the whole distance," and they almost did, but Ruth had held back. "I love you Jim, but I'm just not ready. Not yet. I want the moment when we make love for the first time to be very special, not rushed or accidental."

She could tell he was eager and frustrated at the same time. "Ruth, I love you and I'm sure I can make you happy," he whispered. "Please let me love you." He paused, seeing her hesitation. "Would it make a difference if we were married?" he asked. "I can ask the priest first thing in the morning. If I can convince the priest to marry us, would you...?" Jim let the question hang there, every inch of his body pleading with her to say yes.

"I love you, Jim. More than anyone I've ever known. And I want to spend the rest of my life with you. These are such crazy times. You're leaving in just a few days, and I go back to Boston Sunday morning."

"That's why we should be married now. Right away. Before you leave." He held Ruth close. "I love you so much, and I know you love me. I want to marry you now—this moment. I don't want to wait. Not one day more. I want to know you're really mine and that you'll be waiting for me to come home after this war."

Ruth pushed back a little so Jim could see her face in the dim light. "I love you, Jim," her resistance beginning to waver. "If you can find a priest who will marry us tomorrow, then, yes, Jim Doherty, I will marry you."

"You mean it?" Jim asked, "You'll marry me tomorrow?"

Ruth gave a soft laugh. "Yes, Jim. I'll marry you tomorrow. If you can find a priest to do the honors, then, yes, I will marry you."

"Come here," Jim demanded, pulling her into his arms. "I love you, Ruth. I love you more than my life." They held each other tightly, not wanting to move, not wanting the moment to pass. Finally, Jim spoke.

"If we're going to be married in the morning, I better go find us that priest."

"You don't have to go so soon," Ruth looked at the small travel clock on the desk. "It's only ten o'clock."

But Jim was eager to return to the base, and hunt up a chaplain. "I'll talk to Fr. Murphy first thing in the morning. He'll marry us. I'm sure of it."

As she walked along Main Street in the Saturday-morning sunshine, Ruth was having second thoughts. She had checked with the hotel desk earlier, before breakfast, and then again just after her meal. Jim had not called or left a message. Perhaps finding someone to marry them was going to take a little more time and convincing than Jim had anticipated.

Ruth could understand his eagerness to tie the knot before he went overseas and she was tempted to just say yes to everything he wanted, married or not. But for her, it didn't feel right.

I guess I'm just a stickler for doing things the right way, she thought. She glanced at her watch. It was nearly 11. Jim must have called by now. She retraced her steps and quickly returned to the hotel.

"Sorry, Miss. There is no message."

"Could you check again, please. It's very important."

The clerk behind the hotel desk flipped through the message pad for a second time. "Sorry, no message for a Miss LeBlanc. Did you try calling him?" She gestured towards the wall phone. "You're welcome to use the hotel phone if it's a local call."

"Thanks, maybe a little later." Ruth fiddled with her purse. "Perhaps I'll just go to the base myself."

"Oh, he's a soldier, is he? Well, that explains it." The clerk shook her head. "I hate to be the one to tell you, but those boys are notorious for making promises they never keep."

Ruth felt her face flush with anger. "That's not the way it is with Jim. We're engaged to be married. In fact, we're getting married today."

The clerk look embarrassed. "Well, then, I hope you and your fiancé are very happy."

Ruth was just about to turn away when a familiar voice rang out, "You're getting married today?" It was Alice. Ruth hadn't noticed her standing just a few feet away. "Why, Ruth LeBlanc! You are full of surprises!"

It was too late to escape Alice's enthusiastic bluster.

"Why didn't you say something this morning? I knew there was something different about you at breakfast. You just seemed so, I don't know—more put together. Yes, that's it. You just seemed more put together. And now I know why! You're getting married. And today too! Tony!" she called to her boyfriend who was just crossing the lobby. "Tony! You remember Ruth? She's the one who stood us up at the dance! Shame on you, Ruth. We had such a great time, didn't we, Tony? Well, guess what, honey? She and that beau of hers are getting married. Today!"

Tony looked a little confused at Alice's rant, but nodded and smiled at Ruth. "Really?" He thrust out his hand. "My congratulations. Who is the lucky guy?"

"His name is Jim Doherty. He's at the base right now, making arrangements. I'm just waiting to hear from him."

Alice interrupted. "Are you supposed to meet Jim here at the hotel? Because if you're not, we're heading to the base in just a few minutes. Tony's got a car. We'll be happy to drive you, right Tony?" If Tony was feeling reluctant, her enthusiasm for the idea convinced him otherwise.

"Sure, I guess we could drive you. We were heading in the other direction." He looked at the expression of determination on Alice's face. "I'm sure our plans can wait a little while."

Ruth didn't know what to do. She could wait to hear from Jim and then have to walk or catch a bus to meet him, or she could take advantage of Alice's offer and hitch a ride with them. If she took the ride, her fear was Alice might ask to stay on to attend whatever ceremony Jim had planned and the last person Ruth wanted at her wedding was Alice.

"I don't want to interfere with your plans, Alice," Ruth answered.

"Oh, no trouble. We were just going to ride around the countryside, stop for a meal or something. Nothing special." She took Ruth's arm. "Don't you worry about a thing. Tony and me will drive you to the base. You find that guy of yours and get married. We'll even stay for the wedding if you want!" Alice gave her a toothy grin. Tony looked less than enthusiastic.

In the end, Ruth agreed. It was nearly noon. If she and Jim were going to be married that afternoon, she had better not wait any longer. She left a message for Jim with the front desk, just in case he called, and then followed Alice and Tony out to the car.

Once at Fort Dix, they had to park in the visitor's lot and check in with the registration center, all of which took time. Ruth tried to encourage Alice and Tony to just drop her off, but Alice would have none of it. "I want to be sure you're all set before we leave. Wouldn't want you to be stranded out here on your own," Alice declared. "We'll wait here, you go check if Jim has left you a message."

Ruth went inside to check with the desk sergeant, and returned moments later. "I think I'm all set. Jim left a message. We have a meeting with the priest this afternoon." She gave Alice a quick hug. "Thanks for the ride."

"You want us to stay?" Alice asked.

"No. Thanks anyway. I'll be fine."

"You sure?" Alice asked again.

"She said she'll be fine, Alice," Tony interrupted. "Listen, Ruth, you go have your meeting. I'm sure everything will be just great." He began to ease Alice towards the car. "And congratulations again."

Alice had no choice but to follow Tony. But she couldn't help but give one more piece of advice. "You tell that guy, he's a lucky fella, to snag a girl like you. Make sure you tell him for me!"

Ruth laughed. "I'll tell him," and with that she happily waved the two good bye.

She re-entered the reception center. "I have a one o'clock meeting with the base chaplain, Father Murphy," she told the desk sergeant.

He gave Ruth the necessary pass and pointed her to the far door. "You can pick up a base trolley just outside that door. Ask the driver to drop you off at the chapel."

"Thanks," Ruth answered.

❀

Jim was waiting for her outside the small white chapel when she arrived a few minutes later.

"Sorry I missed you at the hotel. They said you had just left so I thought it best to leave a message at the front gate." He kissed her gently, drawing her to himself.

"Your message said we have a meeting with the chaplain at one o'clock?"

"I told him all about you, and how we want to be married today. He wanted to meet you first." He grinned down at her. "I think he wants to be sure you're not being railroaded into anything."

Ruth laughed. "He doesn't know me. Or how stubborn I am." She gave Jim a friendly poke. "No one railroads Ruth LeBlanc into anything. I'm getting married because I want to, and that's that."

"That's my girl," Jim grinned broadly. "Come on, we're meeting him in his office. It's around the back."

Jim led Ruth towards the back of the chapel to a small low building. A cocker spaniel was leashed to the bench outside the entrance to the office. As soon as the dog saw the two approach, he began to bark.

"Stop it, Dixy. These people are here to visit me." A short stocky man in army fatigues held open the screen door. "Hello there. You must be Ruth." He held out his hand in welcome. "I'm Father Murphy, and you're the fool girl who wants to marry this joker, eh?" He gave Jim a quick jab to the shoulder and grinned. "Why don't you two come in and sit for a spell. I have a few things I need to say to you both."

The meeting lasted a little under an hour but at the end of it, there was no persuading the priest.

"I'm sorry, Jim. I'm telling everyone the same thing. If you're scheduled to ship out in the next few weeks, I'm not going to marry you. I'm not going to marry widows."

Jim tried his best to change the man's mind. "But we love each other. And from what I'm hearing around camp I'll be gone for a good long time. Maybe years. If we don't get married now, it'll be years before we have another chance."

"And that's precisely my point, young man," Father Murphy continued. "You don't know where you are going, you don't know when you'll be back, or if you'll be back." He turned to Ruth, sympathy in his voice. "Our country is in the middle of a war. A lot of these brave boys are about to be thrust into harm's way. Many won't be coming home again." He shook his head slowly. "I am not going to marry you today and have your life on hold for who knows how long."

"But I want my life on hold," Ruth countered. "I love Jim, and I've promised to marry him. If you only knew me, you'd realize I would never give such a promise unless I meant it with all my heart."

"If that is true," the priest reached out and held Ruth's hand, "then there is nothing to fear. Your love will sustain you while Jim is away. And when he returns, then you can marry."

Jim interrupted, "But…"

"There's no changing my mind. It's made up. I'm saying the same to every soldier in camp. Get engaged if you wish, but I'm not marrying widows, and that's my final word on the subject." He raised his right hand. "Now, let me give you my blessing."

Jim and Ruth bowed their heads as the priest made the sign of the cross over them.

"Go in peace, both of you."

There was nothing more to be said.

✦

Jim grabbed Ruth's hand as they quickly walked out of the chaplain's cool office into the heat of the day. "I am so angry, I just want to hit something," Jim exploded. "Who does he think he is telling us we can't get married?"

"He's the priest, Jim."

"Well, he's no priest of mine, I can tell you. I love you, Ruth, and I'm going to marry you no matter what." Jim's face was red with fury, and the veins in his neck looked as if they were about to burst.

"You've got to calm down, Jim. Father Murphy's only doing what he thinks is best." Ruth was surprised at how relieved she was beginning to feel. There was no question she wanted to marry Jim, but she wasn't sure she wanted to do it so fast. She had only said yes the night before because Jim had insisted.

"So you think the priest is right? You think it's okay for him to say no to two people who love each other, who desperately want to marry, before one of them goes away and gets himself blown up? Is that what you think?"

Ruth stopped walking and turned to Jim. "That's not what I'm thinking." She took both of Jim's hands. "I'm thinking that if our love is strong enough, it will survive this war. That if we just stay true to each other, we'll make it through this, no matter what."

"That's not enough for me, Ruth. I love you, and I want to love you now, today, this moment." His anger and frustration were clear. He dropped her hands and walked a few paces away.

"Is that what this is really about?" Ruth confronted Jim. "Is it only about us making love? About sex? Or is it real love you are looking for?"

"What's the difference?" Jim asked, his anger boiling over. "I love you. I want to make love to you. I want to marry you. And I want to do it now. That foolish priest is just plain wrong." He paused, hand on his head, considering his options.

"I'm going to go find a minister. I'll bet Reverend Winslow will do it." He looked at Ruth. "Winslow's the Methodist minister on base. A good man from what I hear. I'll ask him to marry us."

"I don't think so."

"What do you mean? What does it matter? Catholic, Methodist? He's a preacher. It shouldn't matter."

"I mean I don't think so. I'm not going to be married by a Methodist minister, Jim. We're both Catholic. It wouldn't count."

"Of course it'd count. It's a marriage no matter what, isn't it?"

Ruth looked at Jim and saw how deep was his anger and disappointment. She could see how much this marriage meant to him. And how much he wanted her. But there was no way she was going to allow herself to be rushed into a shotgun marriage just to satisfy his needs.

"You need to calm down." She lowered her voice. "You asked the priest to marry us; he said no. That's it. That's the answer."

"It's not good enough, Ruth."

"What more do you want?"

"I want you to be my wife," Jim answered. "I just want you."

"You already have me, Jim." She reached out to him and softly stroked his cheek. "I love you, and I'll wait for you till you come marching home. Besides, having a little time to plan our big day is a good thing. Don't you want all your friends and family to be there?"

Jim just shrugged, slowly becoming resigned to the reality of the situation. "I suppose so."

"Come on, let's go have some lunch. I'm hungry and we still have the whole afternoon and evening to be together. I don't want to waste it standing here."

They spent the rest of the afternoon walking around the base. They stopped at Hostess House for a light lunch and then Jim took Ruth on a quick tour of the one airfield that was open to visitors. They couldn't get close to the aircraft, but he pointed out one of the planes he had trained on.

"The B-17. They call it the Flying Fortress" he explained, "I can't tell you any more about it, but trust me, it deserves the name."

Ruth was impressed. "Do you have any more training to do?"

"Classes are pretty much done. Only maneuvers and combat training now. We're just waiting to get our orders."

Ruth didn't want to think about it.

"I think we should be heading back to the hotel. I still have to pack."

"What time is your bus in the morning?"

"I'm catching the first bus to New York. It leaves the base at 9 o'clock."

"Okay, I'll walk you back. We can grab dinner at that little Italian restaurant I saw across from the Barlow. I think it's called Mama Rosa's. You must be tired of eating at the hotel."

"It's been fine, Jim. But a change of venue would be nice, too."

Jim took Ruth's arm. "Then that's what we'll do."

They walked most of the way back to the center of town in comfortable silence. There was so little and so much to say, but neither knew how to begin. It wasn't until they were almost to the restaurant that Jim said, "I just wish there was something to change your mind before you go. Something I could say to convince you how much I love you. How much I need you."

Ruth squeezed his hand. "You don't have to do or say anything, Jim. I know how you feel. But I think the priest was right. And the more I think about what he said, the more I agree with him."

"Maybe I should never have asked you," Jim wondered. "I never meant to push you into anything you didn't want to do. I thought you loved me and wanted to marry me."

"Jim Doherty!" Ruth stopped abruptly. "I don't want to hear that kind of talk from you again." She pulled on Jim's arm. "Look at me."

He turned slowly, facing Ruth.

"I love you, Jim Doherty." She paused, waiting to be sure he was really listening. "I will wait for you and I will marry you as soon as you come home safe and sound from this war. Never doubt my love, do you hear me?" Suddenly she pulled him close and gave him a very long and deep kiss, not a bit embarrassed by the fact they were standing in the middle of a busy sidewalk.

"Do you believe me now?"

"I won't argue with that." He gave her a big grin. He looked around at the people nearby. "She's my girl," he said out loud to anyone who would listen. People just smiled agreeably.

He turned back to Ruth. "Okay. Well, that's that." He grinned. "You ready for dinner?"

Mama Rosa's homemade lasagna was delicious. They took their time with the meal, sharing an antipasto and most of a bottle of wine. By nine o'clock Ruth was feeling tired. "It's getting late, and I've still got to pack."

"I'll walk you to your room." Jim said.

"Of course." Ruth answered, "but just to the door," she warned him. "I'm really very tired and I still have a lot to do."

"Don't worry, Ruth, I'll behave myself."

But try as he might, Jim could not contain his desire. It was their last night together. She was leaving in the morning. It might be years before they saw each other again and he needed her desperately. By the time they reached the door of Room 314 he was beginning to despair.

Once Ruth had the door unlocked, Jim pushed passed her into the room.

"Jim, what are you doing?"

"This can't be it with us. Can't you see how much I need you?"

Ruth didn't know what to say. "Jim, I thought we settled this." She could see both desire and desperation in his eyes. "There is nothing to be done about it. As long as we are not married..." She let the words hang there for a moment. "I think you had better go, Jim. Before we do something we'll both regret."

"I only want to love you, Ruth," Jim pleaded.

"And I, you," Ruth whispered. "Do you think I don't want to make love to you? Don't you think I have the same desires, the same wants, the same needs as you?" She felt tears beginning to well up behind her eyes. "I want you more than you will ever know, Jim. But it wouldn't be right. Not now, not tonight."

A tear escaped her right eye. She quickly brushed it aside. She had to stay in control. She crossed to the door and opened it. "I really think you should go."

"I can't." Jim said quietly.

"You must."

Ruth held the door open, facing the corridor, waiting for Jim to leave.

"You need to go now," she said, without turning around.

Jim stood quietly, hoping Ruth would change her mind. She did not.

"I'll come by the bus stop in the morning to see you off," he said softly, barely touching her arm as he walked by her into the hall and out of the hotel.

Ruth closed the door slowly. She knew she had made the right decision, but asking Jim to leave had been one of the hardest things she had ever done. Suddenly, all the tension and anxiety of the day hit her like a wave and she collapsed on the bed, sobbing.

How could this happen? she thought. She began to trace the events of the day in her mind: how excited she had been that morning to think she would be married by the end of the day, and how disappointed yet relieved she had been when the priest told them he wouldn't marry them. In the end, the hardest part was dealing with Jim's anger and desire, and her own. It was almost too much to bear, but there was nothing she could do about it now.

She looked at the small travel clock on the nearby desk. It was nearly ten. I've still got to pack, she thought. But she had no energy for it and instead, pulled the bedspread over her head and fell asleep, thoroughly exhausted.

※

It was the sound of passing traffic on the main street below that woke her the next morning. A quick glance at her watch told her she was very late.

No time for breakfast, she thought, as she grabbed her suitcase and began collecting her things. Thankfully she had only brought a few outfits and within fifteen minutes she was packed, dressed and standing at the hotel reception desk, settling her bill. "I need to be at the base by 8:45 this morning, and I'm very late. Could you please arrange for a cab?"

"Certainly, miss. We'll have one meet you at the entrance."

She hated to spend the money on cab fare, but she knew if she missed the 9 a.m. bus to New York she would have to wait until early evening for the next one and that meant traveling all night to Boston. If she was really honest with herself, it was more the thought of spending the day fighting off Jim that she was avoiding rather than the all night bus ride. I just need to go home, she thought.

"I need to get to Fort Dix to catch the 9 a.m. bus to New York," she told the driver.

"It'll be tight," he said, putting her suitcase in the cab's trunk. "But I think we can make it."

The driver was as good as his word. When the cab pulled into the Fort Dix bus stop a large Greyhound bus was still parked just beyond the entrance to the base. A small group of passengers were lined up on the sidewalk, waiting to board, and standing just to one side, was Jim. He looked worried.

"I've been here for over an hour, waiting for you," he said. "I thought you were going to be here earlier."

"Sorry. I overslept." She handed him her suitcase. "Here, can you hold this for a minute? I have to find my ticket."

She began to dig through her purse. "I thought I put it in the side pocket."

"I've been waiting here for an hour," Jim repeated. "When I didn't see you, I thought you might have decided to wait for the late bus." He looked at her, hope still in his eyes.

"Oh, good. Found the ticket." She held it up for Jim to see.

"I thought we might still have today together?" Jim asked.

Ruth gave Jim a long look. "I have to go home, Jim. It's going to take all day to get there, and I have to work tomorrow." She reached out and placed her hand on his chest. "It's been wonderful but I have to go, not only for work, but for everything. You know that," she said softly.

Reluctantly, he nodded, knowing Ruth was right. It was easier to say goodbye now than spend another day longing for each other without any possible resolution.

"I'll write every day," he said. "No matter where I am, or what I'm doing. I'll write every day."

He took her in his arms, their lips meeting for one long last kiss. They held each other tightly, not wanting to let go.

"Hey, miss, you getting on this bus, or what?" It was the bus driver.

"Yes, yes, I'm coming."

Jim handed the driver her suitcase, and turned to Ruth for one last kiss.

"I'll be thinking of you every day, sweet. Every day."

"And I'll be waiting for you, Jim. Every day." She turned and began to walk away. "I love you," she said. "I'll always love you."

He nodded, watching her go.

She climbed the stairs of the bus and took a window seat on the same side on which Jim was standing. As the bus pulled away, she gave him a last wave. He didn't wave back. Instead he clicked his heels together and gave her a quick salute. She smiled, tears beginning to stream down her cheeks. She didn't know it, but the sight of him standing there, so healthy and strong, and saying goodbye, would have to sustain her for the next three years.

CHAPTER 7

BOSTON

It was nearly midnight by the time Mr. LeBlanc met Ruth at the Greyhound terminal on Stuart Street in Boston. "How was your trip?"

"It was fine. Jim is fine. The base is enormous. Met some nice people. Bus ride was long. I just want to get home and go to bed."

Her father knew his daughter well enough to know better than to probe. He could tell she was troubled. Whatever had happened between Ruth and Jim was better left unsaid. He let the conversation drift to local gossip, and finally silence.

For the next few days, Ruth concentrated on her work. When family and friends asked about her trip, she revealed nothing of the pain in her heart and was matter of fact in her answers: "Had a wonderful time. Jim is in fine shape. He sends his love." Nothing more.

Only her best friend Helen knew the truth. "It was not what I expected, Helen. I mean, we had a good time and it was wonderful to be with Jim again. But he had only one thing on his mind. I resisted. So he decided we should be married right away. I would have gone along, but then the priest said no and things got very awkward after that."

"What you're saying is, the man you love, the man you've promised to marry wanted to bed you and you wouldn't sleep with him, unless you were married by a priest?"

"Keep your voice down, Helen. I don't want my personal news broadcast everywhere." They were huddled together in the office break room. It would be easy for someone to overhear their conversation.

Helen took a long sip of her tea. "So, how did Jim take it?"

"Take what?"

"How did he feel about you're refusing to...?" She wasn't going to say the words aloud.

"He was upset," Ruth replied, "But I think he understood." She paused, confusion on her face. "Do you think I made a big mistake, Helen?"

"It's a little too late to worry about that, now. Besides, if he loves you as much as you say he does, maybe the fact that you said no will keep him faithful." She began to rinse out her tea cup. "But who knows? In my experience, men are only thinking about two things: food and sex, and most of the time sex wins. I'd let it be for the moment. There's nothing much you can do anyway. Just see how things go."

"I guess you're right, still I can't help thinking I hurt him terribly, and I don't know how to fix it."

Ruth worried silently until Jim's next letter arrived in the post.

Monday, August 17, 1942- Fort Dix, N.J.

Good morning dearest:

I'm writing this from a corner of the mess hall. By this writing you should be home. Some families just arrived to visit soldiers. They are out parked by the side of the building. I can hear children laughing.

I can't thank you enough darling for coming down. Before another day goes by, I want to apologize in writing for my rudeness at times.

You came down here because you loved me. Thursday night, I can truthfully say was the happiest evening I have spent thus far in my life. You also enjoyed that evening dear, we both were very happy in each other's arms. The dinner together in the hotel and the pleasant walk are memories long to be remembered. Friday, when we finally met for dinner, you seemed a little tired and I can appreciate how you felt just waiting around all day for me to show up.

Friday night I coaxed you into something that I think proved distasteful to you and which is very dangerous to our love. No matter how much people love each other it won't last if it is strained by such stolen moments. I am the guilty one, Ruth, not you. I could make you love me more by holding out and saving you for the future, but no, instead I caused you to be exposed to such temptations and endangered our whole set up.

Ruth stopped reading, recalling the scene. It hadn't been all Jim's fault. She had been both eager and reluctant. The whole awkward scene had ended badly.

I'm so sorry with that whole business with the priest on Saturday and the way I responded to his answer. I am terribly mad and ashamed with myself this morning and ask that you forgive me once more for the weakling that I am. I really don't deserve you.

What I am trying to say Ruth, is that I promise to become the man you deserve from this moment on. I am terribly serious about this dear, because I know you felt differently towards me Saturday evening.

To sum it up, you're worth fighting for and I'm not going to let you escape. I love you darling too much to lose you. All I ask is your faith in me. When I saw you, all I wanted to do was to hold you in my arms.

Ruth, say you understand and that you're behind me 100%.

I am going on guard duty tonight dear and it is raining. But I'll be thinking of you. We leave tomorrow so far as we know. But let me hear from you Ruth if you still are behind me. I want you more than I have wanted anyone or anything before in my life.

Well this is so long now dear. Call my home and try to see them sometime, huh? My love to all.

Your Jim

Ruth re-read the letter one more time before carefully placing the envelope in her bureau drawer with the others. Jim's apology had made her feel a little better. He realized the awkward position in which he had placed her and the fact that he could acknowledge that gave her some sense of confidence that things would eventually be all right between them. She had no desire to prolong the tension by any further discussion about what had happened. Especially if she had to do it in a letter.

Helen was right. Best let the whole matter drop. Besides, if what Jim wrote was true, his squadron was already on the move, and they both had more important things to worry about, like making sure he came home safe.

※

"How are things with Jim?" her mother asked at dinner that night. "I saw you got a letter from him in the morning post."

"His group has just shipped out, I think."

Mr. LeBlanc put down his fork and added a little milk to his tea. "Does he say where to?"

"No, and I don't expect I'll find out 'til he's settled somewhere. Maybe not even then."

"They don't tell your family where you're going?" Justine asked, incredulity in her voice. "That doesn't make any sense at all."

"It does if you're trying to keep things secret," Mr. LeBlanc explained. "You've heard the saying, 'Loose lips sink ships.' Remember what happened to the Brit's Athenia a couple of years ago, and that was a passenger ship. They still can't prove it, but I'll bet the Germans sunk her. Any ship going across the Atlantic today is vulnerable, whether carrying troops or cargo. They've got to keep these things secret to protect our boys."

"I suppose so," Justine mumbled. "So," she looked at her mother who was seated at the other end of the table. "Is there any dessert?"

"I made some pudding. It's in the Frigidaire. Would you serve it, Justine? The small bowls are in the cupboard."

Mrs. LeBlanc turned to Ruth. "Did you and Jim make any plans for the wedding while you were in New Jersey? Anything I need to know?"

"No plans, mother. Everything is so unpredictable."

"I was talking with Mrs. Anderson at the market this morning," Justine interrupted, "and she was telling me about her son, Joey. He and his girlfriend got married before he shipped out in June and now the girl's expecting. I hear a lot of the girls are marrying their sweethearts so they could... you know..."

"Justine!" Mrs. LeBlanc interrupted, her voice sharp with rebuke. "I will not have that kind of talk at the dinner table. Apologize to your sister."

"We did talk about getting married. In fact, we almost did."

All three at the table looked at her, surprised.

"But you didn't." Mrs. LeBlanc stated with conviction. "You're a sensible girl, Ruth, and you must realize marriage at this time would be a mistake."

"Not at all, Mother. I was more than willing to marry Jim right then and there. We even went to his priest on the base. But Father Murphy refused. He said he was not going to marry widows."

"A smart man, if you ask me," Mr. LeBlanc commented.

"What did he mean?" Justine asked.

Her father tried to explain, "It's a risky business for a girl to marry a soldier just before he ships out. If anything happens to him, if he gets killed, she's a widow straight away. Possibly with a child to bring up on her own, like Mrs. Anderson's daughter-in-law."

"These young people," Mrs. LeBlanc mused. "I don't understand what they're thinking. Marriage is a serious commitment. Not to be taken lightly. War or no war. It's not something you do in a hurry." She turned to her daughter. "I'm proud of you, Ruth, for not rushing into things."

"Oh, I was tempted, Mother," Ruth answered. "But to be honest, when the priest refused us, I was actually relieved."

"I bet Jim wasn't so happy about it," Justine commented under her breath, a sly smile still evident.

"Justine," her mother glared, "you can serve the pudding now."

❈

V-MAIL

Sept 4. 1942—HQ & HQ Squadron, 51st Troop Carrier Wing

Dearest Ruth:

This is certainly a quaint country here, so different from ours back home. Everything so neat and in its place. Getting quite a kick out of it all. Everyone here is in very good spirits and best of health.

Please note my change of address. You understand of course, the censorship these letters undergo, therefore my letters will not describe where I am or what I am doing or anything at all in relation to the service over here.

Have you gone to see the folks yet? I imagine they are worried a bit, so I would appreciate you giving them a call and telling them not to worry as I am fit as a fiddle.

Give everyone my regards, and say hello to your mother and family for me.

You're on my mind more than ever before.

Love, Jim

She brought the letter into work the next day and read it to Helen.

"Are you going to go visit Jim's family?"

"I should." Ruth paused, thinking. "I wonder how much he has told them about us? David knows we're engaged, of course, and he may have said something to his father and Hazel."

"I wouldn't worry . They're nice people, you said so yourself. They only want what's best for Jim. Just call them up and invite yourself over for tea."

Ruth flipped through her calendar. "You're right. I should pick a date or two and see if there is a time we could get together. It doesn't have to be dinner. Just a quick hello to share the latest news."

"He doesn't say where he is in the V-Mail, but can you take a guess?"

"I've been following the news pretty closely. I think he must be in England or Scotland. He writes about the place being 'quaint and neat with everything in its place.' I've never been to England, but they do have a lot of quaint little villages, so England is my best guess. In any event, he's someplace safe, at least for the moment ."

She picked up the phone, and began to dial the Dohertys' phone number. "Might as well get this over with."

It took several rings for someone to pick up, but finally a woman with a thick Irish brogue answered. "Hi, Hazel? This is Ruth LeBlanc. I just got a V-Mail from Jim and he asked me to call."

Helen moved towards the office door, but kept one ear listening to Ruth as she arranged a time to visit the Doherty household.

"She's a very nice woman," Ruth said as she hung up the phone. "But her accent makes it difficult for me to understand her. I miss every other word." She made a notation in her calendar. "I think we decided a week from this Sunday afternoon for tea, but I can't be absolutely certain."

"You could always call her back to confirm," Helen suggested, smiling. "Or you could just show up and see how things go."

"I'll double check with David on Wednesday. We're scheduled to do some plane spotting in Hull again and I just received the pictures Jim and I took at Fort Dix. His family can see for themselves how well he's doing, and that will fill up the afternoon." She glanced at her watch. "Almost lunchtime. Let's walk down Washington Street, Helen. I want to show you something I've decided to buy and I want your opinion."

"Give me a second to grab my jacket and I'll meet you downstairs."

A few minutes later, they were heading towards the center of town. "So, what are we shopping for? A new hat from Jordan's?"

"No, I want to buy a ring, and I saw a beautiful one in the window at the Jewelers Building."

"Why are you looking for a ring? Is it a gift? Who's it for?"

"For me. My engagement ring from Jim."

Helen stopped and stared at her friend. "That's right. You're engaged but Jim never gave you a ring."

Ruth started walking a little faster. "Not that he didn't want to. He was in Missouri remember? I thought he would give me one when we met at Fort Dix, but I think he was just too busy to think about it. So now, I'm buying one on my own."

"Jim asked you to buy your own ring?" Helen quizzed. "Isn't that kind of unusual?"

"He doesn't know about it. But I'm sure he'll be happy." She waited to let a car go by. "Come on, the Jewelers Building is across the street."

The two friends used the crosswalk, walked a block north and stopped in front of a large storefront. The window was filled with beautiful jewelry. Watches, necklaces and rings of every design sparkled under the window's spotlight. Ruth pointed to a small gold ring in the third row with a cultured pearl centered stone.

"What do you think?" she asked her friend eagerly. "I've always wanted a pearl for an engagement ring, and this one is perfect."

Helen was surprised at Ruth's choice. "Are pearls fashionable this year?" she wondered. "I thought it was always diamonds."

"I think pearls are stunning. And this is the one I want Jim to get for me."

Helen nodded and agreed. "It's your ring. If you love it, buy it." She looked at the ring again. "It really is beautiful."

"I'm going to put a deposit down today and pay the balance at the end of the week. By the time I visit Jim's family, this ring will be on my finger."

"When are you going to tell Jim?"

"I'll send him a picture. I don't think he'll care what the ring looks like as long as I'm happy. Picking out jewelry is not his strong suit."

Helen thought about the tall, lanky Jim and knew her friend was right. Whatever ring she wanted would be fine with him.

The two women spent the next half hour discussing the value and care of precious jewelry with the owner of Gann Jewelers. Ruth put down a sizable deposit on the pearl ring she had chosen. "It didn't even need resizing," she told her friend as they left the store. "That's a lucky thing," Ruth reflected. "A good sign."

As she predicted, by the weekend, the ring was on the third finger of Ruth's left hand.

As long as Jim had been stationed at an Army base in the states, most of his letters to Ruth arrived within just three or four days of mailing. But now that he had shipped out, everything was likely to change.

The next letter from Jim took almost two weeks to arrive.

September 13, 1942—12th Troop Carrier Squadron

Dearest Ruth:

I wish I could tell you all about where I am and what I am doing, but censorship demands that nothing is to be said about our locality, food, girls or any particulars peculiar to the place we are stationed. I do quite a bit of cycling now. I cannot discuss weather conditions. Gosh, but I miss you terribly.

I feel indebted to you, really I do, for the many nice things you have done for me. Let me know what goes on around home.

I have dropped V letters to practically everyone whom I think will answer them. I hope they do anyway. I miss the old crowd I was with in the Mid West and laugh now to think about some of the crazy things we did just for the h—of it. Over here, even the girls use the word hell as a figure of speech.

In writing to me don't mention the names of places where I trained or where I shipped out of or anything pertaining to my Army life, because I don't want anyone cutting holes into your letters.

Ruth had read about the strict censorship rules. Once a letter was written, the soldier was required to submit it to a soldier to read. Any hint or suggestion of location or Army maneuvers was literally cut out of the paper. Either that, or a heavy black marker was used to cover the writing. Apparently, the same rules applied to letters from home. She would have to be careful.

Give my regards to your friends both near and far. We will pay them a visit as Mr. & Mrs. Someday, if I have anything to say about it. Best wishes to all. And to you, my sincere love and admiration.

Your Jim

Ruth double-checked the postmark on the front of the envelope: September 14. That would have been a Monday. In the month since leaving him at Fort Dix, she had written at least five letters to Jim but he still had not received any of them. She determined to write him again, this time using the new Victory Mail system. She had hesitated using V-Mail because it was guaranteed her letter would be censored before being delivered. But the post office clerk explained that all mail was inspected whether airmail or V-Mail, and using the new system lessened the load on shipping tons of mail.

"We're encouraging everyone to use V-Mail miss. Very simple to use." He handed Ruth an airgraph form. "You write your letter on this form. We send it off to get photographed and then the negative is put on a roll of microfilm with all the other letters being sent that day. We can ship 1,600 letters on one roll of film and the whole thing only weighs 5 ounces. And V-Mail gets there faster. If those same letters were sent individually, the mail bag would weigh over 50 pounds. It'd take up a lot of space on a transport plane that could be used for valuable war materials. It's your choice, but using Victory Mail is really the patriotic thing to do, miss."

"How much is a form?"

"Cost is 3¢ each for ground, same as a regular letter, or 6¢ if you want it to go by air. And that includes the envelope." The clerk folded the form. "You fold it down like this, and it turns into its own envelope."

Ruth did a quick calculation. "I want my soldier to get this sooner rather than later, so I'll take 10 of the 6¢ forms, please."

She thought that might hold her for a month or so.

CHAPTER 8

ENGLAND

It was hard not knowing if Jim was getting any of her correspondence. The next day, another letter from Jim confirmed her concern. It was full of interesting bits of information, but no mention of any letters she had written.

Sept. 18, 1942—12th Troop Carrier Squadron, 60th Troop Carrier Group

My dearest Ruth:

Boy, I'm aching for a letter. There is nothing much I can say about this end of things or where we are. I have sent you a little gift. Lord knows when you will receive it, but it's on its way.

About every week or so, we are able to draw rations on American goods, such as cigarettes, candy, soap, beer in cans, razor blades, tooth powder and tooth paste and a few other small articles

I can hear the soft tone of an accordion coming from the living quarters adjoining. The boy who is playing it, has been with a band that has traveled in New England.

I got me a candle stuck on top of an empty beer can (I emptied it, of course) and it provides both sufficient light and inspiration. Don't think we are living in caves, or the like, it is just that our quarters haven't been wired up yet.

I am just about getting used to crossing these village roads without jumping across like a scared rabbit. They drive on the left in this country and I keep looking first to the right.

Driving on the left? He must be somewhere in England, she realized. I'm surprised the censor didn't black that out.

It seems as though they drive much faster here. It may be due to the size of the roads. They are a lot smaller than ours and their cars are mostly small ones. You can see lots of Fords with right hand steering wheels about the towns. We have movies on the post about once a week and Al Jolsen and a few other Hollywood personnel were here in person.

The hardest thing to get used to is the lack of street lamps and brightly lit thoroughfares. I shall never forget my first experience in the blackout. I went into a building before dark and along about 10 P.M. decided to leave. As I stepped out the front door, I thought, well, something is wrong here. This must be the backyard, so I retraced my steps looking all the while for the front door. Finally, a chap came downstairs and went out that same door whistling all the while, and it finally dawned on me that that was the front door leading to the street. So, I boldly walked up to it, and yanked it open and looked out into oblivion. I stepped cautiously along the edge of the wall, feeling my way as I went. My hand rested on something soft,—someone's coat. It was a girl just standing there in the darkness for some reason or other, but boy I got cold chills at the thought, was this the way it is all the time?

She said, "Hello" and I stammered and stuttered a weak "Hello" and passed on. Gradually, my eyes became accustomed to the ink, (My mind hasn't as yet.) and I began to see forms more clearly as they approached. People carry these little flashlights with the glass covered with paper and a pin-hole allowing light to show. Most of the people don't light it unless they are going to bump into someone. You see, they are going on three years of this stuff and are quite at ease with the whole thing. Now, I carry a flashlight all the time if I go into a town.

There are many things one sees here that appear so strange to an American, yet are everyday occurrences among the British.

For instance, you might see a big transport lorry bearing down on you on the road and go tearing by at breakneck speed, and at the wheel of that big truck, probably 5 or 8 tons, will be a little fair haired girl hardly out of school age, that is, about 20 years of age.

Many of the bus conductors are women and in London the women drive around these little electric baggage trucks they have in RR stations. And they are as capable it seems as the men. What will happen to their femininity I don't know, but for myself, I like my woman all feminine.

Ruth shook her head. Don't worry about women being feminine, Jim. A woman can drive a truck and still be attractive. She was surprised at his attitude.

And I think most fellows prefer their girls that way. They are much more attractive. I can't seem to bother much about a girl dressed in uniform or work clothes, but put her in a cute little house dress, and she catches my eye every time. But that's me.

I do hope you find time to write often. I am looking so eagerly for your letters. Say hello to your mother and family.

With all my love. Your Jim

Re-reading it, Ruth was surprised the letter hadn't been cut up into tiny pieces. There were so many references to life in what was obviously England, she would have expected the censors to do their worst with Jim's letter. They hadn't. At least Jim is safe for the moment. That's all I can ask for.

Throughout the fall, Jim continued to write and Ruth sent him a return letter for each one he posted. It seemed to take forever for her letters to be delivered, and those Jim sent came in bunches.

October 8, 1942

Dear Ruth,

What a glorious day this has been. I received three of your letters and three V letters.

I wouldn't care if I never received mail from anyone as long as you keep them coming. And the letters! They were just what the doctor ordered. They were potent with that certain something that gives one a "lift" when he hears from his one and only.

If you could only see how anxious the fellows are to hear from home, I'm sure the folks would write daily. Mail call is the most popular call perhaps, even more so than mess call, though some individuals would debate that.

Your letters did not arrive in the proper sequence. And boy, let me tell you your letter of Oct 2. had me all mixed up. You asked me how I liked the ring. I said to myself, What ring? Did she go and buy one? Then I got a letter from Eddy telling me of your visit to the house and how you proudly displayed your ring.

I now have the picture of the ring you sent and dearest, I am very proud of it. Do the folks know you bought it yourself? At first I felt rather left out of things, but after thinking the matter over, I'd say you have done the best thing and it makes me feel flattered, knowing you care so much. My only wish is that I could have thought of something like that myself. What I should have done, was to tell you to buy a ring but it looks like you worked it out after all.

I never thought I could care so much for anyone or anything, but to me, Ruth, you are life itself. I can't get you out of my thoughts for more than a few minutes.

I'll come back to you darling just keep praying.

Goodbye for a while.

Your Jim

Ruth called Jim's family and shared his news. They were happy to hear he was still in England and doing well. The newspapers were full of stories about the German bombing raids, but it sounded like he was in a place away from those targets. When Hazel invited her to come by for another Sunday visit, Ruth asked if Jim's sister Brigid might be joining them.

"Jim speaks so highly of his sister, I thought it might be time I meet her."

Hazel hesitated before answering, and Ruth sensed some tension in her voice when she did. "Well, now Brigid 'tis a very busy person. She has those children that keep her comin' and goin' every day. That's how children are these days. So I kin ask her but I wouldn't be expectin' she'd be free to come."

"I understand. Please tell her I was asking for her and that Jim wanted her to know he thinks of her often."

"I'll tell her if an' when I see the woman."

"Thanks, Hazel. I'll come by next Sunday, then?" Ruth asked.

"That'll be the 8th of November. Yes, that'll do. Good-bye."

Ruth stared at the phone. I knew from Jim that Brigid hadn't had an easy time of it after her mother had died. She remembered what he had told her when they were first dating.

"When my father married Hazel so soon after my mother's death, it was hardest on Brigid. She had become the woman of the household and there was a lot of resentment when Hazel arrived and took things over."

Apparently those bad feelings still lingered even after all these years, but Ruth determined not to let it bother her.

On Wednesday evening, David and two other volunteers met Ruth at the Quincy Armory. David had arranged to drive them to the spotter location.

"Did anyone bring a blanket? I forgot to put one in the trunk," David asked.

"I brought a comforter with me." The new volunteer, a tall blonde woman with thick glasses held out a blanket. "It's kind of small, but two of us could sit on it."

"I guess we can take turns," David suggested. "We'll be inside the water tower and there's a couple of benches we can sit on. It can get pretty windy up there. Cold, too."

"I brought a thermos of coffee," the second volunteer spoke up. "And cups, one for each of us."

"I brought applesauce muffins," Ruth chimed in, smiling. "We should be good for a couple of hours, anyway."

"We better get going. I want to reach Hull before it's too dark."

Although the day had been warm, the evening temperatures were heading down into the thirties and everyone was bundled up with winter coats and hats. Sitting in the cold, staring out at a starry sky was not as romantic in the late autumn as it might be during the summer months.

It was nearly 7 o'clock by the time they got to the tower. The four volunteers who had the earlier shift were very glad to see them.

"A steady wind's coming in from the southeast," Mr. Heath, the spotter group's leader reported. "It's getting cold but the sky is clear, and you should have no trouble keeping an eagle eye on the heavens."

"We'll keep a sharp eye out," Thick Glasses said. "Don't worry."

Ruth wondered if the woman was able to see clearly with those heavy lenses, much less keep a sharp eye out. But she supposed it wasn't her place to judge. As the evening wore on, the four spotters took turns with the binoculars, sipped strong coffee and ate all the muffins.

"David, I was talking to Hazel the other day. She's invited me to visit again and asked me to stay for dinner. Will you be there?"

"I'm not sure. Doris has something happening with her family on Sunday and she asked me to take her. I think it's a baby shower for her sister." David rolled his eyes. "Not exactly my cup of tea, but she asked me and you know how it is with girlfriends."

"Kind of like what it is with families, I would guess," Ruth commented, a touch of irony in her voice.

"Hey, here's an idea," David continued. "Doris told me about a couple of great night clubs in downtown Boston. We should get a group together and go."

"Maybe," Ruth replied. "Jim's encouraged me to go out and have a good time but now that I'm engaged it might feel a little awkward."

"Nonsense. If we all go out together it'll be fun. I'll ask Doris to bring her brother. You get your friend Irene and, what's that guy's name you all go with, Sal? Ask Sal to join us. Three guys, three gals, out just for fun. I'll drive. It'll be great."

Ruth thought for a moment. "David, you're right. We should do it. Where and when?"

"I'd really like to go to the Cocoanut Grove. It's right near Stuart Street. But it would have to be a Friday or Saturday night, and I think Doris has to work the next two Fridays. Let me ask her and I'll get back to you."

"That'll be great. I'll tell Irene and Sal."

On Sunday, Ruth went to Jamaica Plain and had dinner with the Dohertys. The meal went well and the conversation stayed away from religion and money, but the war and politics had to come into it at some point.

"David tells me the two of you are doing some of that airplane spotting for the Army," John asked, passing a large plate of vegetables to Ruth. "That must be exciting."

"Not really, Mr. Doherty," Ruth answered. "Most times we are staring at an empty sky. In fact, I don't know of anyone on our team that has ever seen or reported a suspicious plane flying over Boston."

"Well, it isn't likely the Germans could fly a plane as far as our east coast. Still, it's a valuable thing you're doing to keep us safe." He reached for a roll. "Pass the butter, wouldja?"

"It's not the same on the west coast if you can believe what they write in the papers," Eddy declared. "I saw a picture in *The Globe* the other day. Some woman who works for the forest service in Oregon was holding bits of a bomb that was dropped by a Japanese airplane. A Japanese plane! Can you believe it? They're saying it was some kind of a fire bomb."

"Came at just the right time, if you ask me," John added.

"What do you mean?" Ruth questioned.

"This country is getting soft. People think because we've got an ocean on either side of us that we're somehow safe. That it'll never happen here." He paused, took another bite of chicken, and a swig of Pabst to wash it down. "That bomb was just what we needed to wake us up. We need to be on the alert at all times. If we're not careful, we could turn into another Poland."

"I think that's going a little too far," Eddy argued.

"Think about it," John blurted out. "If we're not vigilant, the enemy can overtake us at any time. They've done it in Europe. What makes you think they can't do it here?" He pounded his fist on the table, making his point.

"I think you are crazy, old man," Eddy countered. "We've got the best military in the world ready to protect our shores."

"Then how do you explain those fire bombs in Oregon? Huh? Someone was asleep at the switch, if you ask me." He glared at his step-son. "I don't see you out there doing anything about it."

Ruth sensed an old argument between father and stepson was about to implode at the dinner table. She stood up.

"I just realized the time." She turned to Hazel who was seated at the end of the table. "I'm so sorry, Hazel, I didn't realize how late it was getting and

I have to get my father's car back. I'm afraid I have to go."

Hazel was not a stupid woman. She knew why Ruth was suddenly eager to leave. She had watched too many conversations erupt into heated arguments at her table.

"Well, now, it was nice enough of you to come at'all, Ruthie, dear, and to bring us all the news of Jim."

Ruth stood behind her chair, suddenly feeling awkward. "I'll let you know as soon as I hear from Jim again. His last letter was dated October 8. I haven't heard from him since so he might have been transferred. As soon as I hear something, I'll let you know."

"You do just that, dear. Give Jim our best when you write."

"You should write too, Hazel. I'm sure Jim would want to hear from you."

Hazel waved her hand as if to brush away a bit of dust. "No, no. I have no head fer such t'ings. I'll be leaning on you for writin' to our Jim. Tell hisself we t'ink of him every day 'n miss him."

Ruth promised to let Jim know next time she wrote, but it would be another few weeks before she heard from Jim again.

CHAPTER 9

NORTH AFRICA

Two days before Thanksgiving Jim's next letter arrived, postmarked, North Africa.

November 17, 1942 (Somewhere in Africa)

My dearest darling

I have been kept rather busy and could not find the time to write. I am well and in good spirits. Just a little tired since I work from sunup to sundown. Am writing this by flashlight and hope you can make it out ok. I imagine the newspapers are rather interesting of late. Don't worry, darling, every thing here is hunky dory. Tell the folks I will write as soon as I can find the time.

I trust everyone at home is well and kept busy with war efforts. I am now used to sleeping on the ground and it's making me tough. I extend to you my very best wishes for a Happy Thanksgiving and only wish I could be there with you. You are to me, everything.

With all my love.

Your, Jim

So he is in Africa after all. When she hadn't received a letter in three weeks she suspected his squadron was on the move.

Knowing Jim was safe in England had made everything somehow tolerable. The Brits had their bomb attacks to worry about, but from what she had read in the papers, England was still relatively outside the real battle zone. The Germans hadn't invaded the country like they had in France. But North Africa was a totally different kettle of fish.

For days the newspapers had been full of the exploits of a German soldier they called "The Desert Fox." Rummel or Rumble, or something or other. She couldn't remember. North Africa was now a hotbed of conflict with planes and tanks and soldiers all battling for the oil reserves so desperately needed by the enemy. Allied troops had landed in force all along the North African coastline. The Allies named the invasion "Operation Torch" and now, after reading his letter, Ruth realized Jim had most likely been right in the thick of it.

"You can't let yourself worry about him, Ruth," Helen tried to calm her. "He's safe now, and that's good news."

"I understand, but the papers make it sound so terrible. Listen to these headlines." She held up a couple of newspapers she found in the office break room: "Quincy Gunner Bags Nazi Plane in Raid on Tunis," "Allied Pincers Tighten on Axis in Africa."

"The whole thing is dreadful, Ruth. But it doesn't help to worry yourself sick. The best thing you can do for Jim is to send him your love and tell him you're thinking about him. Live your life as best you can, believing he's all right."

"I know. I can't do anything but pray he'll be okay. It isn't easy. Especially with the holidays coming."

"That reminds me," Helen asked, deliberately changing the subject. "What are your plans for Thanksgiving?"

"I'm sure my mother has everything organized. My aunt and uncle are coming, Justine asked her boyfriend and some of the neighbors will stop by. Mother loves these family get-togethers." She paused, thinking. "On Friday night a few of the crowd are going dancing at the Cocoanut Grove Night Club. We're going to kick off the holiday season in style. You and Gary should join us."

Helen shook her head. "No can do. We're driving to Gary's folks in Springfield for Thanksgiving and won't be back 'til Sunday."

"You're going to miss a wonderful time!" Ruth teased.

"I'm sure I will!" Helen laughed. "But I'm glad you're getting out. Like I said, Jim wants you to live your life, and you should."

Thanksgiving was as grand a family event as the war and rationing allowed. The LeBlanc family had saved up their food ration coupons in anticipation. Mr. Mazzioli had set aside an eighteen-pound turkey for them, and Ruth secured a half pound of precious sugar to make a War Cake. "We'll call it Holiday Pudding," Mrs. LeBlanc told her daughter. "I don't want anyone to find out it's made with lard from the butcher. If anyone asks, you tell them it's a secret family recipe."

Ruth thought her mother a bit foolish about it. The recipe for War Cake had been in the papers for a few weeks and everyone she knew had tested it. Made with bacon fat, or shortening, it was loaded with spices, raisins and a cup of precious sugar. She had made one as a test and the family liked it well enough to serve it on Thanksgiving. But if her mother wanted to call it "holiday pudding," that was all right with Ruth.

It was a great feast. Mrs. Montgomery couldn't help herself from praising the special pudding. "Ruth, you have to give me your recipe," Mrs. Montgomery remarked. "I tried making one of these a few weeks ago, but it was not as good as yours. You must have a secret ingredient."

Ruth laughed. "Nothing secret about it, Mrs. Montgomery. The only thing we changed was the name. Mother wants to call it Holiday Pudding instead of War Cake."

"Well, whatever the secret, your pudding is much better than the one I made."

"What about that boyfriend of yours?" Mr. Montgomery interrupted. "Where is he stationed these days?"

"Jim's in North Africa as far as I can tell," Ruth answered.

"Was he part of that big move the Allies made? Operation Flame, or something. Been in all the papers."

"Operation Torch," Ruth corrected him.

"Whatever." Mr. Montgomery waved his hand as if to swat a fly. "They use such odd names for everything."

The conversation quickly turned to politics and the war effort. Ruth had no desire to join in and began to clear the table. Sensing Ruth becoming uncomfortable with the war talk, Mr. LeBlanc stood and suggested that their guests move the conversation to the living room. "Anyone for an after dinner drink? Follow me."

With everyone else now moved to the front parlor, Ruth took charge of the cleaning up. "Mother, you've done too much. You go sit and talk with Mrs. Montgomery and the others. I'll take care of all this."

Mrs. LeBlanc hesitated but she began to take off her apron, "I'll send Justine in to help."

"No, let Justine visit with her boyfriend, Mother. I'm fine."

The kitchen was in a state of chaos with dishes stacked high on the counter and pots and pans soaking in the sink, but Ruth was happy to be alone. She expected that spending the holiday without Jim would be hard but she had managed to muddle through most of it by staying busy with all the preparations. Once she sat down at the table and saw everyone smiling and enjoying each other's company, she realized how much she missed having him at her side. She felt overwhelmed with sadness and a profound sense of longing and desire to be with him. It was the not knowing where he was or if he was safe that was becoming an ache she couldn't ignore. Scrubbing pots and pans alone in the kitchen was exactly what she needed to take her mind off things.

The party lingered on into early evening with drinks and conversation. Around eight o'clock Mrs. LeBlanc offered everyone a last chance at Ruth's Holiday Pudding. It was her subtle suggestion that the day was winding down and everyone should go home. Mrs. Montgomery took the hint and hustled her family out the door. Justine and her boyfriend decided they'd go for a long walk, and Uncle John and Aunt Cora decided it was time for bed.

"It has been a long day," Aunt Cora remarked. "The meal was delicious, Bertha. You always do such a nice job. I wonder how you manage!"

"I have good helpers," Mrs. LeBlanc answered smiling, looking at her husband and Ruth.

Aunt Cora nodded in agreement. "A lot of work, I'm sure." She turned to Ruth. "I hope you're going to take a little time for yourself this weekend, dear."

"A few of us are going dancing at the Cocoanut Grove Night Club to-morrow night. That should be fun."

"That sounds exciting." She turned to her husband again. "Don't you think that sounds exciting, dear?" Uncle John shrugged. He was tired and ready for bed.

"Well, I guess we'll be going up." She smiled at Ruth. "You sleep in as long as you can tomorrow. You deserve the rest. We'll be leaving early, so if we miss you, I hope you have a wonderful evening with your friends."

"Thanks, Aunt Cora," Ruth answered. "I'm sure we will."

The next evening, David drove his old Ford to Wollaston to pick Ruth up for the evening. Doris was seated in front and Sal, Irene and her latest boyfriend were in the back. Ruth squeezed into the front seat next to Doris and they were off.

The Cocoanut Grove was the "in" nightclub in Boston that season—the place to be seen. The dance floor was one of the largest in the area and the live bands that played there were always the best. Getting a reservation for dinner was impossible, so the crowd decided to just go for drinks and dancing. David found a parking spot on nearby Stuart Street. "It's an easy walk from here," he said. "Just around the corner."

The door to the club entrance was one of those revolving doors with three large glass panels set up like a wheel around a central hub. You pushed from either side and the whole door would turn to let you enter. As soon as they reached the entrance, David and Sal each pushed on opposite glass panels at the same time.

"That's not going to work," Irene laughed. "Only one of you can push if you ever want to open that door."

The two men looked at each other sheepishly. "Go ahead, Sal. You push," David said, stepping back, laughing. "Ladies enter first."

Sal pushed on the glass panel, the door turned and they each took turns going through the revolving door into the small entrance way. Music from the main floor filled the space.

"The Melody Lounge is downstairs," David declared. "Let's go there first, enjoy a little refreshment and then we can hit the dance floor." They all agreed.

A dark, narrow staircase led to the Melody Lounge and Ruth almost missed the bottom step. Thankfully Sal caught her. "Be careful, doll. You don't want to break that pretty ankle of yours. We've got a night of dancing ahead of us. You don't want to mess that up," he teased.

"I'll check the coats, if you want," David said.

Ruth slipped off her overcoat "Thanks, David." She leaned on Sal's arm and looked around. The dimly lit room was crowded with locals and holiday tourists all eager to experience the magic of the Cocoanut Grove. The Lounge was decorated with a tropical paradise theme. Large paper palm trees lined the walls, bamboo and rattan decorations surrounded the bar. The ceilings were covered with hanging drapery to simulate a tropical sky? Ruth could hardly tell in the low light. The room made her uncomfortable. This is a firetrap if ever I saw one, she thought.

David bought a round of drinks and for the next half hour they listened to light jazz from the piano player seated on a raised platform at the far end of the room.

"Ready to dance, yet?" Sal asked, "Or is that ankle still a little sore?"

Ruth laughed. "Don't worry, Sal. I'm ready to go upstairs. I promise to dance you off your feet before we're done."

After one or two drinks in the Melody Lounge, the group moved upstairs to the main dining room. The dance floor was packed and the music, loud. It was exactly what Ruth needed. She grabbed Sal's hand.

"Let's go!" she declared and headed into the center of the crowd. The band was playing Benny Goodman's "Roll 'Em."

"I love this song," Ruth shouted over the music. Sal could only nod and smile.

They all stayed on the dance floor 'til nearly one'clock in the morning, only taking a break when the band did.

"I'm done in." Ruth finally told David. "I hate to be the one to break this up, but I need to go home and go to bed."

"Thank goodness," Sal laughed. "I was tuckered out an hour ago!"

"Told you I'd dance you off your feet," Ruth teased. She liked Sal a lot. They had dated a few times a couple of years before and he had become a good friend she could always trust to give her a good time.

"A good man," Jim would have said.

It took a few minutes for David to rescue everyone's coat from the check girl, but by one thirty they were on the road, heading south to Wollaston and home.

Ruth slept soundly the next morning and spent most of Saturday afternoon running errands. That evening she started another letter to Jim.

November 28, 1942

My dearest darling,

Have not heard from you in a few days, so I can only hope you are doing well. I must tell you all the news from home. We had a lovely Thanksgiving here at the LeBlanc house. Mother made a wonderful meal. I was put in charge of desserts and made an apple pie and then tried a new recipe I think you would really enjoy—a War Cake but Mother insists on calling it Holiday Pudding. Quite tasty and a big hit with everyone.

Last night your brother David, his new girlfriend Doris, my friend

Sal and a few others from the old crowd got together for a night of dancing at the Cocoanut Grove nightclub in downtown Boston. We had a wonderful time. I couldn't help thinking of you, and I know you would have enjoyed it. We will have to go there when you return home.

When she came down for breakfast the next morning, Ruth found both her mother and father sitting in silence, the Sunday edition of *The Globe*, open on the table in front of them.

"What's wrong?" Ruth asked

Her father pushed the paper across the table. "Read," he demanded.

She looked down at the headline. "400 DEAD IN HUB NIGHT CLUB FIRE - Hundreds Hurt in Panic as the Cocoanut Grove Becomes Wild Inferno"

"Oh my god!" Ruth cried out. "I was there. That's where David took us Friday night. We went dancing at the Cocoanut Grove Night Club." She shook her head in disbelief. "Those poor people."

She began to read the article.

"The worst disaster in Boston's history last night snuffed out the lives of 399 merrymaking men and women in the blazing inferno of the famous Cocoanut Grove nightclub amid scenes of utter panic and horror.

"Crushed, trampled and burned as nearly 1000 patrons, entertainers and employees fought desperately to gain exits through sheets of flames, scores of victims were left lying on the floor helpless...."

Ruth had to stop reading. All she pictured was that revolving door they had such trouble using, and how they had all laughed when David and Sal competed to determine which of the two could push it open first.

"Hundreds are dead." Mr. LeBlanc shook his head. "If not from the fire, then from the smoke."

"This is awful. Those poor people," Ruth repeated, sitting down to read more. "I knew it was a fire trap. The whole time we were there I had an uneasy feeling. Couldn't put my finger on it. But, my goodness. This is awful."

"I hope you realize this could have been you, Ruth. You were very lucky not to be there last night." Mrs. LeBlanc crossed her arms across her ample breast. "Let this be a lesson to you. Don't go to such places. They are too unsafe. If David, or Sal, or even your Jim wants to go dancing, you tell them to take you to an outdoor park. None of this underground night life anymore. I don't care how glamorous or famous it all is. It's too dangerous."

"You can bet there'll be an investigation. Heads will roll over this," Mr. LeBlanc added.

Suddenly the phone rang.

"I'll get it." Ruth stood and walked into the hallway and picked up the phone. It was Irene.

"Ruth, did you read the morning paper?" she asked. "That could have been us. We could have died. Oh my god, it's horrible."

"All I can think of are those poor people getting crushed trying to escape. You remember how narrow and dark those hallways were. And that revolving door! The paper says people were crushed up against the glass, trying to get out."

"It's horrible," Irene paused. "They're calling for blood donations. I just heard it on the radio. That's why I'm calling. I'm going to go into town this afternoon and donate. I thought you might want to come."

"What time?"

"About two? I can meet you at the Wollaston station."

"I can do that. See you at two o'clock."

She returned to the kitchen. "That was Irene on the phone. She's really upset. The Red Cross is asking people to give blood for the burn victims. The two of us are going to town this afternoon."

"Good idea," Mr. LeBlanc answered, looking back at the front page of the paper. A picture of a man being carried away from the scene on a stretcher filled the right side below the fold. The man's body was partially covered with a sheet but you could tell from the burns on his face and arms that he was seriously injured. "You should get your sister Justine to go with you. Looks like they're going to need all the donors they can get."

Justine was reluctant at first. "I've never given blood before," she complained. "Does it hurt? How much do they take out?"

Ruth tried to calm her sister. "I've given once before. It doesn't hurt much. They take a pint, I think." She looked at her sister. Her face had gone white. "Don't worry, Justine. You're healthy and with plenty of blood to spare."

🍁

Justine didn't like it, but she had to admit Ruth was right, it didn't hurt. By the time they got home it was close to six and the sun had long since set.

"Have some supper," Mrs. LeBlanc greeted them at the door. "You must be hungry."

"Famished!" Justine answered. She quickly removed her coat and headed for the kitchen.

"How was it, Ruth? Were there a lot of donors?"

"The hospital was mobbed," Ruth responded. "We were lucky to get in line at all. Just after we got to Mass General the Red Cross started telling people to come back tomorrow. It was pretty amazing."

"Well, I'm proud of the two of you," Mrs. LeBlanc answered. "Now go get some supper. I made sandwiches and there's soup on the stove."

It was almost eight o'clock Sunday evening when Ruth finally went upstairs to her room. Her half written letter to Jim was still on the desk. She sat down and re-read what she had written so far.

... Last night your brother David, his new girlfriend Doris, my friend Sal and a few others from the old crowd got together for a night of dancing at the Cocoanut Grove dance club here in Boston. We had a wonderful time. I couldn't help thinking of you and I know you would have enjoyed it.

She sat, staring at the words on the paper. Should she start the letter again? So much had happened in the last twenty-four hours. Would Jim have heard the news about the fire? He was half a world away, but news about a tragedy this serious would certainly spread fast. She thought about removing all reference to her going to the Cocoanut Grove, but if David had written to him and mentioned their going to the club, she wanted to be sure Jim knew she was ok.

Sunday evening, November 29

Darling, it's been a full day since I wrote the passage above. Just in case you've heard the news about the Cocoanut Grove fire here in Boston, know that I am all right. We did go to the club on Friday and had a good time. The fire occurred the next night, Saturday, the 28th. I didn't hear about it until the Sunday morning papers. Hundreds of people were trapped inside the building. The police are saying most died of smoke inhalation. I certainly hope so. I can't think of a worse way to die than being burned to death.

This afternoon, Justine and I and my friend Irene took the train into town to the Red Cross at Mass General and gave blood. There were so many people donating they had to turn many away.

I don't want you to worry about me. You keep writing, encouraging me to stay busy and enjoy myself and I will. But since the fire, I realize I should be more careful and make wise choices when I go out dancing with the crowd. There are some venues that are just too crowded, and I promise to avoid them.

One place I know you would approve is Norumbega Park, where the group of us spent so many wonderful times. I will just have to wait for warmer weather. And who knows, by then, you may very well be home and take me yourself. I'm wishing so, darling.

I see that I'm almost to the end of this V-mail paper, so I'll sign off now, dear. Sending you all my love, please take very good care of yourself and write soon. Know that I am safe and sound and always eager to hear from you. I love getting your letters. I save every one.

Much love, Ruth

She re-read the letter, then folded and sealed the envelope and put it into her satchel. She'd mail it on her way to the office in the morning.

It was nearly Christmas before Jim's Thanksgiving letter arrived. She was surprised Jim didn't mention the Cocoanut Grove fire, or the Christmas package she had sent weeks before. Ruth had put together some very simple things she knew Jim would enjoy: chocolate, several packages of gum, a small box of letter paper, and a red leather wallet she had chosen as her Christmas gift for him. Inside she had placed two small portrait photos of herself that she had the photographer at Jordan's take. But there was no mention of the package. Instead, the letter was filled with Jim's candid reflections on a few of the more mundane aspects of being a soldier.

November 26, 1942—("Thanksgiving Day" – Somewhere in Africa)

My dearest darling:

How I wish I could be with you today! I am confident though in keeping this date for us in 1943. Please don't worry about me, hon, just say a few little prayers now and then but don't worry.

How is the family? Say hello to your mother, father and sister.

The country here is simply beautiful. It's magnificent in color. I have trouble trying to understand the natives but they know we are their friends and they can help us a great deal. This adventure would be so much fun if our purpose was not to destroy lives but, fundamentally, that is what we are here for, to vanquish the foe at all costs.

You'd be impressed with how efficient I have become with one tin helmet full of water (non drinking.) I first wash my teeth, then my face, arms, shoulders, hands, legs and feet, (almost a bath but not quite) then I wash some socks and underwear and then lay aside what's left for another chap to wash his hands.

Of course conditions have improved quite a bit but I wanted to impress on you what can be done in dire necessity. But my hat's off to Uncle Sam. Boy, he has the punch when it's needed. The soldier boys from the States are now soldiers.

Ruth shook her head as she re-read Jim's letter. She was trying to imagine Jim standing over his helmet full of water, washing his clothes! That must have been quite a sight.

Believe it or not, but I haven't heard from you since your letter dated Oct. 15. Things are going along pretty well here and I know you're with me all the way.

You would be surprised as to how much influence you have over my behavior. I'm not an angel by any means but can say that I have kept out of joints by constantly thinking of what you might think of the situation. A simple but quite effective means of keeping out of trouble.

I am writing this sitting on my bedroll and the lighting is very bad. The boys are playing "Blackjack" and they are hogging all the light

Don't worry hon. I am getting all I can learn out of the airplane and engine while I am working on the line. I like the work and that's what counts.

Well darling I'll sign off for the evening and turn in. Many times I lie awake looking up at the stars and it seems to make you nearer knowing that you see the same stars sometime later in the evening.

With all my love, your Jim

A second letter, written several weeks later, was enclosed in the same envelope. Jim had written in the tiniest cursive handwriting.

December 13, 1942—Somewhere in Africa

Dearest Ruth:

This will probably be my last letter to you before Christmas. In order for each soldier to get a letter off before Xmas he is allowed one thin sheet only. I will write very small to get everything in.

Thank you for your picture. You couldn't have thought of another thing that would please me as much (unless you yourself came all wrapped up in cellophane.)

Don't worry about me Ruth. I'll take care of myself. Just you take good care of yourself for me. I can't say anything of activities here, but you have your newspapers and we certainly aren't sitting around.

My friend Jerry is now a 2nd Lt. in the Quartermaster Corps. I don't know where he is right now. So far as I know I am the only one of the old crowd here in the land of the "Zombie." What a place.

If I only had a camera. I think I have seen some of the extremes of human misery. Not among the soldiers but in the natives themselves. Well dear, they're going to put out the light pretty soon, and I must give this letter to a chap tonight to get it off. Give everyone my best regards. My love for you increases in intensity each passing day. I'll write again soon.

Your Jim

A third note was folded inside the second letter, dated just a day or two later and in a much larger hand. How it had gotten into the envelope and passed through the mail system, she couldn't guess.

December 16, 1942—

My dearest darling Ruth,

I was very sorry to hear of the terrible fire in that night club in Boston, and so glad you were not involved. Death from causes like that seems so much more horrible than the death that stalks around certain other places. I am dead tired some nights, I sleep like a log and eat like a horse. That is, all they give me plus what I engineer through certain acquaintances in the chow house. I always said in civilian life that if ever I got in the Army I'd make it a point to get on good terms with the cook, and that is exactly what I have done.

Darling, I'll say good night for now and will write as soon as I can. I'll be with you in my dreams on Christmas night. You're always on my mind.

Your Jim

Ruth double-checked the date on this last letter. Jim had written it on the 16th and the postmark was for the same day. She glanced at the calendar on her bedroom desk: December 23rd. Only seven days later. The Army must have put on extra transports to accommodate the holiday mail, she thought. It just proved they could get things done quickly when they wanted to.

Ruth knew he was somewhere in North Africa, but how close to the fighting she could only imagine. Every news report she had read lately was filled with mixed messages. One day the Allies had won a battle, the next, the Germans seemed to be in charge. Jim's letters only hinted at what was really going on. Not knowing was worse than knowing. But at least he was safe.

"Ruth! Dinner time." Justine's voice calling from the hall below interrupted her thoughts. "It's your favorite! Spam!" her sister teased.

Ruth groaned. The thought of eating one more meal of make-believe meat was almost too much. But she shouldn't complain. She realized how lucky they were to have even Spam on the table. Besides, Christmas was only two days away and she knew her mother had a surprise meal planned.

※

Christmas morning, 1942, dawned sharp and clear. As Ruth opened the front door to get the morning paper, Mr. Montgomery from across the street was walking by with his dog, Peaches.

"Morning Ruth. Happy Christmas. Beautiful day, yes?"

Ruth smiled and waved. "Merry Christmas." She watched as Peaches yanked on his leash and tried to run up the walkway towards her. Thankfully, the leash was too short and held the dog back from jumping on the front porch. Peaches was known to be a biter and Ruth really didn't like the dog.

"Will we see you this afternoon for dinner?" Ruth asked.

"Wouldn't miss it. Your mother makes the best apple pie!" He began to walk away. "Come on, Peaches. Time to do your business," he urged the dog. "By the way, did you see the morning papers? You ladies are making a major sacrifice for our troops!" He gave a great laugh and walked up the street leaving Ruth wondering what in the world he meant.

Justine solved the mystery at breakfast.

"I heard it on the news this morning. You know that big campaign they were pushing to have ladies give up their nylons? Well, it worked. Millions of pairs of nylons are now going to be turned into parachutes and silky things for the troops!"

"Really?" asked Mr. LeBlanc absent mindedly, as he turned a page in the morning *Globe*.

"I'm serious, Daddy," Justine protested. "You men may not think it's a sacrifice, but to those of us who have to go around bare legged in the cold,

170

it's a big deal."

"That's why a lot of women are beginning to wear pants," Ruth chimed in.

"Well, I don't like it. Not one bit," declared Mrs. LeBlanc. "Its just not right. Don't you think so, Frederick?" She turned to her husband, insisting he agree with her.

"What?" he asked, clearly unaware of the conversation that had been going on around him.

"Don't you think it's a shame women are trying to look more like men?" she urged her husband. "Women are giving up skirts, for heavens sake."

"Mother, you're exaggerating," Ruth protested. "Now that so many women are working in factories, they need to wear slacks. And besides, like Justine said, now that we're giving up our nylons to the war effort, pants help keep our legs warm, especially on a cold winter morning."

"I for one, like it," Mr. LeBlanc finally answered. "I think it makes women look very," he paused searching for the right word, "attractive." He went back to his paper.

"Well! I never expected you to say that." Mrs. LeBlanc glared at the top of her husband's head, knowing he was trying to ignore her. "By the way, we're going to ten o'clock Mass this morning. I certainly hope you're joining us."

"I'll be there," her husband mumbled. "I promised to pass the basket at the offering."

"I wish you'd sit with your family for once. After all, it's Christmas!" Mrs. LeBlanc complained. "People are starting to think I'm a widow."

Her husband peeked up over the edge of the newspaper. "Yes, dear, I'm sure they are, but you'd think they'd have more important things to think about." He ducked back behind the pages. "Small minds. That's what. They've all got small minds," he mumbled.

Ruth and Justine exchanged knowing glances across the table. This was a very old argument and there was no point in trying to persuade either parent to change their tune.

"I'm going to get ready for church," Ruth stood up and pushed in her chair.

"But we still have to open our presents!" Justine declared, turning towards her mother. "We don't have to wait 'til everyone arrives, do we?"

"I need your help setting the table, Justine, and getting things ready in the kitchen before church. They'll be plenty of time for presents later," Mrs. LeBlanc explained.

Justine ignored her mother. "I think we should all open at least one gift before we go to church. Everyone gets to pick one gift from under the tree." She looked at Ruth, hoping for support.

"Whatever you want, Justine. I don't care," Ruth answered.

Justine headed for the front parlor. "Come on everyone. It's Christmas present time!"

Reluctantly all three LeBlancs joined Justine at the Christmas tree.

"Okay, Justine. Pick a present to open, but just one!" Ruth exclaimed.

"No, I think you should open one first. Let me choose for you." With that, Justine dug deep under the mound of presents and pulled out a small box. It wasn't wrapped very well and the ribbon was actually just a piece of string. "Here, Ruth. You should open this one." She held the box out. "It's from someone very special."

Ruth looked at her sister, wondering what she could mean.

Justine couldn't wait any longer. "Come on, Ruth, who do you think it's from? Someone very special. Someone very far away who sent this to me months ago so he'd be sure you got it in time for Christmas?"

Ruth felt her face flush with pleasure. "Is it from Jim?"

"Smart girl!" Justine teased. "You guessed!" She held the package out towards Ruth. "Come on, open it up. I've been waiting for weeks to see what he's sent you."

Ruth could hardly believe it. Jim was not the sentimental type. But the fact he had thought enough in advance to send her a Christmas present so she'd be sure to get it in time for the holiday—she didn't know what to say.

"Aren't you excited, my dear?" asked her mother. "Wasn't that a sweet thing for your Jim to do?"

Justine handed her the small box. "Jim is full of surprises." She sat down and looked at the crinkled brown paper wrapping and the knot of string. "It looks like he wrapped it himself." She started to laugh.

"I promise that Jim did that all himself," Justine explained. "He told me to hold onto it until Christmas morning and give it to you before you went to church. Whatever it is, I think he meant for you to take it with you to Mass this morning."

"That's so sweet." Mrs. LeBlanc gave her husband a pat on his arm. "Don't you think so, dearest?" she whispered. Mr. LeBlanc shrugged his shoulders and gave a low grunt of affirmation.

"So open it, already!" Justine urged her sister.

Slowly Ruth unwrapped the small box. Inside she found another box, this one of dark brown leather with a small gold cross embossed on the lid.

She could tell the leather was of good quality. Jim must have paid a pretty penny for it. She unclasped the lid and looked inside at a beautiful string of crystal rosary beads and a small note written in Jim's hand.

Merry Christmas, darling. Pray for me that I
come home safely to you. All my love, Jim.

Ruth felt tears welling up behind her eyes. Her lips began to tremble as she held the string of crystals in her hand. "Look, Mama." She held the beads up so her mother could see. "Aren't they beautiful?"

Mrs. LeBlanc said nothing but reached for her daughter and held her close. "They're the most beautiful rosary beads I've ever seen," her mother agreed. "Beautiful."

Ruth was quiet for several minutes, holding her mother, trying to control her tears.

Finally, Justine broke the silence. "Okay, enough of this. Time for church. If we don't get going, we'll never make it on time."

"Don't worry, we'll make it," Mr. LeBlanc declared. "I'll get the car warmed up. It's a holiday, after all. We can drive to church this morning. It's time we celebrate a little!"

"Hip hip hooray!" Justine agreed.

It was a day of celebration, from start to finish. The church choir sang well, dinner was a big success with root vegetables harvested and stored from the victory garden and a small turkey they had been lucky enough to purchase from Mr. Mazzioli's Market.

That evening Ruth sat at her desk intending to write Jim a thank you note, but the words would not come. She wanted to send him something to let him know how much she appreciated his gift, but her mind was blank. Nothing she wrote or sent could match the feelings of love and gratitude that filled her heart at that moment. It had been a very special Christmas day, and though Jim was on the other side of the world, she felt his presence more now than at any moment since their time together at Fort Dix.

She couldn't write tonight, Ruth thought. Maybe tomorrow. She turned off the desk lamp and crossed to the window, pulling back the blackout curtains to gaze out at the night sky. As her eyes became accustomed to the darkness, hundreds of brilliant stars appeared overhead. Thanks to the war, there was very little ambient light to spoil the view and as she stood gazing at the heavens she remembered a line from one of Jim's last letters.

Many times I lie awake looking up at the stars and it seems to make you nearer knowing that you see the same stars sometime later in the evening. Goodnight love.

Ruth stayed at the window for a long time, looking up at the stars. Finally, she turned away, leaving the drapes open so she could still see the sky from her bed. As she pulled the covers tight up under her chin, she whispered to the heavens, "Goodnight, my dearest, and merry Christmas, wherever you are. Stay safe and come home to me soon."

1943

CHAPTER 10

NORTH AFRICA

As the war dragged on into the new year, mail delivery became sporadic and out of sequence. By the end of January, Ruth had received four letters, but the dates they were written didn't match the order in which they were received. In one Jim was wishing her a happy new year, and in the next, he was anticipating Christmas. In one long letter, Jim had written bits of news, a little every day—a sort of daily diary he wanted to share.

December 27, 1942—North Africa

Dearest Ruth:

Did you have a nice Christmas? I still have yet to receive any mail from you. Christmas went by, as any other day, but we did have an unusually good dinner. One thing is certain, our cooks deserve the greatest praise. They are up against some difficult problems and yet they come through with the goods every time.

I received a package from my sister, Brigid. It contained a can of salted peanuts, 2 packs of Chesterfields, a small box of Overland cigars, a file and comb set with scissors, several rolls of life savers, 2 pkg of gum, and a packet of mentholated nose wipes.

I got a letter from Jerry Brennan—he's now a 2nd Lt. and is stationed at present at the Army Base, state side. He hopes he can get here to lift a few beers with me. Where does he suppose I am? In the middle of a place like Broadway? It would be quite a joke to get where I could lift a few. Africa is a big place.

By the way, it is rumored that any gifts mailed on or before Oct. 3 are in the drink. I hope none of mine was on it. Always thinking of you, your Jim.

When had she sent her Christmas package to Jim? If it was late September that might explain why he had never mentioned receiving the parcel. It could have been on a ship that had been sunk by the Germans.

January 1, 1943—"New Years Day in No. Africa"

My darling Ruth, there was no celebration here of course, but the New Year brings hope reborn.

I wish I could convey to you in writing some of the things I see in this country. Some of these Arabs are the most peculiar creatures imaginable. The Arab children keep running about asking for cigarettes and chewing gum. Their cry is (spelled as it sounds) "Komeradd, Komeradd Cigareat Cigareat Jewing gum." I often carry two and three packages with me and give them to the Arabs with the purpose of spreading goodwill.

An American soldier dare not speak to the Arab Moslem women or even make signs to them or stare. Believe it or not but drastic results have been reported happening to white men who have failed to respect this code of the Arab. He is extremely jealous of his women or perhaps there is something religious about this determination of his.

Ruth tried to recall something she had read in the paper about the cultural norms of the North African people. They had strict laws about mixing with other races and classes of society, especially when it came to their women.

There are classes of Arabs, the same as in other races, and the rich Arabs who own great lands, are as rich as some of our millionaires.

They have the finest of horses and keep great stocks of cattle and employ many farmers in the fields. They do not, however, give in to modern conveniences too quickly but dress and live the same as their fathers before them.

The poorer class of Arabs makes the Bowery in New York seem like Rockefeller Center. I never knew such human misery as it exists in some quarters of this country. It was in this locality that I saw my only glimpse of Arab women. They are too poverty stricken to own enough clothes to cover themselves as they wish. Of course these are the older women, for a young girl is soon spirited away from these environs.

I don't know how much the papers at home describe the country, but when it rains the soil becomes soupy and it bogs everything just where it lays. You walk five or six steps and it is necessary to remove ten pounds of mud from your boots. This is the stuff we early birds had to pitch pup tents in and I shall never forget those early days and the most difficult circumstances.

January 3, 1943

Hello, Dear—I have a few minutes before turning in, so I am going to sit and talk with you awhile. Today I had a few minutes this morning to wash some clothes and air out my blankets. (Yes! Blankets - 4 of them no less.) I had been sleeping in about 10 pounds of dried mud and finally got rid of the stuff. I have a sewing job to be done on my overcoat. A button was torn off when I had to move rather hurriedly.

Ruth tried to picture Jim sitting in his pup tent, or on the ground, scratching out one entry after the next, trying to give her a sense of what his life was like. Everything was so foreign, but he appeared to be handling it all well. He seemed genuinely interested in the people and the country.

That evening she sat at her desk, a fresh box of stationery in front of her, trying to put into words what she felt in her heart. She wanted what she wrote to be special and to have meaning for Jim. It wasn't enough to fill a page with gossip, though she knew Jim enjoyed hearing all that was going on in the family. She wanted to share something more, something deeper.

She needed to encourage him. After several false starts and sheets of paper in the waste basket she knew she didn't have the energy. I'll wait until the weekend, she decided. Maybe it's the weather, or the fact the days are so short and the nights so dark and long. I'm too tired to put any thoughts on paper.

※

On the last Saturday in February the postman dropped off Jim's next letter from North Africa.

February 5, 1943—Somewhere in North Africa

Hello Ruth dearest,

Brr-r it's cold. You may not believe it dear, but the night's temperature comes darn close to freezing. The days are pretty warm though. You see, this is the winter season here and on cloudy days or before the sun comes up, it is bitterly cold. One never knows how to dress to fit the weather. If you dress warm, you have to peel it off about noon and put it back on as soon as the sun gets low. Am hot in front where I face the sun and freezing in back. I sympathize with you hon, about having to wait in the cold for a street car.

Your letters are piling up and hard as it is to do, I am forced through lack of space, to destroy the few early ones. Up to last night I had every one you had sent me overseas. I read them over and got the same feeling of pride knowing how much you care.

We certainly will be happy dear. I don't know where we shall live, but knowing you will go wherever my work takes me, is a big help in planning.

Hard to believe, I've been one year in the Army as of last night. Goodbye for now darling, will write as soon as I can.

With all my love and admiration. Your Jim.

Had it been a whole year since Jim had joined up? Seeing him in Fort

Dix had made the time seem shorter somehow. She smiled as she recalled one of their first dates. It was a few days before Thanksgiving and they had spent the night bowling. For a beginner she hadn't been half bad, but Jim had been downright awful. She chuckled to herself as she remembered how he complained about the finger holes being too small for his hand.

"I can't get a proper grip on the bowling ball. No wonder I'm landing in so many gutters!"

He tried to explain away his poor score, but all she did was laugh. Thankfully, Jim had taken her banter with good humor, and the evening had ended with some lovely time together in the front parlor at Bromfield Street. She recalled the sweet memories now and wondered if they might ever come again.

"Ruth, I need your help!" Mrs. LeBlanc's voice from the kitchen interrupted Ruth's daydream. "I need to make cookies for the church sale."

The last thing Ruth wanted to do right now was bake cookies. But she had promised her mother that she would be home on Saturday to help out. And it was now Saturday.

By the time she got to the kitchen, her mother had every cookie sheet they owned out of the cabinets and all the ingredients lined up on the counters.

"What are we baking today?" she asked.

"Oatmeal cookies for the bake sale." Mrs. LeBlanc handed Ruth a small index card. "Mrs. Murray gave me the recipe. We use molasses instead of brown sugar. She guarantees they were her best seller at the Women's Guild bake sale last fall."

Ruth looked at the bottles of molasses. "Looks like you're ready to make enough for an army. Don't you think we should test the recipe first?"

"If Mrs. Murray says they're good, I'm not going to worry. You remember how picky she is about her bake sale." She handed Ruth an apron. "Come now, you can break the eggs for me."

There was no sense in arguing. Ruth put on the apron and joined in. For the next three hours they mixed, beat and baked over fifteen batches of cookies. Each batch made four dozen cookies. The recipe called for three dozen eggs, three bottles of light molasses, and cups and cups of walnuts and oatmeal.

They were pulling the last of the cookies out of the oven when Mr. LeBlanc arrived. "I knew something special was happening. I could smell cookies baking all the way out to the side yard!" He reached over, grabbed a cookie off one of the trays, and took a big bite!

"Oh! Hot! Too hot." He began to wave his hand in front of his mouth as if he could cool things off inside. He gave his wife a smile. "Hot! But very good, dear!" he mumbled, continuing to chew. "I think I'll have another."

"Don't you dare!" Mrs. LeBlanc held her spatula up, ready to slap his hand if he tried it again. "These are for the bake sale at church tomorrow. You keep your hands to yourself."

"Aren't you making any for us?" Like her father, Justine had followed her nose to the kitchen. "You've got dozens to give away. How about a few for your loving family, huh?"

"The proceeds from the bake sale are to help the war effort. Mrs. Murray is organizing things to go to the USO in Quincy. So leave the cookies alone. I'll make a special batch for us later after we deliver these to the church." She looked up at her husband. "Which reminds me, Frederick, I need you to deliver these to St. Ann's once we have them all packed up."

"Hurumph," he choked back a cookie crumb. "I think that might require me to take another cookie!" he gave his wife a sly smile.

"You take another cookie and you might lose a finger or two."

She held the spatula high and gave her husband a look that might wither another man. Mr. LeBlanc just laughed. No sooner did she turn back towards the stove, then he swiped two cookies off the cooling tray and quickly handed one to Justine.

"Don't think I don't see you two!" Mrs. LeBlanc declared. She didn't turn around. Both father and daughter knew her bark was much more severe than her bite.

"Good cookie, Mom," Justine exclaimed between bites. "Thanks." She turned to go. "I'll be back for the family batch later!"

Ruth watched her kid sister sashay down the hallway. She looks like she doesn't have a care in the world, she thought.

"Are we done here, Mother?" Ruth glanced at the kitchen clock. "I'm going out with the crowd, and I told Sal Marcusio he could pick me up at 7 tonight. I still need to have a shower and change."

Mrs. LeBlanc continued packing cookies into the small cardboard boxes Mrs. Murray had sent over. "You seem to be spending a lot of time with this Sal gentleman these days. Is this the man you were so sweet on a couple of years ago? I do hope you're not forgetting you are engaged to Jim, after all."

Ruth was startled by her mother's remark. "Of course not. In fact, Jim is the one who has encouraged me to go out with other men. He doesn't expect me to stay home and mope because he's overseas. Jim and I trust each other. Sal is a good friend, nothing more."

"I'm not trying to argue with you, Ruth. I'm just reminding you where your loyalty should lie." She turned to her husband. "Isn't that right, Frederick?"

Mr. LeBlanc was busy munching on another cookie. "What? I missed that. What are you two talking about?"

"Mother thinks I should stay home and go absolutely nowhere until the war is over and Jim comes home. Should I lock myself away in a tower?"

Frederick LeBlanc looked at his wife and then back to his daughter. "I think you're exaggerating, Ruthie."

Ruth took off her apron and tossed it at the back of a chair. "I don't know, Dad. It seems as if every time I go out with the crowd these days, Mother gives me one of her special looks."

"That is not true. I have no idea what you're talking about." Mrs. LeBlanc faced her daughter, hands on her hips, ready for a confrontation. "You can go out with the crowd all you want. I'm glad you have good friends to keep you busy but lately, you've been spending more time with that fellow Sal. And I want to remind you, young lady, that an engaged woman has to be careful. You don't want to start something you cannot finish."

"That's foolish. Sal is fully aware of my relationship with Jim, and he's been a perfect gentleman to me. In fact, he's more interested in Louise than anyone else. You're imagining things, Mother."

Ruth turned to her father looking for support. "Do you think it's wrong for me to go out and have a good time once in a while?"

Mr. LeBlanc knew better than to take his daughter's side against his wife. Instead, he chose the diplomatic middle ground. "You're a smart girl, Ruth and I trust you'll make wise decisions. If Jim has encouraged you to go out and have a good time, then, I'm sure he knows you best." He turned to his wife. "I think we can give Ruth the benefit of the doubt, my dear."

Mrs. LeBlanc gave her husband an exaggerated look and turned back to packing boxes with cookies. "We'll see. I hope you're right."

Ruth realized there was little chance of changing her mother's attitude.

"I'm going upstairs to change. Tonight Sal's taking us to a night club in Somerville. Don't wait up."

"Don't be too late, and remember to use the headlight louvers," Mr. LeBlanc warned.

"Don't worry, we'll follow all the blackout rules."

※

Sal arrived at precisely at 7 o'clock. Ruth stood at the front bay window and watched him pull up to the curb. As soon as he stepped out of the car she was out the door and down the walkway. She did not want to risk any meeting between her mother and Sal.

"Let's go!" She slid into the Chevy's front seat. "Where's Louise and the others?"

"Louise is sick. Some kind of cold she said. The others will meet us at the club."

"I hope she's all right."

"David offered to drive as well, so the girls decided to go with him. There wasn't enough room for all of us in either car." Sal turned the key in the ignition. "So that leaves just the two of us. Hope that's okay?"

Ruth hoped her mother wasn't looking out the bay window as the two of them drove away. "Sure, not a problem."

"Whoever gets to the club first will grab a spot for the rest of us. So it's still the crowd's night out. We're just coming from different directions."

He reached into his chest pocket. "Mind if I smoke?" he asked.

"As long as I can open a window."

"In that case I'll wait 'till we get there. It's too cold to open a window."

Sal was one of the few men she knew who would bother to ask a woman if it was okay to smoke in her presence. He was always considerate of her feelings. Now, as they headed in the dark towards Somerville, she realized, especially in light of her mother's recent remarks, that she had come to think of Sal as one of her closest friends. Someone she could count on.

They drove in companionable silence for the next ten minutes.

"How's your business doing? How's Jim?"

"Business is booming. Lots of work from Jordan's of course. We're getting ready for the big spring push. It'll be Easter before you know it. So I've been working all hours in order to keep up."

Sal gave her a long look. "Well, don't go overboard. I sure hope you're not staying alone late at night in that office of yours. There's a lot of characters out there. You want to be careful."

"Stop worrying. I can take care of myself. And I'll be sure to write Jim and tell him how you're watching out for me. I got another letter this morning. He's still in North Africa, from what I can tell. But he's safe. Not in the real battle. He's stationed in the support areas, repairing planes and transporting supplies."

"Still sounds dangerous," Sal remarked. He paused for a minute or two, then continued. "I don't think there is any place over there that is safe. If you read the papers it sounds like things are getting hot."

He took a quick glance at Ruth. "Sorry, didn't mean to scare you."

"Not scared, Sal. It's reality, I guess. We're at war and no one is safe. Not even here in tiny little Somerville, Massachusetts."

She looked out the window as Sal turned into the parking lot of the club. The lot was filled with cars.

"There may be a war going on," Sal observed, "but you'd never know it from the look of it. This place is jamming tonight."

He pulled the car into a slot in the back row. "Come on let's do some dancing." He got out, went around the Chevy to Ruth's side and held the car door open.

"Why, Mr. Marcusio, you are quite the gentleman!"

"Absolutely, Miss LeBlanc," he answered with an exaggerated flourish.

The two friends laughed out loud at how foolish they sounded. Sal grabbed her arm and they hurried into the dance hall. David and the other girls had already arrived and saved them a booth. Vaughn Monroe's band was playing and from the moment they arrived, Sal kept Ruth dancing. It was one of the happiest evenings Ruth could remember in a long time.

February 13, 1943

Good morning hon.

When things have to be done here, they must be done at once. Keep 'em flying so to speak. I am writing this lying down on my straw pile and my head is propped on an empty gas can. Not too comfortable. We are getting so now, that modern conveniences would seem a bother. Good training for times to come. I mean there is a rough road ahead before that punk Hitler is in a cage with the rest of his crazy whacks.

My hat goes off to the Russian army. Regardless of what England or the States publish about their successful operations, nothing could have been accomplished the way it has without Russia.

You probably get all the war talk you can handle over the radio and through your newspapers and people you meet, so I won't bore you with more.

Two mail deliveries have gone by now and no mail yet from you since that last V-Mail. I guess it's just the V-Mail that gets the priorities.

Ruth paused. If V-Mail got priority treatment, maybe it was time to send more V-Mails to Jim.

As soon as I can get to some place that has a store, I will send you souvenirs from Africa. You may think I have forgotten you in this respect, but I haven't,—just can't get them. Our friends that were here before us cleaned out the places of everything worth having.

I made a discovery, or at least it was told me by a little Indian lad, that many of these Arabs are Jews. He also mentioned that they don't care who controls the country, they are interested only in who has the money. Gosh, but they are the greatest people for separating one from his money I have ever seen

The Army is taking them under control however and purchasing their goods in large quantities at reasonable prices and we buy from the Army.

I could witness murder in the first degree if I had a bolt of cotton cloth and take it into the Arab poor quarters. You have seen dog fights? Well you should see how people scrap over an empty tin can. They don't have utensils or dishes and a tin can is a luxury. They come up out of those piles bleeding and yelling like wild animals.

One of the women tried to drag me into her little one room shack with a vile purpose in mind. Morals? Some people will do most anything imaginable for money.

Say, by the way, how is the horsemeat at home? I have been reading in The Globe, where horsemeat has been sold to Bostonians in great quantities and is relished by many of the Back Bay Bankers.

Ruth stopped reading. Horsemeat? In Boston? I don't think so. Maybe in New Jersey? She tried to remember an article in the paper a while back. Horsemeat had been legalized by the New Jersey Board of Health, but its distribution was severely limited. Was it really being sold in Boston?

All the best meat goes to Army camps I guess. Looking back, the chow in those camps was delicious comparatively speaking. I'm not kicking, at least I have time to eat.

Getting around to us again, I darn near bought some lingerie from one of these traders but then thought twice about it. It would be too forward I was afraid. Blushing? I'll bet you are.

Well, must go now. From one who cherishes your love more than any other worldly treasure.

Yours forever, Jim

Ruth folded the letter thoughtfully and replaced it in the envelope. Jim sounded like he was enjoying the challenge of living in a foreign country— meeting new people and cultures. A part of her envied him the experience. But the poverty he spoke of troubled her and she was surprised by Jim's prejudicial tone.

We are so lucky not to be living in a war zone, she thought. Jim might be appalled at how desperate for money some of the native people are. No wonder, if our local newspapers can be believed. North Africa had been in the middle of one battle or another since the war began. These people stole and took whatever they could get their hands on just to survive. Ruth wondered how she or Jim might act if their positions were reversed.

She opened the second envelope. The postmark was smudged but the date of 2/24/43 could still be read.

Dear, got back dog tired this evening. (Refer to your newspapers to find out what's been happening.)

Ruth tried to recall what she had read in the news. Rommel and his tanks had been driven out of Tunisia by the Allies. She would have to go back and check. Jim must have been in the thick of it all. Thank God he was okay, she thought. He never told her any details of what he was doing, but that was probably best.

What a lift I got when I got to my bunk. A letter from you. I am going to keep the letter until I answer it, and then discard it. Wish I could keep them all, but that's out of the question.

You ask if I was near where the big news occurred. If you mean F.D.R. and Churchill, the answer is no. The actual fighting is many miles east. At present things are pretty peppy, but if you pray as hard as you say you do, why "Lady" luck will see me through. Johnnie doughboy has now met up with the Panzer divisions and some have lived to learn by the experience. You can have the fullest confidence in the Yanks fighting ability. He just needs to get warmed up.

Ruth shook her head. She had read the news reports about Roosevelt's meeting earlier with Churchill in Casablanca. A war program for the year had been agreed upon. Any thought that the war would be over soon, vanished.

2/25/43 (6:00 A.M.) You are on my mind as usual. Reread your last letter over again. Gives a genuine lift to my spirits. Big doings on the firing line about this time. Will be pretty busy very soon now.

Don't forget to let me know how you made out with your clients, I hope that whatever new venture you set upon is a big success. I have the fullest confidence in your ability and originality.

I am almost tempted to make a remark about you confining your relations to strictly business affairs, but I would be defeating the ideals upon which we have set our friendship.

I love you so.

Your, Jim

"You worry too much about nothing, Jim Doherty," Ruth said out loud to the letter she held.

"He's just lonely and probably jealous," Helen tried to explain when Ruth mentioned Jim's letter the following Monday at work. "I'm sure he's joking with you."

"I suppose so. It's not the first time he's wondered what I was up to in my spare time."

"You can't live your life in a cocoon while he's gone, and he understands that. So don't worry about it. In fact use it!"

"What do you mean?"

"It might not be a bad idea to let him think you are following up on his suggestion and seeing other people. Might keep him on the straight and narrow."

Ruth stared at Helen. "I don't understand. What do you think Jim's doing? He is one of the straightest and narrowest men I've ever met. Trust me, he is not fooling around."

"In that case you have nothing to worry about. Do what he says and go out and have fun. Have that fellow Sal you like so much take you out dancing again." Helen waved her hand at Ruth as if pushing her out the door.

Settling in behind her drawing table, Ruth started working on some new sketches but couldn't keep her mind from drifting back to what Jim had written. She knew he was teasing her about getting involved with someone else. As far as Ruth was concerned that wasn't an issue. Jim had been the focus of her heart's attentions for more than a year. Still, she couldn't help wondering what she might do if circumstances changed.

What if something happened to Jim or he didn't come home after the war? One of the girls she met at the USO the week before had been all upset after receiving a letter from her boyfriend. Her fiancé had met someone while he was stationed in England.

He claimed it was love at first sight and had promptly dropped the poor woman who had been waiting for him back home. Ruth thought it unlikely Jim would fall in love with someone else, but this war was changing everyone's life in one way or another.

A week later Jim's next letter arrived. He began with how much he was missing her and wishing they could be together, then shifted to news about his stepbrother and his thoughts about his own position. She knew he had hoped to be accepted into Officer Candidate School, but the timing had been all wrong and he was still a lowly private. It didn't matter to her, but it seemed to matter to Jim.

March 2, 1943—Still in No. Africa

I wrote my stepbrother Eddy and extended my best wishes for his getting into Officer Candidate School. The doctors determined his asthma was not as bad as they first thought. So he's joined up. Gosh, if he attains a commission, will I feel small! I gave him a few tips which I thought he could use to an advantage.

One was, to get an inside job if at all possible. The elements raise havoc with one in general. I'm getting toughened to it though. No more office workers hands. Deeply stained and scratched.

I must remember my table manners, even if I do eat off the top of gas drums or in a ditch at times.

Things are going well here. I am learning something every time a plane needs repair. Do you know what type of plane I'm working on? Do a little of your own investigating and see how the particular outfit I'm in will benefit me after the war.

Ruth made a mental note to cross check the date of his letter with the newspapers she had been keeping.

March 4, 1943 - North Africa

As I write this, I can just see you sitting at your desk with not much work at hand, and deciding to pen me a short note. You have on that pretty colored smock which by now should be well splattered with dabs of paint. You're wearing low cut shoes with flat heels and so help me, red ankle socks. Being absorbed in your work, you fail to see an interested observer glance at two pretty knees crossed in a very attractive manner. But one cannot look away without first noticing how well shaped your legs are.

The dress you're wearing is a bit thin for this season of the year and falls about your thighs in a very complementary manner. (If I thought anyone was gazing at you this long I'd bust him in the nose.) The smock hides a great deal more beauty behind its folded front and thus robs one of keener admiration for something that is really attractive. Your hair, prim at the top but very fluffy along the ear and neckline adds background to a well shaped head and countenance.

Ruth re-read the last few lines. He's a regular poet with these flowery words! Did he have one too many beers with his supper? She'd have to make a point of asking him.

There were days many months ago when I saw you sitting at your board in much the same manner. They were days when the slightest attention you gave me came as reward for finding some reason to talk to you.

The sunbeams coming in through the large window at the side of the desk played wonderful tricks brushing across your golden crown. How it did sparkle and glisten. Like gold stained silk ruffling in a light summer breeze. I've always admired your hair as the one crowning feature you possessed.

That confirms it. Jim must have gotten into the hooch, Ruth thought. He's never ever written about sunbeams before!

Your ready smile, hung on a hair trigger, so often put me off guard and left me standing dumbfounded, groping for words and then saying a rabble of perfectly silly remarks. How I cursed silently to myself when something I would say caused you to remove the smile and laughter from your big brown eyes. I envied, and even suffered small pangs of jealousy whenever another male gave you cause to laugh or smile.

Well that was true enough, she realized. Ruth remembered how nervous Jim had seemed in those early days. The other fellows from Cuddahy's office often stopped by with the latest joke or to share a story. Jim always appeared pre-occupied and shy whenever they met.

Darling, I won't tell all, but my love for you has grown through those days when you didn't give me two thoughts in the same day. I won't say how you hurt me, as that is water under the bridge. Only, I hope you never suffer the same as I did on that memorable night.

Ruth stopped reading. What night? What was Jim talking about? When had she hurt him? It must have happened well over a year ago, before they started dating seriously.

She reached for her calendar and flipped back to November of 1941, looking over the entries. There was a notation on November 13 with a star in the margin: The Fall Festival. Jim had sent her a note asking her to go with him, but she had already said "yes" to Jack Shaw, Jim's boss in the accounting firm. Somehow Jim didn't get her message and showed up at the Festival thinking he was her date for the evening. It was awkward but both men shrugged it off as a mix-up, and Ruth had forgotten all about it. Apparently Jim had not. A year and a half later it still seemed to rankle him.

Foolishly I had thought of vengeance but that died shortly after its birth, for something else grew much stronger—my undying love for you. To remove you entirely from my thoughts was like trying to talk myself out of a toothache. It's alive dear, and will continue to live as long as you appeal to me the way you did then.

How I can be so fortunate in having you for my life's partner is more than I can perceive. A trick of fate, I guess.

Knowing you the way I do and having you back there waiting for me is something that gives me the greatest satisfaction and encouragement.

Perhaps something will break for me soon. It must cause you embarrassment to tell friends I am still a private while friends in camp or at home are barging ahead. We may have our little problems I guess, but hon, they are so minute in comparison with what other people are up against. Many boys will be disfigured for life and leave wives and sweethearts with major problems.

Always remember Ruth that I love you and think of you everyday and evening.

Your Jim.

Ruth sat and re-read the last paragraph. Jim was a good and decent man and he loved her. But she could sense an underlying insecurity. He still held on to a hurt from a foolish misunderstanding that had happened long ago, and now he was jealous of his stepbrother and others who were getting ahead of him. He may still be a private, but he's doing first class work in a war zone. She was proud of him, but it didn't sound like Jim believed it.

※

Soldiers have only one thing on their minds, Ruth thought, save not getting themselves killed. Jim's next letter never used the word "sex" but that's what it was all about.

March 14, 1943 - North Africa

Dearest Ruth:

I just have to write to you. It's sort of an escape valve for my pent up feelings. I'm doing pretty good keeping on the straight and narrow, but when I visit small towns with a few buddies and they frequent the usual places, I sort of hang back with some crazy excuse, because they would never understand if I told them the real reason I don't go in. Don't think I'm an angel by any means. I know that if I got drinking and went in a house I would be the worst one in there. That's cold turkey.

Men under war conditions tend to become reckless with themselves. I could see that very plainly in the girls of England. Most of them didn't care any more. They had nothing more to lose. The chase wasn't at all difficult. Very dangerous hunting grounds.

Strange as it seems, the married men I find are the chaps who "go to town" more often. Perhaps because they are wiser through experience and know how to handle themselves. I hope I am not giving you any wrong impression of my comrades. They are the best soldiers in the world and by far the most intelligent.

You know hon, this thing I'm discussing seems like something big to me but to the majority of men it's nothing. I talk like a kid at times. Perhaps if I took a few steps to the side it would wake me up to what life is like. I won't though. You must think that's all I have on my mind. It isn't really, but I wouldn't be human if those thoughts didn't creep up on me once in a while.

Ruth showed this latest letter to Helen at lunch the next day.

"He should just do the deed and get it over with," Helen commented. "What is he waiting for?"

Ruth shook her head. "He's a principled man with deep religious convictions. I think he's saving himself for me."

"Well, it's going to be a very dull wedding night for you if he doesn't know what he's doing. Getting a little experience on the side would be a smart thing to do, if you ask me." Helen popped another pickle slice into her mouth and gave Ruth a wink. "Trust me, you want the man to know what he's about."

Ruth blushed. "I'm sure Jim will figure it out."

"Hmm. Maybe." Helen took a sip of Postum and made a face. "I still can't stand this stuff." She swallowed. "What else does he say?"

"He asks about nylon rationing and then has this whole thing about the clothes women are wearing. I sent him a picture of me wearing the Women's Defense Corps uniform, and apparently he doesn't like women wearing uniforms. Listen to this..."

I sort of dislike thinking of you in a uniform. It detracts from your femininity and you know I like fluffy things. If there is anything that catches my eyes, it's a pair of shapely legs under a fluffy pleated dress. Sort of swishy. There is something school girlish about it.

You would be surprised how much men watch women's clothes. I think the last thing they want to see them in, are uniforms. Business suits are bad enough. When you gals make up your mind, there is nothing more to be said—I've found that out. You're all the same when it comes to making your final decisions.

Helen shook her head. "What does he want you to do? Go naked? If you're a member of the Corps, you have to wear the uniform."

"I'm sure Jim understands that. He's just ranting."

"Well, he has more important things to think about, like winning this war and getting home to you. If he wants you out of uniform, he needs to fight and then get back home fast. You'd think he would want you to wear a suit so that you wouldn't attract any competition. Which reminds me, how are things going with you and Sal?"

"Helen, I've told you there isn't anything between Sal and me. He's an old flame who's become a good friend."

"Hmmm." Helen gave her a sideways look that clearly said she didn't believe a word Ruth said. "You may think I'm buying what you're telling me. You may even believe it yourself, Ruth LeBlanc. But I can tell there's something else there. I have a gift for picking up the vibes."

Ruth laughed and shook her head at her friend. "Helen, you are full of malarkey. I'm telling you, Sal is a good friend. Nothing more. Honest."

"Uh-huh. We'll see."

By the third week of March, Ruth was caught up in a whirlwind of social activities. She had been appointed chairman of the Serviceman's Hop for the WDC. It was her job to not only select the hall, but choose the right band for the event. It wasn't easy. None of the local bands she knew were playing or available. Most of the band members had enlisted months ago or been drafted.

"How am I supposed to put together a dance without a dance band?" she asked Helen. "Have you heard of any good bands that are still around town? Not the big dance bands. I'm looking for a small local group we could afford."

Helen thought a moment. "I did hear about a band that played at the USO in Framingham last month. It's all girls, which you may or may not like. I heard they were pretty good."

"I don't care if the band's all women as long as they can keep a beat and get us all up dancing. What's the band's name?"

"I think they're called the TrueTones. I saw an ad for them in last week's paper." Helen began to go through a pile of old newspapers left on the break room's sideboard.

"I remember seeing it on the right hand side, near the bottom—somewhere in the movie section." She shuffled a couple more pages. "Here it is," she exclaimed. "I knew I had seen their ad."

She began to read aloud: "Dance to the magic of the TrueTones, your all-girl jazz band. From swing to ballroom, the TrueTones play it all. Book your next event now." Helen looked up. "There's a phone number you can call."

"Sounds like just the group we need." Ruth took down the number. "I better check with Sal before I book them. He's helping me with the event. We're meeting at South Station after work today to go over a few details." Helen began to smile. "And don't give me one of your looks. Sal volunteered over a month ago. We're holding the event in the meeting hall at his father's factory. They have a large space they use for trade shows and Sal said he would help organize things on his end."

"Okay. Whatever you say," Helen answered, clearly amused.

"Let it go, Helen. There's nothing there, honest."

Ruth knew she didn't sound convincing, and with good reason. Over the last few months she and Sal had grown closer. Nothing had happened and neither of them had said anything to each other, but Ruth could tell that something in her heart had shifted just a little.

"I'm surprised Sal didn't get drafted," Helen continued. "He's a healthy guy. Why didn't he sign up like your Jim?"

"He wanted to join up back when Jim did. But his father asked him to stay on to help run the business. Sal's one of their top supervisors now and heaven knows they need every man they can get. Apparently the government agreed. His job has been listed as critical to the war effort." She looked at her friend more closely. "I thought you knew all this. You don't think Sal's looking for an easy way out."

"No, not at all." Helen countered. "I knew he was involved in some sort of important work. I just didn't know the details."

"Well, now you do." Ruth reached for her coat and gathered up a few papers from her desk. "I better be going. Got a lot of things to do and no time to do them all. I'll see you tomorrow."

"Okay. Enjoy your meeting with Sal. I'll be waiting to hear all about it."

Ruth gave her friend an exasperated look and headed for the door.

※

It was a short walk to South Station and Sal was already seated at one of the small tables near the coffee shop, waiting.

He glanced at his watch, and gave her a grin. "Right on time."

"Well, I'm aware how valuable your time is, Sal. I appreciate your helping me out with this event."

"Anything for the boys. You know that. Do you want anything to drink? Coke, tea, a cup of that disgusting Postum?"

"Not a thing. I'm fine. Besides I have a long ride home after this."

"I can drive you home, if you like. No trouble. In fact, why don't we head out now. We can stop on the way and you can let me buy you dinner while we chat."

"Oh no, that's too much trouble. This place is fine."

Sal reached out and took her hand. "No, it's not. I should have thought of it before. It's no trouble at all." Ruth hesitated a bit before she began to pull her hand back. "Don't worry. I see the ring on your finger. I know you're an engaged woman," Sal assured her. "This is not a date. It's a business meeting. You've got to get home and you have to eat. And we have to talk about this event of yours. Besides, I'm famished and there's a great place in Quincy we can try."

Ruth considered her options. Sal was offering her a free ride home and dinner as well. "All right, sounds like a good idea."

The evening turned out to be a lot of fun. Not since the night at the Somerville dance club had she felt so relaxed. Sal suggested the Fox and Hounds, a new restaurant not far from the beach. He knew the owner and although it would be busy he was sure they would not have to wait for a table.

The maitre d' instantly recognized Sal. "Good evening, Mr. Marcusio. It is good to see you again." Without hesitation, he led the couple past a long line of people, and seated the two in a quiet corner, far from the bustle at the front of the restaurant.

"What's on the menu this evening, Charles?" Sal asked, as soon as they were seated.

The maitre d' smiled broadly. "We have just added a few special items to our selections. I can recommend the veal or lamb tonight, sir. They are both delicious. Or perhaps a tenderloin?"

"Sounds perfect. Just give us a few minutes."

"Of course." The maitre d' nodded. "Your waiter tonight will be Frederick. He will be with you momentarily. If there is anything more I can do for you, please don't hesitate."

Ruth scanned the menu's right hand column, noting the prices. "Sal, everything is so expensive."

"Nonsense." He reached across the table, letting his fingers barely touch the top of her left hand. "You're worth it. And besides, where else am I going to spend all my money except on a great evening out with you." He grinned at her and winked.

"You are trouble, Sal," she laughed quietly, but did not move her hand. His gentle touch had sent a sudden pulse of warmth through her and she liked the feeling.

Sal smiled, his facing lighting up with delight. "You know, Ruth, if it's trouble you're looking for, I'm happy to provide it."

Ruth shook her head, laughing. "One thing I don't need is more trouble from you." She looked at the menu again. "It's been so long since I've had a steak. I thought beef was almost impossible to get. Everything is being shipped overseas for the troops."

Sal shrugged. "There's always a way, if you know the right people."

"I guess so," Ruth responded, doubtfully. "That's the way it is with most things, isn't it? It's all in who you know. I think luck and good timing have more to do with success than anything else. For example, I know you and you know the owner here, and he knows someone who can supply him with sirloin steak in the middle of a war, so tonight I'm lucky enough to be here and enjoy it with you."

Sal laughed, "Right! And we will both enjoy it thoroughly. Would you like to start with a cocktail?"

"I don't think so. I'm not much of a drinker, but perhaps we could have a little wine with our meal?"

Sal gestured towards a nearby waiter. "Frederick is it?" The waiter nodded. "We would like two of your very best sirloin steaks tonight, and," he paused looking at Ruth, "Is red alright?" Ruth nodded. "And a bottle of your finest Cabernet."

As the waiter left with their order, Ruth took out a pen and notebook, eager to get started on the business at hand. "I have the name of a great girl band we can book for the Hop. They're called the TrueTones. I called them earlier today but didn't want to book them until I talked to you."

"I trust your judgement, Ruth. If you think they're good, I'll go along."

"Well, I haven't actually heard them perform. The woman I spoke to said they can play just about anything. Their fee is something the Serviceman's Hop can afford, and they're not booked for April 3rd yet, so I think we could get them."

Sal pulled a small calendar out from his suit jacket. "Let's do this. Why don't you and I go and see this band on the 20th of March. That's this Saturday night. If we like them, we book 'em. And if we don't, then we'll still have a week or so to find another band for the hop. Besides, according to my notes... this Saturday is your birthday! We can make it a real celebration."

Ruth laughed. "How do you remember these things?"

"It's my job to remember. Details are what I'm good at, and I've learned to pay attention to them. You know the kind of work I'm doing. In my business, it's the little details that can mean life or death to a soldier." He gave Ruth a serious look. "Everything matters when you're building bombs."

Ruth was unsure what to say next. Their friendly banter had suddenly taken a serious turn, and Sal's face was grim.

"Your job is so important to the war effort, Sal. But it must be hard for you."

"It's not what I wanted to do with my life, that's for sure." He gave Ruth a long look. "Don't get me wrong, I'm proud of what we're doing. We supply our troops with the best equipment money can buy and thanks to companies like ours, this bloody war might end sooner rather than later. Still it's a horrible business to be in."

At that moment, Frederick returned with their wine.

"Enough. No more war talk tonight. Let's nail down this Serviceman's Hop of yours." And with that, the two friends began to strategize.

※

"I think it's a great idea, you going out with Sal, and on your birthday, too. But don't tell me it isn't a date. Sal's nuts about you, I can tell. Every time I see you two together, he's drooling."

"It's not a date, Helen," Ruth insisted. "We're going to evaluate the all girl band for the Serviceman's Hop. That's it. Nothing more."

"Are you going to write to Jim about it?"

"I hadn't thought about it." Ruth shrugged. "I have nothing to hide."

"Well, maybe you should." Helen gave her friend a long look. "Jim's been gone a long time. You love him, but distance has a way of making things difficult for people in love. War changes people. I'm sure it's changed Jim."

Ruth crossed her arms defensively. "I love Jim, Helen. I loved him before he went off to war, and I love him now." She began to sort through a pile of papers on her desk in an effort to change the subject. "War can do strange things to people and maybe Jim isn't quite the same guy, but I love him and I'll stick by him." She looked at her friend. "I made a promise."

"And no matter what happens, you're going to keep it?" Helen asked. "Suppose he comes back injured or with some sort of psychological problem? I hear there are a lot of guys coming home now that have shell shock from being on the front lines."

Ruth tried to ignore her friend but Helen kept pushing the issue. "All I'm saying is, keep an open mind. Jim's overseas, far away and who knows what's happened to him. Sal is here. Right here and now and he loves you. I'm just saying you should keep your options open."

Ruth shook her head with exasperation. "Helen, let it go. I love Jim and that's the end of it. Sal is a good friend, nothing more." She sat down behind her desk. "And now, I've got to get back to work. And so do you."

"See you for lunch?"

"If I can finish this foolish ad. Check in later."

For the next three hours Ruth tried to focus on her work, but Helen's questions about her relationship with Jim just wouldn't quit. Had he changed? Was he the same man she had fallen in love with so many months ago?

When they first met she had been impressed with how easy going Jim was. His sense of humor was infectious and he seemed to enjoy everything she loved to do, from weekly dances at the Totem Pole to trying out new restaurants and nightclubs. In the few short months they had been dating, Jim had taken her to every new show in town.

That was all a lifetime ago and the Jim who now wrote her was not the same easy going guy. He was becoming increasingly uptight and judgmental of both himself and her. He seemed to have developed a very moral and righteous attitude of what was right and wrong. What had happened to his sense of humor? Helen was right. Jim had changed, and she wasn't sure how to handle this new person.

It was nearly noon on Saturday when Jim's next letter arrived.

March 15, 1943 - North Africa My dearest Ruth:

Stealing a few minutes from my chow time to say "Good morning Love." But, I have to write. My handwriting is not so good since I have to balance the pad on my knees. We're busy as old Harry. See your newspapers for news about what's happening over here.

She recalled the headlines from the morning papers. A fierce battle had been fought at Medenine where hundreds of German troops had been captured. Rommel had retreated.

I am in good health but haven't gained an awful lot of weight. Too busy I guess.

Please send me some photographs of you. Fellows are always showing me snapshots of their sweethearts and wives taken at random in quite natural poses. It is these little things that count so very much in a guy's life. Probably you think I'm silly, but I spend quite a bit of my writing time admiring your picture.

Gee, but you sure are the busiest person. Chairman of the Serviceman's Hop? Hmm. That job entails lots of sprinting around doesn't it? However it will be a success I'm sure. Lucky guys.

They made me Corporal yesterday. Don't go wondering why now, and assume vacancies were brought about by mishaps. I can't say where the vacancies occurred but all that counts is I am one step higher up the ladder.

Say, is it true that women in war plants are wearing pants? I'd hate that. In fact I detest any show of a masculine habit or quality in women. I don't like them as well in suits, slacks, shorts or uniforms. Just dresses. I don't want you wearing anything but a skirt. You'll get to really know me through letters before this war is at end.

Good night dear. Wish me well. I want always to be—Your Jim

So he doesn't like women wearing pants? She crossed her long legs and studied the new slacks she had chosen to wear that Saturday morning. Slacks were comfortable and she preferred them to wearing a dress on her day off. Sal was picking her up later that evening and she would dress up for that, but she wasn't going anywhere special during the day and a pair of slacks were what she wanted to wear. Jim would just have to get used to them.

"What are you up to?" Justine stuck her head into the bedroom. "Mom's got me shopping for dinner tonight. I'm heading off to the corner market. Do you need anything?"

"I'm okay. Thanks anyway." Justine started to walk away. "Oh, and tell Mother I won't be in for dinner tonight. Sal and I are going to go check out that all girl band we want to book for the Serviceman's Hop next month. We'll grab something on the way."

Justine stopped in her tracks. "What do you mean? It's your birthday. Mom's got a cake planned and everything. You're going out?"

"It was the only day Sal was free."

"The only day, Ruth? On your birthday?" She paused, considering this new information. "Come on. Tell me the truth. Are you and Sal sweet on each other?"

Ruth put Jim's letter aside and stared at her kid sister. "What's with everyone? First Helen, now you. Sal and I are not sweet on each other," she said, putting the emphasis on the word "sweet." "We're working together on the Hop, and this is the one night we could go and listen to the band play." She could tell she was not convincing her sister. "The fact that it happens to be my birthday is merely a coincidence."

"Uh huh." Justine shook her head. "Tell that to Mom. Better yet, tell that to Jim." She pointed to the letter on the bed. "Is that from him?"

"Yes." Ruth picked up the pages and folded them into the envelope. "He's still in North Africa, working hard. They just made him a Corporal."

"That's good news, I guess. What did he have to do to deserve that?"

"He doesn't say. I suspect his promotion was due to a few vacancies above his rank."

"Vacancies? Guys going AWOL?"

"Guys getting killed or wounded, Justine."

"Oh." Justine was silent for a minute. "Well, I better be going. Have to buy flour for that cake you're not going to be here to eat."

Justine walked down the hall and headed downstairs towards the kitchen. Ruth could hear her shouting as she went. "Mom, Ruth's not going to be here for dinner. Do I still need to go to the store?"

Ruth knew the minute she walked into the kitchen that she was in for a confrontation. Her mother was at the sink, scrubbing pots and pans with a vengeance. "So, you're not going to be here for dinner? It's your birthday! We have made plans. We always try to have a nice dinner to celebrate birthdays. Even now, during this war. I am trying to make things nice for you girls." She threw her sponge into the sink, but didn't turn around. "You should have told me ahead of time."

"Mother, I'm sorry, I've been so busy at work, I honestly forgot. Sal and I are going to go listen to a band we are planning on booking for the Serviceman's Hop." She watched her mother's back stiffen. "It's merely business. Sal's helping me out."

"Your sister seems to think it's more than business. And so do I." Her mother turned and wiped her hands on her apron. "I've seen you and this Sal person together a few times now. I am not blind. You may not know this, but I think Sal has feelings for you. I can see it. You may not, but I know these things. You are playing with fire, young lady. Fire. Every time you go out with Sal you are giving him hope. Hope that you will fall in love with him. You cannot do this. You cannot abandon Jim."

Ruth was stunned. "What are you talking about? I'm not abandoning Jim."

Mrs. LeBlanc pointed to a kitchen chair. "Sit down, Ruth. I have something important to say to you."

"Mother, I'm not a child you can lecture."

"Just sit down." Her mother pulled a second chair out from under the kitchen table and sat down. "You are not too old to take your mother's advice. Now sit."

Ruth reluctantly sat down, crossed her arms and waited. Her mother sat opposite, silently studying her daughter.

"Well?"

"I am trying to find the right words." Her mother frowned. "You know I love you and only wish for your happiness. Jim seems like a very nice young man. From a good family."

"He is, Mother. Jim's a great guy, and I love him, I really do. I don't understand why you're all upset."

"Because I see things, Ruth. Things you do not see. When Jim first went away and he sent you a letter, you were all excited. You couldn't wait to read it over and over. You were so happy every time. And after your time with Jim at that Fort Drake?"

"Dix, mother. Fort Dix in New Jersey."

"Wherever it was." Mrs. LeBlanc waved her hand as if brushing away the mistake. "But now, I watch you. When you get a letter from Jim these days, you don't seem to be so excited. The letter will sit at the front door waiting for you—sometimes for hours as if you don't want to read what he has to say anymore. And I watch you going out with this man Sal, and your eyes are all lit up. I see it."

Ruth shook her head. "You're wrong, Mother. It's just that I've been so busy at work and when I get home all I want to do is lie down. I read all of Jim's letters. And I write to him all the time."

"Just don't write him one of those 'Dear Johnnie' letters I hear girls are sending their soldier boys. Mrs. Evans told me her boy Charlie got one. Imagine, that poor boy all the way in the Pacific and he gets one of those 'Dear Johnnie' letters from Rebecca Thomas, the one person he's fighting for. It think it's shameful."

"Well, I'm sorry for Charlie. But things happen. And people change. I know Rebecca, and she's not someone who goes around hurting people for no good reason. If she broke off the engagement with Charlie, I'm sure it was something she gave a lot of time and thought to before she did it."

She glanced up at the wall clock and stood up, determined to be done with the conversation. "I'm going off to do a few errands. Do you need anything?"

But her mother was not done. "Ruth, you listen to me. I know it's not easy being so far away from Jim, but remember you gave him your word that you would wait for him and marry him when he came home. You cannot go back on that, no matter what."

"You are making something out of nothing, Mother. I'm not going anywhere. When Jim comes home, I'll be waiting for him, just as I promised."

When Sal knocked on the front door at 8 o'clock that evening, it was Justine who answered.

"So you're the one who's taking my sister dancing?"

"Hi Justine." Sal shuffled awkwardly. "Is Ruth ready?"

"All set," Ruth called out, sudddenly appearing from the front parlor. "Just need to grab my coat."

"You know, today is Ruth's birthday." Justine continued, "I hope you're planning on something special."

Ruth gave her sister a warning look. "We're off to listen to a band, Justine. Strictly business. No time for special events."

"Oh, I wouldn't say that," Sal winked at Justine. "I might have a surprise cooked up for the birthday girl."

"Please, Sal. Don't add fuel to the fire. Let's just go." As soon as she said it, Ruth realized Sal wouldn't have a clue what she meant. But Justine got the message. Her sister grinned and closed the front door behind them.

"What was that all about?" Sal asked as he pulled the car away from the curb. "What fire?"

"Nothing," Ruth said. "An inside joke. You know how sisters are. Justine is always teasing me about something."

"My sisters are always giving me a hard time, too. But that's family." He checked his watch. "I hope you haven't had dinner yet. I was hoping we could grab a bite to eat before we get to the nightclub."

"I'm sorry, Sal. I've already eaten. Mother was all upset when she found out I was going out tonight. She made a special meal, and, well, I couldn't say no." She looked across at Sal. "But don't worry, if you're hungry, I'm happy to join you. I'll have a glass of wine or something."

"Too bad. The place I was thinking of serves a spectacular lobster feast on Saturday nights. You would have enjoyed it."

"I still can. I mean, I can watch you eat the feast."

"Don't worry about it," he chuckled. "I'm giving you a hard time. I'll pick something up later."

The nightclub was almost an hour away but seemed a lot closer. The two friends spent the time in easy conversation and before either knew it, they had arrived at the club.

"Here we are," Sal announced as he pulled into the Shadow's parking lot. "Looks like they've got a crowd already, and it's only nine. That's a good sign."

"I should think so," Ruth answered. As she took Sal's arm and the two headed for the nightclub entrance, she could already hear music coming from the dance floor. "They sound really good."

"For an all girl band, you mean?"

"For any band!" Ruth pretended shock. "Come on." She pulled on his arm. "Let's hear what a real band sounds like!" Sal grinned and shook his head. He wasn't going to argue with her.

They found a table towards the back so they could have a better view of the room, and watch unobserved. The band was on stage opposite their table with a small, very crowded dance floor in between. Everyone was up and moving to the rhythm of "Peckin," Benny Goodman's jitterbug classic.

"That woman who's playing the clarinet sounds as good as Benny Goodman!" Ruth declared. The high pitched tones of the clarinet soared above the rest of the melody. Ruth knew it was a difficult solo, and she was impressed at the musician's ability.

"She is good," Sal agreed. They sat through a couple more numbers, taking notes and listing songs they might ask the band to play. A waitress stopped and asked if they would like something to drink and Sal passed her a note.

"I wonder if you would give this to the band leader. We have a few requests we'd like to hear, if that's possible."

"No problem," the waitress said. "They love requests." She put the note in her apron pocket. "They're good, aren't they? We were lucky to snag 'em."

"Do they play here often?" Ruth asked.

"This is only the third time they've been here, but every time we've had 'em, they've filled the room. They're very popular."

Ruth looked at the dance floor. Everyone seemed to be up and dancing. "I can see why. They really are good."

"Want to dance?" Sal asked.

Ruth nodded and the two stepped into the gyrating mass of bodies, just as the band started playing a Lindy tune, "Zaggin' With Zig."

"I love this song," Sal exclaimed and spun Ruth around. "You do know how to Lindy Hop?"

"Just watch me. I hope you can keep up," she laughed.

The two were a matched set, and as they danced, Ruth noticed other people on the floor began to watch them. No matter how many moves Sal made, or variations on the usual dance steps, Ruth followed, step for step. By the time the music was done, they were both laughing.

"That was a lot of fun, but I need to sit down for a bit." Sal attempted to catch his breath.

Ruth laughed. "Of course, whatever you say." The two friends returned to their table. Over the next few hours they alternated listening to the band, requesting special numbers and dancing.

"There isn't a tune these girls can't play. I think they'll be great for your hop."

"I'm going to try and get a deal signed tonight."

"Great idea. You should book 'em while you can."

By evening's end Ruth had negotiated an agreement with the band's manager. The TrueTones would be playing at the Serviceman's Hop.

"Thanks Sal, I appreciate your coming with me. It made it so much easier, and a lot of fun."

"Glad to be of assistance." Sal held the door of the car open as Ruth slipped into the front seat of the Chevy. "Anytime, you know that," he whispered. "I'd do anything to make you happy." He held the door open, looking down at Ruth, his face revealing what his words could not. He slowly closed the car door and walked around to the driver's side, got in behind the wheel and started the car, but did not release the parking brake.

"What are you waiting for?"

"Thought I'd warm up the car a bit." Sal turned to look at Ruth. He could barely make out her face in the dark, but he knew she was looking at him.

"Ruth," he paused, unsure how to say the words he had kept bottled up inside all evening. "Ruth, I don't know how else to say this, but straight out." He gripped the wheel as if holding on for dear life. He knew once he spoke the words he could not take them back. His life—their relationship would never be the same.

"I think I'm falling in love with you."

His voice cracked as he finally spoke the words out loud that he had been saying to himself for weeks. He stopped and waited for her to say something. When she did not respond he continued, "Did you hear what I said?"

"I heard you."

"Well? What do you think? Have I got a chance?"

Ruth turned and looked out the car windshield at the club's nearly deserted parking lot.

"You know I'm promised to Jim."

"I know." Sal waited, hoping she might continue. She didn't. "Jim's a good guy. A great guy. But he's been gone a long time, and things change between people."

He paused before continuing. He reached out and took her hand. "I want you to understand that I'm here for you. War can do a lot of strange things to a lot of people. The Jim you knew before the war might not be the same Jim who comes home."

Ruth nodded.

"If somehow things between you and Jim don't go well, if you change your mind, well—I'm here for you. That's it, that's all I wanted to say."

Ruth squeezed his hand. "All I can do is take each day as it comes and do the best I can."

He gave her a quick smile in the dark. "Just wanted you to know."

They drove back to Wollaston in silence.

❧

The following days were filled with work and planning for the hop. Ruth had little time for anything else, but she did find a moment to send a quick note off to Jim. For months she had written him at least once a week, but since that night with Sal and her confrontation with her mother, Ruth suddenly felt awkward writing to Jim.

Thursday, March 25, 1943

Dear Jim

Congratulations on your promotion to the rank of corporal. You work so hard and I'm glad you are finally getting the recognition you deserve.

Spring has almost arrived here in Massachusetts. Mother is already busy planning her garden and the daffodils are poking their heads up along the fence. Spring is on its way!

I've been busy getting ready for the Serviceman's Hop next weekend. My friend Sal and I went to hear the band that will play that night.

It's an all girl band called the TrueTones and they are very good. With so many musicians serving overseas in the military, we were lucky to find them. The Hop should be a big success. I'll write you and let you know how it all turned out.

I had to wonder at your comment about women wearing slacks. We are all wearing them now. Especially when it is chilly out. Without nylons to keep our legs warm, pants have become a real necessity. And for all the women now working in factories, pants are very practical. Trust me, you wouldn't want them wearing anything else. Skirts and aprons get caught in machinery. A good sturdy pair of coveralls is absolutely necessary to keep workers safe. You will just have to get used to it, dear. I still wear skirts to the office and to church, of course. So all is not lost. Don't worry that I've lost my femininity.

Sorry this is such a short letter, but with so much to do, I must run.

Stay well. Write soon. I'll send pics of the dance if I can.

Love you, Ruth.

�֍

It was the third day of April and the morning of the Serviceman's Hop when Jim's next letter arrived. Scrawled on lined paper, the words were all bunched together and hard to read in places. From the strange tone, Ruth guessed he must have been drinking when he wrote it, at least the first part.

March 21, 1943

Dear little Ruth:

Hello honey chile, draw up a flimsy and rest your weary frame awhile. Old pappy's gonna thumb there his "gotta be answered file" and pay you some dividends on your considerate at-ten-chuns.

Hmm- Feb 18 seems the oldest scribblings demanding my concern. Hold up a bit while I get me a wad of gum to exercise my molars.

You're working hard, honey. Get all you can out of some of these customers and make 'em pay on the nose.

You sure get yourself sunk in work. Boy, oh boy. And you want to join the Army to be doing something? Slow down sister, before you go beserk on me. Me-remember me? I'm the guy what loves ya.

Hey you. Stop burning the midnight oil in that shack on Milk St. Wanta grow old on me before your time? Relax honey.

What's this? What's this? Chairman of the Aristos Serviceman's Hop? A social climber, what. I should be flustered.

What the heck's this war coming to? My gal gets all het up about giving some lonely G.I.s a shindig and consequently lets business wait and obvious late working hours keep her from writing?

Ruth re-read the last few lines. He must have been drinking, she thought. He's not making any sense.

She glanced down the page at the passage that followed. It was a bit more logical and must have been written later when the drink wore off.

Let me tell you about the people here. The Moslem women can stay behind their draperies but boy some of these French dames. Phew. Paris is way ahead of New York when it comes to dressing up our women. But a G.I. gets nowhere unless he can converse in French. They won't be seen walking or talking with an American soldier on the street but instead will invite him to their home. I've visited a few homes and enjoyed their hospitality. Don't worry. Like the Italian girls at home, they are strictly chaperoned at home.

Pretty soon I think we will have V-Mail here. Then I will get more notes off to everyone. A letter to anyone except you is an effort. What is there to say? - Jim

Ruth folded the letter and tossed it in with the others in her dresser drawer, struggling against confusion. She was put off by Jim's tone and did not re-read it as she usually did.

I don't have time for this right now, she thought, looking at the small clock on her bedroom nightstand. I promised to be at the hop by six o'clock to help set up. I'll have to think about all this later.

"Justine?" Ruth knocked on her sister's bedroom door. "Are you ready to go? It's nearly four-thirty."

"What's the big rush? We've still got time." Justine was still in her bathrobe and the towel she had wrapped around her just washed hair made her look exotic. "I need at least an hour."

"Well, you don't have it. If you want to go to this dance, I need you to be ready to go no later than five o'clock. I promised the other girls I'd be there by six."

By five o'clock the back seat of the LeBlanc car was stacked high with paper goods, party favors and all the extra bowls and plates Ruth thought they might need.

"Is there anything you're not bringing to this dance?" her father asked, watching Ruth carefully arrange the family's large punch bowl on the back seat between two cardboard boxes. "You be careful with that bowl. It's an antique."

"I'll be careful. I want the table to look nice and grandma's punch bowl will fit right in the center of the buffet table."

"I don't think the boys will even notice. You're going to an awful lot of trouble for a simple dance."

"It's a special event, Dad. Some of the soldiers are only home on leave for a few days. They'll be heading off to war again and I want to make it a night they'll remember later when things aren't so pleasant. It's nice to have nice things to remember, don't you think?"

"I suppose so." Mr. LeBlanc wondered at his daughter's energy. "You do manage to take on a lot of these projects. I hope you have help tonight."

"Justine's coming along, and of course the committee will be there. They'll be meeting us at the factory." Ruth walked back to the front door and shouted up the stairs. "Justine! Come on! We have to go now or we'll be late."

By the time the two sisters arrived at the factory's meeting hall, the committee had set up the long buffet tables and arranged chairs in small groupings along both walls. Sal was preparing the makeshift bar in the far corner. He waved at Ruth but kept on working. He had volunteered to be the bartender for the evening and was busy unpacking glasses and bottles of liquor.

Ruth turned to her sister. "Justine, help me unpack the car. Once we bring everything in, we can see how best to set things up."

For the next hour the women unpacked, arranged and rearranged the hall and by seven o'clock when the band arrived, everything was in place. Grandmother's punch bowl was filled with a rosy red beverage, dishes and bowls were piled high with sweets and Sal had already begun serving drinks to a few of the committee. "Just to get things started."

"Well, don't forget to collect the money," Ruth reminded Sal. "Everything's free for the soldiers, but each of us should pay our own way, or we'll never be able to pay for the band."

"I disagree. You and your friends have worked hard on this event. The least we can do is offer a free drink or two. And don't worry about paying for the band. I've already taken care of that."

"What do you mean?"

Sal looked sheepish. "I took the liberty of speaking to the manager that night at the Shadows, after you had arranged everything. She was prepared to donate some of their fee for the night, but I convinced her they deserved to be paid in full. They're that good. So I've taken care of it. They get their full fee and we," he gestured to the room, "we get to enjoy the night and not worry about collecting quarters. The drinks are on me." He gave her a broad smile.

Ruth was stunned. "Sal Marcusio, you are a man full of surprises."

"Happy to be of service." He looked around the hall as the first few soldiers began to arrive. "It's the least I can do for these boys. If I can't join them over there, the least I can do is make their time here memorable."

"Well, your generosity will not go unnoticed. I'll make an announcement."

"I'd rather you didn't. It's not that big a deal, and I can afford it. I'm happy to do my part to make your dance a success."

Ruth looked at Sal. She could tell he meant every word and she could see in his eyes that he was happy she knew it. Suddenly, without thinking, she leaned in and gave him a quick kiss on his cheek. "That's for being such a great guy."

He grinned at her. "I should be generous more often."

Ruth laughed and shook her head. "You've been a great friend, Sal and I appreciate all you've done for me—for us." She turned and looked back at the hall and the soldiers and sailors that were now streaming through the doors. "And especially for them."

Sal looked out over the crowd as the band started to play its opening number. "Let's make this a night to remember for these guys."

Ruth nodded. "Absolutely."

CHAPTER 11

BOSTON

Spring came quickly to Wollaston in 1943. One day the weather was cold and dreary and the next, tulips were beginning to pop up everywhere. The Red Sox were in spring training at Tufts University in Medford, and it looked like this would be a winning year for the team. A lot of people expected baseball would suspend play while the war was on, but sentiments changed after President Roosevelt had published his famous "green light" letter stating, in part, "I honestly feel that it would be best for the country to keep baseball going."

"The world may be at war, but we shouldn't just shut down baseball because of it," Mr. LeBlanc had declared to Justine over his morning newspaper. "We need something to take our minds off what's happening overseas."

"I didn't know you were a big baseball fan, Dad."

"I am when they're winning and with Bobby Doerr on second base this year, we might have a chance."

"Uh huh. I've heard that before." Justine filled a cup with morning tea and settled herself at the far end of the table.

Mr. LeBlanc didn't answer, his focus set on the front page news. "They're going to start rationing shoes pretty soon. Can you believe it! They've already got us saving stamps for butter and canned food... now it's shoes!"

"It's so we can save all the leather for army boots." Justine tried to explain. "It doesn't mean we can't buy shoes. I saw some new canvas shoes in Filene's window the other day. They had them in lots of colors. They looked pretty nice."

"Canvas is fine for you ladies," her father complained. "But men need leather shoes for work. How am I supposed to wear colored canvas shoes to work?"

"I think you'd look cute!" Justine teased.

"I'll bring my shoes to the cobbler and get them resoled before I put on a pair of your fancy canvas shoes." He rolled up his paper and pushed back from the table.

❀

It was mid-April when Ruth met Sal for dinner at his new apartment on Beacon Street.

"I'm really glad you could come. I need all the interior design help I can get."

"Happy to give you advice. But you should call in an expert. I'm more of a two dimensional designer."

Sal laughed. "Even so, your ideas are guaranteed to be better than mine." He raised his glass and looked out over the city skyline. "Even at night, Boston is a beautiful city, don't you think?"

Ruth moved closer to the large picture windows. This was her first visit to Sal's home and she was impressed. The apartment overlooked the Public Gardens and had a full view of the river and Cambridge from the corner windows. The sunset tonight had been spectacular as the windows in buildings as far to the west as Somerville caught the hot red reflection of the sun as it sunk below the horizon. They sparkled like rubies until finally fading away as darkness descended on the city. If she looked carefully, Ruth could pick out cars on the street below, their hooded headlights barely visible as they made their way across town in the blackout.

"I can't wait for this war to be over. We thought it would be quick when we first started. I remember, it was all bright lights and patriotic songs. Now it's just dreary the way it's dragging on."

Sal moved closer. "It will end someday, Ruth. And we will win. Hitler and his pals will be defeated. I promise."

"I hope you're right." Ruth looked at him. "I can't imagine what it would be like if we lose."

"That's not going to happen. Not with guys like your Jim overseas fighting for us."

At the mention of Jim, Ruth looked away, a wave of sadness washing

214

over her.

"What's wrong? Did I say something wrong?"

Ruth put her glass down on the end table and gazed out at the horizon. "No, nothing's wrong...," she hesitated. "So many things have changed." Ruth crossed her arms and moved closer to the window.

"What are you saying? Have you and Jim broken up?"

"No, nothing like that. At least not formally." Ruth tried to explain. "He's been gone a long time and when he writes—there are moments, I hardly recognize him."

Sal gently put his hand on her arm, reassuringly. "I'm sure that's not true. War does crazy things to people. Look at me. I'm managing a war factory and making electronic triggers for bombs that kill people. Not what I expected I'd be doing with my life. But it has to be done. Your Jim,—I'm sure is doing work he never expected to be doing. He's fixing planes, right?"

"He's actually an accountant, at least that's what he's trained to do. After high school, he took classes at Bentley but now he's fixing bombers in the desert." She paused. "I think he loves what he's doing. He enjoys fixing things and making them work."

"Well I'm glad. He must be good at his job."

"Too good. He hasn't said it outright, but I'm picking up hints. I think he may be looking into staying in the army and making it a career." Ruth looked at Sal. "Not something I want to do."

"So, tell him. Let him know you have other ideas."

"I can't tell him now. He's right in the middle of everything."

"Better to tell him now than wait," Sal countered. "If you don't want to marry a military career man, you have to let him know. It's only fair."

"He wrote to me last month. A couple of the men in his squadron have received 'Dear John' letters and were devastated. He's begged me not to send him one."

"If that's the case, he must suspect that something's not right between you. Maybe he's expecting you to write and tell him it's over."

"But it's not over. At least I don't think so." Ruth shook her head. "I don't know what to think."

Sal stood quietly. "I'll support you, Ruth. Whatever happens. Let's pray he stays safe."

Ruth nodded and gave a deep sigh.

"I think it's time I got you home." Sal crossed to the hall closet and retrieved Ruth's coat. "Don't want to keep you out too late on a work night."

She leaned in close to Sal and without thinking, gave him a quick kiss on his lips.

"What was that for?"

"For being such a nice guy and for a lovely dinner."

During the long trolley ride into work the next morning, Ruth re-played this last scene in her head over and over. *What was I thinking? I'm engaged to Jim and I'm kissing Sal! He's a friend. A good friend. But I'm engaged to Jim. What will Sal think of me? And worse, what will Jim think?*

"Jim doesn't have to know anything about it," Helen assured her friend.

Ruth had arrived at her desk in such a flutter there was nothing for her to do but reveal the entire scenario.

"I didn't mean to kiss Sal. I wanted to." Ruth paused. "That doesn't make sense, does it?"

"It makes perfect sense if you love him, or admire him, or just like him a lot. Kissing is the most natural response in such a situation. It's not life threatening."

"But now I have to wonder what it means? I'm engaged to Jim and shouldn't be going around kissing other men."

Helen gave her friend a long look. "You worry too much. You kissed Sal because you were happy. Besides, it was only a peck on the cheek, right?"

"Actually it was on the lips, but it was quick. Very quick. You don't think he got the wrong idea, do you?"

"I'm not worried about what Sal thinks, Ruth. I'm concerned about you." She gave her friend a long look. "Are you thinking about breaking off the engagement with Jim?"

Ruth slumped back in her chair not sure how to answer.

"It's a simple question with a yes or no answer. Is this engagement of yours in danger of collapsing in on itself?"

Helen waited for her friend to respond. Finally she broke the silence. "I think you know the answer, Ruth. You just haven't admitted it to yourself yet."

"But I have. I feel so badly about it. I don't want to hurt Jim. I do care about him. But I'm learning things I didn't know. He's very rule conscious and he seems to have lost his sense of humor. He's so conservative about.... He's far more religious than I am. If I'm honest with myself, I not comfortable with what I see."

Helen pulled a chair closer to her friend and sat down. "Remind me, how long had you two been dating before he joined up?"

Ruth paused, thinking. "He worked upstairs in accounting. It was in the early fall of 1941. He was so shy It was hard to get him to talk. But then, we went to one or two dances his friend Jerry organized and he was a totally different person, telling jokes and having a great time with everyone. After that, we dated a few more times and then, a few days before New Years, he asked me if we could be exclusive. And I said, 'yes.'"

"Hmmmm." Helen considered the facts. "A month later he left for war and for the last year, the only way you've communicated is on paper. It's been all letters back and forth."

"Except for that weekend at Fort Dix in August."

Helen studied her friend for a moment. "You never had a real chance to get to know Jim before he hopped on that train and ended up in the Army."

"But we fell in love. That was real." Ruth protested. "Jim was kind and caring, and we seemed to like all the same things. His family seemed nice enough and he even liked Justine, and you know how difficult she can be sometimes."

"But it wasn't enough time to really get to know the man." Helen reached out and took Ruth's hands in her own. "Think about it. You dated for a few months, then he goes away. You spend a summer writing love notes to each other and when he finally pops the question you agreed to marry. I'm not saying it was a bad decision. But it hardly gave you time to get to know each other.

"Look at me. When Gary and I were dating, it took us more than six months before we started to get serious, and another year after that before he asked me to marry him. By the time we heard the Wedding March, we had been together for almost two years. I thought I knew him pretty well by then, but believe me, everyday I find out something new. You and Jim? You didn't have a chance. The war made sure of that."

"So you don't think I'm crazy for feeling confused?"

"Crazy? Think about it. You fall in love with a man—a nice guy—an accountant with a steady job. Someone who pushes a pencil and works with numbers. Suddenly he joins up with the Army and is trained to become a soldier who shoots guns and fixes planes that drop bombs on people to kill them. And you think he should stay exactly the same?"

"When you put it like that, of course Jim would change."

"War changes people, Ruth. If it doesn't kill them outright, it's sure to have a major impact on their lives." Helen stood up. "Listen, honey. I've got to get back to work or my boss is going to be after me. We can talk about this at lunch if you want. But I think it's pretty simple. You need to send Jim a letter and tell him you're having second thoughts. Give him a little warning first, though, you don't want to break his heart all at once."

In early May most of the news from the war front was focused on the North Africa campaign. Control of the territories had been a seesaw affair with the Axis and Allied forces battling back and forth from Algeria to Tunisia, gaining and then losing ground. But since the Battle of Medenine, the Germans had been steadily pushed back. Ruth followed the news carefully, knowing Jim was somewhere in the middle of it all. Although she was feeling increasingly ambiguous about their relationship, she continued to send him at least a letter each week filled with local news and gossip but she avoided sharing anything personal. She persuaded Justine to take a few more snaps and sent them off to Jim. It was mid-May before his next letter arrived. It had been written many weeks before.

April 10, 1943

My dearest darling:

Thanks dear for the big smile in your photo taken in your yard. I'd rather have a picture of you than ten letters from anyone else.

Did I mention before that they sent me to a rest camp for a spell? A beautiful spot on the Mediterranean.

Did you ever become so tired you can't sleep? That's the way I felt many a time. It took some of my weight but I'm catching up again. I didn't get up until 9 A.M. in the morning and retired at 9 P.M. Just laid around.

If you could have only been there, we could enjoy that beautiful sunset together. Magnificent coloring. The rest did me lots of good.

Now back again in the routine but feeling refreshed. Things are going along smoothly and on schedule. There is so much happening that I can't write about, it is a shame.

Darling I shall say so long for a while but please write and send more pictures.

I am busy right now and may be unable to write for a while. Wish me luck dear in my daily work.

Your Jim.

Jim's letter was dated April 10, but it had only arrived that morning. Ruth glanced at the calendar on her desk. Wednesday, May 12. It had taken more than a month for the letter to be delivered. She re-read the section about Jim's being sent to a rest camp. What was that all about? She prayed he hadn't been injured.

"Helen, what do you make of this?" Ruth asked her friend when they met for lunch at noon. She read the passage out loud.

"Sounds like they gave him time off for good behavior," Helen surmised.

"Do they do that? I mean, do they give people time off even though they're on the battlefield?"

"I'm sure they have to rotate the men in and out of wherever they are. They must be exhausted working 12 and 15 hour days in those conditions." She glanced at the letter. "Was he injured?"

"No, nothing like that. Jim can't tell me much in his letters, but I know they are working constantly. The battle never stops. His Captain must have just decided he needed a break."

"I don't think we'll ever know what those guys are going through until this is over. Count your lucky stars he's still going strong." She paused and gave her friend a long look. "Have you told Jim about how you're feeling these days about the engagement?"

"Not yet. I don't know how to tell him. And I'm still confused myself. I promise I'll write him when I know for sure." Ruth carefully placed Jim's letter in her handbag.

"Well, I better get back to work. Lots to do."

"Next time you write to Jim, let him know we're all thinking of him and hope he's feeling better."

That evening when Ruth got home, there were two additional letters from Jim waiting for her on the side table.

April 14, 1943

Dearest Ruth:

Things here are humming along pretty good. Much of the chow here is still S.O.S. Be careful what G. I. you ask to interpret that.

Ruth had learned from a couple of the soldiers at the USO what "S.O.S" meant. "Shit On A Shingle," she remembered. Leave it to the Army to come up with creative acronyms for everything.

Got a note from my friend Dick who had been shipped to a postal station. He has made corporal. My letters often come through with his initials on the envelopes. Once in a while he'll scratch a few words on some of yours such as "She's still writing Jim." or "Hope this is the one you're looking for."

I miss you the most when traveling. If only you could see some of the sights I have seen. This country is like a big patched quilt from the air. And the Arabs! You would sure find they demand some of your attention.

I'm counting on your prayers to get me by and don't forget that a good part of these prayers should be for my soul not only for my physical safety. Sometimes I feel a bit lost.

Having left you just when we began to understand each other has made it that much more difficult. Sometimes I crave your company just as though I was kept from food and water.

Rather than hold this letter up any longer I'll sign off soon. I'm beginning to plan seriously for the future. I want to make you happy and most of all to keep you loving me always. Your Jim

The second letter, much longer, was dated a week after the first.

April 21, 1943

Ruth darling:

I want to tell you about the people here.

The French are wonderful painters but poor plumbers. I got a kick out of their equipment for lavatories. No seats at all. I heard lots about privies being on the street but I didn't believe what I actually saw here. I can just imagine one of them in Times Square.

They have introduced many modern conveniences and Paris fashions to this country. The French are the most artistic people imaginable. They paint everything.

Their gardens are magnificent. They do wonders with stones and flowers. The Arab farmer is expert in his line. You can see cultivated lands in the most inaccessible places. This year should bring them bumper crops with all the rain we have had.

It's a shame that I can't speak French. Walking along a road the other day I was overtaken by a hansom cab with three French girls and their mother. They offered me a lift and I accepted. It was good to be with people other than soldiers, but it was so odd sitting between them and not knowing what to say or how to gesture.

They sure put on perfume, these French gals. Their makeup is excellent. I wonder how long they spend in front of a mirror?

I offered them each a package of gum and so help me I'll bet if their mother wasn't there I would have gotten something nice. They were so pleased, just like little kids.

I kept thinking how nice it would have been to be able to speak their language. They are so sociable but just can't convey their meanings the way they want to. Some of the fellows who know a little French have been invited into homes and they say the interiors are well furnished.

This country now has many French refugees. I have met some Frenchmen who were in Paris before the war, and one who could speak pretty fair English described the country there as best he could. He spoke of how pretty the girls were and had something to say about a certain class of girls which I shall tell you in private. I was surprised, but he said the French people were very matter of *fact about this condition and allowed it to be so.*

It seems to me from my observation that the French are not half way about anything. If they believe in a certain cause or habit they practice, they support the cause to the extreme.

Some of my comrades who have been to what they thought were some pretty "hot" places in the states were really educated when frequenting some of the establishments over here.

The same goes for nationalistic affairs. Given the right equipment and supplies and with a leader in whom they can have full confidence, I believe the French Army here will play a major roll before this war is finished.

There are a number of different types of French soldier. That is, you have the Arabian, Senegalese, Zanons and some others. These soldiers are of course the continental type but are terrific fighters. They know Africa and support the French cause. They wear colorful uniforms with long capes. Very suave. I guess here again is French influence. So help me these Frenchmen would paint the Sun if they could reach it.

Mind if I say au revoir for now dear? Still love me? Get lots of sleep hon for you may not get so much when I return. Ahem!

Bye love and please send me more photos of you. They're my only form of pleasure. I love you.

Your Jim

P.S. Well dear, the next letter I must answer is from David Harrington of South Boston. I darn near drowned with him at White Horse beach one summer. I'd like to have him take you out. Would you accept? He might steal you though. He has several girls after him now.

Ruth re-read the post script. Who was David Harrington? She tried to re-member but drew a total blank. And why was Jim trying to set her up with all these men? Her social life was full enough without Jim's friends trying to take her out. She'd have to remember to tell him so in her next letter.

222

🌸

"Jim's is a very observant fellow," Ruth's father remarked, reading over the letter. "So many interesting details."

Justine chimed in. "I like the bit about his meeting those French women. Lucky he doesn't speak their language. He might have been shocked at what they were saying."

Mrs. LeBlanc looked up from her knitting and stared at her youngest daughter over her bifocals. "I think you should go and do your chores, young lady. It's your night to do the wash up." She pointed a knitting needle towards the kitchen.

"I did them last night!" Justine protested.

"And you'll do them tonight as well. Ruth did them all last week if you recall. It's time you took your turn." She pointed towards the kitchen again and Justine, defeated, stood up and reluctantly headed towards the kitchen and a sink full of dishes.

"So what do you think of your Jim now?" Mr. LeBlanc asked, turning to Ruth. "Did he really say he had to be placed in a rest home."

"Not a rest home, father. You make him sound like he's an old man."

"That's what he called it. He wasn't injured and it wasn't a hospital."

"I think what your daughter means," Mrs. LeBlanc interrupted, "is that the term 'rest home' implies he was given time off to rest his mind rather than his body. Sort of an institution, isn't that right, Ruth?"

"It wasn't an institution. It was a rest camp. I think Jim was exhausted and needed time away from his duties. There is nothing wrong with his mind. When a soldier needs time off, the Army sends him to one of these grand houses they've taken over from the locals. It's not a hospital. It's just a place to rest and recoup."

"I see, so Jim's been working too hard?" her mother asked.

"I think every soldier is working too hard, if you ask me. He can't say much, but things have not been as easy as we might think. A lot is happening that we never read about in the papers. I think this war has had a major effect on Jim, and not always to the good."

"What are you saying, Ruth?"

"I get the feeling he is not happy."

"How can you expect him to be happy?" Mr. LeBlanc declared. "He's fighting a war! He's facing death every day. You can't expect him to be all jolly about it."

"I know, father. It's just that..." she paused, searching for the words. "He's not the man I thought I knew. We both still care for each other, but I think we need more time to get to know each other if we're going to get married."

She looked from her mother to her father, waiting for the reaction she knew would come.

It was her mother who spoke first.

"You're not thinking of breaking off your engagement, are you?"

"I don't know, Mother. It's something I've been thinking about for a while."

"What's Jim done wrong to make you change your mind? Has he been dating other women or getting involved in dangerous activities...?"

"No, it's not that. Jim isn't like that. I don't know how to explain it. The longer this war goes on, the longer Jim is away... I realize I hardly know the man. He's seen so many things. He's not the same person he was."

"Of course he's not. How can he be? But that's what happens in life. War or no war. Do you think your father today is the same person I married all those years ago?" She turned to her husband. "Tell her, Frederick. You've changed. You're not the same as you were back then."

"And neither are you, my dear." Mr. LeBlanc gave his wife an exaggerated smile and put his head back into his newspaper.

"You see. He agrees with me. Life changes people."

"But you two had a long courtship didn't you? You had time to get to know each other and spend time together before you were married. Jim and I never had that and now that I have had a chance to think about it, we had no time at all to get to know each other before he signed up. Only a few months."

"Well, you've had over a year since then, my dear."

"But only in letters. Only in words back and forth, and most of those under the eyes of the censors." Ruth clenched her fists in frustration. "I'm not saying I'm calling it off, Mother. I'm just saying we need more time before we make a final decision. This is the man I'm supposed to be with for the rest of my life. I want to be sure he's the right one."

"Good luck with that," Mr. LeBlanc mumbled to himself.

※

As the cool mornings of May turned into the warm days of June, Ruth struggled to make a decision. Should she call off the engagement? At least temporarily? It wasn't as if she was calling it off permanently. She just needed more time. It wouldn't be a final decision. She needed to put things on hold for a while.

Helen sat at her office desk the next day, listening to her friend trying to work things out for herself.

"I've got to write to Jim about this. It's just not fair to let this drag on."

"If that's what you've decided, I think you're right. But you have to let Jim know as soon as possible."

"I'm right, aren't I? You agree with me, don't you?"

"Honey, you've been telling me all this for weeks. It's time you let Jim know exactly how you feel."

"I'll send him a letter first chance I get and explain everything. But not today. I've got so much work to do, I'll write him tomorrow."

"Don't put it off too long, Ruth, or you'll lose your nerve."

"I'll take care of it. Don't worry."

Ruth had intended to write the letter to Jim the next evening but Sal called and wanted to go out to dinner. The next night it was Justine needing help with a volunteer project that put her off the task. In fact, every night that week there was something important to do that couldn't wait.

It wasn't until the second week of June that she finally had the time to sit down and write to Jim.

Tuesday, June 16, 1943

Dearest Jim,

So much is happening here these days. The weather is getting warmer, and Justine and I have been to Nantasket Beach a couple of times. She asked a couple of her friends to join us and my friend Sal and Helen and her husband Gary came along too. We had a wonderful time. The tide was in and the waves were easy to ride. Sal and I took a long walk along the beach. Did you know it's almost three miles from end to end?

Quincy had a wonderful Memorial Day celebration and, of course, I thought of you as the soldiers marched by in parade down Hancock Street. I'm so proud of you and all that you are doing for our country. I pray for you every night that you stay safe and out of harms way.

I've been doing a lot of thinking and praying about us, too. It's been a very long time since we were together, and although I love getting your letters and writing to you about all that is happening here on the home front, it's very hard to communicate all that I am feeling.

I know I've changed from that woman you first met in the fall of '41. And you've surely changed with all that has happened to you.

What I'm trying to say is that during this last year we have both changed a bit and we're not the same people who promised to love each other as husband and wife for eternity. I still love you but I feel I don't know you as much as I should. We need to take time to get to know each other again—from the start.

I know it's hard to say this in a letter, but I feel we should postpone our engagement and take some time before we say we are engaged— to see if you and I are still truly right for each other. Looking back, we haven't had a chance to get to know each other except through our letters, so I'm hoping you understand what I'm asking for is just a little more time.

Let's postpone the engagement until we have a chance to really get to know each other. Once this war is over and you are back safe and sound, we can finally decide with certainty if marriage is what we both truly want.

I hope you understand that I still love you,

Ruth

She re-read the letter several times. It was the best she could do to try and explain all that she was feeling.

"You don't think it's too cut and dry, do you?" she asked Helen the next morning.

"I think you are perfectly clear. You're just asking for time, that's all. It's not a permanent breakup... call it a pause in the relationship."

Ruth folded the letter, inserted it in an envelope and closed the flap. "Do you have an extra stamp?"

Helen reached into her desk drawer and handed over a small purple 3¢ stamp. "My last one." She watched as Ruth licked the stamp and placed it in the top right corner of the envelope. "Now go mail it."

"I'll drop it in the mailbox on my way to South Station."

Ruth felt confident with her decision but no sooner had she dropped the letter into the mail slot, then she began to have second thoughts. Would Jim understand? What would he think? Would he agree? What if he didn't? What then?

It took until the streetcar pulled into Wollaston Station for her to calm down and stop second guessing herself. What was it Helen said? It's just a pause in the relationship, not a permanent decision. But that evening, before going to bed, Ruth quietly removed the pearl engagement ring from the third finger of her left hand and gave a small sigh of relief.

❧

It was nearly six at night when Ruth arrived home from work several days later. Her mother and sister were sitting in the cool shade of the front porch, snapping peas for supper.

"There's a letter from Jim waiting for you on the hall table," Justine teased. "And it's a thick letter too. I bet there are three or four letters in that envelope."

"Thanks, Justine."

Ruth opened the screen door and entered the front hallway. A thick brown envelope covered with army cancellation stamps was sitting on the side table.

It was too soon for Jim to have received her latest letter, but Ruth couldn't help but feel anxious as she carefully unfolded several pages covered with Jim's familiar scrawl. Jim had written one very long letter over a couple of days.

June 13, 1943

Dearest Ruth:

There is something to this business of writing. It does make us closer to each other. May we never part in feelings and spirit. There is always time to think of you and often I am simply overwhelmed at the thought of just how much you mean to me.

You are to be my guide and inspiration for the life ahead. Everything

I do will be one way or another done for a purpose. Either your happiness or welfare...

Ruth paused and reread the first paragraph, thinking of the letter she had sent to Jim.

It's hard to write I know, but it's harder not to receive, we both know that. Recently you were sent the longest letter I have yet written. You have so many friends up in the intellectual stratosphere such as your Harvard Business friends that it leaves me wondering at times. I will have to get on the ball and make you pleased that I can approach that level. I am not exactly self conscious but wide awake to my abilities. Living on the same standards as a graduate of Tech and Harvard will necessitate a lot of grind. I can do it if you show confidence in me...

I certainly will need all your love and encouragement. A wife can make or break her husband. She can make him love her so intensely that he breaks his neck to please her or she can cause him to feel happiness only when he is away from her and his ambitions are stunted through a broken spirit. There aren't many successful businessmen that have homes that are "hells on earth."

Ruth was at a loss, trying to figure out the meaning behind Jim's words. What social circle does he think I'm in? The only person who even comes close to upper class is Sal, and he's so down to earth, I hardly remember how wealthy he is.

Don't work too hard dear for it will get you down. Get out and enjoy the fresh air and sunshine. I expect a picture of the LeBlanc girls frolicking at Wollaston beach, even if they do have male companions. I'll try not to feel jealous of one certain gal in particular. That is, as long as it is isn't a sailor you're with...

June 14, 1943

Dearest Ruth,

The circus is coming to town? I suppose it will be my job to take all our kids to the circus each year. Will I love it? But yes. I remember one year at the circus I bought me a little salamander. (I thought it was an alligator at the time.) I kept it in the attic. One fine day I went up to feed it and caught our cat trying to eat him. I chased that damn feline all over the place. Was I mad.

Finally I caught the cat and carried him down to the cellar. Spitting and scratching, wriggling and clawing, he tried to get loose. I opened the furnace door and was just going to throw him in when the cat's guardian angel held my hand and I decided to let him go. He was no pet of mine after that. Sometime I'll tell you how I used to use him for a live target in my game of darts. Am I crazy? I guess I was at one time.

Well, hon, write some more and I'll answer all. Still love me? You had better.—Your Jim

From the thickness of the envelope, she had expected several more letters, but instead, Jim had included five colored postcards from Tunisia. They were nice, but she would have rather have had a photo of Jim.

"What did Jim have to say?" her mother asked that evening. "How is he feeling these days?"

"Jim's fine. No news."

"I noticed you're not wearing your engagement ring. Is there a problem?"

"The setting is a little loose. I have to get it fixed." She didn't know if her mother believed her or not, but didn't stay long enough to find out. "I'm going to put these letters upstairs, Mother. I'll be down for dinner in a minute."

As she placed Jim's latest letters in the drawer with the others, she couldn't help but wonder about Jim. She knew he had a bit of a temper, but his description of what he almost did to the family pet surprised her. *I can't think about that right now,* she decided.

Between work and excursions to the beach and to nightclubs with Sal or one of the others in her crowd, Ruth had little time to worry over Jim's old stories of cats and salamanders, but he was never far from her thoughts.

❊

"So what did Jim say when he got your letter?" Helen asked a few weeks later.

"I don't know. I've only received one letter from Jim in the last month. I wrote him weeks ago, so you'd think he would have gotten it by now, but he hasn't mentioned my letter."

"You're kidding."

Ruth straightened the sheets of paper on her desk and rearranged the pencils in the large glass jar.

"I've been waiting for a bomb to drop every time the postman comes to the door. I'm beginning to wonder if my letter ever got delivered."

"When did you send it?"

"June 16th. It was a Tuesday. I mailed it from that box on the corner on my way home that night. That box gets regular pickups, so it should have gone right out."

"Mail does get lost sometimes."

"All the mail must be slow. It's nearly the end of August now. The last letter I got from Jim arrived three days ago. He hasn't received any letters lately, but I know I sent several V-Mails at the beginning of July."

She opened the large canvas satchel she kept over the back of her chair and took out one of Jim's letters.

"He wrote this in mid July, but he still doesn't mention my letter from June. He sounds discouraged."

"He has good reason to be. This war never seems to end. It's tough for us, but I'm sure it's a lot tougher for those guys over there." Helen stood up and moved towards the door. "I've got to check in with my boss before I can finalize these reports I've been working on. I'll see you later."

Ruth nodded at her friend and continued to re-read Jim's letter to herself.

July 17, 1943

Dearest Ruth

The news at home must be encouraging. Please try to understand that when you don't hear from me at least twice a week there is sufficient good reason. Gosh I wish censorship permitted more details but you can judge for yourself by what developments have taken place.

Haven't heard from you in a while. Perhaps with the warm weather you don't feel like writing. I'll understand that dear, but when an entire month goes by ... I don't see how it's the mail. But I try not to think things.

We are going to be separated from each other for quite some time to come and it's imperative that our association be nourished by intimate letters and the best news we both can give.

It's only natural that you, living in a large city, are going to be distracted and have numerous social engagements that take up your time. I understand this.

In my case there are reasons also. One is tiredness and another important factor is that the surroundings are such to discourage writing. Dirt, noise, wind and lack of daylight time. Heat also deadens one's vitality.

Am I making excuses? It looks that way but hon, I promise to answer you, letter for letter. I'm greatly concerned over this lack of mail and would appreciate hearing from you one way or another. I even sent a cable hoping it will reach you sooner.

If by some chance you just got fed up with writing, why take a break dearest. Lay off for a month or so if you wish. I'll understand. May our love grow stronger each passing day. If it is to be so, it will be so.

Still loving you,

Your Jim

He sounded so sad and lonely. I'm sorry you're feeling so alone, she thought. I miss you, Jim. I really do. But why haven't you mentioned my letter? Had he even received it?

She could feel tears begin to well up behind her eyes. Sadness? Regret? No, she didn't regret telling him she wanted their engagement be put on hold. She had to be honest with him. But now, it was the not knowing that had her caught up in a mix of awkward feelings.

And there was the matter of Sal. He had become a close friend and con-fidant. They went to the seashore nearly every Saturday. Sometimes Louise or Bettie would join them. Walking the shoreline and taking a ride on the carousel had become regular rituals, and she always looked forward to their get togethers. She suspected Sal still felt more than he let on when it came to their own relationship. Although he knew how ambivalent she was feeling about her engagement to Jim, he never pressed her or tried to persuade her to his side of things, and for that, Ruth was very grateful. She was sure he had noticed her engagement ring was no longer on her left hand, but he never asked about it. His patience and understanding made him all the more attractive.

But Jim was never far from her mind. Since writing the letter in June she had tried to soften the blow with a couple of quick V-Mails filled with local news and stories. After all, she didn't want Jim to think she had forgotten him or had stopped writing all together. But it seemed he hadn't received anything from her in weeks and the absence of communication with Jim and the close friendship she had developed with Sal had her rethinking everything.

Just before the end of August a large brown envelope addressed to Ruth arrived in the LeBlanc's mailbox. There were several letters from Jim dated from late July. Eager for news, Ruth scanned the contents and quickly discovered that sometime in mid-July Jim had been injured.

July 20, 1943

Hon, you can't imagine how anxiously I await word from you. You're like a good tonic. You wouldn't recognize me now. Want a description? OK.

He is not a native. His clothes speak of an American soldier. His hair is short clipped and is this way for coolness, as his mechanics cap must be worn at all times, due to danger of sunstroke. Oh, oh! He just smiled. Who hit him with a rake?

A large scar runs down the left side of his nose and stops about two inches above his lip. Two teeth are missing from the upper set right in front. Upon closer scrutiny, it is discovered that the scar is a skin abrasion and not a deep cut.

What happened to him? Who did this? Teeth missing? Scar down the side of his face? Ruth shook her head and wondered. How can he be so casual about this? He could have been killed.

He is brown from the sun and lean from either improper diet or activities in the heat. He speaks of the latter as the cause. However his body has hardened with the wind and sand. Surprising as it is, he does not sweat.

A light coating of dust evidently absorbs what little sweat he perspires. The height of 6'1" is due largely to the two lean but sturdy legs that have tramped many miles since donning a uniform. He wears woolen socks and G.I. boots.

He has a little pair of pants to cover his amidships from the blistering sun. Otherwise the tendency might be to go native and save laundering.

With all my love, Jim

Ruth wanted to smile at the image Jim's words created in her mind, but she couldn't. He was hurt and injured, and what surprised her, he didn't seem to care. But she did.

July 31, 1943

I have just come in from washing my socks and two handkerchiefs in my helmet. Oh yes, I had my bath in it also. It's rather hard to get up again once you sit down in it. But hon, I do quite well as it is.

You won't have a big laundry for I have gotten into the habit of washing handkerchiefs, socks and underwear as soon as I wear them so I always have clean ones. It's a nice tidy habit but rather hard on the cloth. My hardest piece of laundry is my big towel. I can't seem to get it white anymore, so I just use it as is and tell myself that the sand color is good camouflage.

The army, especially in the field, teaches a fellow to take care of himself and his property, for no one else is going to worry about protecting you or them. By that, I don't mean that we don't stick together, but that in personal habits a man's life is his own. I live out of a little canvas bag and nothing more is necessary in my surroundings.

Hope to get some mail in today. Sent a letter to my cousin Betty. She had Bill home on furlough. She put it in a more novel way. She said, "Jim, I was all wrapped up for a few days. But it was a relief to have him leave in a way," she said, for she couldn't stand such happiness for long. Lucky people to be in love like that. I guess my chances for a furlough are very slim. If and when I do get home, I want to stay anyway.

Guess what? I had some delicious coffee ice cream the other night. What a treat! I got back in line three times and couldn't make the fourth helping to save my life. Whole hog or none, that's me. Things like that help ones morale, but hon, your letters do more for my morale than any other conceivable person or thing, news or hearsay.

Your Jim

Ruth sighed as she folded the letters and replaced them in the large envelope. His injury didn't appear to be a major problem after all, and Jim's sense of humor had returned.

He certainly has a great imagination, she thought. I could learn to love that about him.

"You must think I'm crazy, Helen." Ruth tried to explain the jumble of emotions she was feeling since reading Jim's last letter. "I don't know what to think about the two of us. One minute I've decided I need some distance and time and the next I want to rush to his side to comfort him. He sounds so vulnerable."

"Injured soldiers have a way of doing that to their girlfriends," Helen replied.

"He still hasn't responded to my June 16th letter. It must have been lost in the mail."

"Or he's decided to ignore it." Helen took out an emery board from her desk drawer and began to work on the fingernails of her left hand. "You've written him a lot of letters since then, haven't you? And haven't they all been sugar sweet?"

Ruth nodded reluctantly.

"If he got the letter he's probably going to ignore it, and put it down to a momentary lapse in love. And if he never got it? Then no problem."

"But I'm still confused. I still think we need more time."

"Then take it. Take all the time you need after he gets back. Put off any wedding for a few months until you're ready."

"And in the meantime? What do I do about Sal, who is right here, right now?"

"You haven't promised him anything, have you?" Helen gave her friend a sharp look. "If I were you, I'd enjoy his company, but don't lead Sal on. If he's looking for anything more than friendship you have to let him know where things stand. It's only fair."

"But that's just it. I'm not sure where things stand. I really like him."

"Do you want to marry him?"

"I could marry him. I know I could. And I think we could be happy together. I don't think money is everything, but Sal is a very wealthy man and he likes spending money on me. And I enjoy lovely things."

"Nothing wrong with that. I'd love to be rich and have Gary lavish me with gifts." She carefully studied her nails. "But trust me when I say, it's not enough." She started filing the nails of her right hand. "Marriage is forever, darling. You have to really love the guy before you take the plunge. Do you love Sal that much?"

"One minute I believe I do, the next—I'm not sure. But I know I have to make a choice at some point. I'm twenty-eight years old and I want to have a family. I can't wait much longer or it'll be too late."

"Nonsense. Women are having babies well into their thirties all the time." Helen continued to file her nails. "Look at me and Gary. We want kids, and I'm almost as old as you. There's still time for all that for both of us. I wouldn't worry too much about it all. These things have a way of working themselves out."

"I guess so. It's all up to this horrible war. It's got to end sometime soon so we can get on with our lives."

❦

It was soon after Labor Day when Jim's next letter arrived. Ruth picked it off the hall table and headed for her room to read in private, but rather than answer her anxieties, it left her feeling more anxious and unsettled than ever.

August 4, 1943RR

My darling Ruth

I just received your letters of July 3, July 5 and July 8. Reading them all in one sitting and in chronological order I enjoyed them immensely.

You write about my being shy around Harvard grads. Darling, it isn't that I wouldn't express my ambitions that would cause me to be shy. It's just that I believe in class distinctions. If it were not true, why is it that here in the Army one doesn't mingle with officers. True, it's because of difference in rank, but way back in the early days, it was and has been a tradition that an officer is of a superior quality socially and physically compared to an enlisted man.

Why is he so concerned about class distinctions? I wish he would recognize how clever he is just as he is.

My education has been purely business administration and not liberal. I once started Boston College in the evening but gave it up as too much to handle in my circumstance. I've always had a thirst for knowledge and luckily still possess the desire. I have always yearned to study higher mathematics as preparation for an engineering career.

Looking at the facts as they stand now, too much time and energy and money has been spent on my studies at Bentley to give up a career in accounting entirely. Rather, I shall try to coordinate these subjects with what practical experience I obtain here.

I just received your letter dated June 16. Where it has been all this time the Lord only knows.

There it was, at last! A reference to her letter of June 16.

But reading along my heart skipped a beat upon your asking to cancel the engagement. Don't scare me like that, please.

How about a picture of you? Please remember my soul needs strength, I love you.

Your Jim

Ruth shook her head as she reread the last few lines. He had finally received her letter asking they put their engagement on "hold." But he didn't have any response. It was as if he didn't understand the words she had written. What did he think I meant? Ruth wondered.

She glanced back at the date scrawled at the top of Jim's letter: August 4. Almost two months had gone by since she had written Jim that she needed more time to reconsider everything. He's not taking me seriously. Helen is right. I never mentioned it again, and only sent letters filled with foolish gossip to entertain him. It's no wonder he didn't respond, she concluded. Maybe what Mother said is true? Once promised you can't go back on your word.

Ruth leaned back into the soft cushions of the overstuffed armchair and closed her eyes. So that settles it? I'm engaged to Jim and I just have to accept it? No matter who else comes into my life?

She slowly rocked her head from side to side. I don't know what I want. I'm so tired and confused. I think what I really need is a good night's rest.

Early fall was always one of Ruth's busiest times of the year. It seemed every client had decided on a major advertising campaign for the Christmas holidays. Ruth had little time for anything but work.

"You're going to burn out," Helen warned her. "Maybe you should hire a couple of students to help you with some of the simpler designs."

"Not possible. I can't afford it."

"But you must be making good money, now."

Ruth paused and looked at her friend. It was lunch time and Helen had practically had to drag her to the Devonshire Deli.

"You have to eat. We haven't had a good conversation in weeks. I need to know what's going on with you. Take a break once in a while, will you?"

"I have so much work to do. I can't afford the time."

Helen wondered at her friend's business savy. "So you should bring someone in to help you."

"Like I said, Helen, that takes money up front. I can't hire someone if I can't pay them. The stores are all good for it, but some take more than 30 days to pay their bills."

Helen couldn't help but wonder at her friend's business savy. "So you work your fingers to the bone in the meantime? Makes no sense to me."

She took a bite of her sandwich. "I like getting a steady salary. Every week I get a paycheck. You? You do the work, but never know when you'll get paid. I don't know how you do it."

"It's the curse that comes with working for yourself. If you want to be your own boss, you have to put up with the roller coaster ride that comes with it."

"At least you won't have to do this for the rest of your life."

Ruth took a sip of hot tea and shrugged her shoulders. "I don't know. If I marry Jim, I may have to keep on working. The last letter he wrote was all about how much he was likely to earn if he goes back to his old accounting job. He was a junior in the firm before the war and made $30 a week. Not much to live on."

"And what about if you marry Sal? Would you keep working then?"

"Sal has not asked me, and if he did, I don't know what I'd say."

"But you'd stop working wouldn't you? Settle down and start having babies?"

"Stop it, Helen. You're trying to cause trouble. I have no idea what I would do if I married Sal, and since he has not asked, I haven't given the matter any thought."

Helen looked at her friend and decided to change the conversation.

"Is Jim still in North Africa?"

"I don't know for sure. Now that the Germans and Italians have been driven out of the desert they will most likely move his unit. He can't say much about what they've been doing but I'm sure his squadron was involved during the invasion of Sicily this past summer. He's a crew chief now—some sort of hydraulic specialist. And his health is a lot better. Living in the desert was tough on all the men. They had to sleep under nets to prevent the bugs and spiders and who knows what else from eating them alive."

Helen reached for a pickle.

"I read in the newspaper that between the sand and the scorpions a lot of the men couldn't wait to get out of North Africa. Sicily might be poor and wartorn, but at least the climate is a bit better."

Ruth had to agree. She was glad Jim was finally moving out of North Africa, though he was not out of danger. He was now flying, delivering supplies and transporting troops to the front. That couldn't be safe.

August 30, 1943

Hello dear:

Haven't heard from you for a bit, about 10 days now. Must be the mail I guess. I am writing this sitting in my ship. Yes, hon, since last writing you they assigned me to crewing a plane and it has been my home ever since. But don't tell the folks, for they may worry needlessly. The way I look at it, if my time is due, nothing will prevent it. I like flying and it keeps me on my toes most all the time.

He had enclosed a copy of a money transfer slip. He wanted her to buy Christmas presents for both his and her family.

Please do this for me, for it gives me pleasure as well to make my folks feel happy on that day of all days.

Let's hold Christmas as we always did when I was a kid. And don't bank any of the money. Spend the balance as you will, just as though I were home and taking you places. Buy a hat and remember me every time you wear it. Buy a new dress and know that I feel proud to make you happy.

*I don't care a darn how unconventional this all seems to you. Just do
what I ask for you might as well learn now that I shall be the master
of the house and my word shall be law. Please give me your love as
I give you mine and our happiness can be assured to be everlasting.*

I have always been "Your Jim"

Ruth re-read the last few lines. Was Jim making a joke or was he serious
that he could master her? She'd have to set him straight.

CHAPTER 12

SICILY

Weeks went by with no word from Jim. By mid-November Ruth had begun to worry. Jim never let this much time pass without writing. Maybe his family had heard news and they just hadn't told her?

The streets were nearly deserted by the time she got home from work. Too tired to talk, all she wanted to do was grab a cup of tea, go up to her room and crawl into bed. But the moment she saw the envelope on the hall stand with Jim's familiar scrawl across the front, she gave a sigh of relief. Slipping her fingernail under the edge of the sealed flap she pulled out two dozen sheets of lined paper. There were two very long letters. The first had been written over several weeks.

"Is that you, dear?" Mrs. LeBlanc called out from the parlor.

"Yes, Mother. Just got home."

"There's a letter there for you on the hall table. I think it's from Jim."

"Yes, Mother. I have it. Thank you."

"Nothing wrong, I hope," her mother's disembodied voice continued.

Ruth stuck her head into the front room. Her father was sound asleep in his chair, an open newspaper spread awkwardly across his chest. Her mother sat knitting what appeared to be a sweater, skeins of dark green yarn tucked into large canvas satchels at her feet.

"Haven't had a chance to read it, yet, Mother."

"Well, there's no need to be huffy about it." Her mother glanced down at her handiwork and looked back at her daughter. "You look tired, dear. You work too hard. And you've missed your dinner again. I left a plate on the counter in the kitchen."

"Thanks, but I grabbed something at South Station before I took the streetcar. I'll just have some tea and go up."

Without waiting for her mother to respond, Ruth escaped to the kitchen. While she waited for the pot to boil, she quickly scanned through Jim's letters. The first section was filled with his usual observations of people and the weather.

September 11, 1943 Sicily

Hello there:

I am somewhere in Sicily as you probably know. Lots of interesting things have happened but can't mention anything. Italy surrendered for one thing and that does save some time and a lot of lives. The country would have been wrecked anyhow so it was the smart thing to do.

Ruth recalled a headline she had read in the *Daily Boston Globe:* "Nazis On The Run." In mid-August, the Allies had taken Sicily, forcing the Germans to withdraw to Italy. Since then, Allied forces had landed on the Italian mainland, and were making steady progress Northward. Ruth could only pray that by now Jim was far away from the center of the conflict.

Sicily is a better climate than No. Africa but that's about the only difference. People in the country are friendly but very poor.

The women here don't seem to be as pretty as the French gals on the average. Man! But there are some pretty girls in Algeria.

Honestly, Ruth, Hedy Lamar couldn't hold a candle to some of the young Spanish and French girls of that city. The fellows use to stand on the sidewalk and moan as they went by. But somehow, there aren't too many good-looking middle-aged women here in Sicily so I guess they don't keep that creamy complexion for long. (What a wolf says you!) Well, women are the big thing in a soldier's life when he gets a chance to come in from out of nowhere and sees them.

Men are so predictable, she thought. They all have only one thing on their minds most of the time. Silly.

September 17

Dearest Ruth:

Am I burned up. The gremlins have finally caught up with me I guess. I have been sent back to a convalescent hospital for some R&R... I'm very tired and will write more in a little while...

Ruth glanced at the calendar on the kitchen wall. Tuesday, November 16th—nearly two months since Jim had written. He had been sick again. She quickly continued reading, scanning down the page.

September 23

Dearest Darling:

Well hon, I'm out of the hospital and back in harness. It may be a few days before I fly again but I can still fly. I'm pretty sure of that.

Got your letter dated September 5. Glad to hear that you are getting some fun at least some weekends. I want you to keep laughing. For I shall surely be fed up on grim realities by the time its all over with. Keep young and beautiful as the song goes.

October 19-22, 1943

Hello Ruth old girl: Thought I'd drop a line seeing as how I haven't heard from you for some time. Remember you have someone on this side of the ocean that would appreciate hearing from you.

You want to know about local color? I'll admit I didn't say much about the Frenchys in No. Africa or about those crummy Arabs. But you had Ernie Pyle and even he couldn't tell the truth.

They won't let us tell what we really feel at times so why write a pack of lies?

As I write this, the Italian prisoners are singing their fool heads off. No worries in the world. I'm tired tonight but want to write and let off some steam. You might as well start getting use to me blowing off steam now as well as later. I'm not a fairy prince but right now a dirty, unshaven, toothless, tired mechanic.

Pardon me, my love, while I dispose of a damnable pest namely one field mouse. Charlie I call him. He insists on living in my barracks bag. And now he wants to bring his bride in too. And now you can't blame me for not balking at that.

The darn fool never heard of an outhouse. He takes advantage of me, using my clean clothes for all-purpose convenience. Ah but his very hours are numbered.

"Charlie - if you behave like a good little mouse, I won't deprive your little bride of one more night of bliss. But by gosh, tomorrow I'll toss this big shoe, and won't miss."

Your Jim

Ruth couldn't help but wonder at Jim. With all the troubles in the world, Jim's focus was on figuring out how to trap a tiny field mouse. At least he still has his sense of humor, she thought.

She reached for the third letter that had been enclosed with the first two. It had been written in early November.

Hello dear Ruth: The opportunities to write you are so varied and not always predictable that I write on the fly more or less. Thinking of you many times during the days work.

Have become accustomed at long last to the conditions of living now. I wouldn't know what to do if suddenly I found myself back in my own room with that big bed and soft mattress. The desk in one corner and dresser in another. All my clothes neatly pressed and hanging orderly in my closet.

Will I continue the habit of making up my own bunk and sewing and washing my own under clothes? I wonder.

I should like very much to describe the country but I shall wait until I can tell you in person. Censorship forbids.

There is not much sense, I find in telling anyone at home the gory details of certain occurrences for it's not what you wish to hear.

We all know you people are doing what you can to speed on Victory and so it is part of our job as well to see that your morale is kept as high as possible.

In view of this fact let me say that our boys are doing a fine job. They face a stubborn and well-trained enemy but have proven to be just a bit better all around. It is that old American pride which even in a democracy binds people just as closely as any so called nation of one breed and culture.

We all gripe at times and blow off steam, but who doesn't? It's good for what ails us. Every one of us wants to see the end of this show but the end that will be ours for keeps.

Eating plenty of oranges now. Bought 170 oranges for $1.60 today from an Italian farmer. They are juicier than the African type but not quite so large.

So darling, I am still on that job that keeps me away from you but eventually it will be finished and we can have our day.

Your Jim.

Next day she shared the letter with Helen.

"I'm not sure what's wrong with Jim, but he keeps getting sent back to the convalescent hospital."

"Might be a bug or something, or exhaustion." Helen tried to sound sympathetic.

"Maybe. Jim doesn't complain, and he's already back at work, flying."

"Then I wouldn't worry too much. If the Army Air Force thinks he's well enough to fly, then he is. Be happy he's working in transports instead of bombers."

"I'm grateful he's in the Army Air Force at all. He could just as easily have ended up in the infantry. Those are the soldiers with the toughest jobs."

"Has he had a chance to see anything of the countryside? Sicily is supposed to be beautiful."

"The only thing of beauty he constantly mentions are the women! Apparently gawking at all the beautiful women is a very popular pastime for soldiers."

Helen laughed. "Well, you can't blame 'em."

"I guess not. One thing I can be grateful for is that Jim doesn't seem too interested. He keeps getting photos and letters from those girls he met back in St. Louis when he was at Kessler Field, but he passes them around to the other men."

"I'd say your man is one exceptional creature. Talk about faithful!" Helen couldn't help but tease her friend. "He's handed beautiful women on a platter and rather than play the hero soldier and string them along, he passes the bounty on to his friends. I'd say that's remarkable."

"I think it's kind of sweet. But that's Jim for you. A one woman guy." Ruth replaced the letter in her satchel and reached for her ruler.

"Going to write him right back?" Helen asked.

"I should. But I've got to get back to work. If I don't, I'm going to miss my deadline."

Helen shook her head and wondered at her friend's discipline. "Don't forget to take a break later. There's a sale on at Filene's. We should go at lunchtime."

Ruth didn't respond. Her mind was already totally absorbed in lettering a headline.

❋

Sunday, November 14, 1943

Dearest Jim,

It's cold here this November, and getting colder every day. The holidays are just around the corner, and we are already planning our Thanksgiving and Christmas feasts. We have to plan way ahead to be sure we have all the ration stamps we need. I've invited a few of the old crowd to join us this year. You remember Joyce and Elaine and, of course, Sal? They all promise to come, and I promise to take a few snaps and send them to you.

Justine and I went shopping yesterday and found some nice things to give as Christmas gifts. I have my eye out for something special for you and have been looking for gifts you might want me to buy for your family. I received the money transfer you sent so you don't need to worry about that.

Work has been hectic with all the holiday advertising. I'm grateful for the business and my clients are pleased with the results. I know you have said you don't care if I continue working after we are married. I've decided I would like that. I think it's important for a woman to retain some measure of independence, and I've worked so hard at building my reputation as a good commercial artist, I would hate to give it up so easily. You understand don't you dear?

Must go. I have a busy day at work tomorrow. I'll sign off by wishing you peace and my love.

Your Ruth

Ruth reread the letter twice. She thought it hit just the right tone. Not too mushy but not too distant. Still confused about her own feelings for Jim, she found it hard to write with any real warmth.

I think the letter's fine, she thought. I'll send him another one after Thanksgiving, filled with lots of gossip. He'll like that.

She found an envelope and stamp in the top drawer of her desk and slipped the letter inside. At the last minute she clipped a small curl from her hair, taped it to a second sheet of paper and scrawled a short note:

"Here's something to add to that wallet I sent you long ago. You can think of it as a little Thanksgiving present from me, grateful you are still safe and sound."

She felt a little foolish as she sealed the envelope, but it was the kind of gesture that Jim would appreciate and it took no effort for her to do it. If it makes him happy, then I'm all for it, she thought.

"Ruth dear, are you in your room?" Her mother called out from the bottom of the stairs. "Can you come down for a few minutes? I need your help with a few things."

Ruth sighed deeply. Lately her mother had needed her for a lot of things.

Planning this, organizing that. I don't mind helping, but couldn't she ask Justine once in a while? she thought to herself.

Her mother was waiting at the kitchen table, the family ration tickets and a notepad already filled with scribbles in front of her. "I want to plan out our holiday dinner to be certain we have all the ration tickets we need. I'm making a list of everyone who is coming." She paused and consulted her notes. "I have Aunt Cora and Uncle John, the four of us, and how many of your friends are you inviting?"

"There should be three if they all accept. Sal and two friends, Joyce and Elaine."

"Sal?" her mother asked, surprised.

"His father has to be in Washington that weekend and his mother is going with him. That leaves Sal here in Boston by himself."

"Doesn't he have any siblings he could join?"

"He has a sister who lives in Brookline but she's going off with her husband's family. I thought it would be nice to have Sal join us. You don't mind, do you?"

"Of course not, dear. I'm just surprised, that's all. You'd think with all that money, Sal could take himself on vacation for the holiday."

"I'm sure he would if he wanted to," Ruth countered. "But he's so busy at work right now I don't think he would or could take the time off. And taking a vacation? With all the men his age at the front, fighting, I think taking a vacation is the last thing on Sal's mind." Ruth studied her mother for a moment. "You don't really like Sal do you, mother?"

"What a thing to say. Sal seems like a very decent boy."

"Man, Mother. Sal's a man."

"Man, then. He seems like a very nice gentleman." She took her time trying to find the right words. "I wouldn't want this Sal to come between you and Jim. You are, after all, an engaged woman."

"I may be engaged, mother. But that doesn't mean I can't change my mind."

"What do you mean?"

"So much has happened in the last two years. I've changed, Jim's changed... even you've changed." She pointed to the list on the table and the stack of ration tickets. "Look at us. We can't even buy what we want at the store anymore. We have to plan and plot and use these foolish stamps in order to even buy a pound of sugar to make a holiday pie!"

"We have to do our part for the war effort, dear."

"I understand that, but do you understand that nothing is the way it used to be? In your day people fell in love and spent months, maybe years getting to know each other until they knew for sure this was 'the one.' It doesn't work like that anymore. The war has made everything crazy. People meet, they fall in love and there's no time to get to know each other. Not really. And they make promises they really shouldn't keep."

Her mother stared at her. "What are you saying?"

"Jim and I hardly know each other, except through letters. We had no time at all before he got shipped out. He's smart and clever with machines, but he's very hard on himself and resents anyone who seems to be doing any better. He's not the same man I fell in love with. The man I knew was full of laughter and fun and good times."

"I see. And now, when he's away and fighting for our country, you've decided to find someone else," her mother said, accusingly.

"Don't make it sound so harsh, Mother. I told you, I haven't decided anything. I'm just letting you know what I'm feeling, and it's confused."

"And this fellow Sal helps you feel less confused?"

Ruth gave her mother a sharp look. "There's nothing I can tell you to make you understand, is there?" She shook her head. "I need to take a walk. Justine can help you with the planning." And with that, Ruth stormed out of the kitchen.

✻

Thanksgiving arrived, and the holiday went as well as could be expected. The relatives arrived with their ration tickets; Ruth's friends, Joyce and Elaine, each brought a vegetable dish; and Sal arrived with flowers and an oversized box of Whitman's Sampler chocolates for after dinner, which impressed everyone, including Mrs. LeBlanc.

"How did you manage to get your hands on it?" Justine demanded. "This is the biggest box of chocolates I've ever seen."

Sal gave her a wink. "Oh, I know some people, who know people."

"You know the right people, that's for sure." Justine grabbed a second chocolate before anyone could stop her.

"Don't be greedy, Justine," Ruth scoffed. "You eat too many of those and you'll start putting on pounds before you know it."

"It's been ages since I've had a real piece of chocolate, Ruth. There is no chance that eating two or three pieces today is going to put on weight. I bet I could eat that whole box and not gain one tiny ounce."

Sal laughed. "Give Justine a break. Ruth. She can eat as much chocolate as she wants. After all, it is Thanksgiving."

Justine grinned. "Sal's right. It's a holiday!

Ruth suppressed a sudden wave of anger. There was no point arguing with her sister. She glanced at the clock on the mantel. Five minutes of four. Not much daylight left, but enough for a quick walk if they headed out immediately.

"Sal, how about a brisk walk around the block to walk off some of this dinner?" She turned to her two friends. "Joyce, you and Elaine come too. I need a little air. Justine can help with the clean up."

Justine was about to say something in her own defense but Elaine interrupted. "Oh no, we can't leave it all to Justine. Joyce and I are happy to help out, Ruth. You and Sal go. We'll help clear the table." She turned to Ruth's mother. "Mrs. LeBlanc, you've worked hard all day. You go into the front room and relax. We girls will handle everything." Without waiting for her to protest, the two friends and a very reluctant Justine picked up empty dishes and headed towards the kitchen.

Sal took Ruth's arm. "Looks like it's just the two of us."

Ruth hesitated. She had intended this to be a communal walk with all three of her friends. Not a one-on-one with Sal.

"Come on," he whispered. "Let's escape while we have the chance."

She looked toward the kitchen. "I should really help out here."

"You help more than anyone. Take a half hour off and let them do the chores for once. Come on, grab your coat." He gave Mrs. LeBlanc a smile. "Don't worry, we'll just walk around the block a few times and come right back." He quickly maneuvered Ruth towards the front door, before her mother could protest.

Once outside, Sal led her to the end of the walkway. "Let's head down towards the beach. It must be nearly high tide by now."

The air was cold and the wind brisk as they headed down Bromfield Street towards the ocean. Bright light shone from front parlor windows, and they could see families gathered inside each home as they passed. Thanksgiving dinners were still being served. Once darkness fell, windows would be covered with blackout curtains, and the street would go dark, but at the moment it was filled with streams of warm light falling in bright horizontal lines across frozen lawns and sidewalks.

"The McGoverns have quite a crowd visiting." Ruth remarked as they passed by number 92. There were three cars in the driveway. "Their son Paul was drafted. I think he's going to the Pacific."

"Tough time to go. Holiday time, I mean," Sal remarked.

"No time is a good time to go to war." Ruth said quietly.

The two friends walked on in silence. Finally, Sal asked, "Have you heard from Jim, lately?"

"Not in the last few weeks. The mail is so sporadic. One day they deliver three letters all at once and then nothing for a month."

"But he's okay? He's doing well?"

"I'm not really sure. He likes what he's doing. He's become quite an expert at fixing and maintaining almost every plane engine in the fleet. They've promoted him to chief of inspection, which makes him very unpopular with the guys he used to call his friends."

"What do you mean?"

"It's his job to be sure the engines are working properly on all the transports and bombers. When a plane's engine gets damaged, his crew has to fix it. Sometimes they have to disassemble an entire engine, figure out what's wrong, fix it or replace it—all in record time. It's his responsibility to see that the planes keep flying. And Jim's determined to do just that. He's even invented some gadget to test the engines after they've repaired them and before they put them back on the planes. But he has to push the crew to meet deadlines, and they don't like it."

"I can understand that.'

"He doesn't say it in so many words, but I think he's feeling very isolated, and lonely."

Sal was silent for a minute. "Managing people is hard enough when you are just doing business. I can't imagine what it's like to get soldiers to do their job when guns are blazing and bombs are falling all around you. I really admire Jim."

"He's a good man, Sal." She paused, considering how much more she should add. Finally, she decided she needed to share her concerns with her friend. "The war has changed Jim. He used to be so light hearted and fun. But now when he writes, most of what he describes are the problems he encounters. The poverty, the people... He's become very serious."

"War is a nasty business. There isn't much fun about it."

The two walked on in silence. After a few moments, Ruth said, "I think what I'm trying to say is that the Jim who writes to me now isn't the same Jim I knew back in '41."

Sal kept walking on as if he hadn't heard her.

"Did you hear what I said, Sal?"

"I heard."

"So what do you think? Am I crazy? Am I being unreasonable to think that the guy I promised to marry wouldn't change? In the middle of fighting a war?"

They had reached the end of the block. The seawall was just across the street and beyond it the ocean shimmered in the early evening light.

"Come on, let's sit for a minute." Sal took her arm and led her to a nearby bench.

"How long has Jim been overseas? Since you've actually seen him?"

Ruth thought for a moment. "He volunteered in February of '42 and shipped out last fall. I saw him at Fort Dix in mid-August."

"Almost a year and a half ago." Sal calculated. "And during that time the only communication you've had is through letters. He's in the middle of a war, and he's been in battles all over North Africa."

"And now he's in Sicily."

Sal patted her arm. "Who knows what he's really been through, Ruth or what he's seen first hand." He waited a moment, then continued, "Does he ever write about it?"

"The censors are pretty tough on letters home. They go through every letter and either black out or cut out anything they don't want the soldiers to share. Jim's careful and only had one letter censored, and that was when he first joined up."

"Does he share what he's feeling about all this?"

"He's become very serious and hard on himself."

"Go on."

"Soldiers don't have a lot of time off, but when they do, the men go into town and party. They drink and go dancing with all the local girls. I don't have a problem with that, in fact it's what I would expect but Jim refuses to join them. Only rarely does he drink and he never allows himself to go to those clubs all the soldiers go to. And then he gets sick. He's been in and out of hospitals a few times."

"Sounds like he works too hard and doesn't give himself a chance to relax."

"He's become conservative about life, especially religion."

"Facing death every day on a battlefield can do that to you."

"More than that. He's developed some very conservative views about marriage and children and a woman's place in the world. One minute he praises me for working so hard, and encourages me to keep on working, the next, he wants me to quit as soon as we're married so I can start having children."

"Oh."

"I'm sorry, Sal. I'm just whining on. You shouldn't have to listen to this."

"What are friends for if not to listen when a friend wants to whine? I'm just sorry things are not going more smoothly for you."

He reached out a gloved hand and gently pushed Ruth's hair off her forehead. Ruth smiled at the gesture and shook her head slowly.

"If there's anything I can do to make it easier for you," he hesitated. "... You know you can count on me."

"I know Sal, and I do. I do count on you." She reached out and placed her hand on his arm. "It's good to know I can rely on you."

The moment was filled with tenderness and hidden meaning. Both Sal and Ruth knew more was being said than was spoken. They sat in silence, neither wanting to break the stillness that surrounded them. Suddenly the air was filled with the blast of a car's horn and a rush of seagulls lifting into the sky. A car full of young people raced by.

"I think we should be getting back," Ruth said. "It's getting late."

"Your mother will think I've spirited you away for sure," Sal added.

That's not too far from the truth, Ruth thought to herself, as the two friends quickly rose and began the short walk back up Bromfield Street.

Once Thanksgiving was past, the rest of the holiday season seemed to fly by in a blur. With all her work for Christmas behind her, Ruth spent much of her time buying presents, going to social events at the USO and a dance or two sponsored by the Women's Defense Corps. She was still busy with plane spotting, though the likelihood of a German pilot finding his way to the shores of Boston in December of 1943 were next to nil.

She continued to send Jim newsy notes of all the doings around both the LeBlanc and Doherty households. But Christmas came and went without any word from Sicily.

1944

CHAPTER 13

ITALY

It wasn't until late January that she finally received several letters from Jim that arrived all on the same day. Included were several photos of a very thin looking soldier, a toothless grin spread across his face. His clothes were loose fitting, and his hair cut close to his scalp. Ruth gasped when she saw them. Jim had told her about losing a couple of teeth but she had no idea how extensive the damage was until she saw the photos. Every front tooth in his mouth was missing. Where two straight rows of shining white teeth had been, there now was a large, gaping hole. Sharply pointed molars on both top and bottom rows, barely touched. To Ruth, he resembled a vampire.

November 25, 1943 - Thanksgiving

Darling Ruth,

Here again that old day rolls around bringing back vivid memories of home. We had a delicious dinner today. None of those confounded rations.

I recently returned from a well-needed rest, (as the enclosed picture shows) yes, hon a rest camp. It was beautiful there. And above all things I had a hot bath. Feel like a new man again. The place I was at was a resort of some kind. Slept between sheets and on a spring. Wow! What a sensation a bed is now.

Bought you something while there and mailed it today. It will probably reach you sometime in the middle of January. Hope you like it.

Guess what, I'm looking straight at—a big fat mouse. There he sits on the edge of a box just looking at me. Scram, buddy, can't you see I'm trying to get my girl in her good graces again.

Hope you like the package I'm sending you. In it you will find a silk parachute (part of one) used once by a French pilot. (God have mercy on his soul.) I want a scarf made out of it, for it will be a remembrance of some pretty hectic days. There's more to the story but it can wait until later.

My misfortune with my teeth doesn't worry me exactly, but darling, it will put a crimp in our nest egg. I have been debating with myself whether or not I should send these pictures home. They are terrible. However the rest did me good and I shall guarantee to look better if and when I return to you. Will you greet me with open arms or will I hit you just about the time you have one of your indifferent spells? Open arms I hope.

I love you Ruth, Jim

Ruth re-read the last paragraph and studied the photograph. She felt confused. He was not telling her the truth about what was going on. Clearly, the accident a month or so ago had been a lot more serious than Jim had let on. Whatever had knocked out his teeth could have killed him. He was lucky he hadn't been seriously injured.

And what did he mean by "indifferent spells?" When was she indifferent? She had tried to be attentive to the hidden signals in his letters but it wasn't easy responding to his changing moods.

"I don't know how to respond to Jim anymore," she told Helen the next morning. "Look at this photo he sent."

"Oh, my god. He looks a wreck."

"And that's after he got back from the hospital."

Helen felt sympathy for her friend. "He certainly looks like he took it on the chin."

"Not funny, Helen."

"Sorry. Just trying to lighten the moment."

Ruth tossed the letter and photos on the desktop. "I hope he takes better care of himself from now on and the Army pays to have his teeth fixed."

"It's the least they can do for him," Helen agreed. "What else does he have to say for himself?"

Ruth shuffled the pages of Jim's next letter. "These letters were written before Christmas, but I'm just getting them now. He's an old fashioned guy, writing about building Christmas stables and having just the right tree, and he's annoyed with me for not writing more frequently, or longer letters."

"That's crazy, Ruth. You write him all the time."

"But many of those are quick V-Mail letters. And he hates getting them." She searched a page. "Listen to this... he's referring to V-Mails I sent back in November.

You know when you come right down to it; we are all little boys when mail call sounds. Especially so when packages arrive. Home seems near enough to see the wrappings and stamps, chocolates and cakes, pictures of loved ones and a book or magazines a fellow always had to read while home.

I wanted a long letter that night. One that I could take to my shelter and lie down on the sack and read over and over. The sight of two helpless little white envelopes enclosing just one tiny sheet of paper in each, struck me then as being typical of my popularity among those whom I loved.

"So I don't send V-Mails anymore. And I've decided it's better not to let him know too much about the local gossip. I wrote and told him about my friend Roberta and her husband getting a divorce. She's just one of three that's going through a split up. I made the mistake of telling Jim. He has some very strong opinions about such matters."

Depressing news to say the least. It seems as though all your friends' love affairs are going to the junk pile. Roberta and her husband are both young aren't they? Lets hope he tires of this new "feature" in his life and regains his senses before a tragedy occurs that will make one very sad girl. That old human element "sex" sure causes a lot of trouble.

Men are funny. They show signs of good character but one fault seems prevalent. It isn't the cry of nature, for that is a lot of baloney. It merely is one of the common drawbacks of society today. It's easy to do the wrong thing. And Ruth, the whole business is as old as Jonah. Why worry about three men cheating on their wives. Is it worth talking about? Would you really consider having them in your company? Look down on them for heavens sake. And let them know that they aren't much above the dog in the street that chases after any female.

Helen shook her head. "He has developed a superiority complex. You're going to have a lot to contend with when Jim finally gets home. But I think you can handle it."

Ruth wasn't so sure. "We'll wait and see."

🌸

December 29, 1943

Hello dearest:

Was much surprised and overjoyed at receiving my birthday gift. Thanks very much darling for your thoughtfulness.

Another of your friends break their engagement? What is the war doing to you folks back there anyway?

There probably are differences we must iron out before entering on any such venture as we intend. Clear headedness is my viewpoint. At least I've seen it work more over here. Use your bean over here and you may be able to keep it.

I want to be sure about everything and I've seen enough of the results of battle so that I can really appreciate peace

It's going to be so nice and comfortable having a lovely wife who makes a home pleasant to live in. My drawbacks are numerous and you are going to either learn to disregard them or like them. Don't think you can change any habits I might have. That's a mistake most girls make. Marrying men with obvious faults thinking they can make new men of them.

Oh well, time will tell. I love you darling and want so much to get back to you for good.

Your Jim

She re-read the last long paragraph. She knew Jim had faults and draw-backs. It was good to know he recognized that. But that doesn't mean he can't change or improve, does it? If you recognize a fault you don't just say, "Oh well, that's just the way things are." You work on making things better, right?

Ruth shook her head as more doubts about Jim flooded her mind. They only increased when she turned to the third letter in the envelope.

December 30, 1943

To Ruth—Guess what?

The other night I received the "Journal of Commerce" from my old boss. They still seem to keep in contact with me. I hope I can decide completely what my life's work is to be. Whether it is a white-collar job or one having to do with machinery. Of course you know I haven't done anything but mechanical work for the past year or so and naturally I am becoming proficient with tools.

However, the aviation field will no doubt be crowded. Anyway there is always the W.P.A. Or is there?

Looking back, I did have a pretty nice job. It didn't pay too much but I liked it and I was always clean as a pin.

How about all you femmes in them there factories? Are you all going to vacate or stick around as you did in the last war? Lots of chaps have decided to let their wives work while they mind the house.

Seriously though, I'm going to leave it up to you as to whether or not you keep working. As long as you're feminine when I want you to be and the home isn't disrupted, I can readily appreciate how dull the days can be just sitting around.

Marriage is to make a home and a place where a man can enjoy life normally with care and attention he wouldn't get otherwise. It also fulfills the natural obligation of a woman to bear children. One of the finest attributes of humankind.

Now he seemed confused about his job and about whether he would let her keep working! "Let her?" Ruth felt her face getting hot. And did he really think it was her obligation to have a baby? Of course she wanted children, but she didn't think it was her obligation!

Well darling, I'll say goodnight now, as I have two other letters I must answer. Courtesy demands it.

Love you Ruth, Your Jim

There was a lot she and Jim needed to talk about when he got home and before she would ever marry him. But things would just have to wait. There was no sense trying to settle these things in letters. It was too easy to be misunderstood.

"Are you joining me tonight, Helen?" Ruth asked. "I promised Mrs. Glastnick that I would help out with the buffet at the Stage Door Canteen."

Helen looked up from her typewriter. "I totally forgot." She quickly flipped through her calendar. "I didn't write it down when you told me last week, and I promised Gary I'd meet him for dinner."

"You should call him and tell him to meet us there. Guys are welcome to help out you know."

"Maybe another time. You know my Gary. He needs his Pabst Blue Ribbon at the end of a long day's work. And the canteen doesn't serve alcohol."

"But we always have delicious food and cool music," Ruth teased. "You two could be twirling the night away in just a few hours."

"Another time, Ruth, I promise." Helen turned back to her desk.

"It's a fun way to support the men, Helen. They get some free food and a night of fun with a chance to dance the light fantastic with a local celebrity. The place is packed almost every night. You should come sometime."

"Are you going alone?" Helen asked.

"Sal's going to meet me there."

Helen gave her friend a long and knowing look.

"Don't give me any trouble. He's friends with the canteen's manager, and promised to help out backstage. It's chaos unless there is at least one person in charge of moving people and furniture and Sal's very capable at managing things."

"I bet." Helen looked amused. "Well, have a great time and don't stay out too late. Work tomorrow, you know!"

"I know. I promise to get home early."

In fact, it turned out to be a short night. About seven o'clock the heavens opened and a heavy, cold January rain started to fall on the city. It kept the soldiers away, and the volunteers home. Even the band arrived late and left early. By nine thirty Sal found Ruth in the kitchen putting away food.

"I think it's time I drive you home. This storm has kept everyone away, and I doubt if there will be many more soldiers looking for a sandwich."

Ruth glanced over at Mrs. Glastnick. "You go now, Ruth. You've worked hard, but there are so few here tonight, we can handle things now."

Ruth promised to return the following week and headed out the door with Sal. A mix of freezing rain and snow was still falling as they carefully picked their way across the parking lot. Standing water covered the icy ground, and she felt her feet begin to slip on the black ice. Only Sal's steady arm kept her from falling.

"Driving is going to be nasty," Ruth cautioned.

"Don't worry, I'll be extra careful and go real slow."

With so few cars on the road and no plows in sight, it took them nearly an hour to crawl the ten miles home from Boston to Wollaston. As Sal inched the car up to the curb Ruth could see her mother keeping watch, peeking out from behind the drapes in the front parlor.

"You should come in and stay the night, Sal." Ruth urged. "It's too dangerous to keep driving."

"I'll be fine. It's only a short drive, and I promise to stay under the speed limit."

"You should come in. In fact, I insist. You can sleep in the back room. We have space."

Sal stared beyond the frozen windshield at the icy road ahead. "Maybe you're right. I didn't want to say anything, but the car's been slipping on the icy pavement the whole way." He considered his options. "Okay. I give in. No sense killing myself when we can both be home safe and warm."

"Smart choice. Come on."

Sal turned off the ignition and set the brake. The front door of 180 Bromfield Street was opened before they had a chance to reach the porch railing.

"Come in out of this wretched weather, you two." Mrs. LeBlanc stood back, and let Ruth and Sal shake off the rain. "Be sure you stand on the carpet, now. I don't want you ruining the floor after all."

"Yes, ma'am," Sal answered.

"Don't worry, mother. No rain on the floor."

"Hang your coats on the rack at the top of the cellar stairs and put your boots at the bottom. That way they'll be warm again when you're ready to leave."

"Sal's staying the night, mother," Ruth declared. "It's just too dangerous to keep driving in this mess."

Mrs. LeBlanc looked from her daughter to Sal. "I see." There was no sense in arguing. She could see for herself that the storm was only going to get worse and her daughter had made up her mind.

"Sal's going to sleep in the back room, Mother. I'll make up the bed. Why don't you make us a cup of tea or maybe Postum? I'll just grab some sheets and a blanket from the linen closet." Ruth didn't wait for her mother to answer and headed up the front stairs.

"I don't want you to go to any trouble on my account," Sal pleaded. "I can sleep on the sofa."

Ruth leaned over the stair bannister. "No trouble. Besides, it'll only take a minute to make up a bed." She pointed towards the kitchen where her mother was already setting up the tea service. "Now go get a cup of tea and warm up. I'll get your room ready."

It took a few minutes for the kettle to boil as Mrs. LeBlanc tried to fill the awkward silence with mindless chatter.

"How did things go tonight at the canteen?" she asked. "It's been a difficult winter so far, don't you think? So cold. I don't remember when it's been so cold. One day after the next. Seems like it will never warm up. Ever since Christmas. Don't you agree?"

"It has been cold most days."

"You begin to wonder if spring will ever come again, don't you? I mean that's what it feels like when it gets so cold. These days are so long. And dark. Of course, it's nothing to what our brave boys are facing every day." She rearranged the tea cups on the tray. "I'm glad you and Ruth and all these people are volunteering to help our soldiers feel at home no matter where they're from. I think the Stage Door Canteen is a wonderful idea. It's all for a worthy cause."

Sal nodded.

Mrs. LeBlanc gestured for Sal to sit down. She moved awkwardly around the kitchen table, stopping behind one chair and then another, unsure whether to sit or stand.

"Is anything wrong, Mrs. LeBlanc? I hope my being here isn't a problem."

She ignored his question.

"You're a good man for helping our Ruth and doing your part, Sal. I appreciate that. And I know it wasn't your choice to stay home from the war. You're doing important work here, I know that." She measured her words very carefully before continuing. "I'm sure you don't mean any harm, spending so much time with Ruth. But I have something I've been meaning to say to you, and tonight is the night I'm going to say it."

Sal looked up at her, a puzzled look on his face. "I don't understand."

"You know my daughter is engaged to be married. To a soldier. Who is overseas fighting for his country. She is engaged to a wonderful man, and I don't want you interfering."

"I know—she's engaged to Jim Doherty." He paused, then continued. "Mrs. LeBlanc, there is no way..."

"Enough! I don't want to hear any excuses." She raised her hand as if to stop any further discussion. "I've seen how much time you spend with Ruth, and how much attention you give to her causes. I just want you to know I'm watching you. And if anything you do or say causes Ruth to break her promise to James Doherty, you'll have me to answer to."

"I think you've got this all wrong."

"Really? Are you trying to tell me that your relationship with my daughter is strictly friendship and nothing more?"

"I think that's something for Ruth to decide."

"What do I need to decide?" Ruth stood in the kitchen doorway, a look of anticipation on her face.

Her mother reached for the kettle. "Nothing dear, we're just discussing if you might like tea or Postum."

"Tea, if there's enough to spare," Ruth answered. "You know I can't stand Postum."

"I agree with you," Sal chimed in. "Postum is a poor excuse for a cup of joe."

His words sounded nonchalant but Ruth sensed tension just under the surface. "Is anything wrong? Did I miss something?"

Sal flashed Ruth a quick smile. "Nothing to be missed. We're just talking about what a great program the Canteen is for the soldiers."

"It is a wonderful program, isn't it!" Ruth declared and reached for one of the graham crackers her mother was serving. "I think it's one of the best things we can do for visiting G.I.s," She nibbled on the cookie. "These boys would never have a chance to meet some of these theatre people or see them perform. We didn't have anyone special tonight because of the weather, but we've had some big names come through in the last couple of months." She turned to her mother for confirmation.

"I wouldn't know, dear. I've never been to a Canteen event."

"You should come sometime, mother. They're a lot of fun."

"I think you'd enjoy it, Mrs. LeBlanc. I'd be happy to come by and pick you up sometime if you'd like." Sal reached into his breast pocket and took out a business card. "Here's my number. You call me anytime you want to join us."

Mrs. LeBlanc shook her head. "No, I don't think so. You young people are just fine on your own. You don't need an old woman poking around."

"What are you talking about?" Ruth protested. "There are lots of women your age working behind the scenes. Mrs. Glastnick is the woman in charge of my shift, and she's got to be in her sixties. You'd fit right in."

"No, no, no, it's not for me. I'll bake cookies for you, dear, but glad handing strangers is not something I care to do."

"But these are soldiers and sailors, Mrs. LeBlanc. Men just like Ruth's Jim, who are far away from home. They just want to have a good time. We all want to show them how much they mean to us." Sal stared at the older woman, daring her to disagree.

Mrs. LeBlanc ignored the challenge in his voice. "Well, it's getting late. I think we should all turn in, don't you?" She turned to her daughter. "I'm sure Ruth has everything ready for you in the back room, Sal. Right dear?"

Ruth looked up from her cup of tea. "Everything's all set." She glanced at Sal across the table, his teacup untouched. "We'll just finish our drinks first, Mother. You go on up."

Mrs. LeBlanc hesitated, unsure whether to leave or not. "Well, if there's anything you need, Sal..." She let the thought hang, waiting on a response that did not come.

"All right, then. Well, I expect I'll see you in the morning. Breakfast will be at seven."

"Don't trouble yourself, Mrs. LeBlanc. I'll be up and out very early tomorrow. Have meetings all day."

"Whatever the case. Breakfast is served at seven o'clock sharp in the LeBlanc home."

With that, she turned on her heels and marched out of the room.

Sal watched her leave. "Did I do something to offend your mother?"

Ruth shook her head. "She's fine. She just doesn't like surprises." She sipped the hot liquid. "And tonight, you're a surprise."

"A pleasant surprise, I hope for you," Sal commented.

"It is actually a little exciting having you stay overnight. Something unexpected. It reminds me of the sleep overs we girls used to have as kids. We'd stay up all night, talking, playing games and telling stories. At least we'd try to. We were all asleep long before morning."

Sal laughed softly. "This is not going to be one of those nights. I'm bushed and I have to get up and leave early. I really do have a meeting first thing. If you don't mind getting to work early, I can drive you in. It'll save you a train ride."

"What time?"

He paused, thinking. "Probably need to leave close to six-thirty. You in?"

"Sounds like a plan." Ruth smiled at her friend. "We better get to bed, then."

"Going to tuck me in?"

"I think you can tuck yourself in, my friend."

"Well, at least give me a friendly goodnight kiss," Sal encouraged her.

Ruth stood up and laughed. "You're incorrigible."

"Just a quick one," Sal responded. "It can be my reward for getting you home safe and sound."

Ruth looked down at her friend, all innocence and pleading. "All right." She laughed again. "I guess it's the least I can do."

She leaned over and kissed his forehead. "There. You are rewarded."

Sal stood and took her hand. He moved closer, his lips inches from her ear. "I think something a little more personal is called for, don't you think? I mean, it is a really bad storm out there."

He didn't wait for an answer. Instead he moved even closer. She could feel his breath on her skin as he hesitated. Slowly and with great care he kissed her full on the lips. It only lasted a moment, barely enough time to call it a kiss, but just as their lips parted, Ruth felt the tip of his tongue touch hers. It was as if a bolt of lightning had shot straight through her.

"That was nice," Sal whispered. "Now, which way to my bed?"

Ruth stared blankly at him, confused at the swirl of emotions she was feeling. She attempted to release her hand from his grasp but he held it tight against his chest.

"Uh... Your bed? I'm not sure. I mean, of course. Whatever...."

She pointed to the kitchen door. "It's just down the corridor. Last door on the right."

"Thanks." He didn't move. "You want to show me?"

For the next few moments the two stood facing each other. Neither spoke but they didn't have to. She understood his invitation. And he knew she could not accept it. Not now, not yet, not in this place.

He finally let go of her hand. "I guess I'll see you in the morning."

"Yes. Six thirty. At the front door. Good night, Sal."

Two weeks after the storm, Jim's next letter arrived.

January 25, 1944

Dearest Ruth,

What's this? My gal passing out chow to those wolves at the Stage Door Canteen? Well, hon don't be foolish and pass up any millionaire sons.

Ruth was suddenly overcome with a wave of guilt. How did Jim know about her work at the Stage Door Canteen? And what did he mean about not passing up millionaires? Sal was a wealthy man, but there was no way Jim could know about her growing relationship with him. She certainly had not mentioned it and she was almost sure Justine would not have done so.

Who else could have told him? She looked down at the letter again and suddenly she knew. Mother. She must have written Jim about her volunteering at the canteen, all about the storm and the night Sal had stayed on. She shook her head. Should she feel guilty? Nothing had happened, after all. Her mother was just butting in where she did not belong.

I have invented and built something for my squadron for which I have been commended. Can't say what it is though. At first it was a nightmare but out of that fantastic idea grew a very solid and labor saving device. I'm bragging again, but I just wanted to let you know that I know you're behind me and that's why I try so hard.

You know I hate to think of the post war problems that are ahead. Shipping alone is going to be a headache. And not trying to be pessimistic but practical, unemployment is bound to result due to shutdowns and plants retooling for commercial use. So I wouldn't think of us making any big purchases on credit. Pay as we go, even if we only have one or two pieces of furniture. I do think it best that we plan wisely and together.

Something tells me that no matter what I suggest the final windup is going to be your way anyway. You're like that and I'm like this and I am old enough to treat these differences lightly.

As long as you're happy, you will make a good wife, so who am I to step up headstrong and cause my home to be another battlefield? How frank I am at times! Loving you the way I do isn't anything heavenly or blissful. I love you because you're you. Just Ruth LeBlanc, the girl I always thought to be attractive with a wonderful personality and best of all, of unquestionable character.

Ruth paused. "Unquestionable character?" She was beginning to wonder. Since the night Sal had driven her home in the storm, she had found herself struggling with the real possibility she might be falling in love with him.

You seem quite concerned about whether I have changed. Of course I will have changed a bit. I notice that myself. More and more each day I am becoming more conscious of the fact that I am drifting from the world I used to know: white collars and shined shoes with checkered suits and panama hats.

Can I get back? I often wonder. Could I now walk into the office on Summer Street and speak intelligently with the General Manager? I know for a certainty I would be a regular guy on a bridge crowd, but you didn't fall in love with a steel worker or a rough laborer. Not that my every word reeks of blasphemy. It isn't quite that bad. But it's been so long since I have listened to a quiet conversation that didn't deal with the infamous characteristics of life.

I want to go somewhere and think where it is quiet. I want to rest my head on a soft bunch of grass and look up at the stars and think. You probably can't understand my mood at present.

I sit here, rather tired. My mind is taken up with the problems at hand since I am a department head. My clothes are perfumed of a certain fluid. My hands are hard with many scars, Little slips and scrapes here and there have defaced them to a point of a fisherman's paws.

My teeth, ugh!

Still slim as ever, if not slimmer. The old watch crystal has born the brunt of many knocks. It is scratched a bit. Oh well. Give me another year of this and I'll really be mean.

Still, all my love to you dear,

Your Jim xxxxxx

She slowly folded the letter back into its envelope and carefully placed it in her satchel. She would read it to Helen the next day at work.

"Jim sounds so tired and worn out. I think he's feeling down, Helen, and I don't know what to do for him."

Helen reached for the letter and re-read the section where Jim mentioned his invention. "Sounds to me like he's doing okay. He has the energy to invent some new-fangled machine. And they've commended him for it. So something's going right."

"Still I think he needs a rest."

Helen agreed. "I don't know how they can expect these men to just keep going with bombs dropping all around them and men getting killed everyday. They're living in a nightmare. It's no wonder your Jim sounds a little depressed."

Ruth wondered how much she should confide in her friend. "I told you about the night of the storm..."

Helen looked at her, puzzled.

"The night Sal stayed over."

"Oh, yes. You told me your mother was pretty upset with the whole arrangement."

"She was. And probably for good reason." Ruth fiddled with the buckle on her satchel, unsure how to continue.

"Go on." Helen urged.

"Mother's always suspected I've had a thing for Sal. I've assured her it's not true. I love Jim. But Sal's a friend, and I enjoy his company. We spend a lot of time together at different events and functions. Until the night of the storm, I thought that was all it was. And now, after reading Jim's letter, I'm thinking my mother has written to Jim, warning him about Sal."

"Why? What happened? What have you not told me?"

"We kissed. It wasn't a big kiss and it was only a moment, but it was" Ruth paused, searching for the right word, "exciting. I've never felt like that before."

"Are you talking fireworks?"

Ruth felt her face blush red. "Just for a moment. It felt like a bolt of lightning went right through me."

"And you liked the feeling?"

"I loved it. I wanted it to last. I wanted it to happen again."

"And did it? Did Sal kiss you again?"

"He wanted to. I know he did. In fact he nearly invited me to his bed."

"Oh that would have been sweet."

"Sure, just what my mother needed—to find the two of us in each other's arms bundled together in the back bedroom."

Helen chuckled. "So you didn't go to bed together. In reality, nothing actually happened."

Ruth shook her head. "Nothing. Not then and not since. I've seen Sal twice in the last few weeks and neither of us has mentioned it. Maybe I'm imagining everything."

"From what you're telling me, I think you've been hit by the sparks of love. And when that happens you've got no choice but to give in."

"But I don't want to give in. I still love Jim. At least I think so. And I'm not really sure I want to start a romance with Sal. After all, it was only one kiss. Who knows what Sal was thinking."

"Sooner or later things will become clear."

Ruth looked up at her friend. "I know you're right. I just wish it would be sooner. I don't want anyone to get hurt."

"My best advice: be honest. Write to Jim again and let him know that you still need time to figure things out. No instant wedding when the war's over."

Ruth nodded.

"And in the meantime, tell your mother to stop interfering. And talk to Sal. Let him know how you feel. Give him a chance to let you know what he's thinking."

It was the end of the following week when Ruth finally saw Sal again at the Canteen. She was in the kitchen when the swinging doors to the ballroom opened and Sal walked in, a new volunteer on his arm. She was tall, blonde and very pretty.

"Everyone, I'd like you to meet my friend, Carmen. She's here to join you in serving our brave soldiers a healthy meal." Sal gestured toward the room full of women. "I'm sure you will make her feel right at home." Immediately, there was a welcome buzz and nods of "welcome honey," "certainly," "of course," "glad to have you."

Sal walked Carmen to the end of the counter where Ruth was busy filling small bowls with pickles. "Ruth, would you make sure my friend feels welcome?" He didn't wait for an answer, but quickly leaned over and gave Carmen a quick peck on the cheek. "I'll be working with the band, tonight, honey. I'll come by later and see how you're doing."

"Okey-dokey." Carmen flashed him a broad smile as Sal turned and left.

"So, how can I help out?" Carmen asked eagerly. "What do you need me to do?"

Ruth stared at the new volunteer, taking a moment to process what just happened. Finally, she picked up a bowl and handed it to the new girl. "You can serve the pickles."

"I can't believe it," Helen exclaimed the next day. "Sal has a new girlfriend?"

"That's what it looked like. Her name is Carmen, and she's gorgeous. Looks like a model straight from the cover of Life."

"Well that's a bit of a shocker, considering how he came onto you just a few days ago. Although it shouldn't be a surprise. Sal is tall, dark and handsome and rich." She thought for a minute. "I guess that takes care of your confusion about Sal. He's clearly interested in other women."

"I guess so. I should have known something like this would happen. I haven't been honest with Sal. It's no wonder he would move on. Like you say, he's a great guy and a real catch for some lucky gal."

"And, of course, you're engaged to Jim." Helen reminded her.

"And I'm still engaged to Jim." Ruth sighed. "Are you going to lunch?"

"Not today. I've got to run errands for the boss."

They promised to meet the next day.

Just as well, Ruth thought. I'll have some quiet time alone. Jim's latest letter was still in her satchel. Ruth had already read it once but she had brought it with her to work. She was waiting for lunchtime so she could read it again. She opened the envelope and unfolded the thin sheets of paper.

Two small photos were included in the letter and Ruth studied each closely. In the first, Jim, dressed in a leather flight jacket, was leaning casually on the back end of a donkey. Army humor, she thought. A friend of Jim's must have snapped it as a joke. In the second photo Jim was sitting with other soldiers in some sort of barracks. A small dog sat on his lap, and along the edge of the print he had penciled in the word, "Dopey."

For quite sometime now, I have suspected someone of stealing those sandals you sent me. If what I saw today proves anything, it wasn't a "someone" but a "something." Yes, my little dog, Dopey was caught sneaking off with another chap's moccasin. So I strongly suspect the little beast.

Have I mentioned Dopey before?

Well, when I first laid eyes on him, I was moved with pity. There he was, standing at our chow line, thin as grass, his little ribs sticking out, hair all dirty and matted. His little tail was wagging away at about 500 r.p.m. He gazed up at me with such soulful eyes I couldn't resist, but asked him if he had eaten yet. No answer but a frown with a soft whine coming from what should have been a smiling face. All little dogs should be happy, I thought, and you're no exception. So, I carried him back to my straw pile (Yes, darling I sleep on a pile

of straw.) And now, he is the fattest little pooch and full of life. Yes,
I believe he is the guilty party. But I can't imagine where his hiding
place is.

Ruth paused. Leave it to Jim to adopt a stray dog as a pet. She knew
he had been feeling quite low lately. Perhaps this little dog would lift his
spirits.

Today's mail saw a letter from you dated January 10. Please don't
ask me again where I am. My censor is extremely reserved. I can't
even discuss the weather.

Once and for all I am everywhere in the Eastern Mediterranean.
Wherever my work may take me. I handle emergency jobs so
perhaps that can suffice for my absence of letters.

You ask about my health? Most of the time I'm all soiled, my clothes
covered with a greasy substance (too tired to take a helmet bath)
dirty clothes, mussy hair and guilty conscience. I'm happiest when
all covered with dirt and doing something I feel is important. I know
I'm not getting ahead very fast. I am definitely out of the officer
class with my mug and teeth. I don't give a _____! either. I'm just
another John grease monkey. I happen to have the presence of mind
to specialize in a field best suited to my mechanical abilities.

I'm not promising you anything. I'm not working in a nice clean
air-conditioned office or a well-organized assembly line or any such
thing. I work in all kinds of weather at all hours and for any length
of time it is deemed necessary and expedient to get the _____ !
job finished. I improvise and many times my simple ingenuity has
been put to the test.

War is terrible, Ruth. You people in the States can read the newspapers
and see the newsreels and listen to the commentators, but unless
you can walk down a street of shambles and see for yourself the
skeletons of people's homes and the very people themselves trying
to construct some form of shelter out of the carnage, and smell the
stink of poor sewerage and of rot and musty buildings, you can't
visualize what it must be like.

And noise? They don't give you that in the newspapers! They don't sound off on the radio the awful screech and ear splitting crash of an American or German 1000 lb. bomb.

Ruth, I want to go home, but I don't like the idea of going home and seeing untouched America and then have to turn around to go back to some war stricken area again. I want to go home and forget. I've been thinking about it all too much I guess. But I have let off some steam tonight and feel a little better. Thanks for listening.

Your Jim

Ruth re-read the last two paragraphs. War is a terrible thing. These poor men have been through so much, seen so much, suffered so much. She realized how little she knew of what was really going on. She carefully folded the letter, placed it and the photos in the envelope and gave a deep sigh.

Would this war ever end?

CHAPTER 14

EASTERN EUROPE

T he newspapers and newsreels don't really tell us what's happening," Ruth declared to Helen the next morning when she stopped by her office. "I just got a letter from Jim describing some of the things he's seen, and what the people are really going through."

"Where is he stationed now?"

"I'm not really sure. He can't really be specific—Italy or somewhere near Eastern Europe, I think. They have him flying all over. From what he writes, he's the one they call if a plane is hit or needs repair. Which means he's probably flying into enemy territory, or close to it."

"Don't say that. You'll make yourself all worried for no reason. Jim could be anywhere. If he's that valuable, you can bet the Corps has him tucked in some hanger someplace safe."

"I don't think so. It sounds like he's living in a barn, sleeping on straw and taking a bath in his helmet! Not exactly the Ritz." She tossed her satchel on the desk. "He's got a dog. Some mutt he's named Dopey."

"You're kidding?" Helen asked. "The Air Corps lets him keep it?"

"Jim found him near the camp, nearly starved to death and couldn't just leave him there." She smiled at her friend. "I'm glad he's got a dog. At least that's one friend he can count on. Ever since he got that inspector promotion he's been pretty much on his own. The men look up to him, but they're not his buddies like they were before. He's been sounding pretty down."

"You should write more often," Helen urged her friend.

"I do, every week. I tell him all about my work and family, and the news around town."

"Have you told him about how you and Sal are both working together at the Canteen and just about every other volunteer effort in Boston?" Helen teased. "I'm sure Jim would want all the details."

Ruth was silent for a moment, absentmindedly shuffling papers on Helen's desk. Finally she looked up.

"Do you think I'm spending too much time with Sal? I mean as an engaged person?"

Helen crossed her arms and leaned back in her chair. "Do you mean do I think you're playing with fire?"

Ruth felt her face blush. "I'm not exactly sure I'd call it fire."

"Well, what would you call it?"

Ruth was silent.

"I've been watching you and Sal circle each other for the last year, watching, waiting, wondering and both of you too afraid to make a move. If it's not fire, what you've got between you is certainly burning embers."

Ruth stared at her friend.

"I think that with just a little help, a fresh wind, a new breeze, and those embers would burst into quite a flame."

"And burn us both, badly!" Ruth answered. She stepped back, turning as if to go. Then stopped and turned back.

"You're right of course. There's always been a little something special about Sal. He's the kind of man I always thought I would marry. Successful, cultured, interested in theatre and the arts. He's just so sure of himself. I find that very attractive in a man."

"Not to mention he's filthy rich," Helen chided.

Ruth blushed again. "Money does help, I have to admit. But it's not everything. When I met Jim, all those things I thought were important didn't seem to matter. He was kind and gentle, and considerate. He didn't—he still doesn't—have two nickels to rub together, but whatever he has, he shares. And he loves me."

"It's up to you. I think if you wanted to start something with Sal, all you need is a little spark."

"And then what? What about Jim? How would I tell him?"

Helen leaned forward, resting her head in her hands. "Maybe you don't."

"I don't understand. What do you mean?"

"You love Jim, right? And you agreed to marry him. But that was a long time ago,—a lifetime ago, before this bloody war really got going. You're two very different people from those two lovers who fell for each other one winter's eve three years ago."

"That's not totally true," Ruth protested.

"For the last six months you've been telling me how confused you've been. One day you love Jim, the next, you're unsure. Meanwhile Sal has been a good and faithful friend to you. He's been your rock. You rely on him and, even if you won't admit it to yourself, you love him." Helen sat back. "I think you need to stand back and be honest with yourself, Ruth LeBlanc."

Winter dragged on, cold and raw. For days, grey clouds blocked the sun, and with average temperatures in the low 20s, it was too cold for most outdoor activities, including the ice skating that Ruth loved. She continued her volunteer work for the Canteen and the USO but unless there was a special event, she, like everyone else in the northeast, hunkered down in a warm home, sheltered against the cold. No one ventured out if they didn't have to. By late February, Ruth was beginning to feel claustrophobic.

There was no word from Jim.

"I'm sure if something has happened to him, they would tell us," Mrs. LeBlanc declared. "The War Office would send his family a telegram, wouldn't they?"

Mr. LeBlanc tried to reassure his wife. "Stop worrying, Bertha. I'm sure Ruth's young man is okay." He looked up from his newspaper long enough to nod in the direction of his daughter. Ruth was perched on a stool at the kitchen counter, splitting peas for dinner.

"I can hear you both. If Jim were injured or missing in action, I'm sure they would tell his family."

"I'm certain they would, dear." Mrs. LeBlanc tried to comfort her daughter.

"It's been almost a month since his last letter. The Air Corps had him flying all over. When a plane goes down or gets damaged Jim and his crew are sent out to repair it and get it flying again."

"He should be promoted or at least receive a medal for all the work he's doing," Mr. LeBlanc mumbled.

"It doesn't work like that, Dad. Jim's just doing his job. Although he did write about a month ago and tell me about some invention of his that got some attention from his Major. Some sort of testing device to save time when they are rebuilding engines. But he couldn't say more than that."

"I'm sure you'll receive a letter any day now, my dear." Ruth's mother tried to sound encouraging.

Ruth nodded. But it was mid-March before Jim's next letter arrived. She found the envelope tucked under her bedroom door.

Back in her room Ruth settled into the soft armchair by the window and opened the envelope.

February 10, 1944

Dearest Ruth,

Not much I can tell you right now, at least about my work. Dopey got himself into a pack of trouble recently. He was foraging around in his usual manner when he evidently came upon a mother dog and six of the cutest little puppies. She took off after him and away he went yelping his fool head off.

He is the most stupid beast I ever did see. Big ears, feet just made for a dog three times his size. I can't image what sort of company his mother must have kept. I guess she believed in "variety is the spice of life" for our little Dopey is a variety of dogs. Your Jim

February 16

I wish my letters could tell you of an increase in rank but you know, dear, my lot falls last in line every time.

Yours truly does not seem to make the proper impression with those lofty ones holding the whip. Ah me! Why should I comment on such trivialities? I am confident that my work is correct though my social habits do not including gambling with the "right" crowd.

This game of war is going to get rough sooner or later and someone is bound to get knocked around a bit. Your letters keep me level headed, please, please remember that fact.

March 5, 1944

There isn't much to say about over here. We are all pretty busy now.

I heard from home—my step-brother will be made a Staff Sergeant ahead of me as he boastfully predicted. For some reason or other I just don't seem to get up there. Oh well, I am satisfied with myself in knowing that there never has been any backfires on my work.

There is a personal satisfaction in knowing that one has done his best and the results are up there in the clouds.

You know dear that working along day in and day out—sometimes under rather severe and often uncomfortable conditions—a guy can get so that his nerves are tense and his temper is held on a hair spring release. Well, I have been like this many times but always when I lie in my sack and begin to study the stars and know that those same stars will be above you a little later, it all brings you a little closer.

Darling, I was thinking the other night, how nice it would be if I were where I might turn my head and see your blonde tresses lying on a pillow near me and be able to reach out and touch you. Oh well, no time to think like that now.

Your Jim

P.S. Dopey, my dog is getting big and his hair is becoming shiny, with all the good care given him. He is the squadron pet now.

Ruth glanced over at the top of her dressing table. She had placed the photo of Jim with Dopey up against the mirror.

You little bugger of a dog, she stared at the picture. You keep my Jim safe, you hear me? The dog stared back at her, its head tilted to one side, a twinkle in his eyes, as if asking "So, what's new with you?"

Saturday morning, Ruth decided she had to write Jim a letter before doing anything else. She checked the clock on her bedside table. It was too late to catch the morning pickup, but if she hurried she might make it to the post office before they closed.

For the next hour Ruth focused on filling sheets of writing paper with all the latest news and gossip. She also encouraged Jim to stand up for himself and claim credit for all the good work he was doing.

> *I know how talented you are, Jim and how much you care about doing the best job you can. I'm glad you have such pride in your work. But you must not be shy about putting yourself forward. You have to be willing to brag a little about what you do so that your superiors realize your value.*
>
> *When you come home, you will need to assert yourself. If you want to move ahead in the world of business, and I hope you do, you cannot be afraid of letting your boss recognize how talented you are. Don't worry, I'll be there to give you a pep talk if you need it.*

She ended with a tease and a promise.

> *We're still having trouble getting beef for Mother's famous stew. You boys are hogging it all. (Only kidding.) If it would bring you home safely I would gladly send you the whole cow anytime!*
>
> *Helen and I are becoming fast friends and we can't wait until you are home again so we can all play a round or two of golf. The weather this winter has been very cold and harsh, but we are all looking forward to a warm spring. The bulbs are beginning to poke up around the back fence.*
>
> *Please take care of yourself. Stay safe. I realize you can't tell me everything you are doing, and that's just as well. Ignorance is bliss—I'd rather not know what you let yourself in for. Well, enough of that, I'll mail this immediately.*
>
> *Much love, your Ruth*

Ruth dressed quickly in an old sweater and baggy pants and headed down the stairs.

"And where are you going dressed like that?" Mrs. LeBlanc was dusting the hall table as Ruth flew by.

"Gotta run!" She held up the letter. "This needs to go out in the next mail.

I'll be back before you know it."

"You look like a peasant wearing those old things."

Ruth grabbed her jacket from the hall closet and wrapped a colorful scarf around her neck. "Don't worry Mother, I'm just going up the street, not to the State House. Besides, who am I going to run into at the Wollaston Post Office on a Saturday morning?"

"Well you're just not presentable for an engaged woman. What would Jim think, you looking like that?"

She reached for the front door knob. "I think Jim would be happy to see me looking any which way, Mother." She swung the door open and was gone.

It was a short walk to the local post office at the end of Beach Street. Ruth made the half mile in under eight minutes and was just in time for the last mail pickup of the day. Mr. Schroeder was behind the central counter sorting through a pile of paperwork as she slipped her letter into the slot marked "Military."

"Good morning, Mr. Schroeder. Beautiful day, don't you think?"

The postman looked up over the top of his wire-rimmed glasses, gave a half-hearted shrug and grunted. "Haven't been outside."

"Well, make sure you do. It's a beautiful day. Spring is coming."

"If you say so." The postman went back to sorting his papers. Ruth turned to leave and ran straight into Sal Marcusio.

"What are you doing in my part of town this morning?"

Sal grinned. "Looking for you!"

Ruth looked at him, puzzled.

"I stopped by the house. Your mother told me you were mailing a letter, so I took a chance and came here."

Ruth blushed, embarrassed at the way she must look in her old coat and baggy pants. Sal was impeccably dressed as always. I'll kill mother for sending him out after me, she thought. Out loud she stumbled over her words. "Well, lucky you. You found me."

Sal took her arm and led her towards the entrance. "I thought you might want to go to lunch. It's such a beautiful day and the clam shack down at the beach just opened for the season."

"Isn't it too cold to eat outdoors?"

"They have a small dining room out back. We'll be fine."

Ruth hesitated. "Can I go looking like this?"

"Absolutely. You look fine. It's a clam shack after all!" He took her hand. "Come on, I have something important to ask you."

Sal opened the heavy glass door and led Ruth down the granite staircase. A new Ford Convertible Club Coupe sat at the curb. Its dark maroon body and chrome trim sparkling in the noon-day sun.

Ruth was stunned. "You got a new car!" she exclaimed. "How did you swing that, or should I ask?"

Sal laughed. "I know a guy."

"What else is new?" She shook her head in wonder. "Your job at the factory lets you have special privileges and all. But a new car?"

He held the door open and Ruth slid onto the soft leather seat.

"Actually the car's not new, well, not exactly. It's a '42. One of the last on the line before Ford switched to manufacturing jeeps and trucks for the war. Last month, I was able to snag a permit to buy this baby. It's one of the last ones they had on the lot." He turned the key in the ignition and the V8 engine roared into action. "Shall I put the top down?"

"I don't think so, Sal. It's still a little cold to be joy riding."

"Oh, come on, the beach is just down the road. You can handle a little chill for a few minutes." With that, Sal flipped a couple of levers near the top of the windshield and pushed a large button on the dashboard. Suddenly the canvas top released and began to lift and fold into itself. The roof moved back out of the way, and the car filled with bright sunshine and chilly air. Ruth took her old wool cap out of her pocket and pulled it down around her ears.

As Sal turned the car away from the curb, Ruth couldn't help but feel a sense of privilege and pride. Everyone on the sidewalk was staring at the shiny new Ford and the happy couple inside. It's good to be rich, she thought.

It only took a few minutes to drive to the beach. Sal parked the car in the Clam Shack's side lot.

"Aren't you going to put the top up?" Ruth asked.

Sal looked up at the sky. "No sign of rain or snow. I think we'll be safe for an hour or so." He led Ruth around to the front entrance, passed the open patio and into the small dining area. He chose a table under the windows and away from the drafty doorway.

"I need your help with a special project I'm involved in," Sal explained as soon as they were seated.

"What kind of project?" Ruth looked around the room. The Clam Shack was designed as an outdoor restaurant, catering to the summer beach crowd. This early in the season it was only the die hard clam lovers who were brave enough to face the elements and fill the few inside tables. The one heater in the back wall tried in vain to keep the customers warm but the heat dissipated quickly and never reached the front of the room. Ruth kept both her cap and her jacket on.

Sal ordered two bowls of New England clam chowder and plates of full belly clams with a side of onion rings they could share.

When the chowder arrived, Ruth didn't start eating right away. Instead she grabbed the bowl in both hands and held on for warmth. "Brrr. At least the chowder's hot."

She looked at Sal but he didn't seem to notice the cold. "So tell me about this project of yours. Is it a secret? Am I sworn to secrecy?" Ruth teased.

"No, not at all. It's a project for the WMC. The War Manpower Commission."

"I've heard of them. What do they do?"

"For a long time now, the government has been worried that people are getting really tired of war. We all are. Fewer workers are signing up to work in the war plants, or are leaving after only a short time. Especially women. It's tough work making bombs and building jeeps. At the beginning of the war it was all hands on deck. Everyone wanted to be a part of it. Even you, as I remember."

"I joined the plane spotters, and the USO, and the Stage Door Canteen. I'm still doing my part."

"Not exactly what I mean, but you get my point. It's been almost three years and people are tired."

The clam plates arrived and for a few minutes they were distracted by the meal.

"The thing is, we need to reinvigorate the public. Make them realize there is still a lot more to be done. We need to keep war workers at their jobs."

"And how are you going to do that?"

"I've been asked to head up a committee for something we're calling 'Boston Loyalty Week.' We're planning on a week-long event sometime this coming summer. There'll be speeches and music and parades, and I need you and a few other commercial artists to help promote it. We're even thinking of an Army Air Force show that will feature Japanese and German planes that have been captured. We're thinking of calling it: Shot Out of the Sky."

"What can I do?"

"We've got the Retail Board of Trade involved and more than 100 stores and industries signed up. Most of the stores will make posters and displays for their front windows. We've asked if they can promote war products too. It's going to be a big deal. The idea is to put new life and vigor into Boston patriotism."

"Will they need newspaper advertising as well?"

"Of course. And radio ads, too. Best of all, the stores and industries have agreed to finance the project. We're not asking you or the other artists to work for nothing. You'll be well paid for your time and talent."

"That's a refreshing change." Ruth took a sip of water. "I don't mean to sound cynical, but I've been volunteering for everything for so long, it'll be nice to get paid for my work."

"You're a very talented woman and I would never take that work for granted. I was told to put together a team to make this happen and I want you on it."

"When are you starting?"

"Our first meeting is Monday night. That's why I wanted to meet you today. I need you on board now. Are you in?"

Ruth didn't need to think about it. Promoting patriotism? Creating posters and displays? This was something she could easily do. Not only that but she would be working closely with Sal. She didn't hesitate.

"Of course you can count on me."

"Great. I'd hoped you'd say yes. We're meeting at my factory in the North End. It's an easy walk from your office. Six o'clock sharp, Monday night."

"I'll be there," Ruth agreed. "Sounds like it will be a great event."

That evening at dinner Ruth tried to explain the project to her parents.

"It will be a full week of displays, events, and speeches—we are even try-ing to get a few big name celebrities to perform. The purpose is to remind people that we are still at war. It's not that they've forgotten, but we've all become a bit complacent. As if things are supposed to be this way."

"You don't need to remind me that there's a war going on. Just look at this dinner." Mrs. LeBlanc gestured to the plate of Spam. "I don't know how we're supposed to get on with only this make-believe meat to eat."

"I think it's a grand idea, Ruthie," her father interrupted. "And Sal will be just the person to get it off the ground." He reached his fork towards the meat platter for a second helping, then thought better of it. "That man's got a lot of moxie. If anyone can wake this city up and get us moving, Sal can do it."

"What does he want you to do, dear?" Her mother passed Ruth a big bowl of mashed potatoes.

"They need commercial artists to design posters and help with store displays. There'll be a lot of work to do."

"Another volunteer committee?"

"No, this is a real job. That's the best part. The WMC is going to pay us for the work. All the stores and shops are pooling their resources."

"It's actually good marketing for the stores." Mr. LeBlanc chimed in. "Good press. I'm sure they'll get lots of coverage for this—what did you call it again?"

"Boston Loyalty Week," Ruth replied. "It's happening this summer. Late July to early August. The committee is meeting Monday night to plan and strategize."

"Well, just let your mother and I know. We'll be happy to help out if we can."

"Don't worry, Dad, the whole city will know all about it soon enough. Sal will make sure of that."

Monday evening after work, Ruth made her way to Sal's business in the North End. She had never been to his office, but the doorman was expecting her. "The meeting is in Mr. Marcusio's office on the fourth floor. You can take the elevator on the right." He pointed down the hall.

"Thank you," Ruth responded. "Am I the first or the last to arrive?"

"I think you're the last, ma'am. The meeting started about an hour ago."

As soon as she got off the elevator she could hear laughter coming from the office at the end of the hallway. The door was open and Ruth peeked in. Close to a dozen people sat around a large rectangular conference table, all of them talking at once. Sketch pads and newspapers were scattered across the dark mahogany surface, and one tall lanky fellow was bent over a large pad of newsprint drawing something while the others looked on and commented.

"Ruth, come on in," Sal called out from the far end of the room. "Glad you made it." Ruth looked up to see Sal standing at the head of the table, fully enjoying the chaos before him.

"Tom here is testing out some ideas for our event logo." He pointed at the tall man who was busy sketching. "Perhaps you can help him."

"I'll try." She shrugged off her coat and left it on a side chair. "Sorry I'm late. I thought the meeting was at six."

"A few of the guys arrived early so we decided to just start right in." He turned to the crowd of people and announced, "Hey, everyone. This young lady is Ruth LeBlanc, a very talented commercial artist here in Boston and she's going to help us out." He gestured towards Ruth. "Everyone, say hello to Ruth."

A few heads bobbed up and nodded. But most of the committee were too busy to notice. Ruth smiled at the top of their bent heads.

A tall, very attractive woman was seated just to Sal's left, her hand resting gently on his arm. Ruth recognized her from the Stage Door Canteen.

"Carmen, isn't it?" Ruth asked. "Sal asked me to help with the artistic end of things."

"That's great," Carmen responded. "I'm an artist too, well sort of. Sal asked me to work on ideas for shop windows. You know, patriotic fashions. That sort of thing. I haven't got an idea in my head, but I'm sure yours is packed full of 'em. I'm sure we'll be great friends. I mean, us working together and all."

Ruth didn't respond but turned and gave Sal a quick, stiff smile. "What exactly, Sal, do you need me to do for you and the committee?"

Sal flashed a quick grin. "We need you to run interference between the designers and the production people—making sure it all works together."

Ruth was disappointed. She had envisioned her designs flying high above the crowds on banners of silk,—of life-sized posters in every store window, patriotic scenes of men and women marching towards victory. She was beginning to realize her job would be as a gopher, shuttling ideas back and forth but never making key decisions. Others would do that.

"Whatever you need Sal. That's fine by me. My job is to help the committee."

"Good girl. I know you'll do your best."

The next few weeks flew by. Word was spreading to the public that something big was being planned as a summer event, and while her designs weren't flying all over Boston, Ruth was happy to be part of the buzz.

Jim's next letter arrived a few weeks later. Like the previous letters, it was filled with a series of jottings written quickly in between one battle and the next. Although he was right in the thick of things, Jim couldn't tell her any details about where he was or what he was doing. Instead, he focused on the one thing he could write about—his little dog, Dopey.

April 3, 1944

Dearest,

All is going as well as can be expected here.

The other day, Dopey decided it would be nice and cool underneath the large wheels of a truck and failed to move when the truck did. He came out second best with a few sore spots. We are watching him closely. If he doesn't get better why I'll just have to shoot him.

Ruth re-read the last line. Was Jim kidding or was he serious?

He just sits looking up at me with the most pained expression on his funny little face. His tongue is hanging limp, and his ears are folded back against his head. He's hurt all right for he hardly moves and yelps when you rub him.

Anyhow, if he comes out of this why I'll see if I can't find a good little playmate for him. I don't trust him, he is dopey enough to get tangled up with some fly-by-night lassie and wind up a disillusioned little dog.

April 6 - Dopey was able to eat and drink a little today, but he still can't walk. An animal naturally refuses food when he is ill or injured. He just wants to lie still and be left alone. Nature has a way of healing her dumb creatures.

April 8 - Dopey is getting better. We thought for a while he might not live. He can't even walk much but today he is able to get to his feet.

April 22 - There is a chap here who is feeling quite "high" and he had some touching comments to make on your pictures. Recently his fiancée wrote him that she has fallen in love with another. Now he is a full fledged member of the "Dear John" crowd. They don't give a damn for anything or anyone.

So glad I'm not a part of that.

Ruth wondered if Jim realized how close he was to becoming a member of the "Dear John" crowd.

My work keeps me very busy. That gadget I invented now has the attention of the 12th Command. Me, big shot, huh! What I wouldn't give to be near you just for a while. Somehow your letters keep me feeling close. They help tremendously. As a matter of fact, they are all I have to hold onto.

With all my love, Your Jim

That evening Ruth wrote Jim a long letter full of details of the WMC project, what they were planning and how glad she was to be working for the committee.

May 11, 1944

Dear Jim,

Haven't heard from you in a while. Your last letters were dated from early April. I'm sure it's the fault of the mail service. We hear news from the front, but as I don't know where you are stationed right now I don't know whether to be worried or not. I just pray you are safe, wherever you are.

Lots of things are happening here in Boston. I wrote to you about the committee I have joined? I think this work would meet with your approval.

We are focused on rallying all the people of Boston to remind them how important it is to keep up the war effort, especially in the factories. After nearly three years of war, everyone is war weary. This celebration we are calling "Boston Loyalty Week" will remind everyone of the brave work you boys are doing to keep us all safe and how each of us can do our part too.

Ruth paused, her pen hovering over the flimsy paper. Should she mention her visit to the Doherty household? She had gone to visit Jim's family just before the Easter holiday. It wasn't the easiest of visits. His father had spent most of the time under his car in the driveway, tinkering with his old Ford. That left Ruth alone with Hazel. She offered Ruth a cup of tea and a biscuit, but there was only so much the two women had in common. Jim, of course was the central topic, but after a half hour they had little left to say to each other and Ruth made her excuses and left.

I had a chance to visit your family just before Easter. Both your father and stepmother are fine. No news about your stepbrother Eddy. David and his girlfriend, Doris, were supposed to stop by but never arrived. Hazel said they were visiting friends in Cambridge for the day. I only stayed for an hour or so. They both miss you and wish you would write more often.

Thinking of you every day, Ruth

P. S. I've decided to send you something for Dopey. I hope he enjoys it.

That morning she had mailed Jim a small box filled with packages of dry dog food. It was meant as a joke and she hoped Jim would appreciate it.

"What do you think of Carmen?"

It was a week later, and Sal was driving Ruth home after a particularly long committee meeting. The night air was cool but not unpleasant and Sal had put the top down on the coupe.

"Carmen?" Ruth wondered why he was asking. Does he need my approval to have her as his girlfriend?

"Yes, Carmen. She's been fussing with all these fashion ideas for weeks, but I haven't seen anything concrete yet. I think she may be just spinning her wheels. What do you think of her? Has she got what it takes or should I ask someone else to handle that side of things?"

"You mean, do I think she's got talent?"

Sal glanced across the front seat at Ruth. "You should be a good judge of that. What did you think I was asking?"

"I don't know. She seems a nice enough girl. She certainly likes you." She paused, then continued, "Does it really matter what I think?"

"Of course it matters." Sal gripped the wheel a little more tightly. "I only ask because I trust your judgment. Do you think she's the best person for the fashion angle?"

"You want me to be honest?"

"Of course."

"I think you asked her to join the committee because she's your girl-friend, and she said yes because she wants to make you happy. But do I think she knows what she's doing?" Ruth paused a moment before answering. "The simple truth is no. I don't think she has a clue how to manage the fashion angle. I think you need to find someone else to either replace her or at least help her out."

"That's what I thought."

They drove along in silence for a few more minutes.

"Look, Sal, I know a couple of people at Jordan's who would be perfect for your committee. You should contact Evelyn Connors. She's head of women's wear and has connections with the best suppliers. I'm surprised you didn't ask her before."

"I didn't ask her because Carmen said she could handle it all."

"Clearly that's not true."

He thought for a moment. "Listen, can you contact this Evelyn Connors for me, ask if she'd be interested in working with us? If she says yes, you can set her up with Carmen. Maybe the two of them can work together."

"You should contact Evelyn yourself, Sal. She's a very busy woman and an invitation from you would be far more persuasive than one from me."

"But you know her already. And these are women things. Fashion and fluff and all."

Ruth laughed softly and shook her head. "You men are all the same."

"What does that mean?"

"You want me to handle this so you don't have to tell Carmen she's off the committee."

Sal smiled sheepishly but didn't respond.

"She can't do the work, but you're afraid to tell her yourself, so you're going to have me or Evelyn do your dirty work."

"That's not totally true." He turned the car into Bromfield Street. They were almost at the LeBlanc house.

Ruth laughed out loud. "You are so full of malarkey, Sal Marcusio. Here you are, a big shot vice president of your own company and you're frightened of confronting your girlfriend with the truth that she's not as talented as she thinks she is."

Sal shrugged. "What can I say?" He pulled the car to the curb in front of number 180. "Will you call Evelyn and set things up?"

The two sat for a few moments, neither speaking.

"I'll do it on one condition." Ruth said.

"And what's that?"

"You have to take me dancing at the Totem Pole next week."

Sal laughed out loud. "Is that all?"

"That's what I want. A night out, dancing at the Totem Pole." She paused, waiting, her hand on the door handle. "Well?"

Ruth looked across at Sal, his face in shadow, only his shape against the dim light of the evening sky. She couldn't read what he was thinking from his facial expression, but she caught a hint of surprise and pleasure in his voice.

"Agreed! Next week, just the two of us at the Totem Pole."

"Agreed." She opened the car door and quickly disappeared down the walkway and into the house.

Once inside, she leaned back against the front door, stunned. What had she just done?

❋

It took three phone calls and one face-to-face meeting to convince Evelyn Connors to join the committee. Ruth met her in Jordan's café on the lower level for tea and biscuits.

"It's for a very good cause, Evelyn. You know how important it is to rally the people behind the war effort. Besides, you should be able to sell an entire store full of the new styles. The tailored look is very much in demand this season."

"You don't have to tell me," Evelyn agreed. She took a sip of tea. "We just got in a fresh shipment of skirt suits and they are flying off the racks. Even though money is tight for most of us, those who have it want the very latest. It's my job to be certain it's available. We're busier than ever in Women's Wear."

They spent the next ten minutes chatting about trends and styles. Ruth finally looked at her watch.

"Just one more thing. Sal asked another woman to join the committee as a fashion coordinator. Her name is Carmen something or other. She doesn't have any particular fashion expertise as far as I can tell and I'm sure she will defer to any suggestions you make. Sal wants you to be in charge."

"Is that so? And am I supposed to be the one to tell this Carmen that she is now second in command?"

"I think you need to talk to Sal about that. He can fill you in on all the details, but I'm sure it will be fine." Ruth reached for her purse. "Listen, Evelyn, it's been wonderful to talk with you, and I'm so glad you will be heading up the fashion committee of Boston Loyalty Week. See you next Monday evening?" On that note, Ruth escaped.

"When is your date with Sal?" Helen asked two days later when they met in the office break room. "Now that you've done him the favor of setting up Evelyn as fashion coordinator, when does Sal take you dancing?"

"I'm not sure. We tentatively planned on this Saturday night."

"That's great. Artie Shaw is playing at the Totem Pole."

"I hope so. That clarinet! He's the absolute best." Ruth closed her eyes and began to sway and move to some musical refrain that only she could hear.

Helen laughed as she watched her friend begin to circle the room, holding her arms out as if holding an invisible partner. "I should tell Gary, and we should meet you there."

Ruth stopped in the middle of a turn. "Please don't!" she pleaded.

Helen looked at Ruth, stunned. "And why ever not? Gary loves Artie Shaw, and the two of us haven't been to the Totem Pole since" she paused, thinking, "since I don't know when. It's hard enough to get Gary to go anywhere, but if it's dancing to Artie Shaw, I think I can pry him out of his easy chair for at least one night." She looked at Ruth expectantly. "So what d'ya say? Shall we make it a foursome?"

Ruth didn't respond. Instead she left the room and headed down the hall to her office. Helen followed.

"What's going on, Ruth?"

"Nothing."

"Don't tell me 'nothing'. Something's going on under that thinking cap of yours. What's up?"

Ruth abruptly sat down in the secretary chair. As she unconsciously began shifting left and right, the chair squeeked under her weight.

Helen moved to the desk and leaned in close. "What's going on, Ruth?"

She looked up at her friend, her eyes beginning to tear. "I'm not exactly sure why I asked Sal to take me dancing. I even surprised myself. It was as if somebody else took over my brain, and I just blurted out the question."

"You don't have to make excuses. Sal's a good friend of yours. You did him a favor, and now he'll do one for you. That's all it means. Go dancing Saturday night and have a great time."

Ruth reached for a pencil and began to unconsciously draw circles on a scrap of paper. "There's something else." She didn't know quite how to say it. "I want it to be just the two of us. Just Sal and me. I don't want the crowd along or you and Gary. I just want it to be the two of us." She shook her head, trying to make sense of it all. Finally she looked up again. "What am I going to do, Helen? I'm engaged to one man and I'm falling in love with another."

By three o'clock Saturday afternoon, Ruth was beginning to feel light-headed. There was no reason for it. She wasn't sick. She had taken her temperature earlier in the day and the thermometer had registered a perfect 98.6. But all afternoon she had been feeling uneasy, as if some great weight was suspended from above just waiting for the right moment to fall and crush her into dust.

This is crazy, she thought. Sal's picking me up at eight o'clock. We're going dancing. We're going to have fun. We will have a good time. It doesn't mean anything more than that. She repeated the thoughts over and over like a prayer, hoping the weighty feeling would lift. But no matter how many times she repeated the positive thoughts to herself, she couldn't shake the sense she was somehow cheating on Jim.

By six she had decided to call Sal and cancel. She let his phone ring a dozen times, but he didn't pick up. She tried again at six-thirty and again at seven with the same result. By seven-fifteen she knew she had no choice but to change her clothes and go.

"And where are you off to tonight looking so spiffy?" Justine confronted

Ruth outside the second floor bathroom. "You've been in there for hours!"

Ruth considered telling her sister the truth, but knew that would only cause trouble downstairs. Her mother was still concerned about any relationship between herself and Sal. No sense giving her fuel for that fire, Ruth thought.

"I'm going dancing with the crowd," Ruth lied. 'Sal's picking me up in a few minutes and we're meeting everyone in Newton."

"You're going to the Pole?" Justine exclaimed.

"Artie Shaw's band is playing tonight; it should be fun."

"Can I tag along?" Justine begged. "I won't be any trouble, and you won't have to pay for me. I've got my own cash. I can pay my own way. Please let me come with you?"

"That's impossible, Justine. Maybe another time but not tonight."

"Why not?"

"It just wouldn't work."

"I don't know why not." Justine pouted. "I never ask for anything."

Ruth looked at her kid sister. "Look, I promise you can join us next time. This is just the beginning of the season. We've got a whole summer ahead of us." She could see Justine was disappointed. "Besides, wouldn't you want to go dancing with your own friends?"

"But Sal is so dreamy. If he's going to be there, I'd dance the night away for sure."

Ruth began to walk towards the top of the stairs. "I've got to go, Justine. Sal's going to be here any minute."

"Well, tell your date I said hello!" Justine teased.

Ruth stopped short at the remark, paused and shook her head. No sense giving her any satisfaction by responding to that line, she thought. "I'll see you in the morning."

Ruth stood at the front window watching for Sal's car. Thankfully her parents were still in the kitchen and didn't see the Ford convertible pull up to the curb. As soon as it did, Ruth was out the front door.

"Looking splendid tonight," Sal commented as Ruth came down the porch stairs. He barely had time to open his own door before she was around the car and was seated in the passenger seat.

"Let's go," Ruth said.

"You're in an awfully big hurry," he questioned. "We have plenty of time to get there."

Ruth didn't respond.

"Top down?" he asked, reaching for the clamps above the windshield.

"Not tonight, Sal. I just did my hair." Ruth adjusted the collar of her spring coat, freeing a long blonde curl. She looked over at Sal. "You don't mind, do you?"

"Not at all. You don't want the top down? Top doesn't come down."

"Artie Shaw is playing tonight," Ruth said excitedly.

"That's the icing on the cake," Sal answered. "He has a great band."

She paused, waiting. Finally, "Listen, Sal, I don't want you to think this asking you to take me dancing means anything. I mean between us. I mean, there's nothing between us." Her words fell over themselves. "I know I'm not being clear. I just don't want you to think..." her words faded into silence. "I don't know what I'm saying."

Sal focused on the road ahead and didn't respond.

"Am I making any sense at all?" Ruth asked.

"Not really." Sal gave her a quick smile. "I think you're like most women when it comes to love and relationships. You're confused."

"Love?" she gasped. "What are you talking about?"

Sal kept his eyes on the road ahead. "Nothing in particular, everything in general." He glanced over at her. "Don't worry. I'm just teasing." Ruth wasn't so sure.

At the entrance to Norumbega Park a long line of cars waited to make the left hand turn into the parking lot.

"Looks likes it's going to be a crowd tonight," Sal remarked. "Shaw's band has always been a big draw." He pulled into the first available spot. "Are you ready for a fun night?" he asked.

"Absolutely."

"Come on then. Let's boogie." He took her hand and together they headed up the long path towards the entrance.

Sal checked their coats and they found a small booth just to the right of the main ballroom. No sooner had they ordered drinks than Sal insisted they get out on the dance floor. For the next hour, they stayed there, twirling, sliding and swaying to the big band sounds of Artie Shaw and his orchestra.

"I thought you wanted to dance," Sal teased when Ruth finally begged to take a break.

"If I don't sit down for a few minutes, I'm going to collapse," Ruth laughed, falling back into the comfortable sofa that lined one side of their booth.

"Okay, but only for five minutes. Then we're back up. There's a Two Step contest coming up, and I intend to win it with you!"

"You've got to be kidding?"

"I know you can do it. I've seen the way you dance. We're sure to make the finals."

Ruth laughed and shook her head in disbelief. "I'm not so sure. There are a lot of very talented dancers here tonight. Some of them look like they've been dancing together for ages."

Sal scanned the dance floor and watched as couples twirled by warming up for the contest.

"The competition is high, but I think we've got a chance." He reached for her hand. "Come on, doll. Just follow my lead and we'll do fine."

Ruth was doubtful they would even make the first cut, but she knew there was no saying no to Sal when he had decided to do something. She let herself be led to the center of the floor, as the band started playing Artie Shaw's hit, "Deep Purple." The whole dance floor quickly filled with contestants.

Out of the corner of her eye Ruth could see the judges circling, pointing to one couple or another, gesturing that they were disqualified, and had to move to the sidelines. Ruth was surprised when the music ended and they were still on the dance floor. But there was no time to rest. Almost immediately the band started a second tune, "My Blue Heaven."

They made it to the end of the second dance, but Ruth was exhausted. Half way through the third tune, "Begin the Beguine" she watched as one of the judges approached and tapped Sal on the shoulder. They were out of the contest. Ruth was secretly thrilled.

"Sorry, Sal. I just couldn't keep up with you."

"I think you did just fine." Sal scanned the few remaining couples on the dance floor. "Come on, let's catch some air."

He led Ruth up the aisle, through the lobby and out into the cool night. A nearly full moon hung high in the sky to the east. It was refreshing to be standing under the stars, away from the heat of the crowded dance floor. She looked around. They were not alone. Other couples had the same idea, and Ruth could see several standing in the shadows, heads close together, their voices low. A woman laughed softly.

"Come with me, Ruth, I know where there's a bench, and we can sit and talk."

Ruth let herself be led down a nearby path. It was hard to see as the blackout rules prevented the use of any type of path light. But Sal seemed to know where he was going.

"Here it is. I knew there was a bench along here." He paused, waiting until Ruth was seated.

"You're not cold, are you? I can lend you my jacket."

"I'm fine, Sal. Dancing is hot work. It's nice to be outside."

They sat quietly for a few minutes, just enjoying the moment. Strains of "In the Mood" could be heard in the distance.

"This has been a lot of fun, Sal. I'm glad we did this."

"I didn't really have much of a choice, did I?" he teased.

"I guess not. But it all worked out. You have a new fashion chairwoman, and I got to dance at the 'Pole' again."

Sal smiled, then slowly let his hand brush Ruth's forearm. When she didn't pull away, he leaned forward, closing the gap between them.

"Would you let me kiss you, Ruth?" He didn't wait for an answer, his lips just brushing Ruth's cheek.

Ruth turned her face and looked at him squarely. "Sal, I don't..." Her words were swallowed by his lips as he kissed her again, this time full on the mouth. She pulled back, but only a little. "What are you doing, Sal?" she asked softly.

"I'm trying to kiss you, silly girl."

His eyes locked on hers, his broad smile eager for her response. "Is that a problem?"

Ruth sat still, trying to sort out her feelings. "What's going on?"

"Isn't it obvious?" Sal reached up and gently stroked her chin. He moved closer and this time when he kissed her, he let his tongue caress the full length of her lips. Ruth felt her body flush with waves of heat as his tongue parted her lips and entered her mouth, teasing her, begging her to want more of him.

Ruth closed her eyes and for a moment let the waves of emotion carry her. Her head swam as her body responded to his embrace. But only for a moment. As if a light switch had suddenly been turned on, she pushed back against him.

"I can't do this, Sal. It isn't fair."

Stunned by her response, he sat back and stared at her.

"Isn't fair?" He looked at her closely. "What isn't fair?"

"Loving you this way," Ruth tried to explain. "It isn't fair to you. I love you," she paused, searching for the words, "but I don't love you." She looked at Sal, her eyes beginning to fill with tears.

"It's Jim, isn't it?" It was more of a statement than a question. "Look, I know you love him. He's a great guy. But the fact is, you love me. It's just a question of which one you love more. Jim or me."

He reached out and took her hand. "We've always had a thing going on between us. I knew it from the beginning and so did you. You love me, Ruth. I know you do. And, try as I might, I can't deny it, I love you. The night of the snowstorm when I stayed over?"

Ruth closed her eyes and sat very still, waiting.

"You remember, the night of the snowstorm don't you?"

"Of course," she barely whispered.

"I wanted to make love to you that night, you know that?"

"Yes, I know."

"If it hadn't been for the fact your parents were sleeping in the next room, I would have taken you to my bed that night."

"But you didn't."

"No, I didn't. But I wanted to. I wanted to make love to you more than just about anything I've ever wanted in my life. But I didn't. And do you know the reason why?"

Ruth looked across at Sal, his features barely visible. She shook her head, "no."

"Because I knew you were confused. We both wanted it to happen, but I knew you were still unsure and I could sense that." He looked at Ruth. "I thought by now you would have figured things out. And I won't take advantage of that until you are sure."

Ruth looked down at her hands and said nothing.

"You're right, Sal, about everything. I do love you, but I still love Jim" She paused, not knowing whether she should go on. Oh, what the heck, she thought. I've got to say it sometime.

"To tell the truth, Sal, you're everything I ever wanted in a man. You're smart and ambitious."

"Well, that's something," he chuckled quietly. "And don't forget good looking."

Ruth had to smile. "That goes without saying. Everyone, especially my kid sister Justine, thinks you're just gorgeous."

Sal grinned and pretended to straighten his tie. "Good to know people recognize beauty when they see it," he teased.

"Seriously, you're exactly the type of man that I always hoped I would meet someday and marry. I thought maybe you were the one."

"But?" Sal kept his eyes on her face, waiting for her answer. "I know there's a 'but' in there someplace."

"But then I met Jim and everything changed."

"I see."

"I don't know how to put this so you can understand, Sal. Jim is a good man. He's not rich by any means, but he's very smart and he wants to get ahead someday. He just hasn't met the right people yet. When he comes home after the war, I know he'll get a great job with one of the banks or insurance companies. He's very good with numbers."

Sal didn't respond and they sat in silence for another few minutes.

"Jim needs me, Sal. He needs me to love him." She looked across the bench at her friend. "You have dozens of people, including me, who look up to you, who admire you, who want to be your friend. Jim has no one really, except me."

"What about his family? Surely they care about him."

"His mother died when he was a child, his father's an alcoholic and as far as I can tell the rest of the family is not far behind. He has no real connection with any of them."

"What about friends? Or Army buddies? From what I can see those guys at the front are a tight-knit group."

"Jim doesn't make friends very easily. He has a couple of good pals that he knew before the war. His best friend, Jerry, is an officer serving in Italy but I don't think they've seen each other in a while. Officers and enlisted men don't mix."

"So Jim is alone in the world except for you? Is this what you're telling me?" Sal looked at Ruth, waiting for a response. "And you feel it's up to you to make him happy?"

Ruth nodded.

"You know, things may be very different when he comes home."

"But I made Jim a promise, and I can't just walk away. Not yet. Not without seeing him again."

"And if he is a different man?" Sal let the question hang in the air between them.

Ruth looked at Sal and slowly shook her head. "I guess I'll know when I know."

The last week of May another thick envelope from Jim arrived. There had been no word from him all month. Ruth knew from the nightly news reports on the radio that things were heating up in Italy and as she scanned the first page, she whispered a quick prayer Jim was still in one piece.

May 16, 1944 —— Hello darling, missing you. We must date at the Copley Plaza some evening. The best date is to have you alone in some quiet little roadhouse. I don't particularly like crowds. Don't you think I have been subjected to just that for so long now. Sleeping with hundreds, eating and working.

Boy, what music is playing now! The Club Royal of London is broadcasting to the boys over here. Memories of Totem Pole meander through my head. Nice to come down the river in the moonlight.

Gosh but memories like that hurt a little. I guess I'm a softy. Things here are getting pretty hot. And I'm not talking about the temperature. Summer will be here soon.

My work is becoming more involved. I am now in charge of two departments. Hydraulics and Propellers. Still a buck sergeant with nothing in sight.

Someday I'm going to take off and see if I can't get to a base hospital. My teeth you know? I'm not kidding when I say that if ever my lot fell to getting a bit of leave in the U.S.—my teeth would come first. You will never see them this way.

She recalled the picture he had sent and had to agree.

Enjoy yourself hon, for who can tell when they'll decide this G.I. ought to go home. Listen, stop thinking of things like me coming home, for it doesn't help either your or my morale.

Would they let him go home before the war ends? Ruth tried to remember what Jim had written in an earlier letter. He had tried to explain the difference between taking a leave or a furlough, but he wasn't too clear himself.

You remember when I first came into the outfit? I mentioned then that I would have to start at the very bottom. Well hon, I did, but how. Hours of guard duty, detail after detail. Well, the same system applies to rotation. The older fellows are going home first. Some have already gone and more will go in the next few months. But I seem to be way down on the list. Why? Because I don't cater to the powers that be. I tell them off if I know I'm right. Not the cleverest tactic to get ahead, but I know that some of them think more of me for it.

I am highly technically minded and will stick to my guns to see a job done right even though it takes longer.

One consolation is my past record. None of my engines have bounced back due to faulty workmanship. I derive great satisfaction when the test flight report is O.K. on my line of work. To hell with the stripes. That invention of mine was copied on a drawing and has earned fame for another group of people, but still, I know in my own mind that it was my brain child and I am proud of it.

Nothing like it was ever seen in any theatre overseas. That was the comment of a real big shot. But he never was told who made it.

Oh damn there I go crying my blues again, when there are boys up ahead getting killed off like so many rabbits.

About taking a leave? As long as work is here, I don't think of anything else. To be home and know I must come back to this. This!!! Oh, forget it please. Sometimes I feel as though I've seen the best of whatever my lot was in life. Dammit to hell, anyway.

Keep your chin up pal and we both will get together someday. What's an old war or two anyway? I love you, dearest.

- Your Jim.

Ruth shook her head and re-read the last section. Why doesn't he put himself forward? He should claim the credit for his invention, get a proper promotion and take a chance on getting home before this war is done. If others can do it, Jim should be able to.

May 18, 1944

Yesterday a package arrived and the fellows were sweating me out, as to its contents. Well, when I opened one end and pulled out a box of dog food, that did it. What some of them had to say about you sending a guy overseas dog food isn't writable to a lady. Boy, did I take a panning. Of course I can understand that you can't appreciate just what it really was like.

You must listen. Over here, when a package arrives, it's everybody's interest, for that package is from the U.S. Maybe we get some enjoyment looking over someone's shoulder as he unwraps the expectant prize. These things don't come everyday and they travel thousands of miles.

Ruth pictured a group of GIs all gathered 'round anxiously watching as Jim opened his precious package from home. Of course they were expecting cookies and chocolates.

To see a G. I. pull out a box of "Dog Dessert" is a big laugh and I mean a BIG laugh.

Well we were determined to find that son of a _____ and make him eat it. Would he? Huh! Dogs in Italy aren't that delicate. Boy, we crammed it down his big gullet but up it came. He'll eat it or our friends the rodents will make a meal of his carcass.

I showed Dopey the box and explained to him, but definitely. Told him how a beautiful blonde thought so much of him and that he must oblige or else.

So much for dog food. Oie! What next.

Sorry Jim, Ruth laughed softly to herself. Don't worry, I won't send anymore dog food.

May 20

Dopey is a big hound now and due to his unfortunate tussle with a lorry, he travels along with his rear end all out of kilter. His hind feet keep catching up with his fore feet and as a result he often winds up at the scene of his departure.

He travels in sort of a great circle. I feel sorry for him for another reason. His hind feet won't support him very well. Might as well shoot him as let him live in that condition. His sorry attempts to service a friend of his has brought great laughter from us uncouth individuals.

So much for Dopey.

You ask about my grey hairs. Well, if you really are concerned, they are becoming more numerous and in more places. Probably won't get to a rest camp now that things are popping up.

"Popping up?" Ruth thought about the radio broadcast she had heard the night before. For weeks the bombing of the railroads in Sienna had been the top story. Now the airwaves were filled with day after day coverage of the assault by the Allies on the famous monastery at Monte Cassino. She knew the Army Air Corps must be in the air every day, but Jim never mentioned anything specific about his work, only hinting at the stress and strain all the soldiers were under trying to bring an end to this endless war.

Rumors had been swirling for weeks. Everyone at the office or on the WMC committee was concerned. The allies were planning a major offensive, but where or when it would take place was a mystery.

It was Tuesday morning, June 6, when Mr. LeBlanc stepped out onto his front porch and picked up the morning paper. After one glance at the headline, he quickly returned to the kitchen and showed it to his wife and daughters. The headline splashed across the front page of *The Boston Daily Globe* was set in the largest bold type Ruth had ever seen. It left little doubt that this, finally, was the start of the allied invasion of Europe. 'INVASION OPENS Allied Air-Borne Troops Land Near Mouth of Seine.'

Her father began to read out loud. "The long-expected invasion by the British and Americans was begun in the first hours of the morning of June 6 by landing of parachute troops in the area of the mouth of the Seine..."

He ran his finger across the columns. "Looks like Eisenhower's in charge of everything. Listen to this: 'Under the command of General Eisenhower Allied naval forces supported by strong air forces began landing Allied armies this morning on the northern coast of France.'"

He turned to Ruth. "Do you think your Jim could be in the middle of this?" He gestured to the headline.

"I don't think so, Father. Jim is still in Italy. But they have him flying all over Europe, so it's possible."

"Well, let's pray he stays safe. You tell him that next time you write to that boy of yours. We're all behind him, 100 percent."

"Jim knows that, father, but I will tell him again," Ruth agreed.

"I'm going to turn on the radio. I'm sure there will be reports coming over about this."

"Your breakfast is going to get cold, Frederick," Mrs. LeBlanc protested. But her husband pretended not to hear and headed for the front parlor.

Ruth looked after his retreating back. "I wish I could stay home and listen as well, but I've got to get to the office. The WMC gave me tons of work at last night's meeting, and I still have all the mid-summer promos to create for Polar."

She took a quick sip of the last of her morning Postum, grabbed her jacket and satchel from the back of the kitchen chair and headed out the door. "I've got to go."

It took her a little over a half hour to walk to Atlantic Station, but the time gave Ruth a chance to shake off the uneasy feeling that had been growing since she saw the morning headlines. *I just hope Jim can keep himself out of harm's way.*

Over the next few days it was hard to concentrate on anything except the war effort. At home or at work, it was the only thing people talked about. News from the battle in Normandy filled the newspapers and the radio broadcasts had one reporter after another describing whatever they could find out. It seemed Roosevelt and Churchill were pleased by the invasion. Hitler's Sea Wall had been breached, and the troops were now heading deep into France. But the cost was very high. The casualty lists in the morning papers were long. Almost everyone knew someone who had lost a son or father or brother.

The following Wednesday, Edith Carlton, the neighbor next door got word that her nephew, Mark, had been killed in the second wave that hit Omaha Beach. She was inconsolable. Mr. Mazzioli, the grocer down the street, was very worried. His son, Angelo, was a member of the 82nd Air-borne Division that was assigned the task of destroying the German supply bridges behind their lines. He was reported missing in action.

"I'm so sorry to hear about Angelo, Mr. Mazzioli," Ruth told him. She had stepped into the store on her way home from work and had heard the news. "We'll be praying for you and your family."

"Thank you, Miss Ruthie. That's all we can do now. Is pray." He tried to put on a brave front. "And how's that boyfriend of yours, that Jimmy you like so much?"

"Jim is fine. He's in Italy right now as far as I know."

"Tell him to stay there. Is good country. People very good." He gave Ruth a smile. "My people, you see."

"Yes, Mr. Mazzioli. Jim writes that it is very beautiful where he is. Everyone is very nice." She handed the grocer money for the canned milk she was purchasing. "I hope they find your son right away. Please tell your family we are praying for him."

Walking the few blocks home, Ruth could think of nothing but how sad she was feeling. First, Mrs. Carlton's nephew, now Angelo Mazzioli. The list of casualties never stopped growing. When will this war end? she thought. This cannot go on forever.

She glanced at each of the houses as she passed by. The sound of children still playing outside in the warm evening air brought back memories of her own childhood. She and Justine and their friends would jump rope or play hopscotch for hours, waiting for the clang of an old cowbell. It was her mother's signal that supper was on the table. But those days of innocence were long gone.

As she turned the corner at Billings and Bromfield she looked up the tree lined street. Ruth could see her mother waiting for her on the front porch. Mrs. LeBlanc had moved the long metal glider into the shade and was busily snapping peas for dinner.

"Here's the Carnation you asked me to pick up." Ruth handed the small tin to her mother and sat down. "I just spoke with Mr. Mazzioli. Angelo is still missing. He said to thank you for your prayers."

"The poor man." Mrs. LeBlanc shook her head. "I don't know what I would do if I had a son overseas right now. Of course, your Jim is almost like a son to us. I worry for him." She patted Ruth's hand. "And for you too."

"One of Helen's co-workers just found out her husband was killed," Ruth continued somberly. "It feels like we are surrounded by bad news everywhere."

Her mother looked up. "I nearly forgot. There's another letter from Jim waiting for you on the hall table. Perhaps he has good news for you. He's trying to get a furlough, isn't he?"

Ruth stood up. "Jim deserves one, but I don't think they'll ever let him go now that things are the way they are."

"Well that's a pity." She snapped a few more peas, already distracted by her task. "You can take that tin into the kitchen on your way, Ruth. Read your letter in private, then come out and tell me what Jim has to say."

"Yes, Mother."

Jim's letter was waiting for her on the hall table. She picked it up and walked into the empty kitchen.

Justine was still upstairs, and she guessed her father wasn't home yet. Putting the kettle on for a cup of tea, she settled into the nearest chair, opened Jim's letter and began to read.

June 4, 1944

Dearest Ruth,

Lot of nice songs being made over there now. I don't mean those d— patriotic and flag waving get ups they have. I have grown to dislike any movie or story about this war or anything in relation to "Our boys over there" etc. etc. etc. What a happy lot of ———!

Dopey was shot yesterday afternoon.

Ruth gasped as she read the words.

He took a fit. He only had three pieces of your dog food. Too many vitamins, I guess. Anyway, stopped his clock for all time. Put a detail of locals to bury him. Nice little pooch up to the time he tangled with that truck.

Now I don't have to sweat out any more packages of dog food from you.

The dog must have been out of control for someone to shoot him. The news of Dopey's death was almost more than Ruth could handle. So many men were being killed. And now—an innocent dog. A wave of deep sadness washed over her.

You once asked me if I ever saw anything during my tour of duty at night. Well, I guess it's all right to mention that many moons ago I saw a couple of punks trying to put one over on Uncle Sam. I don't want to write the details but understand, they were stopped.

One learns to hate.

Mr. LeBlanc entered the kitchen, sat down at the kitchen table, opened the newspaper and began to read. "Looks like we've finally got the Jerries on the run in Italy."

Ruth stepped closer and read the headline. 500 U.S. Planes Blast Nazis Fleeing Rome.

"Now that the 5th Army has finally broken free from Anzio, it's all good news. The Italians love us." He glanced at his daughter. "If things keep going this way, it won't be long before that soldier of yours will be home."

"I hope so, Father. I certainly hope so." Ruth studied the paper. Pursuing Allies Seek Destruction of Enemy; Civilians Hail Yankees. "I'm sure they still have a lot of fighting ahead of them. But at least this is some good news. Jim doesn't say much in his letters, but I know he can't wait for it to be over."

"As long as he comes home in one piece, safe and sound. It's the best we can hope for, dear."

"Safe and sound, Dad. That's what I pray for."

Much later that evening Ruth finally had a chance to finish reading Jim's letters.

Why do you ask so many hard questions? Much has happened that I don't wish to remember. I try to keep my letters from mentioning the rough spots. There is nothing glamorous about war. Nothing colorful. That is parade ground stuff. There is a feeling of strength watching large formations of bombers and fighters in the sky but mostly I'm too busy to draw much out of the war aside from a tired look.

The boys at the front want more and better equipment and that's all they need at present. It's not necessary to give them the old malarkey about their being the saviors of democracy etc. etc. etc.

Boy, but I burn up when I read about some of the junk going on back home. A Yank over here published several letters of soldiers who had been overseas two years and found that when they returned home they were treated coldly and subjected to criticisms and to details not warranted. This isn't just a few but many cases.

Ruth knew there had been a lot of bickering reported in the news. Wartime factories were falling back on their commitments, workers were staying home or walking off the job in protest against being made to work overtime without compensation. Stories had been in the papers for weeks, but she had not realized word had spread to the troops overseas.

They are catching k.p. and being drilled all day by "Johns" in the states. If you don't think that makes us want to stay over here where we are together in good fellowship. Men together subjected to the same discomforts for 18 months and more grow to keen friendship.

I'm not a civilian Ruth. Over two years has given me cause to wonder certain things about civilians.

Some of the many departments in Washington are nothing but "war jobs." Making their pile of dough on a good thing. Will they step out and give the returning G. I. a job? They will like hell.

General Arnold spoke critically to the striking foremen at Chrysler. He mentioned their failure to keep production going. Something like 250 fighter planes behind. Do you know, Ruth, that ironic as it is, these same people have lost sons, brothers and friends because a fighter plane didn't keep off an attack. Hell, it's the same old story. They don't think over there any further than their pocketbooks.

I'm afraid my letter thus far isn't very cheerful. I'm not exactly in the best of moods. There doesn't seem to be any end to my work.

But there is a bright side to everything isn't there. The thought that someday you're going to be my reason for forgetting everything in the past.

Just you and I in our own shack or three room apartment whatever it is. That's what I think about every night while waiting to fall asleep. That makes more of a chance that you will be in my dreams. It works sometimes.

We will walk along the beach in the cool evenings and maybe sit together on that bench along the sea wall.

Those things are worth going home for.

Love Jim.

Ruth wished she could reach out and touch Jim. He sounded so sad and lonely and angry. Why wouldn't he be angry, she thought. He's trapped in an unbelievable situation and all the news he hears from home is how much money millionaires are making on the war.

June 9, 1944

As you probably can understand through your newspapers, the places around here have been quite busy. Tiredness seems to be my only set back at present and it's with deep satisfaction I can still say everything else is bright and shiny.

She glanced again at the date at the top of the page. The letter had been written after the big invasion in Normandy. Thankfully Jim hadn't been in the thick of it. As she scanned down the rest of the sheet, it was clear that another situation, this one closer to home, had most of his attention.

A few days ago I received a letter from Jim Sullivan. It made me feel so left out of things. He has a wonderful position with the Peter W. Bronson Co. on Milk Street. He travels around New England and does audits as I have always thought I would like to do. Oh but that letter had me blue. As I read on, I glanced at the dirty mechanics clothes on my bunk and at my hands and of what little of the social life I was missing. Damm it, dammit all.

He asked me if I would like to know more detail of his work. At that, I tore the letter to pieces and felt terribly ashamed at my reaction to what was meant to be a very nice letter.

Darling you're going to have to make allowances for something, but what it is I can't define. Perhaps the actual thought of coming home to you will change this lost feeling but right now my work looms large and long, ahead of me.

I produced another gadget which I think I can say will prevent injury in many cases. But that's all I can say about it.

Next to seeing you, I'd like to have a nice big dish of vanilla ice cream with chocolate cookies. Yowie! That's just a small part of what I miss. The Gods of war sure burn up my energy. The damn thing can't last forever, but our love can live on if we just give it a chance to start living.

Your Jim.

The next day Helen and Ruth decided to walk to the Boston Public Garden for lunch.

"It's just too nice to stay cooped up inside today," Helen complained. Ruth agreed and the two friends headed off down Beacon Street, past the Frog Pond and across Charles Street to the Garden entrance.

As they settled on a bench not far from the edge of the lagoon, the warm July sun filtered through the long feathery branches of the weeping willow trees that surrounded the small lake. A family of mallard ducks paddled by. The drake, attracted by the sight of Ruth's sandwich, swam closer to the shore.

"I just got a letter from Jim," Ruth began. "He sounds really discouraged. A couple of men from their troop who made it back have nothing but bad news to share about life as a soldier returning home. They've heard about all the protests and walk outs happening at some of the factories. They think politicians and big businesses are all about greed and making as much money as possible on the back of the war effort. What can I tell him?"

Helen thought a moment. "You told Jim that you're part of the War Manpower Commission for Boston, didn't you? The whole reason for your committee is to encourage the people of Boston to feel more patriotic and get workers to stay on the job. Tell him about that. It'll make him feel better."

"I guess so. We've been working really hard to pull this event together.

Boston Loyalty Week! The committee finally settled on dates. It's scheduled for the last week of July. Getting everyone to agree on where and when was a hassle, but it's all set now."

"So what's the plan? Any celebrities coming?"

"The Army Air Force is putting on a show they're calling 'Shot Out of the Sky.'

"Sounds intriguing."

"They're going to be showing off some Japanese and German planes that were..."

"Don't tell me," Helen interrupted. "These planes were 'Shot Out of the Sky?'"

"Exactly," Ruth confirmed. "I know it sounds hokey, but the idea is to get people fired up to see what we've accomplished—how we're winning the war. And every day there are going to be speeches and music and a marching band."

"Where is all this happening?" Helen asked.

"It all starts on Sunday, July 30, on Boston Common. A proclamation will be read out at all the churches. Every night there will be a program of music and speech-making. WBZ Radio will be broadcasting it all live. We even have the Boston Symphony Orchestra on a coast-to-coast hook-up, but that's still in the planning stages."

Helen sat back in her seat. "I'm impressed. This little shindig is turning out to be quite the event. Be sure to tell Jim all about it. If he and the boys know we're trying our best to boost patriotism on this side of the Atlantic, it can only lift their spirits."

"I certainly hope so. I don't know what else I can do."

Ruth looked down at her sandwich and ripped off a small corner. The ducks were still poking around in the reeds nearby, hoping for a friendly handout. Ruth stood up, walked to the edge of the lagoon and tossed the bread onto the water. The drake pounced on the crumbs.

"What has Sal got you doing for this extravaganza?"

Ruth tossed another bit of bread towards the ducks, this time aiming just in front of the dark-feathered female. She quickly snatched it up before the drake could get close.

"I'm in charge of getting all the posters and flyers printed and distributed. It's not complicated, but it is time consuming. Thankfully we've recruited a hundred or so high school students to help spread the word. They've been riding their bikes all over the city for the last week. Every store on Washington Street will have at least one large poster in their window. The radio station has been making public service announcements for at least a week and we've sent scads of flyers to every major company in New England to pass out to their workers. Trust me, everyone is going to know about it."

"Sounds like it'll be a success."

"If Sal has anything to do with it, Boston Loyalty Week will go national. He wants every city in the country to imitate what we're doing in Boston. He's even got the president reading a speech on the radio."

Helen laughed softly. "When Sal makes his mind up to do something, he knows how to make it happen. He may be a bit of a show off, but you've got to give the guy credit. He really knows how to promote an idea."

"Unlike someone else I know."

Puzzled, Helen watched as her friend quietly ripped the rest of her sandwich into small pieces and tossed it all into the lagoon. The ducks went crazy, racing to grab each and every morsel before it sank.

"What's eating you?" Helen asked.

Ruth returned to the bench and sat down. "It's Jim. I told you he's discouraged. He's a talented guy but can't seem to get any recognition for these inventions he's developed. Unlike Sal, Jim just doesn't know how to put himself out there. He thinks the higher ups will see what he's done and reward him. But it doesn't work that way."

"You have to encourage him to toot his own horn."

"I do, but you know Jim, he doesn't want to hear it. He's beginning to drive me a little crazy. I think I may need to take a little break from Jim for a bit!"

Helen studied her friend. "That might be a good idea."

Over the next few weeks Ruth was totally occupied with preparations for Boston Loyalty Week. Her days were filled with printing specifications, running to meetings and sending out packages of posters, flyers and promotions.

Meanwhile, most of the news from the European front was good news. Since Rome had been taken in early June, the Allies continued their advance towards Florence and then north towards Bologna. Each night Ruth would join her parents in the front parlor and listen to the radio broadcasts. The news was encouraging. But still no word from Jim.

Early on the third Saturday in July another bundle of letters arrived.

Ruth saw it as soon as she came downstairs for breakfast. She grabbed the packet and headed towards the kitchen. While she waited for the water to boil, Ruth sorted through the letters, placing them in the order each was postmarked.

The first, written several weeks before, was short and made up of several disconnected jottings, one following immediately after another.

June 13, 1944

Hello Ruth,

Quite a bit of water has passed under the proverbial bridge since last posting a letter to you. You must know or at least feel through your own experience that our love is undergoing much of a strain, but proud as I am to say it, my feelings are more defined than they were back at Fort Dix in August of 1942.

June 27

The machine I invented is being used by squadrons of other outfits. It has become popular as a "safety first precaution." I can't mention it in detail but it does away with a very dangerous practice of which I was almost a victim in Africa. This last invention is the safety machine. The one before was the time saver. If I can get the stuff I need, why, there are many ideas I've got way back in my cranium.

July 2, 1944, Rome

Dear Ruth

Now that I've been into Rome about five or six times the place doesn't interest me as much as when I first came here. I must say that Mussolini did a fine job in the construction of new public buildings. They are more of an attraction to me than some of the

315

ancient ruins.

Yesterday, some of our boys discovered that there are deer wandering close to our bivouac area. A few went hunting and it did not take very long for them to bag one. Everyone is looking forward to tonight's meal as it's a welcome change from G.I. beans, sausage and hash.

Bye for now, Jim

Is that all he has to say about Rome? Ruth turned the page over. The reverse was blank as always. She slipped a fingernail under the flap of the next envelope and removed three sheets covered with Jim's tight handwriting.

July 3, 1944

My dearest darling,

I visited Naples shortly after the Allies had taken it and there were still many evidences that it was a lovely city before the armies worked it over. It is impressive the way the Italian builders construct. Very little steel frame is used. They build great stone upon stone walls.

There was a great stone building on the waterfront that just caught my breath. It looked like a medieval fortress but served as a penitentiary. There it stood, majestic above the rubble that lay around it.

Just heard from Jim Donovan. He is still stateside. He cautions me about hitching up too fast. He writes that a guy can be plenty choosy over there right now. I guess that is so, but there is still going to be plenty of guys coming back to get a hold of that stuff which he claims is all over the place. I don't have to listen to the likes of Jim Donovan tell me what I want or don't want. Perhaps he can date all the girls he wants but he can never duplicate a certain gal that I have decided upon.

Ruth paused and re-read the last two paragraphs. She had never liked Jimmy Donovan. He was a classic manipulator. Always looking for an angle to get ahead or meet the right people. She had watched him try and involve Jim in one too many money making schemes. They always failed. Now he's giving Jim advice about romance? Ruth laughed at the thought. No one knows less about love than good old Jimmy Donovan.

There is no one who wants to be surer of a thing than I. And I want you to be sure as well. Have all the fun you can possibly dig up in the time you have to find it. That way you can be sure that it isn't just the idea of me courting you that makes you feel obligated to deprive yourself of the company of other males. Yes, I know that I would be jealous but that is because of my selfish attitude in wanting you all for myself.

She wondered what Jim would think about her evolving relationship with Sal. She turned to the third and final letter in the bundle. It was thicker than the others and a large military postmark was stamped on the outside of the envelope.

July 4, 1944

Italy: (dammit)

This day, being a holiday in the States, and held in memory of those noble and patriotic souls who prevented this country from being engulfed in an imperialistic monarchy, has caused me to ponder over a few isolated thoughts on just why things are the way they are.

To class myself as being a noble and patriotic soul is to make an erroneous gesture. I'm over here because I have to be over here.

If I progress in the next two years at the same slow rate of the past couple, I am afraid that there isn't much to look forward to. It is too late to consider a commission. Perhaps through some unforeseen miracle, they could kind of put me up for another stripe but it's so unlikely to be just a wish that I am perfectly willing to let it rest as just that.

You see, my dear, my personal pride enters into it and I always like to hold to the opinion that if they can't see and judge accordingly, I am not the one to step out and ask. Say what you will, but it is better that you know how I operate than to have any illusions of me as a world beater.

I know, I know, you have said time and again that it pays to blow one's horn once in a while. But in so doing in my circumstances, there is too much chance of being talked about in uncomplimentary terms.

Yes, I do consider public opinion above that of personal opinion. What little I have accomplished thus far is absolutely 100% the result of my efforts as a workman and not one fraction can be accounted as the result of political antics or as they say in rather strong G. I. language———kissing. And that is the way I shall keep the record.

Ruth folded the letter and replaced it in the envelope.

What am I going to do with you, James Doherty? You deserve recognition. You just refuse to play the game you have to play in order to get it. She let out a long sigh.

"Why the long face, Ruthie?"

She looked up, startled. So preoccupied with Jim's letters, she hadn't heard her father enter the kitchen.

Mr. LeBlanc glanced at the package of letters in Ruth's hand. "Looks like you finally heard from that soldier of yours. Hope nothing's wrong."

"Jim's doing okay. He just invented another machine to help prevent injuries while the men are repairing planes. He hopes it'll merit him another stripe."

"It should. That Jim is a real clever man. Has a great knack for mechanical things I wager. You should encourage him."

"I try to. But it isn't easy. He doesn't like to call attention to himself and thinks that if he just does the work, the top brass will notice him."

"He should go right up to his captain and tell him just what's what."

"Jim's not made that way."

"Well, he better learn how, or he'll be left behind. I just read in *The Globe* that when the boys over there finally get back home, competition for jobs is going to be fierce. If he wants to get ahead, he has to put himself forward. No question about it. Maybe you should have that smart guy of yours, Sal, write Jim and give him a little advice."

"I don't think that would be a good idea," Ruth answered quickly. "Sal's in manufacturing, Jim's interested in accounting."

"I thought he was doing well in mechanics and engineering."

"He is, Father, but it's only his job for the war. I think he hopes to go back to accounting when he gets home."

"Hmmm." Mr. LeBlanc looked at his daughter, thoughtfully. "This war may have given him different ideas.

August, 1944

Dearest Jim,

I just received your July 4th letter and I'm a little concerned. You sound discouraged about your chances for advancement. I know you don't want to "play the game" of tooting your own horn to your superiors, but you deserve to be recognized for all the good things you are doing. I want you to succeed and I'm sure if you put yourself forward a bit more, those in charge will see what you have done and will reward you.

For my part, I don't care about your rank and will love you whether you are a private or an officer. But I do want you to be proud of what you have done, and it's not boasting to simply declare the truth of what you have accomplished with those inventions of yours.

If you want to succeed in this world whether in the army or in civilian life, you have to make yourself known to those who are in power. Help them help you move up the ladder.

I am not trying to criticize you. I want to encourage you! You deserve recognition, so stand up for yourself and don't be shy about claiming it.

Wishing you all the best each day. Stay safe and hurry home.

Love, Ruth

In the week prior to the big event, Ruth and the Loyalty Week Committee met each evening at Sal's office to smooth out all the final details. It was a little after ten on the eve of the event when Sal finally dropped Ruth off in front of her house on Bromfield Street.

"Thanks for everything, Ruth, you really came through for me this week. Thanks to you and the rest of the committee, Loyalty Week is going to be a great success." Sal reached out and grasped her hand, pulling Ruth towards himself.

She felt the gentle tug and resisted ever so slightly.

"Don't, Sal."

He looked at her, his face a question mark. Wondering. "What is it Ruth? What's wrong?"

"Nothing's wrong." She slowly released her hand from his. "Working with you, spending time with you. A wonderful cause we can remember and be proud of after all this war business is done and over with." She paused, sorting through her feelings. "But let's just leave it at that."

It was hard to see Sal's face in the shadows, but the edge in his voice revealed an underlying sense of frustration.

"I thought we were friends." He reached for her hand again. This time Ruth pulled it away first.

"We are friends, Sal. Good friends. But I'm engaged to Jim and no matter how I feel towards you, I cannot love you the way you want. I have to love Jim. At least until he comes home."

"You're not making any sense. What do you mean? 'You have to love him?' Ever since..." He didn't finish the sentence but let the silence fill the space between them.

She shook her head. "I'm sorry if I gave you the wrong impression, the wrong signals. I think with everything going on, I've just been mixed up."

"Well, I'm not confused. You know I love you, Ruth. More than I can say." He turned away and grasped the steering wheel with both hands, his fingers turning white with the pressure. "How can I prove it to you? You're in love with a man who doesn't deserve you. Who doesn't even know how wonderful you are. He's been away for almost three years. You hardly knew each other before he left. How can you marry a man you've only known for a few weeks? A few months at best? I just don't understand."

"To be honest, neither do I. It all happened so fast. We dated a few times— went dancing with the crowd, and that was about it until the holidays. At New Year's we went to the company party. I knew Jim was getting more serious, but then he enlisted and off he went to war."

"And you?" Sal asked, "were you getting serious?"

"I was beginning to but we never had a real chance. He was gone and the only connection we've had since have been his letters. Except for my visit to Fort Dix just before Jim got shipped out."

"What happened at Fort Dix? I knew you had gone to see him, but you never told me what happened."

"Nothing happened. Not really." She paused, considering how much more to tell Sal. "Except we almost got married."

Sal looked at her surprised.

"Don't look so shocked. Jim had already asked me to marry him in one of his letters and I had tentatively said yes."

"So you were engaged before you went south?"

Ruth nervously toyed with the latch of her purse. "I guess you could say so. We hadn't made any plans. Nothing was absolutely definite. Jim didn't even think to buy me a ring." She nervously touched her empty ring finger. "I bought one for myself, knowing he was too busy to even think about a ring. But I seldom wear it. It's a small pearl with diamonds and I don't want it to get damaged."

Sal sat silent, shaking his head in disbelief.

"You have to understand, Sal, Jim was off to war. Who knew if he was ever going to come back. I think I was falling in love with him. His letters were so dear, so honest. He really does love me. And when he asked me to marry him, I said 'Why not?' If it will make him happy, I can do that. He was heading overseas and I might never see him again."

"But what about your happiness? Jim's a survivor. He's going to come back from this war and he's going to want to marry you, settle down and start a family. Is that what you want?" He paused before continuing. "You're a professional woman, Ruth, with a great career. Why would you want to get married and leave it all behind?"

Sal was right. If she married Jim, she would most likely have to give up her career. It was clear from his letters that he wanted to start a family right away, and if children came along it was her duty to stop working, and stay home caring for both children and husband. It was what was expected of her.

"I just think you deserve more." He reached out and took her hand. This time she did not pull away. "Don't settle for less than you deserve."

Ruth looked down at their hands, their fingers interlaced so that she couldn't tell which was hers and which, Sals. Did she love Jim or was she marrying him out of some sense of duty or obligation? Or did she love this handsome Italian who declared his love for her every chance he got?

Marrying Sal would be the easy choice. He was good looking, smart and successful. She would never want for anything and if her plan was to keep on working that would be fine with him. He was proud of her success and encouraged her to grow the business.

"I can't talk about this now, Sal. It's late, I'm tired and I know either my mother or my sister is, at this very moment, looking out from behind those front parlour curtains watching every move we make. I need to go in."

Sal shook his head again. "You do whatever you want. I know you'll do it anyway, no matter what I say."

Ruth reached for the car's door handle. "Don't worry, Sal. Just be patient with me for a little while longer. I'll figure things out."

The door latch clicked open, "See you tomorrow? I'll try to get to the Common early in the afternoon."

"See you at the show."

"Good morning, Ruthie, and congratulations. This Loyalty Week event of yours is getting some big coverage in this morning's paper."

Mr. LeBlanc and Justine were seated at the kitchen table when Ruth finally shuffled in for breakfast the next morning. Her father held up the newspaper for Ruth to see, pointing to a large headline and display ad on the bottom of the editorial page. "Looks good, don't you think?"

Ruth squinted in the direction of the paper. It was still early and Ruth had not slept well. The conversation with Sal the night before had played over and over in her mind, leaving her confused and anxious.

"What time is it?" Ruth asked, walking towards the kitchen counter. "Is there any hot water left? I need to wake up." She reached into the cabinet for a cup and grabbed the jar of Postum. "I need to wake up," she repeated.

Mrs. LeBlanc put down her basket. "I've got to arrange these flowers for the woman's club brunch. We're meeting right after the eleven o'clock Mass, and you should all get ready or we'll be late." She turned towards her husband. "Are you joining us this time?"

Mr. LeBlanc pretended not to hear the question.

"Frederick!" she kicked the volume of her voice up a notch. "Are you going to church today or not?"

Lowering the paper just far enough so that he could see his wife, Frederick LeBlanc frowned. "Not today, dear. I thought I'd head into town with Ruth. It's the first day of that big shindig she's been working on, and I promised I'd go with her."

"But that isn't until later this afternoon, Father," Ruth countered. "We can all go to Mass first and then you and I can take the trolley into town."

Mr. LeBlanc scowled at his daughter.

"Well, that settles it then." Mrs. LeBlanc carefully arranged her flower bouquet into a large glass vase. "We'll all attend the eleven o'clock mass and then you and Ruth can go on to this affair."

"You're not coming with us, Mother?" Ruth asked.

"I have no interest in seeing war planes and guns or listening to a lot of patriotic speeches."

"But there'll be music. We have several military bands scheduled to play."

"I'm sure it will be lovely, Ruth, but you know how I hate crowds."

Justine spoke up. "I'll tag along with you two and take some pictures. You can send a couple to Jim and let him know all we're doing to support our troops."

"Well, you three can attend if you want to. I have my women's brunch to attend." Mrs. LeBlanc continued to fuss with her flowers. "By the way, Ruth, did you see the letter from Jim I left on the hall table? It came in yesterday's post."

"I missed it," Ruth responded. "Is it still there?"

Justine took another bite of toast. "When I saw it still there this morning I thought you might not have seen it, so I took it upstairs and left it on the chair just outside your bedroom door."

Ruth quickly left the kitchen and hurried up the stairs towards her bedroom. A large envelope with Jim's handwriting was sitting in the center of the chair just as Justine had described.

The envelope was thick and the military postmark only a few days old. Jim was sending two and three letters at a time now. She glanced at the clock on her dresser. Nearly quarter past ten. She wouldn't have time to read more than one letter before leaving for church. The rest would have to wait. She quickly opened the envelope with the oldest postmark.

July 6, 1944

Darling,

Here I am this beautiful evening in Italy, setting myself down to write my gal.

You know, I have come to the conclusion that you don't know me very well. I mean the real me, as I perhaps do not understand the real you. And I think that it is about time that we straightened a few things out to begin trying to understand one another.

Dearest, I intended to leave the question of your working up to you. Purely to keep peace in the family. I thought that since you have been at the office so long, you wouldn't enjoy staying home alone. But now I can see I made a mistake there. Frankly, I'd rather have my wife give me . . .

Ruth turned the page over. There was nothing on the reverse. She shuffled the other pages but the letter did not continue. Jim had cut off the paragraph in mid sentence.

What does he mean? "I'd rather have my wife give me..." What? Ruth questioned. I don't understand. She quickly turned to the second envelope hoping his thoughts continued.

July 8, 1944

I need to apologize for cutting off that last letter. I discarded the next page for I feel in a different mood today. My feelings or rather temperament is hair trigger now so I have to watch what I write. You may, as you write, not worship the almighty dollar but we differ greatly on our ideas of it. My outlook is not to the opposite extreme but almost. I give money very little thought. Perhaps a shortcoming on my part.

Right now you'd better understand that I am not a world beater. You women have big imaginations. My status is somewhere in the lower half of the middle income brackets, and we must both understand what my capabilities are.

Work if you want or stay home. I don't care. As long as you're a wife and not a stranger and can keep a home. Why? What more can I expect? You bet you're not 16 and I realize I can't change any ideas you have and I was wrong in giving you that impression.

A girl once remarked that I would be the kind of "Yes-Man husband" afraid of his wife. Remember what I said once about my taking flight if life is miserable. You're the type that doesn't give much so there would be no other alternative than to leave you alone for a spell.

Sorry, Ruth, but I do not agree with some of your philosophy. My pocketbook never was my best friend. Many dates cost me dough, but there were a few people who enjoyed my company more than my money. Of course one cannot live without some money, but I can find real friends in the same monetary brackets.

Rather than provoke any wrath (which I bet you can certainly build up) from you because of my coming home drunk, I swear off drinking unless I am out of town. Now I know what the cute saying "battle-ax" means.

Have I figured you out somewhere near right, or am I wrong? You aren't all sweetness and light but tell me, wouldn't life be monotonous if all were sweet and bliss?

Bye for a while dearest, your Jim

Ruth put down the letter, stunned at Jim's tone. What was he talking about? Was he angry at her? She tried to remember the last letter she had written to him. She must have mentioned money at some point and how she hoped they could build a future together. But Jim's letters were filled with a sense of frustration and resignation. He seemed prepared to settle for things as they are. Where is his ambition to make a better life for us? she wondered. Where is his drive to achieve something with his life? If things don't go his way, is he warning me he'll just disappear?

She shook her head in frustration. I haven't got time to figure this out right now. I have to get to church and then into town for the exhibit. Sal's waiting for me.

"Oh, God," she whispered. The contrast between the two men in her life had never been more stark.

✿

Boston Loyalty Week and the special army program 'Shot From the Sky' were huge hits with the public. All week long thousands of people visited Boston Common to view the exhibits, listen to musical performances and hear the dozens of speeches given by prominent politicians and military leaders.

Volunteers from across the state who served in a variety of military support groups gathered and marched in uniform as a sign of solidarity with the troops. Ruth donned her own dark chocolate brown uniform and joined the Massachusetts Women's Defense Corp contingent.

Up and down Beacon Street, front doors were draped in patriotic red white and blue bunting, and the store windows along Tremont and Washington Streets featured special items and souvenirs promoting the war effort. By the end of the week, the whole city was feeling a new enthusiasm.

"Did you get a chance to see the exhibit on the Common last week?" Ruth asked Helen when they met for a morning break the following Monday. It was the first time in a week the two had had a chance to talk.

Helen looked at her friend over the slender edge of her cup as she sipped hot Earl Grey tea. "Planes and guns are not my favorite things, Ruth. But I appreciate all the work you've done. Gary saw the show yesterday with a couple of his friends. They were really impressed. He told me to let you know he thinks you all did a fine job."

"I'm glad. It was a lot of work, but if it fires people up to keep supporting the troops it'll all be worth it. The paper this morning reported more than two hundred thousand people had been to the exhibit before it closed last night."

"You should be proud of what you've all accomplished. Especially Sal Marcusio. He's the one who really put it all together, right?"

Ruth nodded but didn't respond.

"What's wrong?"

"Nothing."

"I know that look, Ruth. You come in here bright and cheery and I mention Sal's name and you suddenly get all moody. Did you two have a fight or something?"

"No, nothing like that." Ruth paused, considering what more to tell her friend. She gazed out the window for a moment, watching pedestrians quickly moving along the crowded sidewalk five floors below. Everyone with a purpose, with a mission, with a direction. What was her direction? Where was she going with her life? Since reading the latest letters from Jim a week ago, Ruth had felt her life in turmoil.

"I got another letter from Jim. A few of them in fact."

"It's about time."

"He's been very busy. He doesn't write about the war, the battlefront is not far from where he is. And his job is to keep the bombers flying, so he's busy no matter where the war is happening."

"How's he doing?"

"He's good. He works so hard." Ruth fiddled with her teacup.

"So what's the problem?"

Ruth reached for her purse and took out the letters Jim had sent. "It's probably all a big misunderstanding. Letter writing is not the best or easiest way to build a relationship."

She shuffled the pages of the first letter searching for the section she wanted to share. "He has some odd ideas about money. He doesn't seem to care much about it. But what concerns me is his attitude towards my working after we're married—or dealing with married life at all.

> *Work if you want or stay home. I don't care. As long as you're a wife and not a stranger and can keep a home why, what more can I expect? You bet you're not 16 and I realize I can't change any ideas you have and I was wrong in giving you that impression.*
>
> *A girl once remarked that I would be the kind of "Yes-Man husband" afraid of his wife. Remember what I said once about my taking flight if life is miserable. You're the type that doesn't give much so there would be no other alternative than to leave you alone for a spell.*

"Oh, my," Helen responded. "He's blunt, isn't he."

"Is that the way things are between you and Gary? Does he take off if things get a little off kilter between you?"

Helen stifled a laugh. "That'll be the day. If he ever takes off, he's not getting back in and he knows it." She paused, then continued, "Look, married life is not a bed of roses. You're bound to have differences between you. But you learn how to deal with them. You don't just run away when things get bumpy."

"I asked Jim what he hoped for in life, what he would like our life to be like when we are married, and this is what he wrote back…

> *Considering that my position at present doesn't foster anything of the finer qualities of life such as culture, high education or keen executive abilities, I must honestly admit my short comings …*

Money fails to beckon me on to great heights. I associate lots of money with too many temptations.

"He goes on from there, but it's a lot of the same philosophy. He writes about following in the footsteps of his mother who died when he was very young, living a good Christian life, dealing with the disappointments of life..."

"Sounds a bit bleak to me," Helen commented.

"He used to be pretty easy going, but he says it himself, he's got a quick temper now. The littlest thing can set him off."

Helen looked at her friend. "I'm sorry, Ruth. I don't know what to tell you. Perhaps the best thing you can do is keep writing Jim, sending him the support he needs. And when he finally gets home, see how things are. You may be surprised everything will go back to the way it was."

"Perhaps. The war can't go on much longer, can it?"

"Who knows?" Helen sipped the last of her tea. "In the meantime I've got reports to fill out."

Hot summer days stretched into warm summer nights.

August 20, 1944

Dearest Jim,

Life has been very busy here on the home front. Since our big success at Loyalty Week, everyone has been pulling out all the stops to support the troops, and yesterday our entire committee celebrated with a day at Paragon Park at Nantasket Beach. It was such a great time.

Sal and I organized everything and we were able to charter a Peter Pan bus to collect everyone so we could all travel together. We encouraged the committee members to invite their families, so you can imagine the crowd! It was the first time a lot of these children had ever been to an amusement park. What fun! Sal and I rode the giant coaster at least three times! Helen and Gary came too, and joined us in a wonderful round of miniature golf. You would have laughed at the way we played. We must go to Nantasket beach sometime after you return home.

I've talked with your stepmother a few times on the phone. She worries about you and hopes you will be heading home soon. She heard from Eddy that you might be up for a furlough soon. Is this true? You should write to her.

Father is busy working with his Victory Garden pals. They have begun to harvest the first of the summer vegetables and we will soon have more tomatoes than we can ever use. Mother will put some up for sauces so nothing will be wasted.

Since working on Loyalty Week I've received a couple of very large commissions that will keep me very busy into the fall. I'm glad for the work as these are very successful clients who are not afraid to spend money on a job well done, and I am pleased that my work is appreciated. I will let you know how it goes.

Meantime, I am doing very well, staying happy, and going out with friends once in a while. Looking forward to the time when we can be together again.

Stay safe. Much love, Ruth

Two days later as Ruth returned home from work, her eyes focused on the hall table. A light brown envelope with military markings was waiting for her.

"That you, Ruth?" Her mother called from the parlour. "You're late."

Ruth picked up the envelope, dropped her sweater on a nearby chair and followed her mother's voice into the front parlour. Mrs. LeBlanc was busy sorting through a small box of buttons. Her father was hidden from view behind his usual evening paper.

"Sorry, Mother. The trolleys were all very slow tonight. Some sort of switch trouble on the line, I guess."

"Well, no matter. I left a plate for you in the oven. You eat and then come and listen to the news with us."

Ruth didn't have to ask what was for dinner. There was no mistaking the odor of boiled cabbage and grilled Spam. Better than liver, she thought.

She rescued her food plate from the oven, and set a place for herself at the kitchen table. As she opened the envelope from Jim, three sheets of letter paper fell out.

It had been several weeks since Ruth had received a letter, but she had no trouble recalling Jim's tone or questions about money, and what he expected of her. She had been living with doubts about their relationship since his last letter arrived.

August 7, 1944 Dearest,

I hope it won't be long before I return to you. This war can't go on much longer. Some of the boys have already begun to receive rotations home. I have read this evening of the homecomings of many of the Rangers who were at the beachheads in Sicily and Italy.

The front line lads deserve to go home and I wish the married men could be home where they could occasionally see their wives. Many of our air crews have had the chance to see home but ground crews are pretty well trained to a high operating efficiency especially in the specialist lines. And of course I am not one of the "old boys" so must await my turn. When I come back to you Ruth, I don't want another goodbye. We aren't getting younger.

About my last letter. Sometimes Ruth, I put my head before my heart. I guess it's human nature. If one of my recent letters brought you down a bit, I didn't mean to be critical. But now at least, you have some idea of what I think about money. Don't ever let money cause us to say things we may regret. Living within our means whatever it may be, will be a guarantee of happiness, I'm sure.

All my love, your Jim.

August 9, 1944

I'm sort of coming around to an idea of just what I can do for work in the future and what would suit me the best. I don't know just how you might take this but I don't think sitting in an office all day would give me as much chance to think up new ideas and sort of experiment. One good thing about my job here as a department head, I can use my own ingenuity. I have invented two pieces of equipment now, which save time and labor and are safer to implement. Recently I pulled the guts out of a big tractor and fixed it up again. I derived a kick out of this for this would have been a big job back there in any civilian garage and here, a former accountant does the job in the field. Damn if I ain't bragging again. I should be ashamed of myself but instead I'm kinda proud.

Darling, you mentioned in your letter that once you almost teetered from me to another.

Ruth, I'm so much sold on having all of you for myself alone, that it hurts to even consider any other condition. There are so many more desirable males than I. Please, dear, stay true to me.

Your Jim

Until they had a chance to really spend time together Jim would just have to live with the uncertainty.

She unfolded the third letter and began to read. It was dated several weeks after the first two.

August 25, 1944

I just received your letter of August 20 with the picture of you and Sal at the beach! I was surprised! All the time that you people go to the beach and you won't let me have a snapshot of you!

By the way you have recently been tugging at those tender heart strings of mine. You know why? Well, all along you mentioned Sal and you doing this or that and I thought Sal was a girl. Holy Smokes.

When did you first meet him? It must have been just after I left. Has he had the pleasure of your company since that time? The lucky stiff.

Ruth struggled to hold back a laugh. All this time Jim thought Sal was a girlfriend? Oh Jim, if you only knew.

But darling I can't feel that you are being unfaithful in the least, for I want you to have fun. But it came as a real surprise to learn that someone else was occupying some of your time. He is a very lucky fellow and I feel guilty holding on to you when there is another chance of happiness so close.

Ruth, after two years, I am more certain of myself than ever, that you are the one I want for my mate for life. But definitely you might drop a hint to Sal. I wouldn't want the poor chum to get false hopes.

Hon I know you won't ever let me down on the mail even if Sal does manage to date you. I actually live half of each day with the hope that at night there will surely be a letter for me. That goes on. It's a cycle one day of happiness, next of disappointment.

Darling, I can't say what it is that I want you to pray for. But something is happening and for my sake, I'll need your prayers in my work for the next few months.

Ruth paused. Jim seldom commented on any military action, but if she read between the lines, it sounded like trouble was not far way. Was he being sent to the front?

Help me succeed. Give me a chance to gain an appreciable background in the Army. So many men will be getting out at the end of the war that it will be necessary to have a little more on the ball than the next guy.

Today I took a very responsible job. I can't mention what it is but it is a lot of work and requires a good knowledge of technicalities. It may mean that I won't see you for a while but I know that you consider our future more important than a short time away from each other.

True we are missing out on some real happiness, but we can't have everything. So you see dear, I shall count on your mail for a spell yet and you mustn't forget that I shall be thinking of you always.

Your Jim.

Ruth sat quietly for a few moments. What did he mean by writing he won't be seeing me for a while? Was he considering the possibility of staying in the service longer than he needed to? She knew soldiers only needed 85 points to be considered for discharge. Jim had volunteered in February of '42. Points were awarded based on the type and length of duty served, and where the soldier was posted. Serving in a combat zone was worth five times the points. Jim had been in one combat zone after another. He must be close to 85 points by now, she thought. He took his work so seriously and now he had taken on a new position. Whatever this new job was, it sounded like it could be dangerous.

When Ruth entered the front parlour Mr. LeBlanc was still sitting in the overstuffed chair by the window, hiding behind his newspapers.

"Father, you've been following all the military reports from the front. Is there any battle heating up in southern Italy?"

Mr. LeBlanc turned down a corner of the paper so he could see his daughter's face. "Why, is that fella of yours getting himself into trouble?"

"Jim never writes anything specific about where his squadron is or what they're doing. But something's up."

"A battle?"

"Whatever it is, he's asking for special prayers."

Mrs. LeBlanc stopped counting her buttons. "Oh, my dear. Well, we will have to light a candle at church this Sunday, and we can each say a rosary for him and his friends."

"From what I've read, Ruth, most of the action is happening near Florence. The Germans are still holed up in the mountains, and our boys are fighting one battle after another. With Rome now in the hands of the Allies, the generals seem to think it won't be too much longer."

"How much longer is 'not much longer'?" Ruth asked. She crossed the room to the sofa and slumped into the far corner. "It's been three years and we're still not done with it."

Mr. LeBlanc closed his paper, carefully folded it and stared at his daughter, a stern look crossing his face. "I'm surprised to hear you talk like this, Ruth. You of all people. I'd think you'd be more behind our troops than anyone."

Ruth slouched even further into the cushions and frowned. "I'm behind the troops, Father, you know I am, but there doesn't seem to be any end to this mess."

"We have to have faith in our leaders. Fighting a war is a very serious and complicated business. You can't just snap your fingers and call it quits because you want your young man to come home."

Ruth looked down, gathering her thoughts. "I'm not sure Jim wants to come home, at least not right away."

Mrs. LeBlanc looked up, startled at this news. "What do you mean, Ruth?"

"This war has been going on so long, Jim's hinting that he might want to stay in the army when the war is over. He's learned so much and he thinks there may be a future in it for him. He hasn't said as much, but I'm beginning to read between the lines."

"I thought he was trained as an accountant?" Mrs. LeBlanc quizzed her daughter.

"He is, and I'm sure there's a job waiting for him with his old firm when he gets back. He just doesn't sound too enthusiastic about it now that he's learned all this mechanical stuff."

She paused, waiting for a reaction from either parent, but none came.

"I just want this war to be over. I'm so tired hearing about battles and people dying. I'm sick to death with eating Spam, and boiled cabbage. I'm sorry, Mother. There isn't much you can do to make Spam and boiled cabbage taste like a prime rib dinner."

She leaned her head back. "I want to wear a new pair of nylons and drive a car with the headlights on at night. I want to go to the movies and not see a newsreel filled with scenes of soldiers dying and bombs exploding everywhere."

Her father took a deep breath before responding. "Those men are far away from home doing a job they never asked for or expected. Each and every one of them is risking his life—bleeding and dying for us back home—for our freedom. Our job is to be here and support them every way we can. And if that means we eat Spam instead of steak so they can stay strong,—well, that's the least we can do."

"I'm sorry, Father. I don't mean to complain. I just want life to go back to the way it was before this whole thing started. I want to stop waiting for life to happen again. I want to get on with my future, with my career, with my life! I'm tired of being in a relationship with someone who is thousands of miles away and the only connection we have is letters."

"You should be grateful. That's more than some people have," her mother interrupted.

"Jim and I have been apart for almost three full years, Mother—for almost as long as I've known him. We need to spend time together if we are ever to marry. If he decides to stay in the army when everyone else comes home, I'm not sure if I can wait."

Her mother tightened her lips and began to fumble in her button box again. "You must learn to be patient, Ruth, dear. Patience is a virtue we must all aspire to acquire. Even you."

Ruth closed her eyes. "I don't know if I can, Mother. I just don't know."

September 1, 1944

Dearest Jim,

I just received your last letter. Sorry you were surprised about Sal being a fellow. I thought I told you all about him? He's been a great friend and support to me since you have been away. His father owns a large factory in Boston and Sal is vice president in charge of manufacturing all manner of supplies for the troops. His job is considered essential to the war effort, which prevents his enlisting or serving in the military.

He's become a regular when the crowd gets together. You would like him, I think. Perhaps we could all play golf sometime together or go to the Totem Pole? He has connections all over town, and I'm sure we would get first class service! Just what you deserve.

I am puzzled at what you wrote about your future plans. Are you intending to stay in the service? You mention how much you enjoy the work you are doing now and how much you have learned. I want you to be happy, Jim, but I have to be honest. A career in the army does not promise a prosperous future. I remember the housing at Fort Dix, and I do not want to live on an army base. I want us to be able to have nice things and enjoy the better things in life. I want to go to the theatre and buy a new dress once in a while.

Perhaps you do not realize the impact rationing has had on all of us back home! Everyone is glad to do it for the greater cause, but it has not been easy. Once this war is over life will be very different, and I want to thoroughly enjoy it.

I've been looking at some real estate magazines. There are some *wonderful new designs being developed by leading architects. After the war there will be new homes built for all the returning soldiers and their new families. It might be possible for us to purchase or rent a new home? Prices start at just $3,000.*

So much has happened since you left. Please write and tell me your thoughts...

Stay safe, much love, Ruth.

"Do you think money is important, Helen?" Ruth asked her friend a few days later.

"What did you ask?" Helen tossed a yellow legal pad onto the tall pile of folders on the corner of her desk and looked up. "Sorry, I didn't hear what you said."

"I asked if you thought money is important? Especially in a marriage."

Helen leaned back in her chair and crossed her arms. "What's going on? Did you get another letter from Jim?"

Ruth shook her head slowly. "I just can't figure him out."

"What's he writing now?"

Ruth reached into the pocket of her smock. "I just got this. I wrote him asking if he might share some of his ideas about our future together."

Carefully unfolding the thin sheets of paper she began to read.

About money... Money's not holding such powers over me as you would expect or like to have hold on me, and has caused me to be the target for many a smart gambler who could smoothly borrow my bottom dollar and never intend to pay it back.

And I wouldn't be bothered to chase him for it for I have always felt that it was more of a detriment to a person's life to have a bad conscience than to have to argue over a few measly dollars, which are only bits of green paper anyway.

"Only bits of paper? I don't think your boyfriend grasps the essential meaning here..."

"He seems to have very fixed ideas when it comes to money," Ruth continued.

> *You can't buy real love, and you can't buy religion and you can't buy a real helpmate, and you can't buy common sense and you can't buy character. So what the hell good is money? Oh yes, you can buy food, and you can buy clothes and you can keep a wife, but if these things were the most important things in life do you suppose I would work just to obtain them? Hell, no. I would be the happiest bum on the railroad. I could always get a hand out and wouldn't need to work for the rest of my carefree life. As a matter of fact if I ever get to the point where money disgusts me, why off I'll go to the nearest hobo jungle or ship on some lazy freighter to the southern climes and live off mother nature. That's the life anyway. Next to mother nature. The ground. Good solid rich black soil. The kind that green things grow out of.*

> *I better quit right now, or you will be sending "Dear Johns" special delivery.*

> *Your Jim*

"I think he must be trying to make a joke, Ruth. Don't take him seriously."

"You think so?" Ruth questioned.

"He's pulling your leg."

"I sure hope so, because if this is his attitude about money and getting ahead in the world, he will be getting a 'Dear John' letter."

"I would just ignore it."

"What I want to know is where do I fit into this picture? If he wants to be a hobo, I say let him. But if he wants a home and wife and family, then he has to wake up and change his thinking."

"I'm sure he's not serious. Wait for his next letter and if he continues to rant, then give him hell!" Helen grinned at her friend. "Come on, it's almost time for lunch."

Ruth waited for another letter from Jim before she responded, but a week passed and the next letter had no mention of money. Instead he let her know that in spite of his length of service he would probably be one of the last of his troop to return home.

Sept 3, 1944

Dear Ruth,

I managed to get off a letter to my stepmother as she was overdue for one. I wish she wouldn't be overoptimistic about my getting home. I guess you can't expect mothers not to wish, but I hate to tell her that many moons will pass before I get released. Somehow she got the impression that I was next in line or in any remote part of the line. I am nowhere near the top of the list, as a matter of fact, to my knowledge I am not even on it. She doesn't realize that the transport planes I work on can be used for many kinds of jobs. We will always be needed wherever there are G.I's to feed and evacuate, and my new responsibilities are in critical areas that are needed now.

Ruth frowned. The husband of one of the women at the Stage Door Canteen had just returned home. He had been stationed somewhere in Italy and had finally reached 85 points—the minimum number needed to be released from service. Once he got his discharge papers he had taken the first transport home that he could. Ruth knew he had joined up several months after Jim, which meant Jim should be eligible to come home soon, or at least get a chance for a furlough. But things didn't sound promising.

I got a letter from my pal Eddie. He just got back recently from a pretty active section. Left seven more buddies under the sod. He could get out of it as it was all voluntary, but the darn fool is afraid of public opinion. I have the best of confidence in Eddie. He has been overseas long enough now to know what the score is. Doesn't take any more unnecessary chances or have crazy ideas of trying to win medals. Losing guys who, the night before were his drinking companions, has sobered him up I guess.

The Air Corps is so different from the infantry. In the infantry the GIs plod along always within rifle shot of the enemy. In the damn

Air Corps, you may be hundreds of miles from action one day and the following day you're too dam close for comfort. Funny damn way to live. You're not a fighter but often wish you were.

Love, your Jim

Anxious, Ruth wrote back to Jim that same evening.

September 14, 1944

Dear Jim,

Please take care of yourself. Your last letter with news of your friend Eddie has caused me to worry more than usual. I won't mention anything to his family or our friends, but please be careful.

When will you be eligible for a furlough? Hazel was asking me the last time we spoke. Perhaps you mentioned the possibility in one of your early letters, or she may have read something in the papers. There was an article in The Globe just the other day, listing the criteria for demobilization. A number of servicemen who joined up early like you, are starting to return home. Tell me your plans when you can, and I will be waiting to greet you when you arrive. Please let me know soon.

Much love, Ruth

She folded the single sheet of air mail paper. Come home soon, she whispered. She placed the air mail letter in her satchel to post the next day on her way to work.

CHAPTER 15

BOSTON

R uth woke to the sound of howling winds and pelting rain across her bedroom windows. She took a quick look at the alarm clock on the side table: 5:38 a.m. Too early to be up and about. She pulled the coverlet closer and tried to block out the sounds of the storm. A muffled radio broadcast seemed to be coming from the front parlour below. Her father must be up early, listening to the latest weather report.

She tried to fall back to sleep, but the sounds of driving rain and wind made it impossible. Grabbing her bathrobe, she walked to the top of the stairs at the same time Justine came out of her room.

"What's going on? Sounds like a real whopper of a storm outside," Justine complained.

"There was nothing about it on the radio yesterday."

"You'd think they'd tell us ahead of time." Justine grumbled. Ruth agreed and the two sisters headed downstairs.

"What's happening?" Ruth quizzed her father. He was bent over the tube set, trying to tune in WBZ. "Sounds like a major hurricane or something."

"I've finally got the weather report. It's a major storm all right, but they're not calling it a hurricane yet. Any news is on a 'need to know' basis these days. I guess they don't want any passing U-boats finding out New England is in trouble."

"Why not? Do they think a submarine is going to wait for a big rain storm to attack Boston?" Justine asked sarcastically.

"Anything's possible these days." He looked at his daughters, standing in slippers and robes. "You two should check the back porch and be sure the awning's pulled in, and start the kettle, too. Your mother will be up most likely."

Ruth shuffled down the hallway towards the back porch, and Justine headed for the kitchen to heat a pot of water and start breakfast.

An hour later the four LeBlancs huddled around the radio, listening intently to the announcer report on the storm. They were finally calling it a hurricane. There was sure to be damage all along the New England coast. Residents, especially those near the shoreline were encouraged to stay indoors until the storm passed.

"Do you think it will take all day 'til this thing blows by?" Ruth asked. "I need to go to work."

"Don't worry about work." Mr. LeBlanc looked up from the radio. "From the sound of things, the streetcars aren't running. Neither are the buses. With this wind and rain, everyone will be staying home."

"You should take the day off, Ruthie. It's Friday after all! Call it a long weekend. I'm going to. It's hot tea and jigsaw puzzles all afternoon for me!"

Ruth had to admit she was secretly glad for the time off. Since Loyalty Week she had been working non-stop. It would be nice to have some time to herself.

"In that case, I think I'll spend the whole day in bed, reading," she declared.

No sooner had she spoken the words, but the lamp on the side table near the door began to flicker.

"If this wind keeps up, we're going to lose electricity." Mr. Leblanc turned to his wife. "You should find some candles, dear. I'll hunt for my flashlight in the cellar."

An hour later the lights went out and the radio died.

"That's it. Must be a power cut." Mr. LeBlanc sounded annoyed. "I'll check the fuse box."

"Be careful, dear, don't go getting yourself electrocuted." Mrs. LeBlanc looked worried. "Perhaps you should ask Mr. Carlton from next door check on it."

Ruth went to the window and looked up the street towards the Carlton home. "They've most likely lost power as well. I don't see any lights on."

"Probably the entire neighborhood," her father replied. "Those old trees up on Hancock were ready to fall over anyway. They should have cut them down years ago. I'll bet they fell right across the power lines. If that's the case, this could last a few days."

"We'll lose all the food in the refrigerator," Mrs. Leblanc worried. "I just bought a whole chicken at Mazzioli's. We'll have to eat it for dinner tonight."

Ruth looked at her mother. "Two problems with that, Mother. One, it's Friday and we can't eat meat, and two, how are you going to cook the chicken? The stove is electric."

Justine started to giggle, but one severe glance from her mother was enough to silence her immediately.

"We can use the Coleman Stove that's in the cellar," Mr. LeBlanc chimed in. "I'm pretty sure there are still a couple of Everdur tanks. Enough to cook a few meals, I should think."

Mrs. LeBlanc looked at her husband, grateful for the information. "You do the cooking, dear. I won't touch that thing. If you can get it to work, that would be wonderful. Just don't burn my good pans."

By lunchtime the Coleman stove and two gas canisters had been rediscovered in the basement, the chicken had been boiled, fresh vegetables peeled and prepared and the four LeBlancs sat down to eat by candlelight. The storm continued to rage outside.

"It's like a picnic!" Justine announced.

"With a special dispensation for eating chicken on a Friday," added Ruth.

"Don't tell Father O'Brien." Mr. LeBlanc reached his fork across the table, selecting a tender white breast and delivered it to his plate. "Although under the circumstances I think the dear priest would agree not to let a wonderful chicken dinner go to waste." Mr. LeBlanc grinned broadly.

"Do you think the storm will last all day?" Justine wondered. "What will we do for supper?"

"Don't worry, dear, there's plenty to eat. I'll use the rest of the chicken to make sandwiches for later and there are tins of tuna and jars of peanut butter."

Justine made a face at her mother.

"I'm aware tuna is not your favorite, but there are plenty of things to eat in the cupboard. We certainly won't starve in the day or two it takes for the power to be reconnected." She turned towards her husband for reassurance. "It will be only a day or two, won't it?"

"I have no idea. This is a big storm. Bigger than anything they may have predicted. Depends on the damage."

Just then the telephone rang.

"Power's back on!" Justine shouted.

"Not necessarily." Mr. LeBlanc reached for the phone. "Phones and power lines are on separate circuits. The lights can go out, but the phone will still work." He paused, and picked up the receiver. "Hello, LeBlanc house.... Oh. Hello Sal... How are you?... Lights out where you are? We've lost them here... That so?... You want to talk to Ruth? She's right here." He handed the phone to his oldest daughter, whispering, "Don't stay on too long, we should leave the lines open in case of an emergency."

Ruth took the receiver from her father. "Hello? Is that you, Sal?... Your lights out too? This storm has turned into a regular hurricane. No, I'm not going to work today. No buses or streetcars... depends on when the storm stops. What about you?... Well, be careful. There must be power lines down all over... Don't worry, we've got plenty of food. We're camped out with a Coleman stove and candles.... Yes, father set it up in the back breezeway... Don't worry we won't burn the house down... We just finished a fine chicken dinner." Ruth listened and started to chuckle. "I know it's Friday, but this is an emergency. I'm sure God will forgive us..." She grinned into the phone. "Oh, that's a good point. I'll be sure to tell my father.... No, we'll be fine. You don't need to do that... really, please don't go out of your way. Maybe tomorrow when the storm clears... Okay. See you then." She put the phone back in its cradle and turned to her father.

"Somehow Sal made it to his factory in the North End early this morning. They're running on backup generators. He said there are dozens of trees down across all the streets, and the power is off in the downtown area."

"What else? Has he heard when the power will be back on?" Mr. LeBlanc leaned back in his chair, waiting.

"He was checking to be sure we're all right. He was worried that we might not have any food, but I told him we're fine. By the way, Sal wanted me to remind you to be sure to only use the Coleman Stove outside on the back porch. Something about dangerous fumes."

"Hmph!" Mr. LeBlanc snorted. "Does the man think me a fool?"

"I think he was just trying to be helpful."

"Seems a little pushy to me."

Ruth shrugged her shoulders. "Sal's a good friend, Father. He called to be sure everything was okay here and said he'd check back later."

"I think it was sweet of Sal to call," Justine added. She turned to Ruth and gave her sister an exaggerated wink! "Is he coming over?"

"No." Ruth shook her head. "At least not today."

"I bet he'll be over first thing tomorrow," Justine teased. "He'll want to be sure you made it through the storm safe and sound."

Ruth ignored her sister's remark, walked to the front window and stood quietly, watching the storm rage outside.

❄

It wasn't until late morning the next day that the rains stopped and they could go outside to survey the damage.

"We're lucky." Mr. LeBlanc told his wife and daughters when he returned. "There's been some wind damage to the flower gardens, and one of the trees in the Carlton's side yard lost some branches. Otherwise things look okay."

"What about the power outage? Any news?" Mrs. LeBlanc was busy sorting through tins of soup, trying to calculate what they might heat up later for lunch.

"I asked Mark if he had heard anything. They lost power the same as us. He suspects those big trees at the corner of Beach and Hancock fell on the wires. It'll take a couple of days."

"What are we going to do? Everything in the Frigidaire will be ruined," she worried.

"We're just going to have to eat it all!" Justine joked.

Ruth was about to respond with a quick remark of her own when there was a loud knock on the front door.

"I'll go."

"If it's the power company tell them the power's out and we need it back on as soon as possible."

Ruth glanced at her mother. "I'll tell them."

As she approached the front door, she could see a figure standing on the porch, two large packages in his arms. It was Sal.

"I came as soon as I could." He grinned at her.

Ruth was stunned. "How did you get here?"

"Easy. I called up a couple of guys." He pointed over his shoulder to a New England Gas and Electric utility truck. "They were heading to your neighborhood so I asked if I could hop a ride."

Ruth had to laugh. "Sal, you are something else. You always seem to know a guy who knows a guy."

"It's the way I am, I guess." He laughed and held out the boxes. "Got a few things here for you and the folks."

Ruth stepped back and held the door open. "Of course, please come on in. Can I help you with these?"

"I've got 'em. Lead me to your kitchen."

Ruth led the way.

"What's all this?" Mrs. LeBlanc stood staring as Sal placed two large cartons of food on the kitchen table. She tried to sound annoyed at the sudden intrusion, but couldn't help being impressed.

"Just a few things I put together. I thought you might be hungry. Bread, three cans of tuna fish, cheese, crackers, peanut butter and a couple of cold salads and a little wine to see you through."

"Wine!" Justine exclaimed. "We can have a celebration."

"Thank you, Sal. Very kind of you to think of us." Mrs. LeBlanc stared at her younger daughter, "but I don't think we will keep the wine."

"Oh, Mother!" Ruth complained. "A little wine is just what we need. In fact, why don't we open it now. You'll stay for lunch won't you Sal?"

Sal looked from one woman to the next. "I wouldn't want to impose."

"Nonsense," Ruth answered. "If you're going to hop on that cherry picker for a ride home you'll have to wait a few hours while they repair the lines. Join us for lunch."

"Okay," Sal nodded. "I guess I will."

"Where's your father?" Mrs. LeBlanc asked Justine.

"I think he's down in the cellar checking the fuses."

"He'd better be careful," Sal interrupted. "Especially if there's been any water damage. I'll go down and see if he needs any help." Sal moved towards the cellar door. "I can ask one of the guys from the truck to help if you want."

Ruth shook her head no. "Let's get power on the street first. Then we can worry about our cellar and fuse box."

"Why don't you ladies prepare lunch and I'll go find your father."

By the time Sal and Mr. LeBlanc returned from the cellar a few minutes later, the table was set, and the wine poured.

"Isn't it romantic?" Justine asked. "I think it's actually quite nice eating without electric lights glaring down at us."

Mr. LeBlanc reached for a helping of cold rigatoni and prosciutto. "Where did you find this salad, Sal? It's delicious."

"I know a guy," and with that he gave Ruth an exaggerated wink. She couldn't help but laugh.

After lunch Justine, Sal and Ruth worked on jigsaw puzzles and took turns playing word games. The afternoon passed quickly.

By five o'clock the power had returned to their Bromfield Street neighborhood, thanks to Sal's influence and his friends in the utility truck. When it was time for him to leave, Ruth walked Sal to the front door.

"Thanks for all your help, Sal. And make sure to thank your friends, too, for the special treatment."

"Anything for my girl."

Ruth tried to ignore the remark. "Be sure to tell them we're all really grateful."

Sal stood at the front door as if waiting for something. Ruth sensed he was expecting a hug or kiss but knowing her mother was watching, she couldn't bring herself to do more than give him a pat on his shoulder.

"Thanks again."

Sal nodded, smiled quietly and left.

"He made it to your house in Wollaston in the middle of the storm?" Helen was incredulous when Ruth told her friend about Sal's visit the following Monday.

"It wasn't during the storm. It seems Sal knew a guy who knew a guy who knew another guy who was repairing lines a few streets north of us. He drove the electric utility truck and Sal hitched a ride."

"He really is something else." Helen looked at her friend closely. "Now I'm certain he's sweet on you. If I ever doubted it." She paused and then continued. "So whatcha gonna do about him?"

Ruth looked down, trying to hide the blush that was quickly spreading across her face.

"Nothing, Helen. You know I can't. It was sweet of Sal to come by, but..."

"He rescued your family from starvation!" Helen cried.

"We were fine with what we had on hand and would have made it through the next couple of days without any help."

"That's not the point and you know it, Ruth LeBlanc. Sal came to your family's rescue! Even your mother will have to be impressed with him now."

Ruth laughed. "True. Mother had to admit Sal was very nice to think of us. But I don't think it changed her mind. She still thinks of him as a rival to Jim."

"Well, isn't he?"

Ruth glanced down at her watch eager to change the subject. "It's almost ten o'clock, and I've got a ton of work to finish before lunchtime. I've got to get crackin'."

"Ok, but don't tell me a few months from now that I didn't warn you!

You're going to have to make up your mind sooner or later. Sal's a great catch."

Ruth didn't respond, but she knew Helen was right.

It took several weeks for all the storm damage to be cleared from the streets. Thousands of citizens had lost power, but thankfully there were very few casualties. After all the excitement of the hurricane, things finally began to settle down.

Helen's challenge to Ruth that she choose between Jim and Sal still lingered. Instead of dealing with the question, Ruth put all her efforts into her work. The holiday season was just around the corner and new orders for promotions and ads came in every day. She headed to the office extra early each morning and left long after sundown each night. She had no time for socializing.

"I don't have time for lunch, Helen. I've got to focus on meeting all these deadlines."

"You are working too hard! You'll wear yourself down to a frazzle," Helen warned. "You have to stop to eat once in a while. Go out, go dancing. I'm sure Sal would love to take you." She waited for a reaction. None came.

"If you keep this up, Jim will never recognize you when he gets home. You'll be a walking bone!"

Ruth frowned. "I hardly think that's likely."

"Well, I'm just saying. You want to keep that svelte figure," she paused, "no matter which guy comes through the door!"

Ruth looked at her friend. "I know what you're thinking. You want to know if I've made a decision? Is it Jim or Sal?" She shook her head as if trying to make the answer come clear. "I'm too busy to think about it."

It helped that there had been no word from Jim since his last letter in early September but Ruth wasn't worried. If anything had happened to him surely someone in the Doherty family would have called her.

On the first day of October, a large envelope containing two separate letters finally showed up at 180 Bromfield Street.

Sept 22, 1944

Dearest Ruth,

I am now an inspector. I like my job very much for it gives me the opportunity to study more than one type plane. I have a good assistant who keeps the records and most of my time is taken up with actual inspecting. The only drawback is no one loves an inspector as he finds too much work for them to do. But I like to see things done correctly.

Jim was right. No one likes a task master, and Jim would be one for sure. He was probably tougher on himself than on any of his crew, but no matter, it wouldn't be easy to work for him.

What have you been doing lately? I try not to think of what distractions you might have in the way of male acquaintances both in physique and rank, ahem!

I know it's only September, but I've been thinking about Christmas gifts. I would like a shaving kit for Christmas if you would. A compact one if possible.

I am not near any place where I could buy things for you folks back there and if I were, I'm sure there is nothing in this hole that would be worth near as much as what you could buy for yourself in the States. But I won't ask you to do all that hard work of shopping for my family again this year. I shall try and write the various stores and see if they won't handle my shopping for me. Sort of take care of things that way. Last year it was most selfish of me to ask you to put your self out in that manner.

Do you ever go out with any of the lucky chums that are around you at home? Honestly darling, I can't expect you to stay home and be lonesome. I will feel jealous but at the same time I will know you are happy at least. I can't tell what is in the future, not over here.

Love, your Jim

❄

Sept. 30, 1944

To my best friend and fiancé:

It seems that with my new job time just isn't sufficient enough. I have so much to do and it seems so little time through the day, to get it all done.

I'm hoping that my news about this new job has not caused you some disappointment. It means I will not be coming home anytime soon.

Looks like I've got to get going over here since my friend Captain Jerry Brennan has advanced so far in this war. I feel like a dumbbell or such a person. You know, perhaps one of my shortcomings is that I seem and act too damn independent. I have had words with about every high non-com in the outfit.

Do you people realize that winter is coming and that winter brings mud? And trucks and tanks bog down in mud. That heavy rains limit the activity of aerial warfare. That with winter coming and the recent temporary setback at Arnhem, it is going to take a bit longer. This is sound sensible thinking. Don't look for the end of the European mess until about the first part of next year at least. I can give you my opinion and that's all.

News of the Battle of Arnhem he mentioned had been all over the papers in the last week. Thousands of British and American soldiers had been killed or captured by the Germans in an attempt to free the Netherlands. It was a significant defeat for the Allies.

Wherever Jim was, it must be cold, and raw, and windy. She looked out her bedroom window. The sun had set an hour before but she could still see the trees in the front yard outlined against a darkening October sky. That morning she had noticed that the maple had only just begun to turn a brilliant red. Despite the damaging winds of the hurricane it was going to be a colorful fall. She thought of Jim sitting on some cold Italian airstrip on the other side of the world and felt a wave of longing come over her.

After a few moments she continued to read...

Perhaps now Churchill's speech about casualties, 90,000 British, 145,000 Americans, will have a sobering affect on the many overly optimistic folk back home. Don't people realize that the Japs are the real problem? That even if the Philippines and Formosa were taken that we still have to prevent the Japs from retreating to Manchuria where they could direct adverse action against us for a long time. That the islands being so far apart will require a great transport system? Let's keep our feet always on the ground.

There is no point in sending experienced and fully trained personnel back home and replacing them with green men just because two years have passed. Hell, we are at war. When I go home it's to stay I hope. If I went home now, I would be overseas again in three months. You wouldn't like that now, would you?

Bye for a while darling. Our love will keep if it's the real thing.

Your Jim

He sounded discouraged and angry. What puzzled her was that he seemed to be angry at all the people back home, including her—as if they did not know what was going on. It was more than time that she wrote Jim another letter.

October 5, 1944

Dear Jim,

I just read your latest letter dated September 30. It came in the mail this morning. You sound discouraged, I hope this message finds you in better spirits. Perhaps the enclosed photo will help you feel better. It was taken at Boston Loyalty Week in August. That's the MWDC uniform I wear when on plane spotting duty. I'm officially an Air Raid Person in the Massachusetts Women's Defense Corps with your brother David. I wrote to you about it some time ago.

Unsure if you heard the news, New England and most of the East Coast was hit by a hurricane a few weeks ago. We lost power for a day or so, and several trees fell, but thanks to good friends we survived the storm without any major difficulties. The seawall by the Wollaston Yacht Club suffered some damage but nothing that cannot be repaired.

You should know we keep up with all the news of the war every evening. Father's taken to listening to the nightly news on the radio in the front parlor. We all join him if we can.

I've been very busy with client work. The holidays are not too far off and some of the biggest retail stores on Washington Street have commissioned me to create advertising campaigns. The work has kept me busy, and I seldom have a chance to get out. There will be plenty of time when you return for us to go dancing or out to see a play or concert. I look forward to a time when we can be together again.

I understand your frustration with your current rank. But you should not compare yourself to Jerry Brennan or anyone else for that matter. You are a very talented man, and I'm sure your superiors will soon recognize your abilities and promote you. In fact, if they don't, I'll write to them myself giving you the highest recommendations! (I'm teasing.)

I met your old boss from the accounting firm the other day. He was leaving the building as I was arriving. He asked to be remembered to you and wanted you to know that your job is still waiting for you when you return. That's wonderful news, isn't it? He seemed very enthusiastic.

If you are thinking of staying in engineering you will need to look for a new job here in Boston and I'm sure it would not be easy. After all you've been through it would be so simple to just go back to the accounting job you enjoyed before you left. It would mean a steady paycheck and a solid future for you. Isn't that what you want?

We have so much to talk about, Jim. Sending you love and best wishes to stay safe.   Love, Ruth

❦

Two weeks later another package of letters arrived.

Oct. 11, 1944

Darling:

Got your letter dated October 5. It contained the most wonderful gift I have received in quite some time: a picture of you in uniform. Ruth, you look simply stunning in uniform. Was I the proud fellow this evening, showing you around to all the fellows!

At first glance some questioned my girlfriend joining the WACS, as that is strictly Taboo. That is for "free lancers," not engaged girls. But upon learning that you were a member of the D.C. they were more than pleased. One chump even kissed the picture for which he owes me his beer ration. You don't mind kissing a strange GI so Daddy can have his beer do you?

"Good old American stuff" he says. "I says, Waddya mean "stuff?"

Oh well, you can't blame a G.I. for anything anymore.

Sam Brown belt and pleated pockets with pleated skirt. What a dish. I'm terribly proud all over, dearest. Say, does that shirt come as part of the uniform? Such a stiff collar. Doesn't it feel odd to wear hard collars all day? What are the shoulder straps for? Do you expect to become an officer of the Corps?

I rather hoped that one uniform in the family would be enough but if you are happier to belong to an organization that requires a uniform, why I shouldn't be dissatisfied.

Boy what I wouldn't give to take you out strolling one of these sharp fall days. Of course I don't measure up to certain of your acquaintances, but I promise to be a better man than when I left. (Even if I have to ask for a rest camp out west before coming home.) Many fellows pick the nearest camp to their homes when they get a furlough, but I shall pick one as far away as possible so that I can get my teeth fixed without giving into the temptation of seeing you, before I am patched up.

October 18, 1944

Lots has happened in the last week and it is difficult to know just what to tell you. Censorship is severe and I don't want to get called to the censors carpet. You capish?

It is astounding to contemplate just what will happen if the people of Germany take up arms and resist against our Armored Divisions. Rather think they won't for it might have terrible results

Ruth thought back to the last week's headlines: Germany had finally withdrawn from Greece and the Allies had entered Athens and liberated the city. Had Jim been a part of that assault? A few days ago the German city of Aachen had been captured by U.S. forces.

I had a very pleasant interruption a couple of days ago. I was called to the line phone from off the field. I was cussing out whoever it might be on the other end, for things were getting rough out here in the wind and rain and I wanted to finish on the deadline.

Well, so help me hanna the party on the other end was none other than Captain Jerry Brennan. He seemed terribly excited, while I found myself surprisingly cool. So cool, in fact, I postponed seeing him until I finished some work. After all, another four hours wouldn't make a difference since it was almost three years since last seeing him.

Our reunion was deep felt. We approached each other, Jerry with his good natured smile and I with my sober face, (self conscious about my teeth) and he almost shook my arm off. He waited a few more minutes while I changed clothes, arranged some work and got a pass and then off we went in his jeep.

It was a thrill to hear someone actually speak about being the last one to talk with you. I almost wanted to touch him to see if I could grasp any nearness of you from him. A crazy notion wasn't it? I'll bet I questioned him about you for over an hour until I realized I was being selfish with the time that we had. I was due back at 11 P.M. for further duties.

He picked out a nice quiet and clean little restaurant where the spaghetti was served with that sprinkled cheese. It was a great meal and we talked our heads off. It was real interesting listening to his many different trips and jobs. He has been over about 18 months now and doesn't know himself when he'll get back.

His apartment once belonged to an Italian countess and it was richly furnished with all carved furniture, plush seats, draperies, thick rugs and great rooms. He and four other Captains have this deal all to themselves. His job, by the way is with some P.O.E. outfit. Jerry is in charge of troop movements but couldn't say much else about details. (P.O.E. is Port of Embarkation.)

Jerry sends his best wishes. I'll arrange to see him again so will have more news. Bye for a while

Your Jim.

Ruth thought back to the last time she had seen Jerry Brennan. It had been a few days before Christmas in 1941. Jim had invited her to meet a few of his friends for dinner at Amrheins, one of the Irish pubs near Broadway Station in South Boston. Jim's brother David was there and one of the clerks from the office named Mark. Half-way through the meal, Jerry Brennan showed up with a girl on each arm and a broad grin across his face.

"Sorry, we're late. I'd like you all to meet the twins, Judith and Blanch Conway. They're dancers with the USO show. Just arrived in the city and I asked them to join us. Hope you don't mind."

The two young women were identical twins and impossible to tell one from the other. Jerry took particular delight in calling each by the other's name, totally confusing Jim and everyone else at the table. It had been a raucous evening of fun and teasing and Ruth had throughly enjoyed herself.

Knowing Jerry was in Italy and took the time to visit Jim made her glad the two were such good friends. If anyone could lift Jim's spirits, Jerry could.

She turned to the third letter in the package:

November 6, 1944

Hello Ruth:

Right now I can hear the shrill singing of Arabs and the dull pounding of their drums, but never fear it's only on the radio. But it does bring me back to those long cold nights standing guard in open country.

If you always thought of Africa as the land of sunshine, you can take my word for it. It's not. The days are warm but that's to be expected, but it sure surprised me that first night on the desert. I froze my—off. I dug a fox hole just to keep warm, and to get down out of the wind. I didn't like sleeping on the ground, because of the infernal centipedes. They are poisonous and give a nasty sting.

And then with the moon shining through a haze and the wind kicking up the top of the sand and flinging it hard against ones face, all this accompanied with that weird noise coming upwind from an Arab camp. Such moaning and carrying on the like of which I never before experienced.

Now and then a shot would ring out from one of the guards on the outposts. Arabs sneaking around to see what they could steal. One night I allowed a flock of sheep to graze close to my post, when I noticed one of the sheep walking off with a gasoline can. I let that hunk of mutton have some lead and he took off like a bat out of hell. After that, the sheep grazed a safe distance from my post.

Do they still expect air raids over there, complete with black outs? Boy, if you people don't give the G.Is a laugh, nothing will. Do you know that Lyons, France is lit up like a Christmas tree every night? Do you know (and sister, this should give the women in the States a hint) that the women of France are the most modern dressed and prettiest the G.I.s have ever seen. They have the most exquisite hairdos. Our WACS look a poor second against some of these French girls. Silk stockings, shoes, the latest styles in furs and hats and every woman—even old women—seem to have their hair as though they just left a beauty salon. That's my idea of a girl anyway. Just as though she had left a beauty salon, for I hold to that old fashioned idea, that women should be feminine.

One of the guys from our unit is now working in a depot in Kansas. He likes the work but he said a few things about the civilians that made us guys get burned up. He tells of how some of the civilians are just taking it easy and dragging up the money on pay day. He says that if they accomplished in a week what our squadron can do in a day they would go on strike for double money.

That's the way it is though, the poor joker in the fox hole pays through the nose while palooka crying for higher wages back in a well lighted and air conditioned plant, sits on his dead ass and collects $1.20 an hour for it.

Boy, I don't love civilians no how, and it's going to take time to readjust myself. And if any of those lunkheads ever start waving the flag for union wages after this war, I'll turn around and join the army again.

Love Jim.

Reading the last few paragraphs, Ruth felt herself getting angry. Civilians were not lazy bums taking advantage of the war to make lots of money and live in luxury. If it wasn't for those factory workers busting their chops every day on endless assembly lines building bombers, jeeps and tanks to ship overseas, they wouldn't be wining the war!

She knew the soldiers had it rough, but so did everyone stateside. She was working harder. She pinched every penny she could, and darned the ladders in her stockings until the stockings were just patches of repairs. She hadn't bought a new dress in ages.

Jim could complain about "lazy lunkheads," but he didn't understand half of what the home front put up with.

She decided to set him straight in her next letter.

Saturday, November 18

Dear Jim,

It's Saturday morning and the neighborhood is still quiet. Father is downstairs listening to the latest news reports on the Philco and I can hear Mother in the kitchen getting out her pots and pans. Today is a big cooking day in preparation for Thanksgiving which is this coming Thursday. We've been saving all our ration tickets for weeks and Mr. Mazzioli at the neighborhood market has promised us a decent sized turkey this year. There won't be any extra special treats, but we should have enough for all the traditional fixings: gravy, stuffing and vegetables.

Of course I'm hoping you boys get the real thing served to your table this Thanksgiving, and that's actually why I'm writing.

I want you to know how upset I was at your last letter. I don't think you appreciate what it has been like for us fighting the war from a distance. We may not be fighting battles with bullets and guns, but we sacrifice our needs, our desires, our time and all our energy in support of the war effort.

Everyone is making a sacrifice. In just our neighborhood, families have lost sons and fathers to the war. Mrs. Carlton next door lost her nephew at Omaha Beach this past spring.

Both men and women go to work every day of the week to help produce whatever it is the army needs. No one is asking for a hand out or special treatment as you suggest in your last letter. Everyone I know is giving their last bit to help win this war and bring you boys home.

I find it very hurtful that you and your buddies think we are just "palookas" and "lunkheads" trying to take things easy and then complain about the low wages.

We are all in this together. We, here on the home front, and you and the rest of the boys fighting on the front lines. We all want this to be over soon. And when you do finally come home you'll find us all eager to welcome you back. But not if you see us as the enemy.

I hope you and all your fellow soldiers have a peaceful holiday.

Thinking of you,

Ruth

She folded the letter into thirds and placed it in an airmail envelope. It was harsh perhaps, and blunt. But she was angry and what she wrote needed to be said.

She thought about not mailing it, but after taking another day to think about it, she dropped the letter in the mail on her way to work Monday morning.

※

Thanksgiving day dawned cold and bright. The LeBlanc family had been planning and saving all their ration stamps since Halloween. It would be a small gathering, but there would be plenty of food. The Montgomery family was invited, of course, and Uncle John and Aunt Cora would arrive before noon. Sal had offered to pick them up at South Station and deliver them to Wollaston so they could relax for an hour before the meal.

Ruth and Justine met the Ford convertible at the curb.

"What a wonderful car, Ruthie dear! So comfortable," Aunt Cora gushed. "And your friend Sal—he's such a wonderful driver." Her aunt handed a large covered plate to Justine. "Here, dear, take this in to your mother. I made some of that War Cake for dessert."

Justine nodded, "Yummy!" She guided the older couple up the path towards the front porch.

Ruth turned to Sal. "Thanks so much for picking them up. It makes the trip so much easier for them." She glanced along the street. "I think you're the last one to arrive. Why don't you park your car in the driveway and come on in, at least for a while."

"I'm sorry, Ruth, but this is the one holiday I have to be with my family. My mother is counting on me to make my special pasta dish! Maybe one day you could join us!"

"Maybe. Who knows what the future may bring, Sal."

There was little Ruth could say. Instead, she leaned over and gave his cheek a quick kiss. "Have a wonderful holiday. Say hello to your family

359

for me."

Sal grinned and pulled the car away from the curb.

Ruth watched as the Ford headed north towards Quincy Shore Drive. She couldn't help but wonder if she would ever celebrate Thanksgiving with the Marcusios.

Oh well, no sense wasting time over what might never happen, she thought as she walked up the path and back into the chaos of another LeBlanc holiday feast.

November 29, 1944

Dear Ruth,

Since I last wrote I have had all my teeth fixed. I have been very self conscious about them for many months and I feel almost like a new man with those old jagged ones removed.

This evening I received a package of treats from my sister. Such delicacies, but I am going to give them to the hungry kids in the neighborhood. They will enjoy them much more than I.

Jerry called me today. He told me to say hello to you. Poor old Jerry. He has "heart trouble" again. Right now she is miles from him and he is feeling sorry for himself. I told him to take courage from me. See how nobly I am standing up under it!

Ruth had to smile. Leave it to Jerry Brennan to fall in love with a pretty woman in every town.

Did you have a nice Thanksgiving? I'll bet you put on weight that day.

I shall never quite forget that first Thanksgiving over seas. I guess it will be okay to tell now. There I sat in my cozy little pup tent. Can of C rations in one hand and water canteen in the other. It was pouring rain. That morning, according to orders, I had dug my foxhole and drain ditch, cleaned my gun and set my pack for immediate movement. None of us knew what the score was. I kept thinking of those G.I.s laid out for burial just across the road next to the big trench. They were alive and excited same as I two days before, but they took the brunt of the scrap to make it safe for guys like me to land. I thought of that quite a bit. The chaplain had all their names. I supposed it would take him weeks to write all those personal letters.

That night it was my lot to stand guard at the extreme end of our bivouac. None of us felt that we could trust those French Legionaries camped close by. Sure, they had turned over to our side, but to us they were our enemy two days before. Let me tell you, I was scared.

Several times that night I let one fly at an Arab prowling near the tents. You just couldn't keep those thieves away. Strange to say they wouldn't steal guns or money. The fools wanted clothing and food. (Winter was coming.) An Arab would do most anything for a can of rations.

I'll tell you in private about the French gal and the parachute. Poor innocent me.

Ruth quickly turned the page over looking for more of the story. It was blank. A gal and a parachute? She could only guess. Seems I'll have to wait till he gets home, she thought.

It didn't take long to see life in the raw. And I mean raw. Things were happening fast those days. At least they seemed so. I finally became accustomed to the Arab tricks. By keeping myself hidden, I would let them close and then do some sneak work myself.

What an odd feeling came over me when I crowned one of them with a rifle butt. I thought the man was dead but he merely was unconscious. When at last he came to, I prodded him with the bayonet until he was off my post. He didn't fool around again that night. There is no sense turning them into the French police. Too much trouble getting things straight.

Boy I was glad when we moved away from those legionnaires. They were rough looking gents. During the day I could see them charging the dummies they had set up. The were always practicing with bayonets. Those same legionnaires were the probable cause of that long line of American boys lying by that big trench that Thanksgiving morning.

Oh, well, as the French always say, C'est La Guerre.

I just re-read your letter from October. You mention our shopping for a home?

I was looking at some pictures of modern homes. I didn't like them at all. Maybe I'm old fashioned but I don't like circular houses. These looked like storage tanks with windows in them.

And just where do you suppose we could dig up $3,000 to pay for a house, anyway? Listen hon, I'll be lucky if I can foresee the future in a two room flat where you hang your shirt tail on the fire escape. But we will figure something. The real important thing is to figure each other out. It is going to be just like meeting each other all over again. You may not like the change in me. But I prefer to be optimistic. I think you will.

Love, your Jim

She paused over the line *"You may not like the change in me."* Was he talking about his new appearance now that his teeth had been fixed? Or his view of life? She couldn't be sure.

Ruth opened the second letter dated a few days after the first. It was written on a different type of paper in blue ink rather than the usual black. The lines of text were penned so close together it was difficult to dicipher.

December 4, 1944

Dear Ruth,

No, it's not to be another one of those letters. The reason I use merely "Dear" is that I feel that I am in the dog house and trying hard not to feel sorry for myself.

Yesterday was Sunday, a honey of a day and working was a pleasure in the mild weather with bright sun in the sky. I had promised Jerry

I would meet him late in the afternoon if I could get away.

Well I was able to manage that o.k. and off I started with your recent letter from November 18 in my pocket. I had just received it and was going to keep it until I could get away some where alone and sort of concentrate. I often do that you know. I don't like to read your letters if its noisy or where I am distracted from giving it all my mind.

Anyway, I got me some transportation and met Jerry at the appointed place. We went to his apartment and had lots of fun talking and drinking. Just an old time gab session. I had to leave rather early as I had a long journey ahead.

When I got back, everyone had hit the hay, but I couldn't' wait to open your letter. I concealed the light under my blanket, took my nail file and opened what I hoped would be a nice "love" kind of letter. But you soon changed that but definitely.

Ruth paused to recall her last letter. She had been upset with his attitude towards civilians back home. He seemed to think no one was doing their bit, and she had given him a bit of hell for his insensitivity to all their efforts and sacrifices.

It's hard to make excuses and have them sound genuine. You mention that there are many neighbors about you who have sons in the service that have been through all the intense fighting since the war started. My hat goes off to those fellows and I earnestly hope they find their way home.

I retreat for those things I said about civilians—I publicly apologize, to you, your friends and of course your family to whom you no doubt are reading this letter.

I stated my complaint on very weak grounds. Having witnessed the sight of tremendous supplies overseas, I should be proud of the fact that our civilians back home have done the almost impossible task of making a peace time army into a first class modern fighting team all done through the effort of those home bodies behind the productions lines.

I don't quite remember what I had said about people in the States, but it's quite evident that it caused hurt feelings.

I'm puzzled to know why you continue to take all or any of my wise remarks as being applicable to you. You're easily hurt aren't you?

It's always been my opinion that a woman on the verge of tears is the sorriest looking individual ever, and it leaves me wondering just how much I had said to get you into that state of mind.

You can be sure that whatever I have said about people back home, I once again retract my statements. For I have been tied up in me so long that I can't speak intelligently anymore on the wonderful things that been done in the way of saving lives.

I am proud of you, and the work you have been and are doing.

Darling, as I sit here with the light shaded from my comrades, I can't help but think of just what a chump I must appear to your family and mine.

Remember how I once said that if ever I insulted you, we would never see each other again, well that still goes. When and if you ever think I have insulted you or caused your family to be ashamed of me, I shall do the noble thing and just fade out of the picture.

Would he really fade away? Ruth thought. I doubt it. Jim is nothing if not dramatic. He swings from one extreme to the next.

You think that I am merely writing words, don't you? You say that actions speak louder than words, you're right I guess. I am at your mercy as far as our love affair goes. I love no one else and have no desire for another.

I guess I gummed things up in general for now.

Soon I shall experience another Christmas overseas. I'll work through the day same as any other day I guess, but hell, you folks back in the States won't take a holiday so why should I? But if I can, I'm going to get feeling good, then the next day won't be so bad for I shall probably be nursing a big head and forget about how much I miss home and you.

I shall try hard, Ruth, to measure up to your ideal, but please be lenient with me in the meantime. You might tell the folks that their son is now a Tech Sgt. Only one more stripe to Master.

Your Jim

She looked at the signature and sighed. What am I going to do with you, James Doherty? You blow hot and cold like the wind.

She re-read the letter and decided it was time to contact his family again. After all, Christmas was coming.

※

"What did you get Jim for Christmas?" Helen asked.

"He was very specific this year. He wanted a DOPP kit—one of those compact toiletry sets made of leather to carry his toothbrush, tweezers, hairbrush—that sort of thing. He lost the one the army gave him."

"Sounds practical."

"Hmmm. Of course I filled his with chocolates and sweets. And added a few pounds of nut crunchies to share with his pals. I hope the candy doesn't melt before he opens the box."

"Did he ask you to buy presents for his family again? That was quite a chore last time."

"One of Jim's soldier buddies just got back to the states and stopped by the office last week with money from Jim to buy gifts. So I guess I'll be buying a few for the family."

"Well, if you need help, ask. There's barely two weeks left before Christmas and I've decided to devote next Saturday to Christmas shopping. Gary is out of town so I have the whole day to myself. Why don't the two of us meet at Jordan's and make a full day of it? Buy everything at once."

Ruth laughed. "Sounds like a lot of fun. One day and done."

"Downtown is sure to be a mob scene. But who cares. We'll face the onslaught together." Helen grinned at her friend. "Make your lists, clip your coupons and be sure to wear decent shoes. We may have to walk every street in downtown and walk into every shop, but if we plan it right, we'll get it all done in a day."

Ruth had her doubts, but Helen was a good strategist. One day to shop for all of Christmas? It might be possible.

Early Saturday morning the two friends met outside the entrance to Filene's. They were the first customers in the store and made a beeline for the most critical departments: the perfume counter for Ruth's mother and Jim's stepmother Hazel, a new comb for Justine, a pair of cuff-links for her father and Mr. Doherty. Before the Christmas crowds began to flood the downtown sidewalks, Helen and Ruth had crossed off more than half of their shopping lists.

"Let's go to The Spanish Shop at Jordan's," Helen suggested. "I need to take a break."

They found a small table towards the back of the café and ordered a plate of sandwiches and a pot of tea. "My treat, Ruth. I insist." Helen held her hand up as Ruth began to protest. "Gary finally got his Christmas bonus, and I have money to burn." Ruth reached for her wallet.

"Don't even try. I insist. It's done."

"Helen, you don't have to do this."

"Yes, I do. Call it a Christmas treat. You're a good friend, and I want to do this. You've got enough on your plate buying all these gifts for Jim's family besides your own."

"Well, I do appreciate the treat, and all your help." She glanced down at the paper lists on the table between them. "I think we've done well so far. I can purchase most of these other items at the local drug store in Quincy."

By the end of the day as dusk began to settle over the city, two very happy shoppers headed home carrying bags full of gifts for their families.

It was after seven when Ruth finally reached Bromfield Street. Perhaps there would be a letter or package from Jim waiting for her? But the hall table was empty.

Maybe later this week, she thought. There's still time before Christmas.

Ruth kept her hopes up, but by the end of the week no letter from Jim had arrived.

"There's still Saturday's mail, Ruth." Helen encouraged her friend. "I'm sure you'll have a letter by tomorrow."

"Well, if not tomorrow, it will have to wait till next Tuesday. They won't be delivering mail on Christmas Day."

"Unless it's a special delivery!"

"Jim would never send a special delivery telegram."

"Well, I'm sure he's thinking of you, even if he doesn't write as often as you'd like. There's still a war going on."

Ruth thought about the news headline she had read that morning: Germans Slash 20 Miles Into Belgium. The radio broadcast the night before described the battle as a last effort for Germany to secure its borders. The press called it "The Battle of the Bulge" because the Allied front line bulged inward on all the maps. The Allies had been taken by surprise when the Germans first launched this latest offensive but the Americans were determined to defeat the Germans once and for all.

"They thought the war would be over by Christmas, Helen. But they were wrong. This is going to go on for months until Germany gives up."

"If they ever do."

※

The winter air was sharp and cold between the holidays of Christmas and New Year. Factories were in full production, but most office workers had been given time off and Ruth had let all her clients know she would be unavailable until after the first of the year. It was a week to rest and celebrate with friends and family.

Each morning when no letter from Jim arrived in the morning mail, Ruth braved the cold as she walked the half mile from home to the post office on Beach Street. Perhaps a package or V-Mail from Jim had gone astray? He had made a mistake addressing a letter once before. It was worth checking. But no package or letter was waiting.

On Friday she called the Doherty home wondering if they had heard anything and spoke with David. He told her Hazel had received a Christmas card a week before the holiday with a new picture of Jim in his sergeant's uniform, a wide smile on his face, showing off his new teeth.

"I'd be happy to show it to you, Ruth, next time you come by for a visit. You should stop by soon; it's been too long."

"I've been so busy at work—getting ready for Christmas sales. But now that the holidays are passed, I'll have time for a proper visit."

"You should come this Sunday. It's New Year's Eve. Hazel and the others would love to see you. We can bring in the New Year together. I'd be happy to pick you up."

Ruth thought for a moment. She hadn't yet made any plans for the holiday and she knew her family would most likely be in bed with the lights out by ten o'clock. Justine had already announced she would be staying at a friends house.

"That might work, David. Is it a dress up affair?"

David laughed. "I hardly think so. Just a few of the family gathered together. My sister and her husband, my girlfriend Doris, of course, and my brother George and his wife. It'll be very simple."

"Can I bring anything?"

David assured Ruth that they had all the food and liquor in hand. "Hazel no doubt will make her special pot pie. Bring a big appetite. I'll pick you up at 8 o'clock."

"What are you doing for the holiday?" Sal asked when he called Ruth the next morning. "I'm sorry it's such late notice. I've been trying for days to get tickets to the New Year's Eve party at the Ferngate's Satire Room. I picked them up this morning."

"Oh, Sal, I wish you had said something earlier."

"Don't tell me you've got someplace else to be?"

"I'm going to the Dohertys for the evening. David invited me just yesterday."

"But these are $5,000 tickets! To the most expensive Jazz Club in Boston. Anyone who's anyone will be there."

"You should have told me."

"It was supposed to be a surprise. It's a big fund raiser for War Bonds, and it's very exclusive. I didn't tell you because if I couldn't get the tickets, I didn't want to disappoint you."

"I don't know what to say, Sal."

"You could change your mind. Tell the Dohertys you'll visit them another time. There are plenty of Sunday dinners. But there's only one New Year's Eve."

"I understand, but the Dohertys are expecting me. The whole family is getting together, and Hazel is making a special dinner. I don't want to disappoint them."

"But this is the Satire Room!" Sal pleaded. "I'm sure the Doherty family would understand." He waited but when Ruth didn't answer, he continued. "Here you have a choice to eat a dinner of boiled ham and potatoes, sitting around telling family stories and looking at old pictures, or you can come with me and celebrate the New Year in one of Boston's most exclusive clubs."

Ruth felt trapped. If only Sal had not waited so long to ask her. She would much prefer to spend New Year's Eve with him, but what could she do? She was beginning to feel manipulated and she didn't like it.

"If you had asked me a week ago—even a few days ago, I would have been eager to join you. But as it is, I've given my word to David and the others."

"So your answer is no? I can't believe your turning me down."

"Why did you wait so long to ask me?" Ruth questioned. "Did you just assume I'd be free?"

"No, no of course not, Ruth. I just didn't think..." his voice trailed off.

"There must be someone else you can ask to join you. What about Carmen? Perhaps Louise Carboni? She's always keen for a grand night out."

Sal didn't respond.

"Are you still there?"

"I'm still here. I wish there was some way to persuade you to change your mind."

"I'm sorry, Sal. I can't do it. I gave them my word I would visit this Sunday. They're making it into a special celebration. I have to go." She paused, then continued, "You should really call Louise. She might be free."

"I don't think so, Ruth, but thanks anyway. Enjoy your New Year."

She couldn't help but hear the disappointment in Sal's voice. "I'm sorry, Sal. Maybe next time?" She knew it sounded silly, but she couldn't help it.

"There's only one New Year's Eve, Ruth. There is no 'next time.'" And with that, Sal hung up.

The New Year's celebration with the Doherty family was a pleasant low-key affair. Hazel had draped brightly colored paper chains above the parlour windows and door frames in an effort to decorate. The only other sign of the holiday was a large cardboard cut-out pinned to the wall above the mantle. A baby in a top hat with a cloth draped strategically across his middle announced "1945" in bold red letters "Happy New Year!"

In the dining room the table was covered with platters of Irish soda bread, slices of Spam, and salmon surrounded by carrots and potatoes artistically arranged. In the center of the table was a steaming pot of chicken pot pie.

"Hazel thought it would be easier to have a buffet rather than a sit down meal tonight," Doris explained. "That way no one would be stuck in the pantry all evening."

Ruth looked around. She could see that Jim's father and his brother George were already enjoying second and third helpings of food as well as beverages. Empty beer bottles were stacked up in neat pyramids against the wall.

"That makes a lot of sense," Ruth answered. "What can I do to help?"

"T'ere's nothing to be done, dearest." Hazel rounded the corner from the kitchen, carrying another platter of crackers and Spam. "It's grand to have you with us." She found a spot on the sideboard for the appetizers and came over to give Ruth a bear hug and kiss.

"Right. Now find yourself a plate and a pint and come into the parlour. I need to know all that's been going on withya."

Ruth circled the table and picked up a few pieces of soda bread and a serving of the chicken pot pie. She avoided the Spam.

"Would you like a glass of whiskey?" David asked. "I recall you're not much of a beer drinker."

Ruth hesitated and then thought, why not? "If you could make me a Tom Collins that would be great."

"I think I can do that. I'll bring it in to you."

Ruth found a spot on the couch by Hazel and Jim's sister Brigid and for the next two hours was regaled with Doherty family stories, many which featured young Jim in embarrassing situations. She doubted if most of them were true, but the family certainly enjoyed telling them. Jim had been the butt of many jokes. It was no wonder, she thought, he had issues with self-esteem.

At midnight the family all gathered in front of the baby cardboard cut-out and lifted their glasses. Mr. Doherty led the toast:

"May the Lord keep you in his hand and never close his fist too tight on you, and may the face of every good news and the back of every bad news be toward us in the New Year!"

"Hear, hear!" "Cheers!" "Sláinte!"

Hazel then raised her own glass: "I want the troubles to be over and Jimmy 'n Eddy home safe 'n sound again. Let's pray that next year they can be with us to celebrate."

"I'm for that!" "Let it be so!" "Cheers!" "Sláinte!"

Kisses and hugs for all and wishes for world peace followed.

It was not quite one o'clock when David caught Ruth's eye. "I think we should probably head out. It's getting late."

Ruth began to say her good-byes. "Thanks for inviting me, Hazel. It was a lovely party."

"Right. It was grand to see ya again. Don't be a stranger now. We're family after all."

As David drove her home, Ruth had time to think. She thought about Sal and wondered if he had made it to the Satire Room. Not that it mattered. The Dohertys were simple people but generous and kind. The party hadn't been elegant or exclusive and the only music had been Glen Miller on the Philco, but she was glad she had chosen Jamaica Plain over Beacon Street. She had made the right decision.

1945

CHAPTER 16

NAPLES

A few days after New Years a large padded envelope arrived. Military markings were stamped across the front. Mrs. LeBlanc handed it to Ruth as soon as she got home from work.

"I've put on the kettle. You go find a quiet spot for yourself to sit and read and I'll bring you some tea. Your father's helping out at his club tonight so he won't be back till after supper."

Grateful for the quiet, Ruth went to the front parlour, settled into her favorite chair and opened the envelope. There were at least four letters inside.

December 12, 1944

Just received your letter.

Received your package all right and was most pleased with the gift you sent. The toilet set is compact and is the ideal type for in the field. Equipment suffers some rather severe punishment but the leather case you sent will stand up for quite some time. Now if I don't lose it I shall consider myself lucky. The candy bars and nut crunch and boxes of cookies I plan to give to the local kids.

How is your mother these days? Give her my best regards and tell her I shall refrain from heaping abuse on the defenseless civilians. She must think I am nuts talking the way I did. Just tell her the guy has been overseas too long.

Tell my folks not to worry one bit about me for there is no reason. The fellow I mentioned before as the one going home with my dough should be there by the time this letter reaches you.

I hope he got there in time for you to buy the folks and the family some little thing by which I give them my remembrances.

I haven't bought you anything for I can't imagine what you want that they have over here in this bare countryside, but I can arrange for some little trinket to make you realize I am thinking of you always.

Any little trinket from Jim would have been welcome. She wasn't looking for anything expensive or fancy. She was disappointed he hadn't sent her something in time for the holiday. Of course it wasn't his fault if the mail was delayed.

I hope you have a chance to get out and meet people for the holidays. I want you to go to parties and have a good time. Find someone to take you dancing, as I know how much you enjoy that.

Well dear, there isn't any news that I can tell you that would pass the censor. Do you like oddities or descriptions of the country? Aside from being generally crummy it isn't a bad place in peace time.

The Germans sure wrecked several of the big factories so that the people will loaf for quite some time before they can get around to making an honest days wages. Their standards of living are far below ours so it doesn't make much difference to the present generation just what happens over here. They have been so used to poverty now, that any change would cause a near revolution over here.

Many people think Italy is highly religious. This is a touchy subject at best, but I will go so far as to say there are more religious minded people in the City of Boston than there are in all of Italy to my knowledge. They have been subjected to some pretty severe changes both in government and politics.

You would get quite a kick out of something that happened to me a few days ago. I was with Jerry Brennan one night and we went into

376

a place to get a drink. I laid 500 lire on the table to pay for the bottle of wine, turned my back just a few seconds and this babe all dressed in furs picks it up and hides it where she knows I wouldn't look. Boy, she was the smoothest operator I ever did see. Jerry got a big laugh out of it, but what could I do? I couldn't take if from her and all complaints are merely answered with a "no capish."

Oh well, it only increases my intense dislike for everyone Italian.

Give everyone at your house my best regards. Heck, I just got to be home before the next Xmas. Tell your folks, I wish them all a Happy New Year and to you darling, I wish it to be our happy year.

Your Jim.

❀

Dec. 27, 1944

Dearest Ruth:

The old holiday is past now and with it all those sentimental verses and carols that did nothing but tug at my heart strings. I didn't think of it as a joyous holiday in the least. We did manage to dish out a little joy to the kids around here but hon, the "gremlins" hit me last Friday and Saturday morning found me in the hospital until Monday afternoon. Nice Christmas. Bah humbug.

But darling, I shouldn't complain, when many a G.I. had to spend his holiday in a foxhole or gunpit. My ailment was an infection in a very touchy spot and it required my spending all my time under treatment lying on my tummy.

He had an infection on his back a while ago. Perhaps it has flared up again, she thought. He has to learn to take better care of himself.

Did you have a nice Christmas? I was thinking of you and home all through the Christmas season. I couldn't get to send everyone greetings this year, but my thoughts were all of home just the same.

Jerry called the hospital and wished me a Merry Xmas. He had a quart of Christmas cheer but I couldn't manage to see him due to my difficulty.

I wrote you that I had spent all of the Christmas season in the hospital. Well to make up for lost time I will have to work all through the New Year holidays

Ruth sat back and closed her eyes. Here she sat, cozy and warm, surrounded by the support of a loving family, the happy memory of Christmas and New Years only a few days old. The whole time Jim had been out flat in some cold military hospital feeling miserable and alone.

December 31, 1944

Dearest Ruth,

If you look at the date of this letter you will realize the fact that I am closing my year of writing to you on the last day of old 1944. I will not write anyone else today for that is a privilege granted only to you. Yours was the first letter I sent out this year, and so it shall be the last. Something nice and sentimental about that don't you think?

Incidentally, in keeping with this tradition, I shall bring in the New Year with the same policy. I shall write my first letter in the New Year to my future wife, for if she is willing for us to join together, then this year of 1945 would suit me fine. If I can secure a furlough we might marry as soon as I get back to the States.

Only an out and out optimist can say there is only one more year of war. I think there are at least two full years counting from this day on. I may be wrong and certainly I hope I am, but I would rather think ahead that far and have my mind accustomed to the long awaited day when it is all finished then to expect it to end in another few months.

Ruth and her father had been discussing this subject the night before. How long could this war go on? News reports from the European front seemed optimistic. But who knew the real truth? And there was still the war with Japan to deal with. Would they ship Jim out to the Pacific?

The recent setback in Germany may result in the final conclusion of that affair before the summer is over, but Ruth if one is to remain levelheaded and practical, the war with Japan can easily stretch out another two years, for those damn Japs are just as liable to take a definite stand in China as well as they have in Yokohama. And if they do, it will take the G.I. with rifle in hand to finally dislodge them. That is the costly part of it. The Air Corps helps tremendously but the foot soldier still has to go in there and take actual possession of the land.

Tonight the boys are planning a little time and I just know it is going to be another brawl but it's not for me, no sir. I have had three of them thus far and that is enough. Let the new men in the outfit get their belly full of lousy liquor and the head of the morning after. I am going to hit the sack at about nine tonight, New Year or not New Year. I will be thinking of you just the same.

Well, darling I am going to wish you a happy New Year and may it see us together again, just you and I - Alone.

Love your, Jim

Ruth wrote back to Jim the next day.

Friday, January 5, 1945

Dearest Jim

First, Happy Birthday to you! This letter comes to you filled with blessings and good wishes to keep you safe and sound.

I just received a large parcel of letters from you dated from mid December through to New Years. I don't understand why it took so long for them to reach me, but I'm very glad they finally arrived.

I was so sorry to hear about your latest hospital stay. And on Christmas too! You work too hard. You need to learn how to take time off whenever you can.

The family were all here for the usual holiday dinner and we said a very special prayer and lit a candle for you and all the boys overseas. Your friend Sergeant Jackson stopped by the office in early December and gave me the money you sent for your family's presents. I was happy to shop for you. Helen came with me and we did it all in one day. I think your family was pleased with the gifts I selected.

I spent New Year's Eve with your family. Hazel put out quite a spread, and we ate and drank until the wee hours. I especially enjoyed spending some time with your sister Brigid. She has a great sense of humor and shared a lot of stories about you and the scrapes you used to get into. I had no idea you were such a trouble maker!

I'm glad you are able to spend time with Jerry Brennan. I remember him from before the war. He is such an optimistic fellow. I'm glad he is near by to cheer you up when you are down.

I need to be honest with you. I don't want to marry as soon as you get back. As I've written before, I think we need to spend a lot of time getting to know each other again. It's been three years since we have been together and we've both changed a lot. I know I have. I expect you have as well.

War has changed us both in ways we don't yet realize. We are very different from those two starry eyed people who fell in love before the war. You sound very anxious to make me a bride as soon as you get back. But that is not possible. I need more time than that.

From what you have told me in the past, it seems you should now have many more points than are required to be furloughed. Isn't that true?

Even if the war goes on for a few more months or even years, haven't you already done your bit? If you have met all the requirements, why would you want to stay in the service?

So the sooner you are able to return to civilian life, the sooner we can begin to get to know each other and make plans.

Anxiously waiting for your answer, - Your Ruth

It only took a week for Jim to respond, but his letter left Ruth with more questions than answers.

January 12, 1945

My dearest Ruth

Glad to hear you managed to get everyone some little thing with the century I sent you. I knew you would do the unselfish thing and spend it on everyone else.

You didn't even get a card from me, did you? Well, I only sent two Xmas cards this year, one to your family and one to mine. I just didn't feel that I had any Xmas spirit left so I acted accordingly. As a result, you suffered and I didn't worry much about the feelings of anyone else at the time. Gosh, but I am frank. Too frank as a matter of fact.

But darling, that old old feeling hit me New Years, but hard. I was in the hospital Christmas and New Years and still have to go for treatments everyday. I got myself an infection and didn't take care of it at the start. One morning before Xmas I woke up with a fever and a very sore back. I knew something wasn't right so I thought I'd see the medics. The doctor ordered me to be admitted immediately. I should have known better. This makes twice I had to lay up due to my own fault. They pretty near buried me, boy—I got me a case of poison that just about put me out.

You asked me about points and whether or not I am eligible for a furlough. I don't know. I am busier than ever and can't even think about all that now. I hope you will wait for me no matter what, but don't stay home. You have my blessing. You should go out and meet new people and have fun.

Darling, keep up the wonderful job you are doing but always keep this thought in mind. Jim loves you entirely for you alone and someday he is coming home to you to live with you for the rest of your life!

I love you Ruth, Your Jim.

"He didn't answer any of my questions," Ruth sputtered. She handed Jim's letter to Helen and pointed to the last couple of paragraphs.

"He doesn't mention anything about a furlough or when or if he might get out. Now he wants me to go find new people and start dating again! I don't even think he wants to leave the service." She shook her head in confusion. "He's impossible to figure out!"

Helen re-read the last paragraphs. "At least he's not trying to tie you down."

"What do you mean?"

"I think you should take him up on his offer. Go meet new people. Start dating. Fall in love with someone new and see what Jim says when you write to say you're done with him!"

Ruth gave a short laugh. "You're joking, right?"

Helen shrugged. "Why not? It's his idea. You've been waiting for him to come home for three years. He's got to have enough service points by now. If Jim wanted to, he could leave the service tomorrow and be on the next transport home. But he doesn't want to. You're waiting for a guy who doesn't really want to come home."

"That's not true, Helen. He's doing valuable work. And the Squad leaders appreciate what he's doing. Maybe his work is so important they won't let him go, even if he has all the points he needs."

"Maybe." Helen didn't sound encouraging. "You have a choice. You can stay home, do nothing, go nowhere and feel sorry for yourself and wait for Jim to finally get discharged or you can get out there and enjoy life."

"I do enjoy life," Ruth protested. "I do things with you and I go out with the crowd once in a while."

"I don't think that's what Jim means. It sounds a little crazy. Maybe it's reverse psychology, but I think he wants you to start dating. Shop and compare! And discover Jim's your best bet, after all."

"The only dates I've had since Jim left were with Sal, and they were mostly for business. You realize how confused I am about Sal. I'm just not interested in the "shop and compare" routine."

"So don't do it if you don't want to. No one's forcing you to. But don't stay home all the time. You've been struggling with the Sal or Jim question for months. Now's your chance. If Sal asks you to dinner, go with Jim's blessing."

Ruth put up her hand in surrender. "Okay, okay. I get the message. I promise to not become a recluse."

She decided to take Jim at his word. It had been weeks since Sal had called or stopped by. They had met once or twice when the crowd got together, but she still felt a little awkward since that mix up around New Years.

"Don't worry about it, Ruth." Sal insisted. "I was disappointed, but it was my fault. I should have asked you weeks before. I won't take you for granted again. I just want to see you. I thought we might try Mother Anna's restaurant here in the north end. It's a small place with great food and best of all it's quiet. We can actually have a conversation."

"Is anything going on? Have you got another big project coming up?"

"No big projects. Just wanted to meet and have a quiet dinner with you. Find out how you're doing. We haven't had a long talk in a while. The restaurant's only about a five minute walk from your office on Milk Street. I'll meet you inside and I'll drive you home afterwards."

When Ruth arrived at Mother Anna's, Sal was seated at the bar keeping an eye on the front door. As soon as he saw her, he signaled the maitre d' and the two were immediately seated at an intimate corner table.

"You look wonderful, Ruth. But you always do."

"It's been a long day of work, so I have to say I doubt the quality of your eyesight."

"Well you look great to me." He reached for the wine list. "Would you like to share a bottle?"

"Sure, why not? I'm done with work for the day."

Sal ordered a bottle of red Chianti. "Jimmy, we'll have a bottle of Roma, and I think we'll have the Steak Pizzaiola and a small antipasto." He turned to Ruth. "I hope that's alright?"

"Sounds delightful. I'll leave it to you to choose."

"I come here often with clients. Everything they serve is delicious."

The waiter returned with the bottle of Chianti and showed the label to Sal who nodded his approval. He then uncorked the bottle and poured a small amount of the brilliant dark liquid for Sal to taste. "It needs to breathe a little, Jimmy, but I'm sure it'll be fine. Leave it. I'll take care of pouring the wine."

Ruth was watching carefully. "You do know your way around wines."

"My father taught me. When you're always entertaining clients and business partners you need to be sure everything is top notch."

"And is it?" Ruth asked.

"Is it what?"

"Top notch? The best of everything?"

"I like to think it is. That's one reason the business is so successful."

Ruth paused and considered her next question before continuing. "Do you ever wonder what would happen if we aren't successful? If we don't win this war?"

"Impossible. Every day we get reports we're winning. I can't share any more than that, but trust me, the Allies are defeating Hitler and the troops will be heading home. Even your Jim will be back." He studied Ruth's face. "You're happy about that, aren't you?"

She avoided looking at Sal directly. "Of course. Jim will be coming home at some point. I just don't know when, or if he'll be staying."

"What do you mean?"

"He wrote to say he might want to stay in the Air Force rather than come back to Boston. He might decide to take a rotation in the states and study more about engineering rather than go back into accounting."

"What do you think about that?" Sal reached for her hand, just touching the tips of her fingers. She did not brush him away.

"It might be the best decision for him, if it's what he wants for his future, but it's not something I want."

"Have you told him so?"

"I've tried to, but I'm not sure the message is getting through." She paused as Sal poured them each a glass of wine.

"Everything is in motion and nothing is fixed." She shook her head. "We'll have to wait and see how things go when Jim gets back."

Sal's fingers gently closed around her hand. "You know, Ruth, if there's anything I can do for you—or for Jim. Just say the word."

"You're a dear friend, Sal, and I appreciate all you've done for my family. You're always there for me." She took a sip of wine. "The war isn't over yet. Who knows what the future may bring."

There were no letters from Jim in the month of February and the dreary New England weather kept everyone inside listening to their radios. Word from the front was filled with news of the bombings of Berlin, Dresden and Prague and the defeat of German troops throughout much of Eastern Europe. Ruth prayed Jim was still safe in Italy, but she couldn't be sure.

"They're starting to talk about post-war spheres of influence," Mr. LeBlanc announced at dinner. "Something called the Yalta Conference. All the big wigs got together to decide the new borders and who gets what after this is all done."

"What do you mean, dear?" Mrs. LeBlanc asked. "Please pass the bread."

"Europe is a big grab bag, Mother," Justine interrupted. "Every country wants to grab every other country and rule the world."

"Not exactly, Justine," Ruth chided. "Every country has been scarred by this war. German troops invaded so many nations that all the borders got changed. Churchill and Roosevelt are just trying to put things back the way they were."

"Don't forget Stalin," Mr. LeBlanc added. "He has a lot to say about it, too."

"I don't like Stalin. I don't like his mustache," Justine added. "It makes him look a little sneaky."

"Don't be silly, Justine. I'm sure Stalin is a good leader for his people," Mrs. LeBlanc commented. "Would anyone like more broccoli?" She held out the platter, but there were no takers.

"Any news from Jim? It's been almost a month." Mr. LeBlanc looked at his oldest daughter. "I hope he's well."

"Last I heard from Jim, he was doing okay. He's been talking to his commanders about possibly getting a furlough. He deserves time off. But nothing is certain."

"Would that mean he would come home for good?" Justine asked.

"No. A furlough is like a vacation—but just a few weeks. Everything depends on whether he can get away."

"Well, make sure you tell him we're thinking of him next time you write, dear." Mrs. LeBlanc said. "Now, who wants dessert? I made an apple pandowdy."

An hour later the dinner plates had been washed and dried and the kitchen cleaned and ready for morning.

"Ruth, if you have a minute, I'd like a word." Mrs. Leblanc pulled a kitchen chair out from the table and sat down.

"What about?" Ruth asked. She had her suspicions but didn't want to initiate the discussion.

"You mentioned Jim might be coming home on a furlough."

"It's possible."

"I want to know your intentions. If he comes home are you planning to get married while he's here?"

Ruth was taken aback by her question.

"The only reason I ask is that if you were going to get married, we need to make plans. I'd have to call Father O'Brien and have the banns of marriage read out from the altar. It takes three weeks. So if you were thinking of marriage, I need to know."

Ruth shook her head, dumbfounded. "Mother, I have no idea. Jim is only talking about getting a furlough or a rotation. He hasn't even asked for one. And even if he gets one, I have no idea when that would happen."

Her mother looked crestfallen. "These things are very important to me, Ruth. You may not agree with every church tradition, but there are rules that have to be followed."

"I understand what you are trying to do, Mother. But I can't help you. I have no answer. If Jim does come home, we need—I need—to take time before we can even begin to talk about marriage again."

"Have you changed your mind?" She studied Ruth's face. "Is it Sal? Have you thrown Jim over for that Italian?"

"Mother!" Ruth exclaimed. "How can you say such a thing? Sal is a friend, and he's been very good to me and to this family." She stood up. "I have not thrown Jim over for Sal or anyone else."

"Then you won't be getting married when Jim comes home on furlough?"

"There is no furlough, Mother. There may never be a furlough. When Jim comes home, we'll decide if and when we'll be married. I can guarantee you one thing for sure. It won't be in a hurry. So don't worry about announcing banns of marriage or anything else."

"I see."

Ruth paused to catch her breath. "Jim's been overseas for more than three years. He needs to find his footing again. He needs to find a job, for heaven's sake." Ruth looked at her mother. "Don't rush us, Mother. You won't be hearing wedding bells for a good long time."

It was mid-March when Jim's next letters arrived, bundled with a page ripped from the 12th Squadron Newsletter.

March 7, 1945.

... we are sad to have lost our most able Inspector T/Sgt Jim Doherty, to the office of the Group Air Inspector, but we are proud that a member of our Engineering Department should be selected for that position, and our best wishes go with you, Jim.

Ruth reread the clipping. Jim had been reassigned? Was he still in Italy? She quickly opened the letter and began to read.

March 12, 1945

To the sweetest gal, I have been promoted from Squadron Inspector to Group Inspector. Busier than all h—. With this new job there's a chance I'll be offered a commission but I'm not sure if I should accept it.

It may mean more money and prestige, but it puts the wet blanket on my chances of getting home for awhile. I am telling you but just don't know how to tell the folks. I reckon they were sort of expecting me this summer. See what you can do to break the news, gentle like.

She knew it! This new promotion was going to keep him overseas a lot longer than she had hoped.

Hell, no one has any kick coming. I could be under one of those countless little white crosses I have seen in these battle areas overseas. I don't have a d—thing to be sorry about. I feel God has spared me thus far and if it's only anguish for home that I must suffer, I guess I can take that.

I want to see you very, very much. I believe around August, I can get home. I shall bitch to the high heavens at any rate.

I have kept you away from others for over three years now, it is time we married. I want to give you a husband and perhaps a family and I know you want the same and the sooner the better for both of us.

But, there is that other side of the question.

The war looks as though it may have two years more duration. If not over here, at least in the Pacific.

Please Ruth, always keep uppermost in your mind this one thought: "Jim loves me and wants to get home to me."

Now I can't shape words like a romanticist. I can describe airplanes and write about them, but when it comes to thrilling a women with endearing words of charm I fall far short of my target. In my blunt fashion, Ruth, I want to say that many many times, as I work, eat, write, fly or am just waiting, my thoughts drift across the wide expanse and creep into that garret to a little table in the corner next to the window. They are right there my darling, but you can't see them. Cherish the thought that "he loves me deeply."

Your Jim.

That night Ruth did not sleep well. She went over Jim's letter again and again. Next morning before going to her desk, she went straight to Helen's office and handed her the letter.

"You're the only one I know who can help me straighten this out," she declared. "I feel like I'm being pulled in two directions at once."

Helen quickly glanced at the letter and then at her friend. "You look like you need to sit down."

Ruth slumped into the overstuffed wing chair Helen kept in the corner for the occasional client visit.

Helen took her time studying Jim's scrawl. It was not the easiest to discipher, but after reading it through a second time, she folded the pages, handed them back to Ruth and declared, "It sounds like he loves his job, he loves you and he definitely wants to come home, but, I think for Jim, it's a matter of pride. He thinks you'd rather have him home as an officer than an enlisted man, so he's confused and can't decide what to do next. He's convinced you'll wait for him until he figures it out."

"He should come home! I don't care whether he's a lieutenant or not."

"But I think it matters to Jim." Helen studied her friend. "Haven't you told me he's always comparing himself to that friend of his, Jerry something or other? The one who lives in the mansion and can get anything he wants."

"Jerry Brennan. He's a captain and a quartermaster. Jim does envy him."

"He wants to do as well as his buddy. You can understand that."

"I do, but it doesn't matter. Jim is talented. I'm sure he won't need to be an officer to get a good job once he gets out. Before he enlisted he had a good job at Cuddahy's. He's an excellent accountant."

"But does he want to get a job as an accountant when he gets home? From what you've told me, he loves being an engineer and working on planes, getting his hands dirty. It doesn't sound like pushing a pencil is the career he wants for the rest of his life."

Ruth paused before answering. "If becoming an engineer, working on planes and inventing new gizmos is what he wants, then Jim will stay in the military. If he really wants that for a career he should stay in Italy, or go to California, or wherever the Army Air Force sends him. But if he loves me and wants the two of us to be married, then he has to come home."

Helen studied her friend. "If he comes home and doesn't become an officer or go on to study engineering, he'll probably take the first accounting job that comes along. Would that be okay with you?"

"Of course. Accounting is a fine profession."

"It doesn't pay much and you have to admit you have expensive taste, Ruth."

"Jim won't be at entry level for long. I believe he will advance quickly. Maybe even open his own office someday."

Helen was skeptical. "Whatever you say. But don't be surprised if he doesn't come home on the first boat. I think he's taking it for granted that you're prepared to sit around waiting for him to show up no matter how long it takes. He's clearly got more than enough points to get out. Another man would have been back months ago. If you really want to get on with your life, you need to make it clear to Jim he's not the only fish in the sea. You need to keep in circulation. Tell him he has competition."

Ruth listened but did not respond.

"Jim loves you but he's not rushing home to your arms, is he? I think he's taking you for granted, and you're crazy to let him. You should tell him more about Sal."

She looked down at the letter from Jim, then back at Helen. "I guess I better answer this right away."

March 26, 1945

Dearest Jim,

I received your latest letter dated March 18, and have to admit, upon reading it, I was upset and confused.

I feel you are taking my love for granted. I have waited three very long years. It is time I get on with my life. I would like you to be a part of that life, but not if you take that love as a foregone conclusion. I have had many opportunities to meet other suitors while you have been away. Remember, you encouraged me to stay busy and have fun. I have remained loyal to you but there is a limit.

I don't care if you become an officer before you return home. It's not important to me. Just come home safe and sound. As far as your future career is concerned, there are many opportunities for accountants here in Boston. I'm sure your old office will have an opening for you.

Enough of this. I don't want to argue, especially in a letter. I'm proud you were promoted and considered for officer training. You work so hard at your job. Congratulations. But please don't follow this path. It's time for you to come home. I promised to wait for you to return and I have. It will take time to get reacquainted after you are back, but I look forward to the day when you step on USA soil again.

Work is very busy. Helen invited me to her house for dinner. Her husband, Gary, gave us each a bottle of perfume as a special spring gift. Helen is so lucky. He is a very charming man. The office will never smell the same after this!

I will write again soon with more news, but wanted to get this off to you before any more time passed.

Come home soon,

Ruth

She mailed the letter the next morning on her way to work.
"I think I communicated my concerns to Jim in the most gentle way," she

told Helen when they met for morning tea. "I think he'll ask my opinion the next time he has to make a major decision."

"Or he'll suffer the consequences?" Helen teased.

"Believe it."

✿

Ruth's intuition was confirmed by the end of the week when a letter from Jim arrived. She read it as soon as she arrived home from work.

"So what's the big news from Jim?" Justine asked.

Ruth put the letter back in its envelope. "He needs to decide if he'll take a furlough or a rotation if he's asked, and he wants my opinion."

"Well, tell him from me to get his bony tail back here whichever way he can. He's been overseas way too long. Time this war was over if you ask me."

"It might not be too long before it actually is over. The newspapers this morning were filled with stories about the capture of German troops by the Allies."

Justine frowned. "There are all kinds of rumors. I heard one of the women at Mazzioli's market say that some of the top brass in Hitler's army were running for the hills."

"Don't believe everything you hear, Justine. Those madmen won't be giving up so easily."

Their conversation continued at dinner that evening.

"Good news," announced Mr. LeBlanc. "There are signs of Germany's defeat everywhere. Even the German prisoners they've got locked up at Fort Devens are calling for Hitler to stop the war. Just listen to this:"

He unfolded his *Boston Globe* and began to read.

1391 Nazi Prisoners at Devens Appeal to Fatherland to Quit -

An appeal by German prisoners of war in the United States to German soldiers and people to "put down your weapons immediately" is being broadcast to the Reich. The War Department made public the text of the message tonight saying that the petition was signed voluntarily by 1391 of the 3102 German prisoners of war held at Fort Devens, Mass.

"Do you think anyone will pay attention?" Justine asked. "I actually wonder if there's anyone in Germany even listening anymore." She reached for more mashed potatoes. "I read in the paper General Eisenhower believes all the leaders have scattered to the four winds and there's no one left to make a decision."

"Well, someone has to decide," Mrs. LeBlanc responded. "If not, the fighting will just go on and on."

"Don't worry," Mr. LeBlanc attempted to reassure his wife. "President Roosevelt knows what he's doing. One way or the other he'll get General Eisenhower to stop this horrible war."

"I certainly hope so, Father. I long for the day when things are back to the way they were, when we don't have to save ration books or count out stamps for sugar."

"Or eat Spam." Justine chimed in.

"I want to be able to order a cup of coffee at the corner deli once in a while. I am so sick and tired of drinking Postum," Ruth added.

"It won't be long now, girls. The Allies are moving forward. Hitler can't hold out much longer. Thank God we've got a President in the White House who knows what he's doing."

A week later Sal phoned and asked if he could stop by her office. Ruth wondered if Helen had somehow suggested the meeting. No matter how Ruth protested, her friend seemed determined to get her back into the social scene, and managing to place Sal directly in her pathway was one tactic Helen was likely to try.

"Ruth, I need your help with something special," Sal explained. "And I know you are the best one for the job. Please let me take you to lunch." I need to do some shopping in town and wondered if you would help me." Sal urged.

"I'll help you out and even join you for lunch, but you have to let me pay my own way."

Sal sounded offended. "Do you really think I'd let you pay? I'm taking you to Locke-Ober's."

"Oh!" Ruth instantly realized the famous restaurant was far above her budget. "Isn't that a men's club?"

"I made reservations for the second floor dining room. Women are allowed."

"Well, that's awfully kind of them," Ruth teased. "Locke-Ober's an easy walk from here and it's a beautiful spring day to be outside. I can meet you there. What time?"

"One-thirty if that works for you."

They met outside the restaurant and Sal escorted Ruth past the entrance to the first floor and its private dining areas and bar, and upstairs to the second floor dining room.

"Could we get a place by the window, Sal?" Ruth whispered. "It's such a dark room."

Sal passed the request on to the maître d' and they were quickly seated. Ruth's back was to the windows so it was easy to scan the large room. Diners filled linen covered tables and waiters dressed in black tuxedos and crisply starched dress shirts quietly scurried about carrying trays filled with beautifully designed entrées and deserts. One curious thing: all the waiters had grey hair. Of course, she thought, all the young ones are off to war.

Sal opened the oversized menu as their waiter approached. "Hello Johnson. Good to see you."

"Good afternoon Mr. Marcusio, Miss." He nodded towards Ruth. "We have some wonderful new items on the menu this week."

Ruth looked over the selections. It was a very full menu. Even in war time it seemed everything was available for the Locke-Ober patrons.

Sal offered a suggestion. "Their clam chowder is excellent, and I can recommend the broiled scallops without reservation. Unless you prefer the sirloin?"

"No, scallops sound wonderful."

The waiter nodded. "Would either of you care for a cocktail?"

Sal glanced at his watch. "Too early for me," Sal remarked. I want to have a clear head today. I've got some important shopping to do." Sal ordered two club sodas.

Sal had a very smug look on his face as if he were keeping a grand secret. "Tell me what this is all about," Ruth urged.

"You'll see soon enough."

"Can you give me a hint? At least tell me who we're buying for."

Sal shook his head no. "You'll just have to wait and see."

Ruth knew she would get nothing more out of him.

While they waited for their meal, Sal told her the history of the restaurant. "It's one of the oldest in Boston. Opened sometime in the 1870's I think. It's always been famous for wonderful French cuisine." He gestured towards the ceiling. "There are private dining rooms on the third floor. It's a great place for businessmen to meet. I often bring clients here."

"I'm surprised they let women in. I'd heard it was an exclusive men's club."

He laughed. "It is sort of, but women are welcome here, on the second floor. Just don't try to go in the main bar downstairs though, or I think they'll politely escort you out the door."

"I'm happy to stick by you for the duration."

"Hopefully we won't have long to wait. Service here is excellent."

No sooner had Sal made the comment then Johnson arrived with their clam chowder. The entrée course soon followed. The food was excellent.

"Would you care for dessert, Ruth?"

She held her hand up in protest. "I couldn't, but thank you." She glanced at her watch. "We should be going. I can help you do some shopping, but I really have to be back in the office no later than three-thirty."

Sal settled the bill and the two friends headed towards the center of downtown.

"Let's go this way." Sal said. "The store I want to take you to is just a few blocks up the street." Ruth let Sal lead the way. The sidewalks were filled with shoppers, and it took a few minutes to make their way. Finally Sal stopped in front of a multi-storied office building and pointed to the sign at the entrance. "Boston Diamond Jewelry Building."

"This is it." He opened the door and they stepped into an elegant marble lined lobby. Brightly lit crystal chandeliers filled the space with a warm welcoming glow. After the crush of the sidewalks, the quiet of the foyer was a relief.

"The store is on the seventh floor. You don't mind walking up, do you?"

"Seven floors?" Ruth gasped.

"Only kidding. The building has an elevator." He took her hand and led her to the far end of the lobby where a slim, uniformed woman stood waiting.

"Which floor, sir?"

"Seven please. Ohanian Jewelers."

The woman pulled the large brass lever, closing the elevator doors.

Ruth turned. "Sal, you want me to help you pick out jewelry for someone?"

"Don't worry. You're the right person to help me."

"Are you sure? Jewelry is a very personal thing. Is this a gift for your mother or a new girlfriend I don't know about?" Ruth was beginning to feel a little nervous.

Sal didn't respond.

The lift seemed terribly slow. The operator stopped at every floor, checking to see if anyone needed the lift. No one did. Finally, the doors opened at the seventh floor and Sal led the way down the corridor to a glass door with the name "Leon Ohanian Sons Co., Fine Jewelry since 1919," etched across the pane.

"Here we are."

Sal opened the door and led the way into the brightly lit shop. Glass counters filled with sparkling jewels set in gold and silver lined three sides of the small rectangular room. Shelves set into the dark mahogany wall panels, each lit with a bright spotlight, showcased the finest rings and pendants.

An older gentleman, Ruth assumed it was the owner, immediately asked how he could assist them.

"I'm interested in purchasing an engagement ring. A diamond of course," Sal answered.

"And is this the lucky lady?" the man asked, turning to Ruth.

"Yes." Sal answered, turning towards her. "She doesn't know it yet, but this is the lucky lady."

Ruth was stunned. "Sal, what are you doing? What are you talking about?"

"I love you, Ruth. And I want to marry you. Now. Today, this week, this month. Soon. I don't want to wait until this crazy war is over. You said it yourself. What if we're not successful? If we don't win the war? Or if your Jim doesn't come home to stay? I'm here for you right now. And I'm not going away."

"Sal, you don't realize what you're saying."

"You love me, Ruth. I know you do. And I'm crazy in love with you."

"But I'm engaged to Jim. I love you, Sal, but I can't marry you. I'm supposed to marry Jim. I made him a promise."

Sal reached for her hand. "But do you love him? It's been three years since you last saw Jim, and all you've got are letters to show for it. I thought we'd talked about this. How many times have you told me how unsure you are? Jim's been gone so long."

Ruth stared at Sal, her mind trying to sort through what she was hearing. Sal was a wonderful man,—a good friend. One of the crowd. Someone to go dancing with or walk the beach with on a summer's eve. But could she marry him? He was wealthy and handsome and she knew he could give her all the things she might want out of life. But was it enough?

"Well, what do you say? Will you marry me?" Sal asked. "I've wanted to ask you for more than a year, but there's never been a right time." He squeezed her hand. "I'm tired of waiting for a right time. I was planning on asking you at New Years, but that didn't work out."

"Sal, I don't know what to say."

"Say 'yes'."

Ruth closed her eyes. Faced with the question, she realized what her answer must be. "I can't marry you."

"Please don't say no to me, Ruth, I love you. More than anything." He held her hand between his two, his fingers caressing the soft skin of her ring finger. "When you took off your engagement ring last year, I thought I might have a chance. I never asked you about it but I thought it meant you had finally made a decision." He paused and looked into her eyes, pleading that she agree. "I've wanted to put my ring on this finger for so long."

She pulled her hand away. "I'm sorry, Sal. It's just not possible."

"I don't understand. You told me you loved me. That night in the spring? after dinner at my place?" Sal pleaded. "You told me you loved me."

She shook her head and took a step back. "I'm so sorry, you misunderstood what I said. You're a wonderful man, Sal, and I do love you—but as a dear friend."

She paused, trying to find the right words. "Right now, I have to think of Jim. I made him a promise and I mean to keep it. I told him I would be here waiting for him when he came home."

"But Helen told me..." he paused, his voice trailed off into silence.

"What did she tell you? If she gave you the impression Jim was out of the picture or I was available... She was wrong to say anything to you, Sal, and I will tell her so."

Embarrassed, she turned to the jeweler who had been listening to the entire exchange, a look of utter confusion on his face. "I'm sorry, sir. But I don't think we'll be buying anything today. Sorry for your trouble, sir. There is not going to be an engagement."

Once in the corridor it took a moment for Ruth to find her way to the staircase. She was determined to avoid a scene. Tears blinded her as she slowly made her way down the stairwell. Once she reached the ground floor, she deliberately waited a few extra minutes to compose herself before opening the door into the building's lobby.

It was a short five minute walk back to her office on Milk Street and

Ruth made it in record time. She went straight to Helen's office on the sixth floor.

Ruth threw her satchel into the middle of Helen's desk, scattering papers everywhere.

"What the heck!" Helen stared at her friend. "What's wrong with you?"

"You told Sal I was done with Jim!"

"I never did. What gives you that idea?"

"Because Sal just asked me to marry him. He thought Jim was out of the picture and that he had a clear shot."

Helen looked at her friend. "I think there's been a big misunderstanding. Sal asked me how you and Jim were doing and I told him what you told me, it's been difficult with him gone so long and that you still loved him, but were having a hard time with it all."

"Well he took that to mean that Jim and I were done with each other."

"I never told him anything of the sort."

"But it's what he heard." Ruth crossed her arms and stared at Helen. "You've got to straighten this out!"

"What do you want me to do?"

"Tell Sal he misunderstood whatever it was you told him. I am not done with Jim. I promised him I would wait for him and that's what I'm doing."

"Even if you don't love him?"

"I never said I didn't love him. I never said I stopped loving him."

She reached over and snapped a tissue from the box on the corner of Helen's desk. "I need time to find myself again. It's been so long... I just don't know."

Her eyes began welling up with tears and she quickly wiped them away. "What I do know is that I can't make any decision right now. And it's not fair for you to say anything to Sal about any of this. Whatever you told him, he was convinced I was free. He was so sure I would say 'yes', he even asked me to marry him right in front of the jeweler. It was embarrassing."

"I'm so sorry, Ruth. I had no idea. Sal asked me how you were doing, and I guess I said you were feeling confused about Jim. He didn't tell me he was about to pop the question." She looked at her friend for some sign of reassurance and understanding.

Ruth stared back.

"I was just trying to be honest with Sal."

Ruth shook her head and reached for her satchel. "I know you were trying to help, Helen. We're good friends but what I tell you in confidence is not for you to broadcast all over the place, especially to Sal Marcusio.

Telling Sal about my love life only made things very messy."

Helen leaned back in her chair. "I'm sorry, I really am." She watched as Ruth opened the office door. "But I still think it's a shame. You and Sal would make a great couple."

Ruth pretended not to hear.

It took a couple of days for Ruth to cool off. By the following Monday she determined to confront Helen again.

Helen held up her hand to protest. "Stop it right there, Ruth. You were right, I was wrong. I had no business talking with Sal. I was way out of line. I'm sorry. I thought I was helping and I totally messed up. I really am sorry. Will you ever forgive me?"

"I'm still upset, but what's done is done and there's nothing either of us can do about it. Let it go. There are too many more important things to worry about."

Four days later, as workers were heading home from the office and factories and housewives were preparing the evening meal, news of Roosevelt's sudden death hit the airwaves. Ruth heard it first from one of the secretaries in Cuddahy's office as she was leaving the office for the day.

"Did you hear? President Roosevelt collapsed this afternoon at his home in Hot Springs."

By the time Ruth reached South Station, FDR's death was the only thing people were talking about. Travelers huddled in small groups on the station platforms, exchanging whatever information they had. The newspaper kiosk in the rotunda was surrounded by a crowd straining to catch the latest news broadcasting from the small radio the owner kept behind the racks of papers and magazines. Men and women stood in silence as the news of the President's sudden passing spread from person to person. Ruth saw more than one man wipe a tear from his eye.

No matter where you turned, evidence of Roosevelt's death was everywhere. The Quincy Wollaston Council ordered a large black banner be draped across the front of town hall. Men and women wore black armbands, and every day newspapers ran oversized headlines related to the President's death or to his successor, Harry S Truman.

By Saturday the 14th, word of Roosevelt's death had spread to every nation around the globe. The newspaper was filled with messages of sympathy from every national leader in the free world. On Sunday, *The Globe's* front page headline made it all very real: "Roosevelt Goes Home." The body of the fallen president was being taken by train to his home in Hyde Park on the Hudson. The world was in mourning.

In an effort to shake the overwhelming feeling of gloom that had settled over the LeBlanc household, Ruth decided she needed a long walk. She packed her writing kit and a thermos of water in her satchel. If she found a quiet spot, she would write a long letter to Jim. She wondered if he had heard the news. He must have, she thought. The troops would be the first to be told.

Bromfield Street was quiet as she walked down the sidewalk towards the seawall. Usually the sound of laughing children playing in back yards would pierce the afternoon air. Neighbors would be sitting on front porches or visiting one another over garden gates. But on this afternoon Ruth saw no one. Everyone was inside their homes, gathered around the family radio, eager for the latest news about their fallen leader. By the time she reached the crosswalk at Shore Drive only one or two cars had passed by, and every bench along the walkway was empty.

She headed for her favorite spot across from the Wollaston Yacht Club. On a typical Sunday at the start of the season, the docks would be busy with families getting their boats ready for a sail around the harbor. But today, only seagulls circled the gangway, their lonely calls and cries echoing across the water.

Ruth took out paper and pen and began to write.

April 15—Dearest Jim,

By now you must have heard the terrible news about the President. It has been a time of real grief for all Americans and I'm sure it has been difficult for you and the troops to hear of his death. I feel the most sorrow for his wife, Eleanor. She has been such a pillar of strength for both FDR and our country during the whole of this war.

And now she must carry this burden for us and her family as well. The new President, Mr. Truman has already been sworn in. Father believes he's a straight arrow and will do the right thing for us. I pray he does.

Father O'Brien at St. Ann's has held a prayer vigil for our country each night since the President's death. I've been once and although I know it's for the President, I put in a good word for you so you come home safe and sound.

So much has happened in the time you have been away. I look forward to spending a lot of time together before we marry. It's such an important decision and should not be taken lightly. I want to be sure it is the right decision for both of us.

All my love, Ruth

Ruth reread the letter twice before sealing the envelope. She added a stamp she had brought and dropped the letter in the mailbox on her walk home. Jim should get it within the week.

It was Friday the 27th before Ruth heard from Jim again. This time there were several letters in the envelope. Written over several days, and he finally answered some of her concerns.

April 16, 1945

My darling Ruth

Yesterday we all had memorial services for the deceased President. A shock to the nation wasn't it? We are all hopeful Mr. Truman can lead us to a peaceful end to this terrible war.

Keep me posted on what is cooking on the home front, will you? I am most interested in what things are shaping for the homecoming of veterans, or is it too early to note any change? Will the girls give up most of their factory jobs or enter into competition with the men?

We have so many things to discuss when we get home that I am almost afraid to ask you to take the plunge until we get to know each other all over again.

At last, she thought, he seems to be getting the message! He finally realizes we can't just jump into marriage.

You go to a lot of shows and plays. Well, I like them all right, but not too often. I tell you Ruth, that since I have been working this past year I have become an awful bore to most people. I know very little of what is going on outside of my little circle of friends. I do know myself fairly well, and that is what counts.

I am afraid that I can't really say what I am going to like or dislike or have a relish for whatever things you care to do. It's really going to be like meeting each other all over again. Three years is three years.

If there had not been a war, I think we would have married at least within a year from when we first met. Sweet dreams, Your Jim

She unfolded the third letter. He must have been running out of paper, she thought. The sheet was filled with Jim's tight scrawl—so small it was difficult to decipher.

April 23

Dear Ruth,

I'm ready to start making plans for our future. Where would you like to live if we stay around Boston?

You know the G.I Bill of Rights will give me one year education at any college school that is within the administration's list. I could get one year at Bentley's again if I wanted to. Up to $500.00

I don't know what we will do for income.

"I'm working, James Doherty!" Ruth declared out loud. "I've got a successful business. Of course we'll have an income," She suddenly realized Jim didn't think of her work as "a real job."

> *Besides the $500 maximum allowance, which will include tuition plus fees for books and other incidentals, they will give me $50 a month for subsistence. And of course there is the mustering out pay, which will amount to about $300. Plus what I am able to average a month over here in savings. What do you think?*
>
> *One thing that school might do for me is get me in the groove again. I want to forget most of the habits of the Army when I get out and the schooling will do it I believe. The only thing that worries me right now is will I be able to concentrate on anything after the war? That is what I like about my present job. It requires me to use the noodle quite a bit so that I don't believe I will grow stale.*
>
> *With me in school though, would that be enough to support you and the folks? And another thing... perhaps by that time we will have acquired some little "responsibilities."*

Ruth felt herself begin to blush. Children! Of course, Jim would want children right away.

> *Gosh darling when I really sit down and think of you and what is ahead, it scares me at times. Not the grindstone, but what you might have to go through. I don't want to have anything happen to you or I think I would lose my mind.*
>
> *To lose you would be the most tragic thing in my life. This sounds pessimistic but I am a realist and try to look at the facts. That is why it is a good idea to have a little one as soon as possible. Any other following will not be so hard on you.*
>
> *It will be so nice to have you at my side for all times, always there to help me over the rough spots and give me encouragement when I need it most.*
>
> *Do you suppose it would be wise to invest in a car? Those luxuries are going to go up in a few years. Maybe we could buy a broken*

down jeep. I could fix up a body over it, take off the front wheel drive and put lighter tires and shock absorbers on the body. Remove the transfer case in the transmission and make a light little Bantam out of it.

Ruth re-read the last couple of lines. A broken down jeep? Would this be the best they could afford? She couldn't help but think of Sal and his elegant Ford convertible.

I can't start making comparisons, she berated herself. Jim and I will do just fine with or without a car. Sal might be rich but Jim is clever.

They will probably be selling Bantams for about $800 after the war. Someone just has to start the ball rolling. You know the American public. If they don't buy them, I bet England will take all the excess cars we've got. Well darling, again I say goodnight.

Love Jim

April 23... Just a few more thoughts, dearest, before I hit the hay

The news is pretty good, but being a dyed in the wool conservative, I won't say that it will be over soon. There is a lot of hard fighting ahead yet, though I will not see it directly.

Sometimes I think that it is my duty to go into something where I can actually strike at the enemy, but my work as an inspector is so indirect. I have to remember good inspections make for good airplanes and good airplanes make for a good war

You don't think that I am slacking off in my war effort do you?

We liberated this country, and now, by heck, the higher ups are going to make it as comfortable as possible for us. Sure, things are a lot easier than they were when I first hit Africa and Sicily but that is to be expected. The Air Corps has caught up with itself so to speak. I bet they have plenty of stuff on Iwo Jima right now that we would never dream of having back there in Algiers in December of '42.

Tell me all about yourself in the next letter will you? I am going to close this now dearest, for it is time to sleep and I've got to be rested for a certain lovely blonde who likes and wants her man to be a man not just a resemblance. You bet.

Jim, with lots of love.

❈

It was early Tuesday morning, May 1, when word of Hitler's death hit the airwaves.

"I can't believe it! This is the best news I've heard since this damn war began," Mr. LeBlanc announced to his wife as he strode into the kitchen. "It's all over the radio. They've just announced that Hitler is dead."

"Oh my." Mrs. LeBlanc didn't know how to respond. She reached for the nearest chair, sat down and stared at her husband.

"It's good news, Bertha. With that tyrant gone, the end of the war in Europe can only be days away!"

"Oh, my," she repeated.

"What's going on? What's all the shouting about?" Justine stuck her head in the doorway.

"That damn fool Hitler is dead, thank goodness."

"You've got to be kidding. When did it happen?"

"They found him in his bunker yesterday. The war isn't over yet, but the end can't be more than a few days away." He reached for his hat. "I'm going to walk to Mazziolis and buy another paper. You need anything?"

"You can pick up a can of baking powder for me. I need it to make biscuits for tonight's dinner."

"And can you see if they have the latest issue of Photoplay?" Justine begged.

Mr. LeBlanc studied his youngest daughter. "Is that all you're thinking about? Major events are happening in our world right now and all you can think of is that nonsense." He pulled on his sweater and headed for the back door.

"Please look for it, Father? Greer Garson's on the cover for May."

"I'll look, but no promises."

"Who's promising who, what?" Ruth asked. She entered the kitchen just as her father was closing the back door.

"Your father is eager to hear more news about Hitler's death. He's going to the market to pick up another newspaper."

"Hitler's dead? When did this happen? Who killed him?" Ruth asked.

"We only just heard the news, dear." Mrs. Leblanc fiddled with her apron. "We don't have any details, just that he's dead, and the war in Europe should be over soon."

"I don't know whether to laugh or cry."

"Exactly, dear."

"If there was ever a man filled with hate, it was Hitler. He wanted to rule the world and he didn't care how many people he killed in the process."

"We can only be grateful that our country had the will and strength to stop him. Soldiers like your Jim, Ruth." She looked at her daughter. "God willing, they'll all be coming home soon."

❁

All the way to work that morning, Ruth kept hearing her mother's words. "They'll all be coming home soon."

Jim would be coming home. Finally. Was she ready for him?

He had been gone so long, she couldn't remember what it was like to have him near. For more than three years they had written letters, shared intimate details of their lives. But it was so much easier to write a thought than to say it aloud. She had become used to his absence and wasn't sure she knew how to deal with his presence. Would they even recognize each other? Could they just pick up from where they left off before he headed off to war?

"That's silly, Ruth. Of course you'll be fine." Helen challenged her friend when they met for morning break. "And don't worry if you'll have enough to talk about. Talking is the least of your problems." She gave her friend a sly smile.

"Oh, Helen, stop it. I'm serious. I don't know if I'm ready. It's one thing to have him overseas and me waiting here... but once this war is over, he's going to be back and things are going to get very serious."

"Aren't they serious enough?"

"I know, I know." She paused, sorting out her thoughts. "But where do I begin?"

"When is he due back? Do you have a date? Is he flying in or coming by troop ship?"

"I have no idea. His last letter was dated April 23 and he was still in Italy. I should get another letter before the end of the week."

She spent the rest of the day working on a large display ad featuring the latest summer suits for men. With the number of soldiers returning from war and looking for work, sales of business suits was going through the roof. She was busier than ever designing ads where every figure was tall, dark and handsome. She imagined Jim wearing an elegant double breasted suit jacket with extra wide lapels. She was certain he would be a knockout. She sighed. She would just have to wait.

On Friday, another thick envelope arrived with a long letter inside.

April 26, 1945

My dearest darling Ruth,

Just received your letter dated the 26th of March. Don't know why it took so long to get here. A whole month!

You believe I am taking your love for granted. That is far from the truth.

Don't think that I am taking you for granted again and visualizing you home with thread and needle knitting for the Red Cross. I don't have any lease on you Ruth. My ring on your finger represents that part of your life that is mine, but I don't take it for granted that you live solely for me to come home. I don't take it for granted that nothing else matters to you but that I get back. I only wish that, but I don't take it for granted. We are all human and there are many men at home that could give you far more happiness and a better life than I ever could.

Every letter I get from you makes me feel very proud of myself that I still have you interested in me. But it wouldn't surprise me if someday you told me that so and so entered your life and there is nothing you can do about it.

It has happened all around me Ruth and the law of averages plays funny tricks. There are many men getting out of the Army that will be looking around for a good girl. You have hosts of girlfriends that might introduce you to ex infantry men or officers or men who have lived through the valley of death. Their stories will impress you and their manners compared with mine, may just be the straw that breaks the camel's back.

No, Ruth, there is every possibility that a girl as attractive as you are can very easily arrange to make herself wanted by these men who are looking for someone far from the past Army life they have experienced.

You are both a good conversationalist and a good listener, and it is with the latter tool that you can do the most. These men are going to want a girl that listens to them. They will want to tell you things and watch your reactions in the most feminine way you can muster. Things that to you should be alarming or horrible or fascinating. You will not have experienced these things before or become hardened to the frequent sights of charred bodies in a wrecked aircraft or wounded men being transported to the rear. There is much competition for me back there in the old U.S.A.

Now that I have dumped the chances of a commission overboard, I can be expected home in the next few months, so I earnestly hope we get this mulled up situation straightened out.

Don't you think that once I can get home and into your arms, that everything else will be forgotten, and that the world revolves around just us two?

I am sure that is what I need. I need, most of all, YOU. To live with you even for a short period will give me the rest that I feel I should take. It will give my mind compete rest, just being with you and letting you take care of me for awhile. I'm tired whether you realize it or not.

I may not be fighting the enemy, but I have been over here close to 33 months, and in that time, I bet I haven't taken more than 10 days relief. Believe it or not.

Your Jim.

Ruth added the letter to the pile of be-ribboned envelopes she kept in her dresser drawer.

Saturday morning, Ruth headed down Bromfield towards the corner grocer. She was trying to remember all the things her mother had asked her to pick up and was carefully ticking them off her mental list when the full blast of a car horn brought her quickly back to the present.

"What the—!" she turned, ready to give the driver a nasty look.

"Hi there!"

It was Sal, sitting pretty in the front seat of his shiny Ford, a wide grin on his face. The convertible top was down and his face was tan and as handsome as ever. He pulled the car towards the sidewalk and slowed down. "Need a ride?"

"No, thanks. I'm just walking to the end of the block."

"I'll come with you, anyway."

"Really, Sal. You don't need to."

"No trouble. Give me a sec." He parked the car, jumped out and started walking in the same direction as Ruth. "I'm glad I caught you. I've been meaning to come by your office. We need to talk."

"Why? I don't think we have anything more to say to each other."

Sal reached out and tried to take her hand. She pulled it back quickly.

"But I do, Ruth. I still have something I need to say. Last time we were together I really made a mess of things and we didn't part company very well. I want to apologize. I never should have put you in that position. It was very insensitive of me and awkward for you I'm sure."

"Awkward?" Ruth questioned. "Try humiliating." She turned away and continued walking.

"Ruth! Don't walk away. We've been friends too long to let it end like this."

She stopped mid stride and tried to gather her thoughts.

"Where have you been for the last few weeks, Sal? If you felt so badly about the situation, why has it taken you so long to get up the nerve to say anything?"

"Because—because I was embarrassed. I don't know what I was thinking, but I really thought you would say yes. That you would marry me. I thought I had a real chance. Helen had told me how confused you were."

Ruth held up her hand to stop him. "Helen shouldn't have said anything. It wasn't her place. And it wasn't true."

"Not any of it?"

"I'm not certain what Helen told you, Sal. It's true, I wasn't feeling so sure about things. I may have been confused for a while. But I'm not anymore. I love Jim and when this war finally ends and he gets home, I'm going to marry him."

Sal reached for her hand. She backed up.

"Please, Sal. Let's leave it at that."

"But do you love him? Really love him?"

Ruth began to walk away again.

"Please don't go like this. I know I could make you happy if you would only give me a chance. Jim will never be able to satisfy what it is you want out of life. You and me. We both want the same things and I know I can give you what you want. I don't think Jim Doherty ever could."

Ruth stepped back, anger seeping into her voice. "You don't know what Jim Doherty is capable of, Sal. He's a very smart guy with big plans for the future. For our future. And don't be too sure you know exactly what I want in my life. He may be poor now, but Jim's a good man. He and I are going to be just fine."

Sal stood, stunned into silence by her words.

"Now, please, stand back and let me go."

"I'll let you go now, if that's what you really want. But if you ever need anything... if you change your mind... if things don't work out for you and Jim..."

She looked at Sal and slowly shook her head. "You have to let me go, Sal. Maybe I'm crazy and maybe I'll be sorry someday. If I've learned anything from this war, it's how important it is to do what's right—being faithful and keeping promises. The only reason why we've nearly won this bloody war is that people were willing to stand up and fight for what they believed in. I made a promise to Jim and I have to keep it." She took a step back. "And you have to let me go—now."

Ruth didn't wait for Sal to respond. She turned away and headed towards the corner store, leaving him standing alone on the sidewalk. Later she would admit to Helen that it was this last encounter that finally settled her heart on Jim. In defending him against Sal's protests, Ruth realized she had finally made her decision.

※

It was the next Monday morning, May 7, when the ringing of church bells brought everyone out of their offices and into the streets of Boston.

Ruth had only just sat down at her desk when Helen rushed in.

Ruth looked up, startled.

"Truman's on the radio. He just announced the war with Germany is over! Come on!" Helen raced away up the stairs. Ruth quickly joined her friend.

The hallway outside Cuddahy Accounting was jammed with workers, all straining to hear the news. At the back of the pack, neither Helen nor Ruth could make out what the new President was saying, but those in front did their best to pass the word back.

Germany had surrendered to General Eisenhower in the early hours of May 7. A full surrender of all troops and land taken during the war. It was all over in Europe. The troops were coming home.

"Isn't it wonderful?" Helen asked.

"I can hardly believe it! Is it really over?"

Helen grabbed Ruth's hand, pulling her towards the stairwell. "Come on, let's celebrate!"

It seemed the entire city was in the streets! Everyone was smiling and shouting. Drivers in cars leaned on their horns, blasting the air with endless cacophony. Ruth covered her ears but couldn't help grinning at the sound.

A passing soldier suddenly grabbed her, landing a kiss on her lips before she had a chance to protest. Not that she wanted to. Everyone was kissing and hugging each other. Total strangers embraced in the sheer joy of the moment.

Someone with a trumpet started playing a boogie woogie tune and a group of women she recognized from the office steno pool began dancing in a large circle. In seconds others joined in, the circle increasing in size till it reached both sides of Milk Street and spilled beyond the sidewalks and into the nearby storefronts. Someone shoved a small American flag into Ruth's hand and saluted. She saluted back. After that, the rest of the workday was lost to joyous chaos.

By the time she walked the final block of Bromfield Street to number 180 it was nearly dark. An unfamiliar car was parked out front. It couldn't be Sal. She would have recognized his convertible immediately. In the evening light she had a hard time figuring out the car make or model.

Maybe one of father's friends? she wondered.

It was only when she was hanging up her coat in the front hall closet and heard David Doherty's hearty laugh coming from the parlor did she realize who had come to visit.

"Well hello there!" David exclaimed as she entered the room.

"Hi, David. It's been too long."

"Not since New Year's, I think!" David stood up and gave Ruth a quick hug.

"Has it been that long?" she wondered. She glanced at her mother who was seated on the overstuffed armchair, looking for confirmation.

David laughed. "Don't you worry. We'll be seeing a lot more of you now that this war is over. Jim will be home before you know it and you two will be married." He turned and grinned at both Mr. and Mrs. LeBlanc. "We'll be one big happy family soon enough."

Mr. LeBlanc smiled and nodded without comment. Mrs. LeBlanc began to gush enthusiastically.

"Ruth is already making plans, I'm sure." She turned to Ruth. "Isn't that right, dear? There are so many things we must decide. The hall, the caterer, if you want music, and of course, we have to let Fr. O'Brien know so he can post the bands."

"Slow down, mother. Not so fast. Jim and I have a lot to talk over before we start making plans."

"But you can't delay. Now that the war is over, everyone will be coming home and wanting to get married. All the best dates will be gone if you wait too long."

"I'm sure that's not true."

David smiled. "You never know, Ruthie. Hazel is getting anxious too. We heard from Jim a few days ago. He's still in Italy but expects to be on a troop ship heading home soon enough. She's got big ideas for a wedding."

Ruth looked from David to her mother. "Everybody, slow down. Let's let the man get home first before we start any major planning."

"That's a good idea," Mr. LeBlanc chimed in. "Let the poor man get his bearings first. Once he's back, they'll be plenty of time to sort things out."

"Did Jim say when he was leaving?" Ruth asked David. "I got a letter a few days ago as well, but he didn't have any specific date."

"Then, you know as much as we do." David looked around the room. "I just wanted to stop by and say hello and share the news, but it seems you know it already."

"Jim writes to me pretty regularly."

"Well then..." David stood awkwardly not knowing what to say next.

"Have you had your supper, yet?" Mrs. LeBlanc asked. "I'd be happy to make something up for you. Ruth hasn't eaten yet, have you, dear?"

"Please, don't go to any trouble on my account, ma'am. I'd best be going anyway. When I left, the party in Jamaica Plain was only just getting started, and Hazel will be needing my help." He turned to Ruth. "You want to come, Ruth? I'm sure they'd love to see you."

"I've been celebrating in the streets of Boston since morning. I'm beat. There's only one place I want to be right now and that's in bed."

David laughed. "Can't blame you for that." He turned to the others in the room. "Well, then. Glad to see you all on such a happy occasion. Let's get together once Jim is back."

Everyone agreed as David reached for his hat and coat and headed out the door.

"So he's coming home on a troop ship?" her father asked once David was gone. "Why isn't he flying home in one of those transport planes he works on? You'd think he deserved a first class ticket after all he's been through."

"I'm not sure how Jim's getting home. He promised to write as soon as he could and let me know."

But it was nearly a week before another letter from Jim arrived.

May 9, 1945

My dearest darling Ruth,

Well, the paper came out today with two inch headlines: "ITS OVER OVER HERE." Boy, oh boy but that was what I was waiting to see for so long.

Do you realize that I have been overseas throughout the time of the whole European scrape? I can tell my grandchildren, that their grandpop saw the whole conflict in the European theatre from the beginning to the glorious end. It is a time for thanksgiving and prayer.

Yes, dearest, I have been put on orders to go back to the states on permanent rotation. It's done and finished for me over here and nothing else is on my mind but to get back to your arms as fast as I can.

The war was really over for Jim. He was coming home at last. Permanent rotation?

"It means his job is done, Ruth," her father attempted to explain. "I was reading about it in *The Globe*. The military have developed a point system for discharging soldiers. Priority goes to those who have served the longest in the most dangerous locations. I think your Jim has been gone long enough to qualify. Which means when he finally does get home, he'll stay put. No chance to get redeployed. He might even be free to leave the service. Unless, of course, he signs up again."

"I don't think he'll be doing that, Father." She turned to the letter once again.

> *Ruth, I want you to have the nicest wedding you can have, for it will be your day and you will look back at it many times. I would be making preliminary plans and preparations now for I am pretty sure you will be a June bride.*

Ruth glanced at the kitchen calendar. June was only a few weeks away. I think you're dreaming, Jim Doherty. I need more time. We need more time.

> *Get a blood test and get whatever clothes you will need and make the preliminary preparations and God willing I will reach you soon.*
>
> *But always keep this sober thought in mind: This is still the army and there is still a war on and anything can happen. Up to now I can merely hope for the best and let you know something of what's cooking.*

Ruth paused, rereading the last paragraph. The war against the Japanese was still going strong. Ruth had heard that some soldiers were being sent directly from Europe to the Pacific. They wouldn't send Jim would they?

> *It can only be about 21 days at the most, unless I can finagle an extension, so darling, let us save time and make some temporary plans now. First of all it will take about a week to get everything set up, the license, church plans and letting whatever friends you want to have come. Oh yes, and get me a best man. (One that will not show me up at the wedding.) Not knowing what is in store for me after rotation, I want to have every possible day with you as my wife.*

I love you very much Ruth, and feel that it is best to get married now, if ever we do intend to get married. For I want to make you happy as soon as possible. And it won't be so bad being away from you again, knowing that you are mine, all mine.

I expect to be home sometime around the twentieth of this month, but please don't worry if you do not hear from me for as much as ten days after that. I can't definitely say what time I will be leaving over here. However I shall write every day until I leave so you can gage from my last letter when I will get back.

I wonder what I must wear at the wedding? I don't have one of those dress jackets. My jacket looks like the British type battle dress. I do hope that khakis are not in order, but they probably will be.

The honeymoon. Where? Up north to New Hampshire somewhere? Do you think we can decide that in the first few days. I think we can.

I know darling that this isn't the ideal way to ask a girl to get ready for marriage, but you know the circumstances and besides it will be something to tell our children. Kind of fun, isn't it?

Oh yes, the welcome home. I want first of all to get an olive oil shampoo before seeing you. My hair is a sight. I want to see my old barber alone and then knock down one on the town, and darling, I would like to meet you somewhere where it will not be so crowded that I can't hear your voice when you whisper certain things that I hope you will say.

Gosh I hope my leave isn't canceled.

Where could I see you for the first time? I don't like railroad stations, because it will be in a railroad station that we may say goodbye. Oh that word. That awful, final word, "Goodbye." We shall never use it darling, it will be just "Bye darling, I will see you again soon. Please write."

Can you tell from this letter how excited I am? I never thought that I would feel so happy in anticipation of anything, but honey, I can say right here that it is almost worth being overseas, it's so good to know that I am coming back to you.

We have so much to say to each other. Please choose the day, honey, and let this poor guy know for he is on edge just waiting for the time when he can say you're his.

Your loving admirer, Jim.

She shared most of the letter with Helen when she got to work the following day.

"He just goes off in flights of fancy, writing about what to wear, where to go on a honeymoon. He even wants me to choose his best man for him!"

Helen chuckled. "Sounds like he's pretty excited."

"He's out of control if you ask me. I've written him time and time again that it's not going to happen that fast. I think he actually expects that the wedding party will be there to greet him at the dock or on the train platform, the priest and witnesses at the ready! Let's say our 'I dos,' and off we go to Shangri La! for days of unbridled love making."

Helen couldn't help but laugh out loud. "I think you've got the idea!" She gave her friend a wide smile. "Don't take it all so seriously, Ruth. The man's excited. He's coming home and all he wants to do is run into your arms and never leave again. You can't blame him."

Ruth tried to control her frustration.

"Don't forget you're the one in charge of the situation. He's asked you to do all these things, but you don't have to do anything. Take all the time you need. You've certainly let him know what you want.

"Don't rush anything. Trust me, Jim will wait for you. You do what you need to do. And tell him I said so, if he gives you a hard time."

Ruth didn't think that would persuade Jim. But she agreed to try and take it easy and not worry about it.

Early Saturday, two letters arrived with military stamps in the upper right corner of the envelopes.

May 12, 1945

Darling Ruth, I am in the American Red Cross at Naples on leave. I am waiting for Jerry to come pick me up for I want to see him before I head out. He will write to you as soon as I have left and then you can gauge the time for yourself.

It may be a few days or it may be real soon before I leave.

I have gone through most of the processing so am about ready. When I get to Devens I will call you from there if I can, and we will decide if you can meet me at North Station or at your office.

If I land South, why I naturally will arrive at South Station and go by truck convoy to the North Station then to Devens. At any rate, I will pass right through Boston, but I don't want to see you then. I will be tired and dirty. I want to be fresh and clean when I take you in my arms.

Do you know darling, that I am very happy to know you are there to come back to. I love you dearly Ruth. It won't be long now, honey,

Your loving fiancé, Jim.

Ruth opened the second envelope, eager for news. It was dated two days later than the first.

May 14, 1945

Hello darling

Haven't left sunny Italy as yet. This waiting makes me very restless. I go to sleep early and get up about 6:15 A.M. but I am still tired. Perhaps when I get aboard ship I won't feel so exhausted. Incidentally, darling, I turned down the chance to fly home. I know it would have meant seeing you sooner but I feel that perhaps I can get rested up on the trip back. You will understand, I'm sure.

I want you to have the kind of wedding you will like and cherish. You deserve all the happiness I can possibly afford so darling if a big wedding will take up some of our furlough time, I will gladly give it up to make you the happiest bride.

I don't want you to think that I just want to get you married as quick as possible. If I implied that, I made a mistake. I want your wedding to run off smoothly so that you can feel that you were really married. Whatever pleases you darling, pleases me.

"What would please me, is if you would stop going on about a wedding," Ruth said out loud. What's with the rush of time? I thought you were on permanent rotation. Are you going to stay in the service or not? Ruth was confused.

Even if the wedding preparations take two weeks and we have one week left together I shall still be much satisfied only I certainly hope our timing is in our favor. Perhaps that is a selfish thought but it means much to be able to have you for myself at that time.

Gosh, but I am beginning to feel nervous already. This sort of thing is new to me.

Darling I don't ever want you to regret anything. All I ask is that you be patient with me until I find myself in civilian life. It may look cloudy for a while and there won't be much money in the teapot but I have the ability and confidence and if you love me and keep me in love, why I can get ahead, I am positive. I need your attentions very much. There has been something lacking from my life for the past three years and I am pretty sure I know what it is. It's a pair of soft arms around my neck and a body very close to mine. A man needs a woman.

Well, darling, I can't say when I'll leave here but am looking forward to your arms.

With all my love, your Jim

Ruth slowly folded the letter and replaced it in the envelope just as Justine shuffled into the kitchen, still in her bathrobe and slippers. She looked at Ruth and the letters in her hand.

"From Jim?" she asked.

Ruth nodded.

"Where the heck is he?" Justine asked. "Is he on his way home yet?"

Ruth shook her head 'no.' "He wrote from Naples on the 14th. Today's Saturday, the 19th, so that was five days ago. He's decided to take a transport ship home rather than fly."

"Why would he do that? Doesn't he want to rush home to you? A ship takes a lot longer than a plane ride. What's his problem?"

"No problem. He decided he needed to take some time to rest before he got home. It's probably a smart idea. He's going to have to start looking for work right away or go back to school."

"And get married?" Justine teased.

"Not right away. We need to wait a while, take some time to get to know each other again. It's been over three years, after all."

"I suppose." Justine looked thoughtful. "But you are still going to get married, right?"

Ruth placed the two letters in her satchel and turned to leave. "As of this moment, the answer is 'Yes. We're still getting married. I just don't know exactly when."

"As long as it's not a winter wedding. Too cold."

Ruth had to smile. "I can assure you, it won't be winter."

"Good. Because I just bought a new spring frock that would be perfect!"

"Don't hold your breath waiting for an invitation. It may take a while before we're ready to name the date."

"That's okay. Whenever works for me." Justine reached for her cup of tea and shuffled back to her bedroom.

True to the promise he had made to Jim, Jerry Brennan called the LeBlanc family the afternoon of May 24th. Ruth's father answered.

"Hello?"

"Hello? Is this the LeBlanc home?"

"Yes, who's speaking, please? You'll have to talk louder. I can barely hear you."

"This is Jerry Brennan calling from Naples, Italy. Hello?"

"Did you say Italy?"

"Yes sir. I'm a friend of Sergeant Jim Doherty. He asked me to call you."

Mr. LeBlanc frantically waved at his wife who was sitting in the front parlor, listening to the radio and knitting something very long and bumpy.

"It's a friend of Jim's on the phone. He's calling from Italy!"

Mrs. LeBlanc immediately dropped the ball of yarn she was holding and crossed to where her husband stood, phone in hand.

"What can we do for you Mr. Brennan?"

"Captain Brennan, Mr. LeBlanc, I'm Quartermaster here in Naples. Jim's a good friend and he asked me to let you and the family know he's on his way home. I put him on a troop transport ship headed for Boston this morning. He should be home in 4 or 5 days depending on the weather."

"That's wonderful news." Mr. LeBlanc turned to his wife. "He says Jim will be home in 5 days."

Bertha LeBlanc could hardly contain her pleasure at the news. She grabbed at the phone. "That's very good news, Mr. Brennan. Very good news."

"Do you know the name of the ship?" Mr. LeBlanc asked. There was no answer. "Captain, did you hear me? What is the name of the ship Jim is on?" The lined was filled with static. They had been cut off.

He placed the phone back in its cradle. "Well, at least Jim's safe and sound and on his way."

"But without the name of the ship we won't know which day, or dock he's coming into." Mrs. LeBlanc protested. "Don't you think he'll want his family to meet him when he gets home?"

He looked down at his wife. "I think there's only one person he really wants to see when he steps off that boat. And it isn't either of us."

"You should call Ruth and tell her the news."

CHAPTER 17

BOSTON

How can I find out which ship Jim is on?" Ruth asked Helen. "Is there some transport office I should call?"

"Try Fort Devens. They should have a record of all the troops coming home."

It was a good idea, but no matter whom she spoke with, Ruth could not find anyone with the information she needed.

"I'm sorry, Ma'am. We're trying to manage hundreds, no, thousands of soldiers all coming home at once. We just don't have that information for you right now. Perhaps you could call back next week?"

"He'll be home by next week."

"Well, then, that's good for you, ma'am. I'm sure he will call as soon as he arrives."

She heard confusion in the background. "I'm sorry, ma'am. I must answer this next call."

"Well, that was a waste of time."

Helen was sympathetic. "I wouldn't worry too much, though. Jim already told you he doesn't want to see you until he's all spiffed up. I'm sure he'll call as soon as he gets to Devens."

Ruth had to agree. It would only be a matter of days before he was home. She could wait.

But the transatlantic crossing took longer than expected. Jim's call didn't come until the afternoon of May 30. Ruth almost missed it. It was Memorial Day and a work holiday. She was heading out to meet a few of the crowd at the seawall for a long walk when the phone in the hallway rang.

"Hello."

"Is Ruth LeBlanc at home?"

At first she didn't recognize his voice. It was deeper than she remembered.

"Jim? Is that you?"

She heard a quick intake of breath. "Ruth? It's Jim."

"Hello." She didn't know what to say. She gulped and waited.

"Darling, are you there?"

"Yes," very softly. "I'm here. I've been waiting for your call."

She could hear the smile in his voice as he quipped, "Well your waiting is over, dearest. I'm home now, and pretty much all in one piece."

Ruth felt tears well up behind her eyes. "When did you get in?"

"The ship docked in Boston, sometime last night, then we all got shipped off to Devens."

"You must be tired."

"Not really, I've been here all day going through the motions. Just a few more things that have to be done and then I'm free as a bird."

"That's wonderful."

"My discharge is scheduled for tomorrow morning. It shouldn't take too long. And then I'll take the first train I can catch to Boston. Will you be in town? Shall I meet you?"

"Of course. Do you know what time you'll arrive?"

"No way to tell at this point. But I'll call you once I know. Is the office the best place to reach you?"

"I think so. Let me give you the direct number. Do you have a pen and paper?" Ruth waited until he was ready, then recited the number. "The train from Fort Devens goes to North Station, I think," she said. "From there it's just a short walk to Milk Street and my office."

"I remember. Listen, darling, I can't talk now. I have to get off this phone. There's a long line of very eager soldiers waiting to use it."

"Okay, then, I'll see you tomorrow?"

"Can hardly wait, sweetheart."

And he was gone again.

⚜

She didn't know what to do next. She stood in front of the phone, just staring at the receiver.

"Who was that, dear?" her mother asked as she crossed the hall from kitchen to parlour.

"Jim," Ruth answered. "It was Jim. He's at Fort Devens."

"Thank the good Lord. He's home safe at last." Mrs. LeBlanc was not a demonstrative woman but at this happy news she couldn't help but hug her daughter. "When will you see him?"

"Sometime tomorrow. He can't leave Devens until he's discharged in the morning. He's going to take the train into the city and I'll meet him at the office."

"Does his family know he's back? You should call them."

"I'm sure Jim will do that."

"They'll want to see him right away. Perhaps David could drive you and his family to the Fort? David has a car, doesn't he?"

Ruth couldn't imagine driving all the way to Devens in an overheated car filled with the Doherty clan.

"Jim wants to take the train into town and see me first, Mother. He'll probably go right on to Jamaica Plain after that."

Her mother paused before continuing. "Of course, you're right, dear. What am I thinking? Jim will want time with you first. After all, you are engaged." She gave her daughter a broad smile.

Ruth decided against meeting the crowd at the seawall. She knew once they found out Jim was on his way home, her girlfriends would be asking a million questions—most of which she couldn't answer. She needed some time alone to think. Jim was home at last.

She went upstairs to her bedroom and opened the top drawer of the tall dresser. The ring box was still there, the pearl and diamond engagement ring waiting for this moment.

She placed it on the third finger of her left hand. It felt as if her life was finally going to begin again.

"You should wear that brown dress of yours. The one with the gold buttons," Justine remarked at supper that night. "I think you'll look smashing."

"You want to look your best for Jim, dear," her mother added.

"I don't think it makes a fig of difference what she wears. The man just wants to see her." Mr. LeBlanc put in his two cents, reaching for the bowl of carrots. "You're going to meet at your office tomorrow?"

"Yes. Jim will take the train to North Station and walk up from there."

"What time?" Justine asked.

"I don't know. Whenever he gets there."

"You must be a nervous wreck! I know I would be," Justine said. "Just imagine. It's been three years. I bet Jim's got a mustache!"

Ruth laughed. "Don't be silly!"

"Well, you never know."

Ruth looked at her sister and shook her head. "I don't think Jim would have changed that much!"

"I bet he has one!" Justine insisted. "I'll bet he's going to walk into your office with a big handlebar mustache! You just wait and see."

"The Army doesn't allow handlebar mustaches, Justine." Mr. LeBlanc corrected his daughter. "Stop teasing your sister."

Ruth shrugged off the remark. Justine was just trying to cause trouble as always.

The next morning she dressed carefully in the brown dress with the gold buttons and caught the early trolley into town.

Helen was just approaching the entrance to the Sunley Building when Ruth turned the corner on Milk Street.

"What are you doing here at this hour?" Helen looked at her watch. "It's only eight o'clock."

"Jim called me. He's at Fort Devens and is getting discharged this morning. He's coming to the office."

Helen gave her friend a broad smile. "Wow! That's a surprise."

The two friends entered the lobby. "I don't mind telling you, I'm a nervous wreck."

"I don't blame you. I'd be a basket case. Do you know what time he'll be here?"

"All depends on when he gets discharged. He said he'll take the first train he can out of Devens."

Helen considered the distance. "From Devens to North Station will take at least two hours. If they discharge him by 9, Jim should be here by noon."

"That's what I was thinking."

"You can take him to a fancy lunch!"

Ruth laughed. "Maybe."

But noontime came and went and no phone call from Jim. By two o'clock when Helen checked back, Ruth figured things at Devens must have been delayed.

"He'll be here by four, I'm sure of it," Ruth declared. "He would call if it's going to be later than that."

But four o'clock came and still no phone call from Jim.

"I have to head out, honey," Helen said. "I'm meeting Gary in town for an early supper and then we're going to the seven o'clock show at the Paramount, Flame of Barbary Coast. Gary loves John Wayne."

"Have a good time."

"Say hi to Jim for us. I'll give you a call over the weekend to find out how things went. And don't worry, honey. You look gorgeous."

"I hope so." She turned back to her desk and tried to concentrate on an ad for women's bathing suits. She was so absorbed in her drawing she didn't hear the sound of approaching footsteps in the hallway.

"I can't wait to see you in one of those!" Jim declared.

Startled, Ruth looked up, and there he was. Jim, standing tall and handsome in his Army Air Force uniform.

"Tech Sergeant James Doherty, ma'am, at your service." He stood at attention and saluted as Ruth burst into tears.

He quickly reached down and took her up into his arms. She fell against his chest, sobbing.

"Don't cry, dearest. I'm here. I'm finally home."

He held her tight in his embrace, their faces close, his mouth seeking hers. She felt his lips part, his breath soft against her face as his lips brushed her cheek. His arms supportive, demanding, drawing her ever closer, his heartbeat echoing hers; faster, quicker, more urgent with each passing moment .

Finally, with his first passion satisfied, she leaned back, just far enough to see his face through her tears. All her resistance and doubts seem to fall away as she looked into his eyes.

It was as if a road map had suddenly been laid out before her. The way forward was clear and she finally understood what it was she had to do.

She had been confused for so long. But here he was, home at last. Her Jim. Her decision, her destiny. Her pathway. He was home and in her arms at last.

EPILOGUE

Although Jim was eager to tie the knot as soon as possible, Ruth was reluctant. After much discussion and soul searching, they agreed to take the time they both needed to get to know each other again before they set a wedding date.

During the months following his discharge, Jim tried to find work in the field of aeronautics that he had grown to love. An opportunity presented itself but it meant he would have to re-enlist in the Army Air Force as a commissioned officer. Re-enlisting would mean moving to California for training. Ruth refused to leave her family and friends on the East coast. If they were ever to marry, Jim would have to find other work.

Reluctantly, he returned to the accounting firm he had worked for before the war.

Ruth continued to run a successful business as a commercial artist in Boston until their wedding in April of 1946. After a short honeymoon in Canada, they returned to Boston. She closed her business and focused on starting a family.

The couple moved into a third floor flat in Jamaica Plain. Their first child, a son, was born in 1947 and within a year, Ruth was expecting again. When Ruth's parents decided to leave Wollaston and move to a smaller house in Weymouth, Ruth and Jim bought the Bromfield Street home. They both loved living by the ocean and took long walks pushing a baby carriage along the seawall. By 1952 there were three children and with a growing family to support, Jim took a job as an accountant with a major manufacturing firm in Grafton, Massachusetts.

They moved to a city two hours west of Boston. A fourth child arrived in the winter of 1954.

It was not the marriage "made in heaven" Ruth had always hoped for. Like most, theirs was a marriage of compromise. They each gave up hopes and dreams in order to build a home for themselves and their children. Not an easy marriage, but somehow they made it work.

She remained best friends with Helen for the rest of her life. She never saw Sal again.

TIMELINE OF WORLD WAR II

Jan 30, 1933 • Hitler Becomes Chancellor
Adolf Hitler becomes Chancellor of Germany.

Oct 3, 1935 • Mussolini Invades Ethiopia
Italy, under the leadership of Prime Minister Benito Mussolini, invades Ethiopia.

May 1, 1937 • Neutrality Act
President Franklin D. Roosevelt signs the 1937 Neutrality Act, which bans travel on belligerent ships, forbids the arming of American merchant ships trading with belligerents, and issues an arms embargo with warring nations.

Jul 7, 1937 • Japan Defeats China
The Japanese defeat Chinese forces in a clash near Peking, taking control of North China.

Sep 14, 1937 • Roosevelt Limits Ships to Asia
President Franklin D. Roosevelt forbids U.S. ships from carrying arms to China or Japan.

Oct 5, 1937 • Roosevelt Quarantines War
In response to Japanese action in China, President Franklin D. Roosevelt delivers a speech in which he calls for peace-loving nations to act together to "quarantine" aggressors to protect the world from the "disease" of war.

Dec 12, 1937 • Attack on the Panay
Japanese warplanes dive-bomb the American gunboat Panay in the Yangtze River in China. Japan apologizes and pays reparations for the lives lost.

Jan 21, 1938 • March of Time
Time Inc. releases an anti-Nazi propaganda newsreel entitled March of Time in Nazi Germany.

Feb 20, 1938 • Hitler Supports Japan
German Chancellor Adolf Hitler announces support for Japan.

Feb 1938 • U.S. Against Japan
In the United States, popular support for American action against Japan far exceeds support for action against Nazi Germany.

Mar 13, 1938 • Anschluss
German Chancellor Adolf Hitler declares Austria part of the Third Reich.

Mar 26, 1938 • Hermann Goering Warns Jews
Hermann Goering, marshal of the Third Reich and Hitler's second in charge, warns all Jews to leave Austria.

Apr 6, 1938 • U.S. Recognizes Austria
The United States grants recognition to the new Austrian government.

May 14, 1938 • Mussolini Joins Hitler
In a speech in Rome, Benito Mussolini, fascist leader of Italy, promises to fight the democracies alongside Adolf Hitler's should war break out.

May 17, 1938 • Naval Expansion Act
The U.S. Congress passes the Naval Expansion Act giving President Franklin D. Roosevelt one billion dollars to enlarge the navy.

Sep 12, 1938 • Hitler Aims for Sudetenland
Adolf Hitler is poised to invade and conquer the Sudetenland region of Czechoslovakia.

Sep 29, 1938 • Sudetenland and Appeasement
Leaders of France and Great Britain meet with representatives from Germany,

including Adolf Hitler, to discuss Germany's demands, ultimately granting Hitler the Sudetenland in the hopes of gaining "peace with honor." The Czechs are not consulted.

Sep 29, 1938 • Hitler Promises Peace
Adolf Hitler, in return for the Sudetenland, promises to leave the rest of Czechoslovakia alone.

Nov 10, 1938 • Kristallnacht
During the German Kristallnacht (Night of Broken Glass), 7500 Jewish businesses are looted, 191 synagogues are set afire, nearly 100 Jews are killed, and tens of thousands are sent to concentration camps.

Jan 2, 1939 • Hitler is Time Man of the Year
Time magazine prints its 1938 Man of the Year edition choosing Adolf Hitler for the title, but does not show the Nazi leader's face on the cover of the publication.

Mar 15, 1939 • Hitler Annexes Czechoslovakia
Adolf Hitler reneges on the promise made in September of 1938 and takes all of Czechoslovakia.

Apr 1939 • Roosevelt Writes Hitler and Mussolini
President Franklin D. Roosevelt writes letters to both Adolf Hitler and Benito Mussolini, requesting they promise not to attack a list of nations for at least ten years. Hitler would respond on behalf of the Italian leader and himself, assuring Roosevelt that he had nothing to fear.

May 1939 • Senate Blocks Aid to Allies
A group of U.S. Senators block the President's request for permission to offer economic aid to Britain and France in case of war.

Jun 6, 1939 • St. Louis Refusal
Passenger ship St. Louis, containing 907 Jewish refugees, begins its journey back to Europe after the United States refuses to grant it permission to dock.

Aug 23, 1939 • Stalin and Hitler Sign Nonaggression Pact
Germany and the Soviet Union agree to a nonaggression pact leaving the Soviets free to strengthen their western frontier, and Hitler free to attack Poland.

Sep 1, 1939 • Germany Invades Poland
German troops invade Poland on the ground while Hitler's Air Force bombs Polish cities from the sky.

Sep 3, 1939 • Britain and France Declare War
Britain and France declare war on Germany honoring their commitment to Poland. President Franklin D. Roosevelt invokes the Neutrality Act but notes, "Even a neutral cannot be asked to close his mind or his conscience."

Nov 3, 1939 • Congress Lifts Aid Embargo
Congress grants President Franklin D. Roosevelt's request to revise neutrality laws, to repeal an arms embargo so that munitions could be sold to Britain and France, and to prevent American ships from sailing into war zones.

1940 • *For Whom the Bell Tolls* Published
American author Ernest Hemingway publishes *For Whom the Bell Tolls*, a novel about a young American in Spain who joins an antifascist guerrilla force in the Spanish Civil War.

Apr 1, 1940 • Hitler Seizes Low Countries
Adolf Hitler takes neutral Denmark, Norway, Belgium, Holland, and Luxembourg.

Apr 1940 • Germany Pummels France
German fighter planes and ground troops pummel France.

Apr 1940 • Hitler Defeats France
Britain forces retreat from France and Adolf Hitler's armies defeat French forces.

May 1940 • Allied Support Grows
The Committee to Defend America by Aiding the Allies is founded.

May 1940 • Fleet Moved to Pearl Harbor
President Franklin D. Roosevelt moves the United States Pacific Fleet base from San Diego, California to Pearl Harbor in Hawaii.

May 16, 1940 • Roosevelt Increases Defense Spending
In a speech to Congress, President Franklin D. Roosevelt requests new defense spending, an enlarged army, and an expanded air fleet. Public opinion favors the new defense program.

Jun 10, 1940 • Italy Attacks France
Benito Mussolini's Italian forces attack France from the south.

Jun 22, 1940 • France Surrenders
France, crushed, surrenders to Germany and signs an armistice. Great Britain now stands alone against the Axis powers.

Jul 26, 1940 • U.S. Withholds Gas from Japan
The United States orders gasoline withheld from Japan sparking protest from the Japanese government.

Aug 1940 • Congress Enacts Draft
Congress appropriates $16 billion for defense needs, and enacts the first peacetime draft in American history.

Sep 1940 • America First Committee Formed
The America First Committee is formed.

Sep 3, 1940 • Roosevelt Aids Britain
President Franklin D. Roosevelt makes a deal to give Great Britain 50 destroyers in exchange for naval bases in Newfoundland, Bermuda, and sites in the Caribbean and the South Atlantic.

Sep 25, 1940 • U.S. Extends Japanese Embargo
The United States extends the Japanese embargo to include iron and steel.

Sep 27, 1940 • Japan Joins Axis
Responding to the embargoes imposed by the United States, Japan joins the German-Italian coalition.

Oct 29, 1940 • Draftees to Camps
The first draft numbers are drawn, sending thousands of draftees to drill camps all over the country.

Nov 1940 • Roosevelt Reelected for Third Term
In the presidential election, Democrats break with the two-term tradition and renominate Franklin D. Roosevelt for a third term. Republicans nominate Wendell L. Willkie, a public-utilities executive who shared FDR's views on the war in Europe. Franklin D. Roosevelt defeats Willkie by nearly 5 million popular votes.

Dec 1940 • U.S. Cracks Japanese Code
United States Naval Intelligence cryptographers crack Japan's secret communications code and learn that Japan intends to conquer China.

Dec 29, 1940 • Arsenal of Democracy
President Franklin D. Roosevelt delivers a fireside chat to the American people announcing, "We must be the great arsenal of democracy."

Jan 6, 1941 • Lend-Lease Program
Before the U.S. Congress, President Franklin D. Roosevelt proposes a "lend-lease" program, which would deliver arms to Great Britain to be paid for following the war's end. Congress approves the bill.

Mar 30, 1941 • U.S. Seizes Axis Ships
President Franklin D. Roosevelt orders the United States Coast Guard to seize German ships that sail into American ports. 65 Axis ships are held in "protective custody."

May 15, 1941 • Robin Moor
In the South Atlantic the American merchant ship Robin Moor is sunk by a German torpedo. President Franklin D. Roosevelt responds to the German attack by declaring a national emergency.

Jun 16, 1941 • Axis Consulates Closed
President Franklin D. Roosevelt demands Germany and Italy close their American consulates located in the United States.

Jun 22, 1941 • Germany Invades Soviet Union
Germany invades the Soviet Union violating the Nonaggression Pact. U.S. Secretary of War Henry L. Stimson estimates that it will take Hitler less than three months to conquer the Soviet Union.

Jun 24, 1941 • US Aids Soviets
The United States extends lend-lease aid to the Soviet Union.

Jul 7, 1941 • US Defends Iceland
President Franklin D. Roosevelt announces that the United States will take over defense of Iceland for the duration of the war.

Aug 9, 1941 • Roosevelt and Churchill Draft Atlantic Charter
On a British battleship, President Franklin D. Roosevelt meets with the Prime Minister of Great Britain, Winston Churchill. The two leaders write up the Atlantic Charter.

Aug 17, 1941 • Roosevelt Warns Japanese
President Franklin D. Roosevelt warns the Japanese government to cease all aggression toward neighboring countries or else face United States forces.

Sep 4, 1941 • Greer
Provoked by the American destroyer Greer, a German submarine fires on the ship. In response to the attack, President Franklin D. Roosevelt orders the navy to shoot any Axis battleships they encounter.

Oct 17, 1941 • U.S.S. Kearny
German submarines damage the U.S.S. Kearny in a skirmish near Iceland, killing 11.

Reuban James Sunk • The U.S. destroyer Reuben James is sunk near Iceland, killing 115 seamen.

Nov 1941 • Merchant Ships Armed
In response to the destruction of the battleship Reuben James, the U.S. Congress authorizes American merchant ships to carry arms.

Nov 1941 • Lend-Lease to Soviets
The United States extends "lend-lease" to the Soviet Union.

Nov 3, 1941 • Japanese Decide to Attack
The Japanese government decides to attack Pearl Harbor if negotiations with the United States fail.

Nov 29, 1941 • U.S. Learns Japanese Plan
U.S. Naval cryptographers learn from secret code that Japan plans aggressive action if an agreement with the United States is not met.

Dec 1, 1941 • Japan Ignores US Requests
Japan dismisses American demands to withdraw forces from China.

Dec 7, 1941 • Pearl Harbor
Japanese fighter planes attack the American base at Pearl Harbor destroying U.S. aircraft and naval vessels, and killing 2,355 U.S. servicemen and 68 civilians.

Dec 11, 1941 • US At War
Germany and Italy, Japan's axis partners, declare war on the United States. The United States declares war on Germany, Italy, and Japan.

Jan 6, 1942 • Largest Budget in History
President Franklin D. Roosevelt delivers his State of the Union address in which he proposes a massive government spending budget, the largest in American history.

Oct 23, 1942 • North African Theatre
In the first major Allied offensive, British and U.S. armies attack Germany's Africa Korps on the Mediterranean chasing forces back toward Libya.

Nov 8, 1942 • US Troops Land In Africa
Under the leadership of General Dwight D. Eisenhower, U.S. troops land in Algiers, Oran, and Casablanca in North Africa.

Jan 1, 1943 • Chuchill and Roosevelt Plan
Prime Minister Winston Churchill and President Franklin D. Roosevelt meet in Casablanca in North Africa to plan attacks on all fronts, to invade Sicily and Italy, to send forces to the Pacific, and to better aid the Soviet Union.

Jan 31, 1943 • Russians Trap Germany
The Russian Red Army traps and captures German armies that had invaded the Soviet Union.

Sep 8, 1943 • Italy Surrenders
The Italian government officially surrenders to the Allied powers; still, German forces occupy much of Italy.

Sep 28, 1943 • Allies Capture Naples
The Allies capture German holdings in Naples.

Dec 1, 1943 • Cairo Declaration
The Allied powers announce the Cairo Declaration in which all three declare their intention to establish an international organization to maintain the peace

and security of the world.

Jun 1, 1944 • Allies Assemble
In England, the Allied powers assemble 2.9 million men, 2.5 million tons of supplies, 11,000 airplanes, and hundreds of ships in preparation for D-Day.

Jun 4, 1944 • Rome Falls
Rome falls to Allied forces.

Jun 6, 1944 • D-Day
D-Day: The first of nearly 3 million Allied soldiers arrive in Normandy, on the northern shores of France.

Jul 24, 1944 • Normandy and Brittany
Allied troops take large portions of Normandy and Brittany initiating a German retreat.

Aug 25, 1944 • Paris Liberated
U.S. forces, aided by a Free French division, liberate Paris from Nazi control.

Feb 11, 1945 • Big Three in Yalta
The Allied powers meet in Yalta to negotiate Soviet dominance in Eastern Europe. The Yalta Conference would result in the dual administrations in Berlin, the break up of Germany, and the prosecution of war criminals.

Apr 12, 1945 • FDR Dies
President Franklin D. Roosevelt dies of a cerebral hemorrhage in Warm Springs, Georgia.

Apr 28, 1945 • Mussolini Dies
Italian insurgents capture Mussolini, murder him, and mutilate his body.

April 30, 1945 • Hitler Commits Suicide
Adolf Hitler commits suicide in Berlin.

May 2, 1945 • Germany Surrenders
The German army signs an unconditional surrender.

May 5, 1945 • The Pacific Theatre

The American Air Force in Europe heads for the war in the Pacific.

May 1945 • Demobilization Begins
Demobilization of the American army begins.

Atomic Bomb Tested
An atomic bomb is successfully detonated in the New Mexico desert.

Jul 26, 1945 • Big Three in Potsdam
Allied leaders meet in Potsdam, Germany to send an ultimatum to Japan. Japanese military leaders ruling the government issue no surrender.

Aug 6, 1945 • Hiroshima
The United States drops an atomic bomb—the first to be used in warfare—on Hiroshima, killing 75,000 people instantly, and injuring more than 100,000.

Aug 8, 1945 • Soviet Union Enters Pacific
With still no surrender from Japan, the Soviet Union enters the Pacific war as promised in Yalta, defeating Japanese forces in Manchuria.

Aug 9, 1945 • Nagasaki
A second atomic bomb is dropped in Nagasaki.

Aug 10, 1945 • Tokyo Petitions for Peace
Tokyo asks for peace on the condition that Emperor Hirohito will retain his throne. The Allies accept.

Sep 2, 1945 • World War II Ends
A formal surrender ceremony is conducted in Tokyo Bay on the U.S. battleship Missouri. World War II officially ends.

Timeline provided by Shmoop.com
http://www.shmoop.com/wwii/timeline.html

www.ingramcontent.com/pod-product-compliance
Lightning Source LLC
Chambersburg PA
CBHW030538260626
47157CB00006B/2084